# INDEFENSIBLE

A Novel by

Thomas Banks

Copyright © 2015 by Thomas Banks

ISBN-13: 978-1517306687

ISBN-10: 151730668X

Thomas Banks
indefensible.novel@gmail.com

6.3

www.indefensible.org

Library of Congress Cataloging-in-Publication Data is available upon request.
Printed in the United States of America

# Dedication

◆

Like so many book dedications, there are simply too many people to acknowledge and thank. Generally, I want to thank everyone that has believed in me throughout my career as an entrepreneur, technology innovator and visionary.

Most importantly, I want to dedicate this book to my wife, Melinda. Since meeting twenty-seven years ago, she has been the most unwavering supporter of everything I have done—successes and failures. Until Melinda came into my life, I can honestly say I lacked focus and purpose. If it weren't for her faith and constant prayers I would never have achieved anything. More importantly, I owe her my salvation for without her prayers and encouragement I would never have found a relationship in Jesus. This book, my dear wife was only made possible because of your unjustified belief in me. You are, and will always be the much needed anchor in my life, my one true love, and the wind beneath my wings.

I cannot begin to express the importance of my two sons, William and Jeremy, who both came into our life through the miracle of adoption. My oldest son, Willie is truly a miracle child. Not only was he adopted at birth, he was also delivered by my wife Melinda who is a Board Certified OBGYN.

When Willie was born, his birth represented a turning point in my life. Briefly, his birthmother, who was also my wife's obstetric patient, had initially considered an abortion. After much thought, she told my wife during a subsequent office visit she decided to put her unborn child up for adoption. After much thought and soul searching, Melinda and I decided to propose that we be considered as the adoptive parents. Each day I look upon my amazing son and am reminded that he could have been aborted. I cannot imagine my life without Willie Banks. But, thanks to intervention by the Holy Spirit, he was placed in our life and didn't become just another abortion statistic. When I watched my wife perform the Cesarean Section to deliver her new-born child, I am certain I am one of the few fathers in history to have the honor of witnessing my physician-wife perform her art while delivering our son. What a remarkable experience. The birth of Willie changed my view on abortion and provided the foundation for my walk with Christ. This singular event will forever be the most amazing and impactful experience in my life.

As a young man, now serving this great country in the United States Army as a Combat Medic, Willie continues to affect my life in amazing ways. He is one of the most faithful men, young or old, I have ever known as well as being an amazing patriot. God bless you my Son.

In January, ten years after Willie's birth, one of my employees asked if Melinda and I were interested in adopting another child. My first response was that at 53 I think Melinda and I were a little old to consider adoption, and a newborn at that. But after chatting over the phone with yet unborn-Jeremy's birth-mother and his birth-grandmother (who happened to be two years younger than I) it was suggested that the three of us have a moment of prayer. Within a few minutes, they said that the spirit of the Lord came upon them and this unborn child was meant to be with us. Jokingly, I explained I needed to tell Melinda first. Within the hour, Melinda was on the phone. Four months later, Melinda, Willie and I found ourselves in Idaho Falls, Idaho for Jeremy's birth.

Albeit only nine, Jeremy is an amazing human. He is loving, funny, bright and has incredible love of the Lord. He has and continues to impact my life in amazing and interesting ways. This loving child provides a new level of purpose and focus I had never imagined possible at sixty-two.

To my older brother William, fourteen years my senior, who succumbed to heart disease twenty-one years ago I too dedicate this book. It is after him that we named our first son. My brother Bill was an amazing gentleman with a double doctorate in Anatomy and Veterinary Medicine and was a dean at the Texas A&M University College of Veterinary Medicine & Biomedical Sciences. Bill always believed in me and cherished the relationship that developed way too late for the both of us.

Throughout life one has many acquaintances we so easily call friends. However, it is the rare acquaintance met totally by accident that defines a new and meaningful relationship—a person that becomes a true friend. A friend so close, that the word brother is inadequate. To this singular individual, Mitch Teich, I wish to dedicate this work. The loss of my brother William left a void I believed would never be filled, that is until Mitch, my 'best friend' was placed smack-dab in the middle of my life. Mitch, my friend, my brother. Your faith, character, patriotism and values humble me and make me a better man. Thank you Mitch.

# Table of Contents

◆

# Indefensible

## *On the Web*

www.indefensible.org

## *On Twitter*

@Droneon1

# Preface

———————◆———————

Every leap in technology brings with it opportunity—both beneficial and detrimental.

Today, the effects of drones on society are not limited to toys or theaters of war. In a short time, drones have become an integral part of pop-culture thanks to their use by every warring faction ranging from air forces to the CIA.

Drones, however, are finding their way into everyday life from hobbyists discovering new and exciting ways to pass idle time on to retailers such as Amazon who recognize the cost-effectiveness of unmanned automated delivery of their goods and products. As unmanned vehicles prove their value, their use will quickly become as widespread as smartphones. In fact, as time goes on, it will become increasingly difficult to imagine how one will exist without the other. The blending of smartphones, drones and GPS will change the way we do everything…even terror.

In *Indefensible* we are introduced to a new terror regime—Lone Wolf Technology-Jihadists. Although operating independently, these Lone Wolves will be coordinated and lead by remote leadership from all corners of the globe through social media. Leadership invisibly guiding their operatives' separate efforts into coordinated armadas as swarms of drones wreak terror and destruction.

Imagine drone warriors milling about within cities in innocuous soccer-mom-mini-vans who only need to maneuver their lethal and stealthy weapons within a few miles of their targets, open their sunroofs then let their merciless vehicles begin their autonomous treks to destruction.

The threat and effect of a C4 laden drone in itself is dramatic. Not to mention the possibility of more dastardly assaults with biological contaminants such as Ebola, Anthrax or RICIN. Regardless of its armament, the effects of a swarm of twenty plus drones will be nothing short of catastrophic. Weighing only a few pounds flying low to the ground, these devices are literally invisible to radar detection. These unmanned instruments of terror and destruction are unstoppable and make for a truly sinister attack strategy. No venue will be safe or immune from this new-age attack system. Imagine an assault of twenty, thirty or more explosive laden drones as they swarm buildings, sports arenas or outside gatherings of innocent and unwitting citizens. But yet, buildings are not the only viable targets for this unmanned instrument of disaster. Freeways, bridges, tunnels, cruise ships and even fully loaded airliners on final approach to any airport are all viable targets. Drones have not only changed the fabric of warfare, they usher in a new era of remote and impersonal terror.

Indefensible doesn't require the suspension of disbelief but rather embracing the inevitable.

# Prologue

◆

**"Autonomous weapons represent humanity's next great threat. Their versatility could make them 'the Kalashnikovs" of tomorrow," Stephen Hawking, August 2015**

The unmistakable tones of the computerized lock on the Boeing 757's cockpit door pierced the ever present drone of the big jet's engines as Captain Jack Sanders juggled two cups of coffee as he closed the door behind him.

"Skipper, welcome back. Coffee? Outstanding! I could use a pick-me-up before shooting the approach into John Wayne," declared First Officer Richard Bradshaw.

"I figured you would. What's our status?" asked Captain Sanders.

"Skipper, we'll pass the Hector VOR in about fifteen minutes. LA Approach confirmed the Kayoh Five arrival and advised us to expect thirteen thousand by Dawna intersection. John Wayne is currently reporting winds calm, ceiling three thousand broken, one thousand scattered and to expect the ILS 20 Right. Also, tops were reported at two thousand five hundred by a Citation departing toward the east with mild chop," reported Richard.

"Great. That gives us a few minutes to enjoy the coffee and set up for arrival. Early morning cross country flights make for a long day. Richard, why don't you enjoy the privilege of making the pre-landing public address to our passengers?"

"Will do skipper," said Richard as he rotated the audio switch over to PA and retrieved the microphone from the clip located on the bulkhead to his right. Like hundreds of times before, Richard brought the stale smelling microphone to his lips and began the boring yet obligatory pre-landing commentary. "Ladies and gentlemen, this is the first officer speaking. We are about to begin our descent into Orange County. Please return your trays and seats to their stowed and upright positions. We expect to land at John Wayne on time. From the cockpit and the entire crew of Central Airlines Flight 1423, it has been a pleasure to serve you. Thank you for flying Central Airlines. Flight attendants, prepare the cabin for landing," followed by the subtle noise of the microphone sliding back onto its clip as Richard released the button.

"Central 1423, LA approach."

"LA approach, Central 1423, go ahead," replied Richard.

"1423, you are cleared for the Kayoh Five arrival. Upon passing Hector descend to and maintain sixteen thousand. After crossing Paradise, you're cleared for six thousand. John Wayne altimeter is two niner niner five, over."

Jane Crandon unlocked the cockpit door and quickly slipped inside. "Captain, may I take your coffee cups? I need to stow them."

"Yes. Yes, of course. Jane, your coffee is just what I needed," said Captain Sanders as he looked deep into her eyes for a long moment and smiled.

Blushing slightly, Jane smiled back and invisibly squeezed his hand as she took the half-filled cup of airline brew. Pausing for a short moment, she envisioned Jack and her lounging at the beach before heading back tomorrow.

The morning sun created a truly surreal character to the puffy tops of the thick local overcast, or marine layer as it's affectionately called in Southern California.

"Skipper, crossing Paradise VOR," called Richard.

"Thanks Richard."

Richard depressed the microphone button on the Boeing's massive control yoke and called the Los Angeles Approach Controller. "LA Approach, Central 1423 crossing Paradise. Descending to six thousand."

"Central 1423, traffic two o'clock eight thousand. Bonanza east bound."

"Roger approach. Traffic in sight," replied Richard.

"Roger Central 1423. Turn right two five six degrees, descend to three thousand five hundred. When established, you're cleared for the approach. Contact John Wayne tower on one twenty-six point eight."

Captain Sanders turned the Boeing right two five six degrees as Richard pulled back the throttles beginning the descent to three thousand five hundred feet.

"Approach, Central 1423, heading two five six, leaving six thousand for three thousand five hundred. Cleared for the approach. Have a good day," announced Richard as he changed the radio over to John Wayne's tower.

"John Wayne, Central 1423, four thousand five hundred, inbound to Sager," announced Richard.

"Roger Central 1423. Radar contact. Continue."

"Roger, Central 1423," replied Richard.

Captain Sanders maneuvered his craft, deftly following the flight director as he began a gradual left turn to intercept John Wayne's instrument landing system that will guide him to the runway obscured by the morning overcast.

"John Wayne tower, Central 1423, inbound from Sager," announced Richard.

"Roger. Central 1423. Winds calm, altimeter two niner niner two. Cleared to land two zero right."

"What was that?" asked Sanders.

"What was what skipper?" asked Richard.

"I don't know. It looked like a bunch of bees skirting across the top of the deck."

"I didn't see anything," as Richard peered intently over the Boeing's dashboard.

"John Wayne, Central 1423. It seems we have some sort of traffic at our twelve o'clock just above the deck. Any information?" asked Richard.

"Negative Central 1423. We're not painting any traffic."

"Thanks approach. I don't know what it was, but it looked like a flock of very tiny birds just skirting the cloud deck in front of us."

"Sorry Central. I don't see it."

"Oh my god! Skipper, pull up! Pu....." yelled Richard as the Boeing was engulfed in a wall of fire. The Boeing's skin glistened in the early morning sun as it plummeted toward the ground.

## The Evening News

"Good evening, I'm Jeff Stoddard here with my co-anchor Gretchen Chen. Welcome to United News Network's Evening Edition. Tonight we sadly report on a tragedy in the skies over Southern California. For no apparent reason, a Central Airline's 757 suddenly crashed into the community of Tustin killing one hundred eighty-seven passengers and eight crew members. According to local reports, the airliner crashed into a quiet neighborhood around six fifty AM, killing at least ten people on the ground. According to reports, the crew observed what they thought might have been a flock of birds while on approach to landing into John Wayne airport. In an effort to understand what happened, we are fortunate to have with us this evening FAA Director Thomas Gomez. Director, welcome and thank you for taking the time to come on the air. What can you tell us about this horrific accident?"

"Jeff, it's my pleasure. It is unfortunate, however, that I'm here tonight because of the Central Airlines' tragedy. Candidly Jeff, we don't have any information at the moment. All we know is Flight 1423 hadn't reported any problems but, asked about what appeared to be a flock of birds in its path."

"Director, it's my understanding the pilot asked about what appeared to be birds above the cloud deck. According to reports, the cloud tops over Orange County this morning were reported to be two thousand five hundred feet. As a pilot, it's my understanding that birds usually don't fly that high. Is it possible what they saw weren't birds?" asked Stoddard.

"Jeff, at the moment we don't know what the pilots observed. And yes, with the exception of migrating birds, most birds fly at or about five hundred feet above the ground. According to our experts, there were no reported bird migrations in the area."

"So, what happened Director Gomez?"

"What we know is the John Wayne tower controller observed, on his radar screen, Flight 1423 began a steep right climbing turn at about two thousand six hundred feet then just as quickly began a high speed spiraling descent crashing about eight miles north of the airport. Unfortunately, as you know there were no survivors."

"Thank you Director Gomez. We're confident the FAA and the NTSB will figure out the cause of this terrible accident."

"You're welcome Jeff. I promise, we will get to the bottom of this."

"Ours is a world of nuclear giants and ethical infants. If we continue to develop our technology without wisdom or prudence, our servant may prove to be our executioner," General Omar Bradley

✖ ✖ ✖ ✖ ✖

# Chapter 1

———————◆———————

### New Age…New Idea

The early morning Wisconsin sun peeked through the tamarack and glistened against the frozen surface of Lake Mendota dotted with fifty plus ice fishing houses. Each streaming blue-grey smoke from the wood burning stoves deep within warming the bones of these most ardent mid-winter fishermen. A couple of adventurous speed skaters zipped by breaking the serenity followed by three ice sailors in tight formation tacking north with their starboard blades raised high into the air sparkling like lasers from the early morning sun.

"Joe, think about it," said Dave Turner. "For the one thousand dollars it cost me for this six rotor drone I'm in business delivering beer, bait and food to ice fishermen and never have to leave the warmth of my RV. If I only deliver twenty-five six packs of beer a day for a paltry five dollars each, I'll earn over thirty-seven hundred dollars a month. That's almost twenty thousand dollars for the fishing season. Cash! You want in?"

Joe Duke, Dave's childhood friend, looked skeptical, stared Dave down pondering his friend's entrepreneurial spirit and exuberance. "Hell no Dave, you can barely drive a car, how are you going to fly one of these contraptions?"

Reeling from his friend's assault, Dave fired back, "hell, these things fly themselves. I just flip this switch and my iPhone does the rest. Watch." Dave reached down and flipped the power button and his new drone came to life, motors whirring yet barely making a sound. Dave tapped the screen on his iPhone and his personal drone delivery system came to life gently lifting off rising to ten feet with a six-pack of beer suspended below. Pausing momentarily, Dave's drone swiftly zips across the frozen lake followed by an almost imperceptible shadow. A few minutes later the drone landed softly near an ice house while Dave talked on his iPhone announcing the arrival of the order. A moment later Dave tapped the screen of his iPhone and the drone released its precious cargo and leapt into the air and began its journey back to Dave's RV. Just as Dave's drone lifted off to return home a heavily bundled creature emerged from the warmth of his shelter to gather his cold and refreshing six-pack of beer. "There you have it….I just made five bucks."

## *A Truly Different Agenda*

The cold desert air plucked briskly at Moktar Barakat's cheeks while he talked about using drones to attack America. "Imagine, for only one thousand dollars each, we can command an armada of attack drones invisibly and safely from here." With one tap on Moktar's smartphone, eight drones, each laden with a half-pound package of C4, lifted off from around the compound. As they rose up, Moktar's smartphone commanded them to assemble in a tight and efficient formation and speed away silently and swiftly. Two minutes later, the attack armada approached their assigned target and then broke into four two-drone attack flights. Once aligned as commanded, they paused for a moment then each flight approached from their assigned quadrant. Without a command, they began a coordinated dance around their target then merged together ending in an impressive explosion leaving only dust and rubble. The attack demonstration was followed by the unmistakable and all too familiar repeated clacks of twenty-plus AK-47s cheering the success.

"Our operatives around the world can perform invisibly, embedded in communities, appearing to be regular mini-van drivers enjoying a simple hobby," said Moktar. "Yet, from anywhere we will command coordinated attacks. All our operators need do is park within twenty-minutes of their assigned targets, open their sunroofs and dispatch our indefensible aerial attack force of craft too small to detect with radar and too slow for American jets to engage and subdue."

Moktar put down his iPhone and turned his attention to his energized team of future drone commanders. To a man, each leaned forward enthusiastically awaiting instructions for unleashing an incomprehensible plan to strike not one, but thousands of blows against the American infidels. Blows so numerous and devastating the mighty force of the Islamic State will resonate worldwide.

Moktar's plan for his jihadist drone armada is to rain terror and devastation unlike that since Al-Qaeda's attack on 9/11. Buildings, cruise ships, sports arenas and even airliners departing and approaching airports are all easy targets. Targets too numerous to identify and more importantly, impossible to defend.

"My friends," said Moktar, "in a few months, hundreds of drones like the ones you just witnessed today will arrive in America invisible to the watchful eye of the infidels and into the hands of our brothers waiting to carry the fight to their doorsteps."

## *Four Months Later — It Begins*

It's 7:00pm Eastern Time, Saturday night April 11th. Embedded Islamic State cells across America received notices from the numerous social media sites they monitored. That night, a message awaited them. That night, Twitter carried the deadly instructions.

@SmallTalk So many have so little to say #ALITTLETALK.

@WinterWonders The joys of winter are never ending #WINTERTHOUGHTS

@RelaxandEnjoy Don't forget to take time to exercise #TAKETIMETOENJOY.

Once received, each agent of doom entered the accompanying hashtag into the coupon field in any of one hundred e-commerce websites maintained by supporters of the Islamic State. In moments, the websites returned confirmation that an assignment awaited them along with highly encrypted targeting codes to be downloaded into their smartphones and attack drones. As quickly as the coded package was delivered, each patient attacker's smartphone immediately decoded the detailed attack plan and displayed the dates and times for receipt of their attack drones and ultimate delivery to their assigned targets. Seamlessly, two innocuous calendar entries were created; one entitled "Package Receipt" for Wednesday April 22nd at 2:30pm and the other entitled "Package Delivery" for Sunday May 3rd at 9:00am. Just as quickly, each assigned attacker's smartphone's navigation software was programed with both the Jihadist's rendezvous point to receive their drone and his assigned attack launch point.

At 2:30pm Wednesday afternoon Adnan Boulos, like dozens of his counterparts scattered along both the northern and southern borders of the United States, patiently waited in his van in a secluded park outside of Fabens, Texas. His phone chirped the all-to-familiar sound announcing arrival of a new text message. A message letting him know his wait is almost over. As Adnan scanned the low southern horizon, he got his first glimpse of his assigned vehicle. "Amazing!" thought Adnan. "This is just too easy." Three minutes later the buzzing sound of the multi-rotor miniature drone passed about fifty feet overhead. Adnan tapped the screen on his smartphone and almost immediately the drone stopped in mid-air, reversed its course and headed directly toward his van. Adnan stepped out of his blue mini-van and moved about thirty feet toward the oncoming drone. Once again Adnan tapped his smartphone. Like magic, the drone arrived overhead, stopped in mid-air directly over Adnan and slowly began its descent landing softly on the desert floor only a few feet from Adnan and turned itself off. Adnan swiftly, yet gingerly picked up the drone, as if it was a prized possession, and returned it to the safety of his blue mini-van. In one swift and single motion Adnan opened the side door of his van and deliberately, yet carefully, placed the drone on the floor and covered it with the blanket he had at the ready.

Adnan climbed back into the driver's seat and turned the key in the ignition. As swiftly as it all began, Adnan put the van in to drive and without drawing attention began his trek back to his home.

### Readying the Package

On Saturday at 11:00pm Eastern Time Adnan, like other assigned drone operators, quietly retreated to his garage and began the process of preparing his drone with its deadly payload. After carefully removing the prescribed quantity of C4, which had been securely hidden for months behind a secret panel in the garage, Adnan delicately folded in thousands of deadly stainless steel ball bearings. Once the mound of C4 was laced with stainless steel ball bearings, Adnan gently formed the plastic explosive into a cube and set it aside to be attached to the drone.

Prior to attaching the deadly package, Adnan flicked the power switch on his drone to the on-position and awakened his smartphone with a tap on a playful icon in the middle of its home screen. Immediately, Adnan's smartphone connected to his drone and began the pre-attack diagnostics. One after the other, each of the six small rotors on Adnan's drone came to life confirming all was well with the motors, computer, GPS and battery pack. Just as the drone completed its diagnostics, Adnan's smartphone began downloading the targeting information. Like clockwork, the drone's LED flashed red then blue each time it successfully received a portion of the targeting data. In less than sixty seconds the drone's LED glowed steady green indicating the targeting instructions were successfully loaded into memory.

Once the drone's programming was complete, Adnan turned his attention to the explosive payload. Perspiration streamed down his face as he gently attached the deadly payload to the base of his drone with a few tie-wraps and carefully inserted the computer controlled detonator. In just under thirty minutes of preparation and programming Adnan's drone was setup and ready for its morning mission. After tidying up his workbench, Adnan picked up his drone and returned it to the safety of his blue mini-van and covered it with the blanket shielding it from prying eyes.

## Number 1: Lincoln, Nebraska: April 19: 7:00am

It never seems that we recover from terror. Whether it is personal like the murder of a loved one or something that strikes at the core of society like 9/11 or the Boston Marathon Bombing, the aftertaste lingers. A taste that forever colors our perceptions and interferes with our ability to find joy or peace. No matter how one tries, terror changes us forever.

The blue Chevy mini-van moved smoothly out of the suburban driveway in Lincoln, Nebraska. Its departure never caused an eyebrow to be raised for the simple fact it was one of many similar vehicles that filled the early morning streets. This morning a convoy of mini-vans, SUVs and sundry other vehicles migrated away from their sleepy little burgs toward the center of town to either participate in or be witness to the Lincoln Annual 10K Run. Every year, like clockwork twenty-five thousand adults and children came together to bring awareness to developmental problems, raise some money and have a great time. Today the agenda is no different except for four souls who are party to a plot to forever taint the aftertaste of this historically joyous annual occasion.

Sheriff Graham Johnson has been the head of Lincoln's law enforcement for more than ten years, having succumbed to the pressure to seek public office. Being in the public-eye was a path inconsistent with his personality and years of Special Forces training. Prior to joining the force, Johnson served ten years in the Navy as a SEAL with a number of deployments in the Middle East. Rumor had it that Johnson was a member of SEAL Team Six. But, when asked, his only response was, "I was in the NAVY."

"I hate these large gatherings," announced Sheriff Johnson standing before his staff in the morning briefing. "There are simply too many loose ends to track. What intel do we have from the FBI and Homeland Security?"

Leonard Michaels, Johnson's second-in-command raised to his feet to share information he received during his five AM security briefing with the feds. "According to both the FBI and Homeland there isn't any credible threat that warrants escalating our status. Just your typical 'nut-jobs' that always gravitate toward public events."

"Well," said Sheriff Johnson, "let's keep our eyes open and ensure the safety of our good community. Dismissed!" As the staff disbursed, Johnson walked up to Michaels and placed his hand on his shoulder, "Well my friend, I don't know. Perhaps it's the anxiety that accompanies these events paired with the constant memory of 9/11 and Boston, but, I'm always waiting for the next shoe to drop. I pray it doesn't drop today. And, not in my town," lamented Johnson.

Michaels softly utters "Ditto" sharing his boss's angst.

As Sheriff Johnson exited the briefing room he saw Bonnie, his wife of twenty years, his twelve year old daughter Karen and his dog Bodie. The German Sheppard too was a NAVY SEAL Johnson rescued after the dog was seriously injured by an improvised explosive device in Iraq. "K noze! Sedni!" commanded Johnson in Czech and Bodie dutifully sidled up alongside his master and sat down. "You and Karen better make your way to the starting line or you'll miss the beginning of the race. I'll catch up with you later for brunch." Johnson kissed his wife, daughter and pated Bodie on his side "take care of my girls boy."

Unlike a marathon, a Ten K run doesn't take a very long time and isn't spread over a large area. The city had defined, cordoned-off and implemented every conceivable security measure from manpower to Lincoln's own fleet of mini-drone video platforms. Today, no one will slip through and threaten the security of Lincoln and the safety of its citizens. Unfortunately, the mounting treat is not about someone, but rather some things that waited patiently at the ready to begin their journey to terror.

Two miles outside of town a nondescript mini-van pulled into a quiet and empty parking lot with a view of downtown Lincoln. The driver of this particular soccer-mom chariot knew that this morning was different from any other. As his van invisibly assumed its position, three equally invisible and non-descript vehicles pulled into their respective parking lots. The uniqueness of this morning's activity is that although the drivers were operating in unison, they were totally unaware of the existence of each other. They were simply lone-wolf jihadists following their tiny piece of Moktar Barakat's plan orchestrated from afar. On time and in unison, at 8:30AM, thirty minutes from the start of Lincoln's special event, each driver slipped into the back of his mini-van and uncovered his vehicle of terror— a black six-rotor drone looking like any other. These, however, were equipped with video cameras programed to automatically upload images in 'real-time' to social media sites across the world providing everyone a front-row seat to Barakat's plan. As the clock ticked, each drone's 'human' flipped the power button. Automatically, requiring no further action on the operator's part other than to open the sunroof and drive away, the drones came to life with a short series of beeps and tests of the rotors. Once the tests were complete, a blue LED began blinking indicating that target information was being loaded from the operator's smartphone into his drone's memory. Thirty seconds later, the blue LED changed its color glowed steady red. The drones were ready and in full autonomous mode.

At 8:40am, twenty minutes from the start of the event, twenty-five thousand Nebraskans and visitors enthusiastically engaged as either a participant, fan or vendor. Sheriff Johnson, however, could not allow himself the luxury of enjoying the race and its associated festivities. He awaited the start of the annual event from the warmth of his mobile command center. Not because he couldn't handle the cold, his SEAL training assured him of that, but because the command center was the only place where he could keep an eye on 'everything.' From his command center Johnson got to see the big picture from body cameras on his deputies' uniforms, street cameras, Lincoln's Sheriff helicopter, news feeds and four images from each of the department's camera drones operated from the back of the van.

At 8:50am, four sunroofs opened in unison and invisible to one another. The drones, albeit not fast, were swift. At thirty miles per hour, they would each arrive at their destination in about four minutes, or approximately 8:54am, only minutes prior to the race's start. Eerily, each drone began to rise up, quietly slipping through its sunroof until reaching its assigned three-hundred-foot cruise altitude. Once at altitude, the drones paused for only a moment to confirm GPS signals. Once positioning was confirmed as on cue the drones began their short two mile, five minute journey. Climbing back into the front seats, Barakat's deliverers of evil pulled away and began their trek back to their suburban existences living the American Dream.

As scheduled, one minute from the kill zone, each drone's video camera began broadcasting its trek. The drones' video feeds, uploaded by their own dedicated burner cell phones, began propagating across the globe; Seeking 'Likes' from the Islamic State's supporters.

At T-minus one minute the four drones arrived on station, joined up and descended to fifty feet above the crowd at race central. "Look mom, drones," shouted one little boy. Unfortunately, unlike the Sheriff's camera laden observation drones, Barakat's four drones were each heavily laden with pounds of C4 embedded and stainless steel ball bearings.

T-minus 5, 4, 3, 2, 1….The video feeds went dark, yet the intensity of the explosion is felt a mile away. The Sheriff's command center rocked and chaos and confusion became the new normal for Lincoln, Nebraska.

Barakat would not find out until later that day, until the carnage had been assessed, the impact of his plan. He, along with the rest of the world, will learn that Lincoln lost one thousand fourteen of its citizens and three thousand suffered injuries. Unfortunately, the survivors will be injured for life. Each will carry with them forever the aftertaste of terror.

## Number 2: Chicago, Illinois: April 19: 9:00am

The First Officer of Central Airlines Flight 224 from Buffalo completed the landing checklist and as directed by Chicago Approach Control, contacted O'Hare Tower. "O'Hare Tower, Central 224 on the ILS 9,000 inbound from MOTTT."

"Central 224, Radar Contact, winds 270 at ten, cleared to land on 28 Right."

"Roger, Central 224 cleared to land," acknowledged Stan.

Captain Landers deftly commanded the gigantic Boeing 757 as he tracked the invisible radio beacon of O'Hare's Instrument Landing System to land on Runway 28 Right. Landers called out to his First Officer for this flight, Stan Barrett, to extend the flaps ten degrees.

"Roger Captain," replied Barrett. "Flaps ten degrees. Don't you just love arriving into O'Hare over Lake Michigan in the early morning? Captain, Altitude 4,000 crossing ADAME."

"Roger Stan. Absolutely, this is just a beautiful morning."

"Captain, Altitude 2,200 crossing WILTT …did you see that?" asked Stan a little startled.

"See what Stan?"

"I don't know, it looked like a flock of birds down low."

"Stan, keep an eye out for them. If necessary we'll call a missed approach."

"Roger Captain. Crossing the Inner Marker at 800 feet."

"Captain! Look, those aren't birds. What the hell? They look like something mechanical, hovering below and ahead."

The Captain called for a missed approach. Stan pushed the throttles to full power, unfortunately, moments too late as the swarm of eight attack drones converged on Flight 224 exploding into a fireball in the Boeing's path delivering its deadly cargo of pounds of metal shrapnel. "Mayday! Mayday! Ma...."

"Ladies and gentlemen, this is United News Network breaking news. Central Airlines Flight 224 crashed on landing at Chicago O'Hare airport thirty minutes ago. No news as to survivors. However, from the mobile phone video footage we have been provided, it shows the airliner flying through a ball of fire just before landing. From this video footage, it seems obvious the airliner was attacked. As to how, why and by whom we can only speculate. But it's obvious that Flight 224 encountered a massive airburst of some sort and suffered enough damage to cause it to crash. We will follow this news closely and keep you updated as new information comes in."

## Number 3: Central Park, New York: April 19: 9:00am

Central Park, located in Manhattan, is a truly unique destination for New Yorkers with an average of two hundred thousand visitors on any Spring Sunday. Today, like any other Sunday morning in May, thousands of New Yorkers and visitors were jogging, walking, riding bikes, and doing any number of outdoor activities for which Central Park was famous. Yet, today is not like any other Sunday morning in April. Today, at 8:30am, six Islamic State Jihadists moved into position. Each Soldier of Islam, arrived in his nondescript mini-van or SUV at his assigned point of engagement positioned within three miles of Central Park. The cadre of Jihadists encircled Central Park from Union City, Long Island City, Harlem, Murry Hill, Cliffside Park and Astoria. Just like their counterparts in Lincoln and Chicago, these culprits had at the ready their personal attack drones each loaded to capacity with four pounds of C4 and thousands of stainless steel ball bearings. All of which selected for its weight, power and lethality.

Each drone had been preloaded with a flight plan that allowed them to navigate at one hundred feet above the ground weaving in-between New York's labyrinth of concrete and steel over the Sunday-quiet streets in stark contrast to the hustle and bustle of a New York weekday. Even the smaller crowds that made their way through New York were unaware of the six drones just above their heads or outside their windows. Each drone's faint whisper from its propellers and small presence were overwhelmed by the enormity of the Big Apple and cacophony of the city's sounds. But yet, six drones were about to deliver a wakeup call to the 'City That Never Sleeps' not heard since 9/11. The Islamic State was about to let the other shoe fall on New York.

"Becky, is there anyone who doesn't like Central Park in the spring, especially on a beautiful Sunday morning?" asked Char, Becky's twin sister.

"So true sis. I only wish dad were still alive to enjoy this with us. He and mom so enjoyed bringing us here as kids." Becky and Char Waters, New York high fashion models, enjoyed their Sunday morning tradition of jogging through Central Park, visiting with old friends and meeting new ones. Today, will be just a little different.

"Char, what's that sound? Bees?"

"I don't know Becky. But it's coming from over there."

"No Char, it's coming from over there. I think they're drones. I bet someone is filming a movie or something. Let's follow them and get discovered," suggested Becky.

The two beautiful New Yorkers turned right and began heading to what looked like the squadron of drone's destination; directly over the most heavily populated area.

Becky wasn't completely wrong. The drones were filming, but not for a movie or a commercial. Each drone carried with it a video camera broadcasting live on the World Wide Web its trek through Central Park, documenting every second of its unspeakable mission.

As Char and Becky arrived at what would soon become ground zero, they joined a growing throng now thousands strong. Each looking up, in typical New Yorker fashion, with their sun-glassed-eyes wide and mouths open pointing up at the ballet of six innocuous little vehicles orbiting in harmony fifty feet above the crowd broadcasting video of thousands of onlookers. Unfortunately, curiosity is even more dangerous to these unwitting New Yorkers than to the proverbial cat. As the drones orbited, their autonomous programming initiated a synchronized count-down to 9:00am, the same time as Lincoln and Chicago.

5, 4, 3, 2, 1….the drone video feeds immediately go black, no longer broadcasting their journey, not broadcasting the chaos and carnage wreaked by twenty-four pounds of C4 embedded with twenty thousand deadly stainless steel projectiles each capable of killing anyone in its way.

This morning, New York lost more of its family. In one swift and invisible blow, five thousand innocent visitors of Central Park laid dead and thousands more injured. The bitter taste of terror, long since begrudgingly pushed to the back of our minds, has now come to the fore. A taste that will not soon go away.

### Langley

Deep in the bowls of Agency headquarters the twelve-person antiterrorist task force, including White House Chief of Staff Roger Kerns and Vice President Terrance Colby, sat quietly around the massive semi-circular conference table basking in the bluish glow of digital displays depicting every corner of the globe. Richard Grant, CIA Station Chief responsible for leading today's meeting quietly stood at the podium, shuffling papers and adjusting the barely visible wireless microphone clipped over his right ear.

"Ladies and gentlemen," said Grant, "thank you for being part of what I believe will prove to be the most important meeting since 9/11. As you know, yesterday Lincoln, Nebraska and Chicago joined New York as the latest cities to experience terror first-hand. Today's topic is the result of intense intelligence gathering from satellites, drones, ground-based Agency assets and the NSA. This morning we are going to discuss Indefensible Lone Wolf Automated Terrorism."

"You may recall, eighteen months ago a Falcon jet operated by Autonomous Systems, Inc., carrying their leading technologists and CEO was lost and presumed crashed in the Bay of Bengal on its way from Mumbai to Kuala Lumpur to participate in a conference on robotics and autonomous systems. The last communication with the aircraft was from its Captain declaring an emergency reporting a fire in the cabin and loss of two of its three engines. After an exhaustive search, no wreckage or sign of the aircraft were found. The search efforts continued for three months and was finally terminated declaring the aircraft as lost, presumably crashed in the Bay of Bengal. However, ninety days ago, a posting on an Al-Qaeda message board stated that a new age of autonomous jihad was about to begin. Aside from the odd reference to 'autonomous jihad' the more interesting aspect of this posting was that it was signed by RC. We believe RC is Richard Chambers, former CEO of Autonomous Systems."

"Please direct your attention to the screen behind me? What you see here is video from an Agency drone operating at thirty-five thousand feet and two hundred miles northeast of Kandahar. A longtime suspected training area led by Emir Moktar Barakat. The drone images clearly show a group of Al-Qaeda operatives encircling whom we believe to be Barakat. His image can be seen on the screen to my left. Supporting this belief is the ground-based video recorded at the same time as the drone video from one of our embedded Agency operators. As we zoom into the man at the center, facial recognition gives us a ninety-eight percent confidence that the man is Barakat. Even more interesting is the man to his left. Again, facial recognition analysis gives us a ninety-nine percent confidence that this person is Richard Chambers."

The group stirred nervously. Vice President Colby couldn't contain himself and blurted, "How is this possible? How can a bunch of backwards towel-heads accomplish this?"

"First," replies Grant, "considering Barakat's education, he is far from backwards. More importantly, if our theory is correct, Barakat's organization hijacked a leading-edge team of developers to do the heavy lifting. As I said, Chambers had six members of his team on the plane. Our experts believe if Chambers only retained two or three of his team members they possessed enough brainpower to achieve Barakat's objectives."

"Barakat is not your run-of-the-mill third-world terrorist. In 1995, Barakat earned his undergraduate degree in electrical engineering at the University of Edinburgh. Four years later, he received his masters and doctorate in autonomous systems at the same university. For a very long time, we have suspected Barakat as being the brainchild of Al-Qaeda's technological terror initiatives including cybercrimes such as hacking commercial and government computers. More interesting is Mr. Barakat's passion for technology applications specific to robotic autonomous systems. Systems we believe are at the core of his indefensible Aerial Strike Force and, the modality employed in Lincoln, Chicago and New York."

"As you watch Barakat, it's clear he is performing some activity with a device in his hand. Yet, very shortly everyone's attention turned to the east appearing to be watching some activity near a small building. After two minutes there was a massive explosion and the structure became a pile of rubble and dust. As we zoom into the area where the explosion occurred and move backward in time you can make out what are clearly eight multi-rotor micro-drones operating in a coordinated pattern. According to our lab, the explosion is equivalent to approximately sixteen pounds of C4. More than adequate to cause substantial damage to any structure."

"After reviewing this footage, we concluded that Barakat, with the aid of Richard Chambers and some number of Chambers' team have implemented a micro-drone aerial attack capacity of remarkable proportion. A capacity that is likely fully autonomous, inexpensive and capable of coordinated scheduled attacks on any target. Just as we witnessed in the video. Ladies and gentlemen, I cannot over emphasize when I say any target. More disconcerting to us is that the size, speed, low cost, and inherent stealth nature of this technology making for a massive and indefensible attack strategy."

Grant picked up a second binder and placed it on the podium. "Now, let's take a look at the recent attacks in Lincoln, Nebraska, New York and Chicago." He pressed the start-button on his hand controller and turned his attention to the main screen. "Shown here are composite images drawn from a variety of sources throughout Lincoln, New York and Chicago, the day of the three attacks." The images flashed from one perspective to another. "Until now," said Grant, "none of the images revealed any information about the attack mechanism. The final sequence, taken from Lincoln's helicopter orbiting over the event, local surveillance video at Chicago O'Hare and traffic cameras in New York proves more revealing. Here we see four multi-rotor drones in Lincoln and six similar drones in Chicago and New York. Each craft is approximately two feet across. The Lincoln video sequence clearly shows the four drones arriving overhead at about three hundred feet above the ground. The drones then joined up into a tight diamond formation above ground zero and began descending at a high rate of speed to about thirty feet above the ground. All at once the four drones leveled off and then the explosives were detonated spraying steel ball bearing shrapnel in every direction. In New York's Central Park, six multi-rotor drones approached from different directions and joined in formation over the most densely populated area of the park. Precisely at 10:00am Eastern Time, in sync with the other attacks, these drones descended to within fifty feet of the crowd gathered below, as shown in the drones' videos. The video feed went black and five thousand New Yorkers lost their lives. Similarly, six drones gathered together from low altitude and positioned themselves on the approach path of Central Airlines Flight 224 into O'Hare. In unison the drones' explosive payloads were detonated in the path of Flight 224. The concussion and ensuing fire ball caused substantial damage. As in the Lincoln and New York attacks, evidence of stainless steel ball bearings was detected which exacerbated the concussive effect of the explosion further damaging Flight 224 and causing it to crash killing all 227 souls on board. As you can see, these drones operated together, seamlessly. More interesting, after reviewing cell and satellite logs, it appears no communication took place between the drones or ground-based facilities. We believe these aircraft are operating on a fully autonomous basis and demonstrating a heretofore unseen degree of adaptability consistent with artificial intelligence."

"But these are just toys," commented Vice President Colby. "How can they pose a threat?"

"On the contrary Mr. Vice President," snapped back Grant. "These devices are as much toys as your iPhone is *just a phone!* Today, off-the-shelf drones available from general retailers and websites have tremendous capability. They have GPS navigation, real-time video uplinks, programmable flight planning, speed and amazing payload capacity—upwards of ten pounds. Toys or not, Barakat's systems are effective and functionally invisible." Grant put up a radar screen from Chicago Center the morning of the attack. "As depicted on these radar plots recorded at the time of the attacks, there is no discernible radar reflection from these drones due to their size, minimal surface area and low operating altitude."

Exasperated, Grant moved to sum up his presentation. "Ladies and gentlemen, we are witnessing a genuine paradigm shift in terror. The technology and deployment operatives are clearly working under the radar both figuratively and literally. This technology enables the attackers to begin an attack miles from their intended targets making the area to monitor too immense for existing surveillance techniques."

Vice President Colby, wiped sweat from his brow, "what in hell am I going to tell the President? Al-Qaeda has a weapon made from toys against which the most powerful nation in the world is defenseless!?!"

"Mr. Vice President," replied Grant "everyone here at the Agency, the FBI and the FAA are working the problem. We will develop a solution to neutralize this threat. We have to!"

# Chapter 2

———————◆———————

*Eighteen Months Earlier*

Richard Chambers, CEO of Autonomous Systems, Inc. and six of the best and brightest members of his team comprised of software, electrical and aerospace engineers awaited in the VIP lounge at the Mumbai Executive Terminal while the Falcon 900 was being refueled and readied for departure to Kuala Lumpur for the first annual conference on Robotics and Autonomous Systems. It was a long trip beginning early yesterday morning from San Francisco. After a six-hour layover, the team was anxious to board the plane in anticipation of the upcoming conference. Like any other trip, it's a combination of enthusiasm seeded with boredom from the demands of traveling half-way around the world.

The alarm sounded on Captain Skip Taylor's ten thousand dollar Breitling Emergency watch, bought during better days flying for the airlines, awaking him from his all too short slumber in the pilots' sleeping rooms.

"What time is it?" asked Becky Reynolds, Autonomous Systems' Flight Attendant and Taylor's current love interest. Becky flipped on the overhead light and saw Skip standing over her as she admired his rugged 6+ feet tall frame and craggy face reflecting each of his fifteen thousand hours of flying.

"It's time to gather the troops," said Taylor.

Scrambling to get dressed, Becky embraced Skip, kissing him deeply and nodded her understanding that they couldn't leave the room together.

Skip entered the lounge and informed his passengers that they would begin boarding in thirty minutes. Chambers and his six travel companions began to rise from their rest and slumber, a little sore but more stiff from hours of sitting in one place. They began the familiar ritual of turning off their tablets and cell phones and gathering their personal items that naturally come out of one's carry-on while coping with a long layover.

Within a few minutes the team was assembled at the base of the jet's stairs and began shuffling like cattle toward the comfort of Autonomous Systems' luxury private jet. One-by-one they clambered up the jet's stairs and made their way to one of the eight comfortable seats distributed throughout the luxury jet. After five minutes of obligatory bobbing and weaving retrieving reading material, gathering electronic entertainment devices, tablets and notebooks each team member settled into his or her seat, anticipating an uneventful six-hour flight to Kuala Lumpur. A walk in the park compared to the twenty-six plus hours they just spent on the legs from San Francisco to Mumbai.

Chambers leaned in toward Liz Collins, Autonomous System's Drone Project Manager, seated next to him and asked "What's the status on the latest firmware for the drone?"

"I spoke with Richard at the office thirty minutes ago, he assured me the update would be available for download upon our arrival," replied Liz.

"Great" snapped Chambers, "I hope they tested it this time. We get one shot at showcasing our technology. One hundred million dollars in follow-on funding by Rain Tree Ventures is tied to our successful demonstration. We need this money badly."

"I understand," said Liz. "We all need this money."

The Falcon's three jet engines came to life as Carey James, Autonomous Systems' First Officer called Mumbai ground control: "Ground, Falcon One Alpha Sierra at the Executive Terminal with Echo ready to taxi."

"Falcon One Alpha Sierra" replied the Mumbai Ground Controller in almost comical broken English. "You are cleared to Runway Three Two Left, hold Short at Charlie Ten. Follow the American 757. Contact the tower on one one eight point five."

Captain Taylor advanced the throttles and the Falcon began its lumbering yet majestic dance toward Runway Three Two Left.

"Roger. Falcon One Alpha Sierra Cleared to Three Two Left, hold short at Charlie Ten going to Tower on one one eight point five," responded the enthusiastic young, yet seasoned First Officer. A quick flick of a switch and the First Officer tuned the radio frequency to the tower and announced "Mumbai Tower, Falcon One Alpha Sierra ready for departure holding short at Charlie Ten."

"Roger Falcon One Alpha Sierra, continue holding short of Runway Three Two Left at Charlie Ten, you are number two for departure" replied the Tower Controller.

Liz Collins, a Stanford graduate in Computer Science, is far from a seasoned traveler. Other than the typical junkets to Dallas or Los Angeles, Liz has not traveled all that much. Regardless of her engineering degree and absolute understanding of the physics making it possible for the Falcon to fly, her stomach tightened as she tried to hide the fact that she was griping the armrests a little more tightly than a moment before.

"Falcon One Alpha Sierra, cleared for takeoff."

The First Officer smoothly advanced the throttles as Captain Taylor positioned the Falcon for departure. Seamlessly, the First Officer and Captain Taylor moved the throttles to takeoff power and the three engines of the Falcon came to life. With authority, the jet began its takeoff roll and in moments this glorious private jet accelerated toward the end of the runway which Liz felt was not long enough and imagined the jet running off the end to her fiery demise. But Liz's fears are soon quenched as the Falcon rotated skyward beginning the dramatic climb to its thirty-seven-thousand-foot cruise altitude.

After completing the complicated departure procedure and pausing the Falcon's climb to cruise altitude to avoid traffic conflicts, Captain Taylor, in harmony with the Falcon's leading-edge autopilot settled in to the 37,000-foot cruise altitude only five hours from Mumbai. "The plane is yours Carey, I need to visit the lavatory," said Taylor as he extracted himself from the tight yet comfortable left-seat. He grabbed his carry-on and exited the cockpit heading to the forward lavatory.

The solid click of the lavatory lock, consistent with the quality of the Falcon's sturdy manufacturing, assured Captain Taylor of his privacy. Reaching into his carry-on, Taylor removed his shaving kit. With a slight press, the shaving kit popped open and Skip retrieved two syringes filled with a white liquid. Pausing a moment, Skip recalled that the white liquid was Diprivan, the brand name for Propofol, the drug that brought pop singer Michael Jackson's life to its untimely end.

As much as he tried, Taylor couldn't avoid his accusing reflection in the lavatory's mirror. "I know. I'm a son-of-a-bitch. But, what am I to do?" Sixty years old and about to lose his medical certificate thanks to a physical performed by one of the many off-line physicians professional pilots use before they visit the official FAA Medical Examiner. According to Taylor's underground doctor, his EKG was abnormal and passing his next FAA exam, scheduled in two months, would be unlikely.

"Ok. Ok. Asshole. My story reads like a dime-store novel or a network mini-series," thought Taylor. "Too many marriages paired with costly divorces. Too much alcohol and more importantly, no savings. The bottom line was simple, it was either them or me. How can I turn down twenty million in gold? Solid pure gold. All the 'employer' wanted is to have this arrogant team of computer nerds work for them and solve some technology problems. Then they would be released. At least I hope they'll be released. Unfortunately, I'm in too deep. If I don't follow through, the consequences are unthinkable. My employer may seem like regular guys, but who am I kidding? These guys are despicable rats and assured me that once I accepted their proposal there was no turning back. No turning back what-so-ever."

"I am not a murderer," muttered Taylor. "Just a delivery boy. I was assured numerous times the injection would only sedate the individuals, not kill them." All Taylor had to do was inject both the First Officer and Flight Attendant, lock the cockpit door securing his human cargo in the comfort of the Falcon's passenger cabin then head to his new destination only eight hundred ninety nautical miles away—Islamabad.

Skip slipped the two syringes into the right pocket of his jacket and stowed the shaving kit. As he exited the lavatory, he felt eight pairs of accusing eyes drilling into his back.

"Coffee captain?" asked Becky, followed by a sultry wink.

"No. No thank you. Not for me."

"I'll take a cup up front for Carey," offered Becky.

"Don't bother, you need to attend to our important passengers. I'll bring Carey his coffee." Becky handed Skip a cup prepared just the way Carey liked it, black and sweet as she slid her hand down patting his ass. Just as quickly, Captain Taylor took possession of the coffee then retreated into the sanctity of his all too familiar flight deck leaving Becky curious about what just happened.

"Welcome back Captain," said Carey. "We were just handed off to the first Viet Nam controller. How is everything back there? Yum. Is that coffee I smell?"

"Yep, and it's on me," said Skip as he handed the steaming hot cup of black ambrosia to Carey. For a moment Carey turned his attention to his coffee and savored the special blend that Autonomous Systems prefers to serve onboard the Falcon. "This coffee smells great," proclaimed Carey. "Corporate flying certainly beats schlepping around in regional jets. Their coffee sucked!"

"I couldn't agree more" replied Skip as he stowed his carry-on, locking the cockpit door and quietly retrieving one of the syringes from his pocket. As seen in hundreds of movies, Skip removed the cover from the needle with his teeth and ejected it to the floor of the cabin. Leaning over Carey's left shoulder, agreeing that the coffee smelled marvelous, he quickly reached across the unsuspecting First Officer's face from his left and cupped his hand over Carey's mouth and brought his head back sharply against the headrest as Carey struggled in terror. Regardless of the thousand times he practiced this maneuver in his mind, it took longer than expected to position the needle, slip it into Carey's jugular vein, or whatever was close, then deploy the milky white sedative. Thankfully, Carey was small in stature and the large dose began to take effect immediately. In spite of Cary's futile resistance, muffled grunts and protestations in one long exhale Carey quickly ceased to resist as his arms fell limp toward the deck and the needle slipped from its target.

"Damn!" Skip exclaimed almost loud enough to be heard by the passengers in the rear cabin. "What the hell am I doing?" He leaned in close to Carey to confirm he was asleep only to discover that a restful sleep for Carey was not in his employer's plan. Carey James was dead. There's no turning back now. Skip felt the other syringe still in his right pocket, awaiting its delivery into the neck of his sweet innocent lover. "What choice do I have?" His employers were clear, they only wanted the passengers. The rest of the crew was unnecessary. Delivering the sedative into Becky's vein would be more humane than delivering her into the hands of his barbaric employers," rationalized Taylor.

Skip decided to not think about Becky's future and settled into his familiar captain's chores, but before doing so he took Carey's suit jacket and placed it delicately over his limp lifeless body. Once settled into his seat, Skip began the process of hiding the big Falcon. First, he disabled the transponders making the Falcon invisible to the air traffic controllers, then he turned his attention to the breaker panel where he disabled the automated engine tracking system ending the constant broadcast of the aircraft's location and engine status to Pratt and Whitney. Confident the Falcon was functionally invisible, Skip turned his attention to his new destination, Islamabad. With a few keystrokes, the new course was set into the GPS navigator and the Falcon automatically turned northwest.

Simultaneously, Skip instructed the autopilot to begin an accelerated emergency descent at fifteen thousand feet per minute and level off at four thousand feet, well below the radar veil of Viet Nam Air Traffic Control. Skip then pressed the mike button. "Mayday! Mayday! Viet Name Center, Falcon One Alpha Sierra is declaring an emergency. We've lost two engines and have a fire in the cabin. Mayday!"

At the same time, a frantic intercom call comes in from the passenger cabin. "Captain, Becky here. What's going on?"

Skip replied "everything is fine, we have an emergency and are diverting back to Mumbai. Have the passengers fasten their seatbelts and await further instructions."

The Falcon jet continued its hasty descent to the target altitude and in only two minutes the autopilot began to slow the descent and level off at four thousand feet while making progress toward its programmed destination, with an expected time of arrival in six and half hours.

Becky called again. Even more agitated. Skip concluded in haste that Becky was going to be a problem and decided to continue with the original plan. "Becky, come up to the cockpit, we need to talk" responded Skip. Immediately, Skip jumped from his seat and positioned himself behind the cabin door with the syringe in hand just as Becky knocked. Releasing the lock, Skip opened the door and allowed Becky to slip in, then he quickly closed door behind her. Before Becky had a chance to ask a question or put up a fight, Skip grabbed her from behind and slid the white-liquid filled syringe into her neck. Unlike Carey, Becky was very petite and put up very little resistance against Taylor. The Diprivan took effect almost immediately and Becky went limp in Skip's arms as he gently placed her on the cockpit floor behind the co-pilot's seat.

Standing alone in the cockpit, with two dead bodies and seven hysterical passengers on the other side of the door, Skip needed to complete the process prescribed by his employers—the passengers needed to be subdued to avoid any possible challenges for Skip and more importantly, communication with the outside world. Skip, once again, reached into his carry-on and retrieved an innocuous container camouflaged as shaving cream. Once in hand he donned his oxygen mask, opened the cockpit door and pressed the button on top of the can. Immediately a gaseous cloud emerged and Skip tossed the canister into the passenger compartment and once again secured the cockpit door. As expected, one or more passengers futilely began banging and clawing at the cockpit door. Regardless, the gas took effect and the sounds in the cabin soon subsided. Skip concluded the passengers had been neutralized. According to his employer the effects of the gas would last only fifteen minutes demanding that he act swiftly and execute the final step in the nefarious plan to take over the Falcon. Again, Skip reached into his carry-on and retrieved a handful of long white tie wraps. Skip opened the cockpit door for the final time and entered the cabin to find the seven passengers on the floor or slumped in their seats. One-by-one he secured their feet and bound their hands behind their backs and belted them back in the seats. For the sake of his personal sanity, he added an additional step of his own and created makeshift gags for each of the passengers. "After all, who really wanted to listen to what any of these people had to say," thought Taylor.

As expected, within fifteen minutes the passengers began to stir. Groggy and confused and likely terrorized. "Christ," thought Skip, "I am a terrorist!" Fortunately, in spite of their protestations and efforts, the passengers were secured and do not pose a threat to Skip or the mission.

Finally, seated in the cockpit, Skip pressed the public address system's button and addressed his passengers. "Ladies and gentlemen, this is your captain. By now you're aware that there has been a change in our flight plan. By now the outside world has come to the conclusion that our flight experienced a catastrophic event and likely crashed in the Bay of Bengal. However, as you know, you are all safe and secure and we are on to a new destination. Since our flight attendant is no longer with us, I am sorry to inform you that inflight services will not be available." In spite of his effort to be humorous, Skip realized he sounded more macabre and psychotic than funny. "What the hell, it is what it is," mused Skip.

### The Employer

Emir Moktar Barakat, leader of Al-Qaeda, operating in Islamabad approached his Shura (advisor) Abdul-Ghaffar Fadel. "Sabah el kheer (good morning) Abdul. When does the plane arrive?"

"Emir, according to the plan, the plane should have diverted from its course and headed direct to Islamabad at 6:45am our time with an estimated flight time of six and a half hours. We should expect its arrival around 1:15 this afternoon. As planned, the Captain is to maintain radio silence until five hundred miles before landing. The Pakistani Defense Forces are in position and are prepared to take possession of the hostages. I assure you, we are prepared for their arrival."

"Very well Abdul," said Moktar, "nothing can go wrong. These people are of extreme importance to our mission. The only one to die will be the infidel pilot. The fool shall not leave the airplane."

"Certainly Emir," replied Abdul.

Moktar retired to his room and took refuge atop his family's Majlis (cushion) that he brought with him from Afghanistan and began puffing on his hookah. As many times before, Moktar reflected on the genius of his plan to create a world-wide air force of thousands of attack drone operators wreaking havoc across America. The only unknown factor was, would these American engineers do his bidding? "In reality," Moktar mused, "what choice do they have? They either provide him what he wanted or they will face his wrath." Something Moktar knew few had the strength or character to do.

Sixteen kilometers North of Islamabad, via the Khayaban-e-Iqbal, laid the Margalla Hills where, buried thirty meters below the surface were Moktar's people completing final preparations of the secure dormitory and laboratories which will house Moktar's drone engineering team until they bring to life his vision for an indefensible attack force. The facility consisted of a central work area, with simple desks, desktop computers and a less than well thought-out collection of printers, machines and tools. The work area was surrounded by eight gated sleeping cells each not more than three meters square appointed with a sleeping mat, blanket and pillow. In the north end of the laboratory was a common toilet and shower adjacent to a Spartan meal room. Consistent with Moktar's need for control, the facility was monitored around the clock with video cameras strategically placed everywhere.

Abdul approached Moktar's room and knocked softly. "Emir, it is noon and the jet's captain just called via his satellite phone to announce his arrival within the hour."

### Arrival

The hours seemed to crawl by slowly thought Skip. Probably having two dead bodies in the cockpit had done little to enhance the flight experience. At one point he considered moving Carey and Becky into the passenger cabin but quickly dismissed the idea for he just didn't want to face his seven frightened passengers...err, hostages.

Once again Skip's alarm on his Breitling watch began to beep, this time informing him that it was time to make the dreaded call to his employer. Reaching behind his seat, Skip retrieved his carry-on one last time and quickly withdrew a satellite phone. He suspected that the number he was about to call was likely attached to a burner phone, as criminals liked to call them, making it impossible for anyone to track or monitor calls. Ironically, less than six months earlier, Skip would have referred to them as terrorist phones used by crazy Islamic State jihadists. Amazing how the theater of one's life changes in such a short time. "Six months ago" Skip mused to himself, "I hated terrorists, now I am one." Before dialing the number, skip reflected on the totally unpredictable turn of events in his life. Quietly, Skip chastised himself, "I can't believe it. I'm a hypocrite!" Yet, just as quickly Skip justified his actions, "Why beat myself up over this situation. Someone was going to do it. It was inevitable. Why not me?"

The unique beeping of the satellite phone announced each of the numbers of his employer's anonymous phone. Moments later, after one ring, a non-descript voice answered. "Speak!" Skip was instructed to limit his communication to one simple phrase. "On time" responded Skip as he waited for the listener to acknowledge his message, but none was offered. After a few seconds, Skip pressed the end button and turned his attention to the approach and landing into Islamabad.

Skip tuned the radio to one two nine point six megahertz, Benazir International airport's automated terminal information service (ATIS). He listened carefully to Benazir ATIS.

*"Benazir Information Oscar. Zero Six Hundred Zulu weather. Wind three zero at eight, visibility five. One thousand two hundred scattered, ceiling three thousand overcast, temperature one five, dew-point eight. Altimeter two niner eight seven. IFR approach ILS or visual, runway three zero. All aircraft read back all hold short instructions. Advise controller on initial contact that you have information Oscar."*

For most, this litany of words, phrases and numbers were meaningless, but to Skip it contained all the secrets necessary to bring his craft to a safe and efficient landing. Now that Skip knew which runway he will be landing on—Three Zero—he changed the radio frequency to one two four point nine megahertz, Benazir Approach Control, and began the radio dialog all too familiar to every pilot. At any other time and circumstance Skip would simply call the approach controller and happily announce all the details about his flight. However, his employer once again gave him a very specific phrase to use that likely was provided by the Pakistani Intelligence Service. Skip pressed the microphone button on his control wheel and announced, "Benazir approach control. Cargo One fifty miles southeast of the airport, four thousand."

With barely a pause, the approach controller responded, "Cargo One, Roger. Cleared for the visual to Three Zero contact the tower on one two three point seven."

"Roger Benazir. Cargo One is cleared for the visual to three zero. Going to the tower on one two three point seven," responded Skip. Just as quickly, Skip once again changed the frequency on the radio to Benazir tower and made what was likely his last radio call as pilot-in-command of any aircraft. "Benazir tower, Cargo One, twenty miles southeast at four thousand with Oscar. Airport in sight."

The Benazir tower controller, sounding like every impressionist trying to imitate someone from India or Pakistan replied simply "Cargo One, Cleared to Land." Hmmmm, thought Skip, "That is too easy."

Skip tuned in Benazir's Instrument Landing System and turned south to two one zero degrees to intercept the approach course and glideslope. Within minutes, his instruments showed he was on course and he began his descent. Gear down, flaps twenty degrees, fuel pumps on. Skip couldn't help but smile. Ironic, even in the last moments of his flying career he flew his craft like the professional he was. "I will really miss flying," but, laughing out loud, "twenty million will soothe my loss." Skip watched his instruments and looked intently over the nose of the beautiful Falcon as the inviting ten thousand feet of Benazir's Runway Three Zero laid before him. The threshold approached quickly and just as he had done thousands of times before, Skip deftly landed his craft with barely a bounce and applied the thrust reversers bringing his beautiful steed to a graceful stop. As Skip languished in the glow of a perfect landing, the Benazir controller broke the silence.

"Cargo One. Continue your taxi to end of Three Zero. Exit to your left and park on the apron. Await arrival of security."

Skip responded quickly and smoothly, "Roger."

Upon reaching the end of the runway, Skip maneuvered the Falcon and brought it to a stop on the apron as directed. As expected, a convoy of sinister black SUVs, a bus, and military vehicles, each sporting what looks like fifty caliber machine guns, approached the Falcon and pulled to a stop. Just then, the back door of the lead SUV opened and out stepped what appeared to be a Pakistani military officer. He pointed at Skip and motioned with his hands for Skip to open the jet's stairway. Extricating himself from the comfort of his captain's seat, Skip opened the cockpit door to find seven humans gagged and bound like animals. Skip was a little unsettled as his passengers sat in luxury seats of Autonomous Systems' forty million dollar private jet. "I guess life has no guarantees" mused Skip. "Yesterday these people were on top of the world expecting a big pay day when Autonomous Systems went public. Now, I'm certain each of them is praying that they will be alive tomorrow." Fortunately for them, if they followed his employer's instructions, as he has, they will live to see another day. How many more days? "Only time will tell" thought Skip as he released the lock on the Falcon's massive door and pulled the lever to extend the stairway.

The gentleman from the SUV swiftly ascended the jet's stairs followed by a half dozen soldiers dressed in dark camouflage and carrying what Skip recognized as AK-47s. Before Skip could extend his hand and get a how-do-you-do out of his mouth, his worst nightmare came to life. Like every cheap spy and gangster novel, Skip was confronted with the immediate realization that his employer wanted no loose-ends. Just then, Liz emitted a muffled scream through her gag and reeled in horror as the lead Pakistani Security agent swiftly pulled out an automatic pistol and put two rounds into Skip's head spraying the cabin, as well as Liz and Chambers, with Skip's blood and brains.

The leader waved his arms in the air and yelled commands in Urdu, the national language of Pakistan. The six soldiers quickly gathered the Autonomous team along with their computers, laptops, cellphones and tablets. The soldiers covered the passengers' heads with black cloth hoods and cut their legs free and began hauling them to their feet. Struggle as they might, Chambers and his team were mustered into the aisle of the Falcon and prodded toward the jet's stairway. One-by-one they struggled blindly down the Falcon's stairs and were quickly and forcibly ushered into the waiting bus.

Just as quickly as the soldiers and passengers deplaned, three more soldiers rushed up into the jet with backpacks. The leader shouted more instructions and the three men began their morbid task of deploying incendiary improvised explosive devices throughout the craft. Within minutes the leader and the bomb squad deplaned and boarded their respective vehicles. As the convoy pulled away, the leader pressed the microphone on his handheld radio and shouted in Urdu, "tabaan karna" instructing that the explosives set in the Falcon to be detonated. Moments later, as the convoy continued its journey out of Benazir airport, the sounds of three explosions filled the air and Falcon was engulfed in a raging ball of fire followed by the ignition of the remaining jet fuel in its tanks. Looking over his shoulder, the leader saw that this phase of his mission was completed and was now on to the facility buried deep beneath and secure in the Margalla Hills with Emir Moktar's precious cargo in his possession.

# Chapter 3

———————◆———————

### *Develop or Die*

The smell of fear combined with sounds of struggling and sobbing permeated the bus. Liz leaned in close to her seat-mate for a little solace, not knowing who it was thanks to the black hood covering her head. The warm dampness of her breath and the smell of fear and nausea filled the hood.

As the bus rumbled along, Chambers surmised from the heat, humidity, and the overwhelming stench of impoverished humanity paired with the duration of the flight placed them in Pakistan. As he struggled with his fear, he thought to himself, "Now what?"

Chambers was a proven executive and leader. An innovator who had overcome every obstacle he'd ever encountered. From corporate takeover to the death of his wife and four-year old daughter in a home invasion robbery gone awry five years earlier. Now he was presented with a challenge for which no one could plan. Airplane hijackings had been rare for a very long time. Unfortunately, the security efforts employed with corporate private jet travel pales compared with the airlines. Other than a customs check, TSA is all but invisible when boarding a private jet.

"By now, an all-out search must be underway to find the Falcon," thought Chambers. As a private pilot, he guessed that the Captain's decision to initiate such a rapid descent from cruise altitude was to get the Falcon below controlling radar services and give the impression that the plane was crashing. Regardless, the Captain had an agenda which played out in the Autonomous team's abduction and his much deserved demise. "I hope he rots in hell," thought Chambers.

For a moment, Chambers was distracted by one question; "Who are these people that think they can cooperate with terrorists and expect a positive outcome for themselves? As for the Captain, what a fool! Yes, I hope he rots in hell." In a funny way, Chamber's found comfort knowing that there was justice. Yet, the Captain's death did little to assuage fear for himself and his team.

"Certainly by now, the U.S. had initiated an all-out search for us," pondered Chambers. Unfortunately, they would be looking for wreckage that would not be found. Clearly, the abduction of their jet was done in a way to throw off search efforts. Truly a brilliant strategy to confuse search parties flying low over the Bay of Bengal looking for signs of the Falcon's untimely end. Unfortunately, the search parties will find no debris, no luggage or bodies for the only survivors are in this stinking bus and the jet, Chambers believed, was likely consumed in fire at the end of a runway. Regardless of the fact that Chambers was blinded by the hood over his head, he guessed that the sounds of explosions in the distance as the bus sped away marked the end of Autonomous Systems' beautiful Falcon jet. Their abductors were clearly not amateur rogue terrorists. This was a highly coordinated and professional effort that likely required the involvement of a government. A government that had the ability to cover up and lie about the burning hulk at the end of a runway of a major airport.

Chambers heard familiar sounds. Sounds of anguish and fear. Sounds of someone struggling futilely against his restraints. Regardless of how much he struggled, thought Richard, the restraints would hold fast. Even if one or all of the Autonomous team were to break free, they would have little chance against an armed force. A force clearly committed to achieving their objectives. "Just what were those objectives," pondered Chambers "one can only guess. Ransom seems unlikely. Perhaps they are part of a bigger agenda. A trade for prisoners?" Chambers kept his mind busy in an effort to ignore the obvious motive deep in his subconscious — somebody wanted him and his team.

After what felt like an eternity, Liz realized the bus came to a stop and the engine shut down. She heard what she recognized as the bus door opening. Soon after, booming voices speaking Arabic along with loud footsteps and the unmistakable clattering of metal swarmed the bus. Just as she tried to reposition herself in the seat, she felt a firm grip on her arm followed by a loud voice as she was pulled to her feet. Still blinded by the hood over her head, Liz whimpered and futility tried to resist her captors. As she struggled to steady herself and fight her knees collapsing under her weight, she shuffled along, presumably to exit the bus. One-by-one the Autonomous team was driven from the bus and assembled outside in the unbearable heat and humidity. In unison, the hoods were removed from their heads as they winced, struggling to accommodate to the stark artificial lighting. As Chamber's eyes adjusted, the image of a blend of concrete and rock walls came into view. Obviously they were in a cavernous underground complex. More disconcerting were the dozens of disheveled men dressed in Arab garb with only their dark eyes visible and each sporting the expected AK-47. Even though the Autonomous Systems team didn't put up any resistance, they were not treated gently as the soldiers thoroughly searched each member. One-by-one, soldiers confiscated wallets and watches leaving them with only the clothes on their backs, glasses and murderer a semblance of humanity.

One man stepped forward and introduced himself in English giving the clear perception that he was educated abroad. Probably England. "I am Emir Moktar Barakat, your benefactor. You are prisoners of the Islamic State and in my custody. Today you have a simple choice to make. Consent to my bidding or die where you stand. The decision is yours."

Chambers attempted to step forward, but was confronted by a gun wielding soldier and pushed back into line. "I'm Richard Chambers and…" "Shut up," shouts Moktar. "I know who you are. I know who each of you are. I don't wish to hear anything from you other than your decision to live or die."

Kent Anders, a software engineer leaned forward demanding to know what they wanted from them. "What I want," replied Moktar, "is for you to work for me or choose to die. You have ten seconds to make your decision." Immediately, seven weapons were raised and firmly pressed against the back of each frightened team members' head. "The clock is ticking" Moktar said coldly. Kent, being the most outspoken of the team, struggled and demanded to speak with the U.S. Embassy. "I'm an American citizen. I have rights and…" before he could finish his sentence the undeniable sound of an AK-47 echoed throughout the cavern as its deadly package penetrated Ander's head, spraying blood on his compatriots as his body fell to the ground bleeding profusely. "Does anyone else choose to dine now?" asked Moktar. The remaining six terrified people just stood in silence.

Accepting their silence as their answer, Barakat acknowledged their assent. "Good. Take them to their quarters. We will discuss your future in the morning. Good night."

### The First Night

Even though the sleeping quarters had locking cell doors, the captors didn't lock them. Who knew why? Perhaps it was a statement of good faith, or someone lost the keys. Regardless of their captor's motives, Chambers and his remaining five team members were free to congregate and consider their future. The clock on the wall indicated 8:35 and bowls of food, bread and water were on the dining table. "We have to eat folks," announced Chambers. "Let's get some nourishment and put our heads together."

The team sat around the simple table seated upon less than comfortable chairs gazing down at the meal. "First," said Chambers, "I want to apologize. Other than Liz, I don't know any of your names and roles in the company. Let's go around the table and get to know each other."

There was a long and uncomfortable silence before anyone spoke. Chambers decided to bite the bullet and began the introductions. "I understand we're all frightened and confused, but, we need to pull together if we are going to survive this challenge. I'll go first. As you probably know, I'm Richard Chambers, CEO and founder of Autonomous Systems. I'm forty-eight, a widower, and have my degree in electrical engineering from Rutgers. Next."

Everyone looked at each other, still in shock from the events of the day. "I'm Gary Sasaki. I don't understand what's going on. Who are these people? What do they want from us?"

"Let's pull together and focus on holding it together" said Chambers. "Please, continue Gary.

"Okay. As I said, I'm Gary Sasaki and I'm a software engineer specializing in integrated adaptive systems and artificial intelligence. I'm thirty-one, single and did my undergraduate and graduate studies at MIT."

"It's good to know you Gary," said Chambers. "Who wants to go next?"

"I'm Akio Chan. I received my Masters in electrical engineering from UCLA. I'm twenty-nine and single. I feel the same as Gary, what do these people want from us?"

"I'm Jeff Chaplain, forty-four, married with three children, eight, eleven and twelve. I'm a software engineer specializing in autonomous systems and like Akio, am a graduate of UCLA."

"I'm Will Schmidt, my degree is in Aeronautical Engineering from Embry Riddle. I'm thirty-six, divorced and have two children. A boy, eleven and a girl, eight."

"Liz, please tell us something about yourself," suggested Chambers. "Everyone knows I'm Liz Collins. I'm twenty-seven, never been married and have an undergraduate degree in Computer Science from UC Irvine and my MBA from Stanford."

"Thank you everyone. I know this is probably the most difficult and frightening situation we have ever experienced. But, if we're going to survive, we need to work as a team. Clearly these guys are serious and abducted us for a reason. Since they killed … Liz, what was that young man's name?"

"His name was Kent Anders and was a systems engineer at Autonomous Systems."

"Thank you Liz. Since they didn't hesitate to kill Kent, it's obvious to me they are not holding us for ransom, but hope to intimidate us to do their bidding. Whatever that is."

Chambers and the others pushed their food around nervously eating very little. One-by-one they excused themselves to find solace in the privacy of their humble sleeping quarters. The evening passed slowly and the Autonomous Systems team fell asleep. A sleep that was far from peaceful.

Liz, in her own cell, tried to sleep, but was overwhelmed by fear. Rising from her cot, she made her way through the dimly lit area to Chamber's cell and slipped under his blanket, her shivering body seeking comfort. "Richard, I'm frightened."

Stroking her hair he whispered, "Liz, we're all scared. But, Barakat abducted us for a reason which makes us more valuable to him alive than dead."

"But, Richard, they killed Kent in cold blood," responded Liz.

"Liz, he was trying to make point. I'm certain we'll learn more in the morning." Maybe out of habit or need for a diversion, Chambers' hands began exploring Liz's body as they have done so many times before. As he pulled her in closely, their lips met. Richard could feel Liz shudder and gasp. If they were in their regular suite at the Fairmount, his intellectual young lover's reaction would be one of unbridled passion.

As Liz slept, Chambers laid quietly wishing he and Liz had opted out of going to the damn conference and had gone to Cancun as planned.

### Day One

The sound of their captors entering the underground prison probably meant it was morning. Unfortunately, without their watches and smartphones, time couldn't be confirmed. They were abruptly mustered into a straight-line and forced to their knees waiting patiently for whatever was to come. From behind them they could hear loud authoritative footsteps approaching. As Chambers glanced over his shoulder he was grabbed forcefully "keep your eyes forward, infidel swine!"

The man that greeted them the night before, approached and took a position before the frightened team surveying each of them. "By now," said Barakat, "you have surmised that we have captured you for a reason. You are here because you are the best in your field. And, if you want to live, you will now work for the Islamic State."

"What?" asked Chambers. "What do you want us to do for you?"

"Mr. Chambers, you and your team are going to implement your technology in creating a highly integrated and leading-edge micro-drone attack system. That's all we want." Barakat, looked each of Chamber's team directly and intensely in their eyes. "Anyone that does not wish to do so speak up now and you will be taken outside and shot. It is a simple decision and yours to make."

Gary Sasaki, the first to speak, "If we do what you want will you release us?"

Barakat, clearly amused, looked Sasaki in the eyes. "Mr. Sasaki, I find it impossible to believe that you are so naïve. This isn't a negotiation. You either commit to servicing the needs of Islam or die here and now. I don't really care what decision you make. But, do not deceive yourself into believing that you have any choice beyond that which I have offered. You will give me what I want, or die."

"Your government believes that all of you died in a plane crash in the Bay of Bengal. The facts are simple. One, I assure you, no one is looking for you. Two, your State Department is not negotiating for your release. Three, your fate is in your hands. I caution you, think before you jump to a decision that has only one outcome. Your death!"

After a long pause, "I presume your silence is your answer. Very good. Please stand up and let us begin."

Barakat walked over to a table covered in a black tarp. Gesturing to who appeared to be his number two man, the tarp was removed revealing eight black six-rotor drones.

"Here we have our basic drone platform. These units have the capacity to cruise at fifty-six kilometers per hour for upwards of ninety minutes. More importantly, they have a payload capacity of two point eight kilograms, or approximately six pounds. You may or may not be familiar with these units. Regardless, your job will be to implement the following design changes," explained Barakat as he lifted the cover of a large note pad propped up upon an easel revealing six handwritten features:

- Full Autonomous GPS Navigation
- Visual Imaging and Mapping Supplemental Navigation
- Ultrasonic Ground Tracking, Avoidance
- Ultrasonic and Infrared Inter-drone Communication
- Live Video Streaming into Social Media
- Cell Phone and Impact Based Triggering Systems

Turning the page, "additionally, you will implement the following software services:"

- Web-based Operator Communication System. Disguised as e-commerce websites.
- iPhone Command and Programming Applications.

"All of this will be completed in four months and be ready for field testing. Any questions?"

"Yes." replied Chambers. "These design parameters represent a tremendous effort. I don't know if we can complete them within your timeframe. Also, why not have the manufactures of these drones do the work?"

"Mr. Chambers, you have four months. Not a day more. Understand that I have an advanced degree in electrical engineering. I caution you, do not try to get away with anything. I will be watching you."

"As for the manufacturer, they will implement your design changes and do all manufacturing. Your job is simple. Implement the design features I have explained. You have four months," Barakat turned around and quickly walked out of the room, leaving Chambers, his team and a half dozen armed guards.

"Fuck!" declared Gary. "How in the hell are we going to get all this done in four months? It's impossible."

Chambers, sensing frustration and foreboding among the team, "I share your frustration. But, what choice do we have? Let's get to work. Liz, put together a project plan ASAP. Gary, you get on the app development and web services. Akio, you handle visual imaging, ultrasound and cell phone connectivity. Will, you take on drone inter-communication and navigation. We'll convene at dinner and lay out our development timeline."

## MONTH ONE

It's been thirty days since their abduction and Chamber's team had acquiesced to the demands of their captor. Back at Autonomous Systems, they had the ability to fabricate and prototype anything they dreamed up. Just 'give it to Pete,' was a common phrase, for Pete Cram could piece together anything from junk scrounged up around the office. He was amazing. Too bad for the others (but lucky for Pete) he wasn't on the Falcon with Chambers and the rest of the Autonomous Team. To Chambers' elite team, Pete just didn't fit in. Now, without Pete, it's time for them to 'get their hands dirty.' Something they hadn't done for a very long time.

Since the team was given limited, yet highly supervised access to their tablets and portable computers, they were able to access Autonomous' servers and cloud-based storage enabling them to retrieve entire software libraries, eliminating the need to 're-develop' everything.

"I'm amazed we still have access to Autonomous' services. Isn't Barakat concerned we'll try to get a message to someone?" asked Gary over lunch.

Truly savoring his cup of coffee Chambers, pondered Gary's question for just a moment. "Gary, since everyone thinks we're dead, I'm not surprised no one has dealt with our account access. As hard as our security manager tried. Hmm…what is his name? Yes, I remember. I believe it was Deeb. Arman Deeb. As hard as good old dedicated Mr. Deeb tried to implement better security controls, he was never taken seriously. Obviously security paled in comparison to the excitement of making billions of dollars when we went public. Fortunately for us security was never a priority and we have access to everything we need. At least for the time being."

"Sure, this will make our job easier. But what about contacting someone at Autonomous. Isn't Barakat concerned?"

"Gary, I don't think Barakat cares. I am certain if we try to make contact one of us will be killed on the spot. I for one don't want an AK-47 round flying through my brain," replied Chambers. "Do you?"

### The Seventh Member

Will was logged into the Autonomous server when he noticed something odd. "Akio, come here quick!"

"What is it Will?"

Moving his right index finger across the display he pointed intently holding his left index finger against his lips. "Shush! Be quiet. Take a look at this file I found just off the root directory."

"What file Akio?"

"Be quiet. This file. The one titled Readme_Deeb.txt,"

"Interesting. Did you read it?" asked Will.

"Of course I did. Take a look at what it contains."

'October 15, 2014: Guys…Arman here. I noticed some odd network activity. Akio, I recognized your backdoor access code and started monitoring the system. At first I wasn't sure what you were doing. Now I know you have been accessing the code libraries. I knew you were alive. Are you ok? I don't know what you are up to, but I presume it's important. What can I do to help? You can reach me as Deebinator on Facebook. If you can't use Facebook, then leave a readme file here titled deeb2.txt.'

"Holy crap," exclaimed Will. "This is great. Arman knows we're alive and maybe he can get us help. Have you communicated with him on Facebook yet?"

"No. Not yet. I wanted to talk with you first. Do we tell Chambers?" asked Akio.

Will, scrunched up his eyebrows as he always did when he's thinking. "I don't know. Is this something we can use to our advantage? You know I don't trust Chambers. I think he's a rat and Liz is a kiss-ass. I think Chambers would sell us out if it benefited him."

"I was thinking the same thing. Back at Autonomous, we worked our asses off and he took all the glory and the money," whined Akio.

"You're probably right. But, what can Arman possibly do for us from the states? You really don't believe a hundred Navy SEALS are going to come charging in over the horizon and rescue us. Since we don't know where we are, how can Deeb help us? If we don't handle this correctly, we could wind up dead. I think we're better off keeping this to ourselves and just get as much technical help from Deeb as we can. Let's let Arman feed us as much code as he can so we can get this project finished then hopefully get out of here. Do you agree?" asks Akio.

"I agree. What next?" asked Will.

"Let's leave Arman a message with specific technology needs and see how he responds," suggested Akio.

"Sounds good to me. I'll keep everyone else distracted while you prepare the 'read me' file for Arman. Let me know when you hear from him," said Will as he headed back to the other room to draw attention away from Akio.

### MONTH TWO

Time in captivity seemed to move at a snail's pace. Unfortunately, based on the objectives and timeline set by Barakat, the days clicked by at warp speed and milestones loomed on the horizon.

Chambers was the last to find his way to the common room for breakfast. Gary, made his way through the unappealing fare. Not convinced by Chambers' and Liz's timed entrance he leaned over and whispered to Akio, "Do they really think that coming in at different times will lead us to believe they aren't sleeping together?"

Not saying a word, Akio simply nodded in agreement.

"Good morning everyone," said Richard. "We're at one month and counting with three more to go. Liz, what's the status of the various projects?"

"Richard, we were just discussing that," replied Liz. "We have been able to access Autonomous Systems' development libraries including motor control, GPS and image navigation as well as collision avoidance. The good news is development and integration has progressed more rapidly than expected and the drones are almost ready for testing. Also, version one of social media and web interfaces are complete. Finally, according to Gary, the Alpha version of the iPhone app has been tested and is ready for Alpha testing."

"Wow! That's great progress. Barakat wants to see a field demonstration as soon as possible. When do you think we can have these drones reconfigured?" asked Chambers.

"According to Will and Akio, we can have a demonstrable configuration in two to three weeks," replied Liz.

"This is very good news. I have a meeting with Barakat this afternoon. I anticipate he'll be pleased with our progress and hopefully will be inclined to release us after our task is complete," said Chambers.

Gary, agitated as usual "Getting released is the farthest thing from my mind. I'm just trying to stay alive. I don't believe he has any intention of releasing us. Except for you, I think we are all dead. It seems like you have a special relationship with Barakat."

Seeming more than a little self-conscious, Chambers rebuffed Gary's assertion. "I don't have any better relationship with these people than either of you. Since I'm the CEO....uh...former CEO of Autonomous Systems, my guess is he presumes I have my fingers on the pulse of all activities. All I'm trying to do is ensure Barakat appreciates the work being done and hopefully, he'll release us."

## MONTH THREE

Like all technology deadlines, the two to three weeks for a multi-drone demonstration slipped a few weeks into month three.

Chambers, Barakat and his lieutenants watched with anticipation as eight drones were positioned on the floor of the underground compound.

"Emir, these eight drones have been configured with our latest firmware. Gary will now initiate real-time programming via an iPhone," explained Chambers.

Gary, nervously fumbled with the iPhone. As he tapped on the screen, each drone's LEDs began blinking red and green. Gary explained that each drone was being uploaded with a navigation profile to demonstrate control, video broadcast, formation flying and collision avoidance. Within thirty seconds the last drone was programmed. All at once the drones' LEDs changed to steady green as rotors spun up to speed. Quickly and seamlessly, the eight-drone squadron lifted up off the ground in unison and began hovering at five feet above the floor. The video display on the table showed the lead-drone's video feed as they began to slowly orbit in a tight circle, separated by inches.

The programmed flight profile continued as the drones flew around the cavernous space. Like a school of fish, the squadron spun, turned and orbited around the large room avoiding each other as well as walls, pillars and furniture. Even Gary, who placed himself strategically in the squadron's flightpath was unscathed as the squadron split into two groups of four flying past him then forming up again once they passed him safely.

"Amazing," exclaimed Barakat.

The demonstration continued for another ten minutes at which point the flight of eight drones aligned themselves in front of Barakat and the other observers. All of a sudden photo strobe lights attached to each drone flashed in unison demonstrating that the explosive triggering sequence had been executed. Satisfied with the demonstration, Gary tapped his iPhone once. Again the flight of eight drones backed away from the audience and returned to their original launch point, landed safely, and powered themselves down.

Clapping, Barakat exclaimed, "Very good! Very good indeed. Thank you everyone. This is very exciting. I want to see a real-world demonstration as soon as possible with the drones loaded with explosives. How soon can we take these aircraft outside for a field demonstration?"

Standing proudly, Chambers decided to answer this question. "Emir, all we need are explosive payloads and to transport the drones to a test range. Gary, am I correct?"

"Yes Richard. We also need the attack profile and mapping parameters. Basically the latitude and longitude of the intended target," replied Gary.

"So, Emir, as soon as your people can provide Gary with the targeting coordinates and mapping information he can set up the attack profile and have the drones ready in a couple of days," continued Chambers.

"Very good," exclaimed Barakat. "Abdul, see to it that the necessary information and explosive packages are provided to Chambers as soon as possible. I want to see this demonstration the day after tomorrow. Also Abdul, make arrangements for transporting the drones and Chambers' team to the test range."

"Mr. Chambers, please follow me. I have things to discuss with you," said Barakat.

"Yes Emir," as Chambers followed Barakat from the demonstration.

Arriving at Barakat's private residence in the underground compound, "Mr. Chambers, I am very pleased with the work you have accomplished. Praise Allah."

"Allah Akbar," replied Chambers as he bowed to Barakat.

If only Chambers' team were present at this meeting, Gary's suspicions that Richard had a special relationship with Barakat would be confirmed. Truly a very special relationship.

## The Test Range

Over two hours, under the direct supervision of a half dozen of Barakat's armed soldiers, Gary and Will loaded the eight prototype drones each with two-pound packages of C4 explosives. With beads of sweat covering their foreheads, they carefully connected each detonator to the onboard cellphones. Once completed, Gary, Will and Akio carefully loaded the eight drones into a black transport van.

"Don't drop these damn things," warned Will.

Soon after, Chambers, his team and a half dozen of Barakat's soldiers climbed into the all-to-familiar bus whose windows, with the exception of the driver's, had been blacked out. Once seated, the door was closed and they began their journey to the test range located far from the underground compound.

Chambers and his team sat quietly and hoped for a successful demonstration.

"Akio," asked Chambers. "Did you encounter any problems in preparing the eight drones with the explosive payloads and their targeting parameters?"

"Of course not Richard. None at all," replied Akio. "Everything is ready to go."

As usual, due to the lack of smart devices and watches it was difficult to know how much time passed since leaving the underground compound. Try as they might, the heat and uncomfortable ride of the bus and the ever-present fear made it impossible to sleep. This journey of a lifetime felt like it took forever. But, how long it had been since leaving the compound was anyone's guess. At least the better part of a day. The long ordeal, however, seemed to be coming to an end when the bus stopped for what seemed like an eternity. As the bus sat dormant, Gary and Will could hear numerous men outside in conversation speaking Arabic.

Without notice, once again the bus began to move and followed a winding road up and down a few hills until they finally arrived at a flat area at which time they came to a complete stop. The door swung open allowing six angry looking compatriots of Barakat to board. In typical hostile fashion, Chambers and his team were mustered off the bus and lined up outside to await instructions.

Abdul stepped out of an SUV and walked over to Chambers. "The Emir will be here shortly. Are your people ready for the demonstration?"

"Everything is ready. Where are we?" asked Chambers to Abdul.

"Kandahar," replied Abdul.

Gary leaned over to Akio, "Damn! Were in Afghanistan."

Gary, Akio and Will began unloading the eight drones from the van. The three of them were more than a little uncomfortable as they handled enough C4 to blow them to smithereens. "Fuck!" said Gary. I'm a software engineer not a munitions expert. I don't know what the hell I'm doing."

Trying to settle Gary down, Akio looked him in the eye, "perhaps blowing us up and these God forsaken things would be the best possible outcome."

"Forget it," moaned Gary. "I am not some fucking hero!"

As the last drone was added to the squadron assembled on the valley floor, another SUV pulled up from which Barakat exited and moved swiftly over to the assembly. "Well Mr. Chambers, are we ready?"

"Yes Emir. All systems are go."

Turning to Akio, "Gary, why don't we let the Emir have the honor of initiating the demonstration," suggested Chambers.

"Certainly." Without hesitation, Gary handed the unassuming iPhone to Barakat. "The units are charged, programmed and ready to go sir. To initiate the sequence and arm the payload just tap the 'GO' button on the display."

Barakat took the phone from Gary proudly. "Thank you."

Barakat held the iPhone high in the air with his head bowed, uttering a prayer. Once done, he looked at his assembled forces and yelled "Allah Akbar!" then pressed the 'GO' button.

Just as in the Islamabad compound, the eight drones came to life and swiftly began their ascent. Ironically, the team couldn't help but feel a little pride in their accomplishment and the beauty of these devices as they came to life. It was an amazing demonstration of the team's technological prowess.

Upon reaching the predefined loitering altitude of three hundred feet, the drones joined up into a tight and elegant formation. The drones maneuvered inches apart from each other thanks to the ultrasonic sensors that ensured collision avoidance. The onboard ultrasound and imaging technology provided the additional benefit of ground tracking in the event GPS signals were lost.

As before, the lead drone began broadcasting live video via social media displayed on the iPad held by Chambers.

"As you can see Emir, the lead-drone is broadcasting its video in real-time," said Chambers.

"Fantastic," exclaimed Barakat. "What is next?"

Chambers turned to Gary, "Please describe for the Emir the sequence of events."

Uncomfortable with Chambers dumping this task on him, Gary reluctantly explained the flight profile. Before he could finish, the eight drones pitched forward ever so slightly heading east and instantaneously accelerated to their thirty-five mile per hour cruise speed. The beautifully choreographed sequence was a sight to behold as the squadron swiftly followed their programming to the target a mile away. To demonstrate the powerful navigation capability, the drones did not fly directly to their intended target but followed a very complex and circuitous route ascending and descending together as if making their way through a metropolitan area. In less than three minutes the squadron arrived on station and paused for a moment as if taking pride in what was about to happen. Without any further instruction, the flight of eight drones descended to five feet above the ground tightly hugging the terrain thanks to their ultrasonic sensors. Sharing his attention between the target a mile away and the iPad held by Chambers, Barakat watched with great interest and pride as the flight of drones plunged into the building. Instantaneously the iPad's video went black as twenty-four pounds of C4 was detonated creating a fire ball hundreds of feet into the air reducing the targeted structure to a pile of rubble.

Immediately, dozens of Barakat's troops raised their AK-47s high above their heads and fired hundreds of rounds into the air applauding what they believed to be a glorious demonstration of the Islamic State's new and mighty weapon. "Allah Akbar! Allah Akbar!"

Unbeknownst to Barakat, yet suspected, the CIA's drone loitering thirty-five thousand feet overhead captured the demonstration of the Islamic State's newest, transformative and incredibly devastating weapon in minute and vivid detail.

# Chapter 4

◆

### *Eighteen Months Later... The Reaction*

"Good evening, this is United News Network Evening Edition. I'm Jeff Stoddard and this is my co-anchor Gretchen Chen. Tonight we are broadcasting from Lincoln, New York and Chicago, the sites of the most recent, heinous and frightening acts of terror since 9/11. This morning, over one thousand people in Lincoln were killed and three thousand seriously injured when America was blindsided by a new form of terror—a fleet of self-guided micro-drones loaded with pounds of the highly explosive C4 embedded with thousands of stainless steel ball bearings. Upon detonation, these micro-drones rained down a barrage of deadly shrapnel.

"As in Lincoln, Central Airlines Flight 224 on final approach to Chicago O'Hare airport was similarly attacked by a flight of six to eight micro-drones exploding in the airliner's flight path killing all two hundred twenty-seven souls on board. And finally, at about the same time, six killer drones gathered above Central Park in New York and detonated an explosive force that killed thousands and injured thousands more. Our guest tonight is the Sheriff of Lincoln, Nebraska, Graham Johnson. Sheriff Johnson, what can you tell us about what happened today?"

"Jeff, thank you for having me on this evening. Currently we're conducting an investigation along with the FBI and Homeland Security. What we know is a group of micro-drones, each approximately three feet in diameter, merged on downtown Lincoln. When they arrived at race central, at approximately 9:00am this morning, they hovered over the crowd for a couple of moments then their deadly explosive payloads were detonated creating tremendous chaos, killing over one thousand of our citizens and injuring thousands more."

"Do you know who was behind this attack? Has any organization taken credit?" asked Gretchen.

"According to the FBI, Al-Qaeda and the Islamic State are claiming credit for the attacks on Lincoln, Chicago and New York. However, at this time we don't know who actually commanded the attack. Clearly there were numerous embedded operatives launching a coordinated attack from multiple locations," replied Johnson.

# INDEFENSIBLE

"Sheriff Johnson, I would like to draw your attention to your video monitors," said Stoddard. "Here we see footage broadcast in real-time from the attack drones in Lincoln, New York and Chicago that was distributed worldwide via social media. Sheriff, what is your reaction?"

Sheriff Johnson, shook his head, "Jeff, this is a clear indication of the bold character of the leadership that mounted these attacks. The videos clearly revealed their intent, as well as their ability to carry out these attacks in plain daylight with impunity. We must move quickly to ensure that no other such acts of terror can occur."

"Sheriff Johnson, what is your next step?" asked Gretchen.

"We will continue our investigation. More importantly, tomorrow, Nebraska's State Legislature will convene an emergency meeting to assess the situation and formulate a response. I expect an all-out ban of drone operations will be brought before the legislature and a bill will be passed."

The camera panned to Gretchen, "Sheriff Johnson, what is the precedent for such an action. After all, drones are not illegal and thousands of law-abiding citizens use them safely every day. Isn't this an overreaction since we know terrorists will not obey the law?"

"There is substantial precedent. For example, in September 2013 the city of Philadelphia outlawed 3-D printing of guns. Citizens deserve the right to feel safe. Allowing 'anyone' to operate a drone over populated areas is simply too dangerous. In light of today's events, drones clearly represent an unacceptable risk."

"But, isn't an outright ban analogous to throwing the baby out with the bath water?" asked Stoddard.

"Jeff, certainly there is the risk of overreaching regulations. But, and I cannot over state this fact, drones can be launched miles away from their intended targets and cruise at very low altitude making them completely undetectable. I was at ground-zero this morning and we didn't receive any advance warning. As quickly and invisibly as these attack drones arrived, they detonated their explosive payloads, killing and injuring Lincoln's citizens."

## White House

The morning sun cast an artificial air of brightness over the Oval Office occupied by President Carlton Bennett, Vice President Terrance

Colby and Chief of Staff Roger Kerns. A climate that was not representative of the feelings shared by the three men.

"Mr. President, Chief of Staff Kerns and I attended the CIA briefing yesterday and sadly have to report that we are facing a truly dangerous and likely indefensible terror threat. These automated attack drones, as witnessed in Lincoln, New York and Chicago, represent the most diabolical military threat we have ever witnessed."

President Bennett stood up behind his desk, walked to the window and gazed out for a very long time. "Gentlemen, these god-forsaken machines, and their operators, can literally strike with impunity any target they choose. We have to take drastic measures. And do so immediately."

Chief of Staff Kerns stood up, more out of nervousness, "Mr. President, I've scheduled a meeting with Speaker Teasdale and Senate Majority Leader Palmer. Rest assured, they are at the ready to engage in unified discussion in order to counter and defend against this threat."

"Good," replied President Bennett, "only God knows how many of these heinous contraptions and their operators already reside within our borders. I want legislation on my desk by the end of the week or I will invoke my Executive Order rights and solve this problem myself."

The afternoon continued uneventfully until 4:00pm when the nation's leaders convened in the Oval Office. In addition to legislative leadership, President Bennett invited General Garland James, the Chairman of the Joint Chiefs to join in the discussion and ultimate solution.

"Gentlemen, we are at a crossroads and must formulate a plan to neutralize this threat. General James, what if anything can the military do to protect our citizens?"

"Mr. President, the Joint Chiefs has huddled on this matter for the past twenty-four hours. Our defense strategies have never considered an attack by toys. It is our opinion that our first step should be to fortify our defenses to protect Washington as well as mount an all-out attack on the Islamic State's command and control to neutralize this threat. Today, it's explosives. Tomorrow, it could be biologics. We have to make a decision and do so quickly."

"General, what do you suggest?"

"Mr. President, as you know we've successfully deployed the LaWs, Laser Weapon System, on the USS Ponce and a number of mobile ground-based platforms. We believe LaWs should immediately be deployed in Washington as well as key vital interests such as airports and major metropolitan areas. Candidly we've not tested this technology on such small targets, but our advisors believe the targeting mechanisms can be refined to meet this challenge."

"Can the Lasers neutralize this threat?"

"Mr. President, we don't see any other response at this time. Conventional defensive weapons would be useless and likely cause immeasurable collateral damage. We believe our energy weapon systems, including laser and electromagnetic pulse, can neutralize drones by effectively creating an energy shield. In doing so, the combined explosive effect will be minimized while the drones are at altitude and not joined together. Basically Mr. President, we suggest creating an energy weapon defensive shield."

"General James, thank you. Gentlemen, I don't see a viable alternative to General James' suggestions. We need to authorize appropriations to fund the expansion of America's energy defenses to protect our citizens and the American way of life. Just as importantly, we cannot sit idly by and allow this to occur. The State of Islam must be put on notice immediately. General James, we need a war plan immediately. Gentlemen, can we count on legislative support?"

"Mr. President, Speaker Teasdale and I have meet in advance of today's meeting and agree with General James. We can assure you swift bi-partisan approval. The only question is; how long will it take to deploy this solution?" asked Palmer.

"General James," asked Bennett, "what do you need and how long will it take to immediately protect Washington?"

"Mr. President, we can move a LaWs battery into position to defend Washington in three days. Our contractors are prepared to step-up manufacturing and turn their development efforts to address the unique nature of this threat. The current technology costs approximately $40 million per implementation. We should be prepared to appropriate twenty to fifty billion dollars to deploy defensive batteries in five hundred to one thousand selected communities."

"We need to move quickly," said Bennett. "I believe yesterday was just a taste of what is to come. Gentlemen, as soon as you deliver a budget for energy defense to my desk, I will sign it. Let's not let any grass grow.

General James, we need a plan of attack to neutralize the Islamic State. This is a paradigm shift to which we need a swift and effective solution. Can I count on you to move quickly?"

"Mr. President, Senator Palmer and I will have a budget on your desk in twenty-four hours. You have our promise," assured Teasdale.

"Mr. President, the Joint Chiefs will have a war plan on your desk within twenty-four hours as well," replied James.

"Thank you gentlemen. May God have mercy on our souls."

## *Joint Session*

Tension was palpable throughout the House Chamber as the clock slowly progressed toward 7:00pm Eastern Time. It was two days since the attacks on Lincoln, Central Park and O'Hare and every congressional and senatorial phone never stopped ringing. Mostly driven by fear and confusion, constituents across the land simply wanted one question answered: "Is our government going to protect us?"

It was the uncommon, and likely truant high school civics student that wasn't aware of the four basic responsibilities of the United States Government: Make Laws, Print Currency, Provide for National Defense and Enact Foreign Policy. Fifteen plus years since 9/11, the nation's citizens are frightened and want their leadership to do their job—protect them.

The Sergeant at Arms stood at the back of the House Chamber and announced "Mr. Speaker, the President of the United States." President Carlton Bennett emerged onto the floor and began making his way to the front of the Chamber. Unlike so many joint sessions of Congress before, smiles and handshakes were replaced by solemnity, the likes of which few remembered. Deliberately, President Bennett made his way into the Chamber and climbed the steps and approached the Speaker's Rostrum shaking both Vice President Colby's and Speaker Teasdale's hands. President Bennett took his position at the lectern on the central tier immediately below the Speaker's rostrum and prepared to address this historic joint session of Congress.

All in attendance stood and greeted President Bennett with the customary persistent cheers and applauses. On this day, however, traditional excitement and enthusiasm for a Presidential presentation to a Joint Session of Congress was tempered by nervousness and overshadowed by the pall of fear and sadness that hung over all in attendance. All hopeful that the President had a plan. A plan to bring forth the might of this great nation to protect it from these most heinous and insidious acts of unfettered brutality.

After giving the audience time to express their enthusiasm for President Bennett, the Speaker of the House rapped his gavel three times and announced, "Members of Congress, I have the distinct honor of presenting to you the President of the United States." Once more the crowd rose to their feet and applauded vigorously for their President.

*"Thank you. Thank you. Please sit down. Please sit down. Let us get on with the matter at hand."*

The members of Congress and the gallery become quiet as President Bennett began.

*"Mr. Speaker, Mr. Vice President, members of the United States Congress, distinguished guests and fellow Americans, thank you very much for your warm welcome. We gather this evening in response to the most unimaginable, reprehensible and destructive act of terrorism to touch this great land since Al-Qaeda's cowardly attack on September 11, 2001. That day, we lost more than three thousand of our brothers and sisters. Two days ago, once again this great land fell victim to terrorism. Not terrorism we anticipated, but a twenty-first Century lone-wolf high-technology form of terror that went beyond computer hacking. The Islamic State's use of lone-wolf autonomous drones pose a threat beyond imagination. Two days ago, upwards of eighteen micro-drones attacked our country, undetected, in a most brutal and cowardly fashion. Two days ago, these three acts of automated lone-wolf terror caused the death of six thousand two hundred twenty-seven innocent people and injured thousands more. Today, we take the gloves off. Today, we say no more!"*

The crowd broke into applause.

Bennett waited for the applause to subside. "Thank you. Thank you."

*"As we all know, throughout history, war has been a main component of international relations. Since this nation's founding, a major responsibility of our government has been and continues to be protection of its citizens. The Constitution clearly places this responsibility to defend our nation in our hands—yours and mine—the hands of the federal government. As much as we may detest war, our options have become limited."*

*"Perhaps it has been too easy to forget the pain of 9/11 or suppress feelings as we witness innocent citizens of America and our Allies tortured and beheaded. We can no longer sit on the side lines because once again, our enemy has brought war to our land. Tonight, I come before this joint session to call upon you, the United States Congress, per Article I, Section 8 of the Constitution to declare war against our enemy—the Islamic State."*

*"Ladies and gentlemen, we can wait no longer. The possibilities of this new aggressive and heinous act of terror is devastating and indefensible. Our path is twofold. First, in no uncertain terms, we must reign hell onto the Islamic State. Secondly, we must protect our people and this great land. As such, just as important as confronting the Islamic State where they live, tonight per Article II, Section 2 and Article 1, Section 8 of the Constitution I am exercising my authority to call upon the states and territories to form militias that will be directly under federal control with the express purpose of suppressing insurrections and repel invasions.*

*"My friends, like you, I despise the thought of war and the reality of sending our young men and women into harm's way. However, if we have any chance to ensure that this great experiment of freedom and democracy continues to prosper, we can no longer sit on the sidelines and wait for a solution. We are the solution. May God bless you and this great country! Good night."*

## Fusion Cells

"Good evening, this is United News Network Evening Edition. I'm Jeff Stoddard and this is my co-anchor Gretchen Chen. Tonight, three days after the Islamic State's brutal and devastating attacks on Lincoln, New York and Chicago, we once again have as our guest the Sheriff of Lincoln, Graham Johnson."

"Jeff, thank you for having me on this evening. I hope I will be able to share with you relevant information about our investigation and response."

"Sheriff, Gretchen and I understand that you experienced a grave personal loss two days ago. All of us here at United News Network want to express our heartfelt condolences for the loss of your wife and daughter."

"Thank you Jeff and Gretchen. It's difficult for me to believe that my wife Bonnie and my twelve-year-old Karen were snatched from me in this utter act of brutality. As the Sheriff of Lincoln Nebraska, I am sworn to enforce the law. It is unfortunate for the perpetrators that their actions have made this a personal matter." Johnson glared into the camera, "I know you're out there and can hear my voice. You have pissed-off the wrong Sheriff. You will regret the day that you brought your unholy mission to me and my family."

Gretchen stirred uncomfortably in her chair as Sheriff Johnson personally confronts the Islamic State. "Sheriff, Jeff, I and our viewers understand your pain and are very sorry. Also, we certainly understand that you and thousands of law enforcement professionals have turned their complete attention to the Islamic State's new threat. Can you tell us what initial steps have been taken?"

"Gretchen, as part of the plan set in place after 9/11 local Fusion Cells across the country have been activated."

"Excuse me Sheriff, what is a Fusion Cell?" asked Gretchen.

"I'm sorry Gretchen, the past two days have been a whirlwind. Allow me to explain.

"Fusion Cells are strategic law enforcement venues operated by local and state governments which by-in-large are invisible to the average citizen. As of this morning, approximately seventy-five Fusion Cells have been activated coast-to-coast and border-to-border supporting thousands of federal, state and local law enforcement personnel committed to addressing threat risk and formulating response options in their local community. I believe Homeland Security demonstrated brilliant insight in recognizing that future threats may be more distributed and conducted as independent lone-wolf attacks like those of this week. As planned by the Department of Homeland security, Fusion Cells are primary focal points for the receipt, analysis and sharing of threat-related information among federal, state and local partners. In anticipation of the need to distribute threat response locally, Fusion Cells empower front-line law enforcement, public safety, emergency response, and private sector security personnel to gather and share threat-related information and formulate plans for their community."

"Sheriff, last night President Bennett addressed the joint session of Congress. In addition to his call for the Congress to declare war against the Islamic State, he called for the creation of a National Militia. What role do you see them playing in this war against the current threat?" asked Stoddard.

"Jeff, as you know, two days ago an unidentified number of lone-wolf Jihadists launched a coordinated attack against three very public targets. Based on our analysis of the data, each assailant was upwards of two miles away from their assigned target and the bomb-laden drones tracked in from numerous directions. Their size and altitude makes them fundamentally indefensible with conventional military grade weapons. Imagine the collateral damage resulting from launching shoulder mounted missiles at a three-pound target. Today, every citizen needs to become vigilant and keep an eye out for other attacks. Unfortunately, we don't know the next target nor its launch points. Our plan is simple and manageable. Fusion Cells have been ordered to coordinate and train, under my direction, tens of thousands of shotgun carrying militia members who will stand at the ready as our first line of defense to destroy these evil craft on sight."

"The use of cheap, miniature 'everyman' drones needs to be banned by international treaties before such devices fall into the hands of private users including terrorists," Eric Schmidt, CEO Google

✖ ✖ ✖ ✖ ✖

# Chapter 5

---◆---

***Six Months Earlier***

Chambers, wearing his everyday Thobe, paced the floor as yet another futile discussion erupted between Gary Sasaki and Akio Chan about escaping. "Haven't you guy's figured it out?" groaned Chambers. "There is no escaping. Nor is there a rescue. It's been more than a year and there hasn't been any evidence that the State Department is negotiating for our release. No one! And, I mean no one is looking for us. To the world we are not hostages. To the world, we're dead. We have one answer…continue giving Barakat what he wants ensures our long-term value."

Liz, cloaked in the typical Jilbab, spoke up, "Richard, we have been working night and day giving this beast everything he wants. The systems are operating. The distribution technology is deployed and tested. Even the drone control software is finalized. Tomorrow is our final demonstration. Once he sees that the system is working, what's to keep him from killing us?"

"Liz," said Chambers, "when are you going to learn that software is never complete? And, more importantly, complex systems are never bug free. The more complex we make these systems, the more valuable we are to Barakat."

Chambers leaned in close to his five team members, raised his right index finger to his mouth as he spoke softly, "Shush! Our ace in the hole is the embedded and coded messages. As long as we know this we have leverage. Quiet! Someone's coming."

The guard peered into the drone laboratory. He paused for a moment, glancing at each of the hostages, then turned and walked away.

"I don't know when it will matter, but our best strategy is to ensure that we ultimately have control over the technology," said Chambers.

"How can you be so sure that this is our insurance?" asked Gary. "If they get wind of our plan they are just going to beat us and kill us."

"Sure," said Chambers, "that's our risk. What choice do we have? If there is even a remote chance one of us gets free, the world will need our help to contain this threat. Anyone of us can take down Barakat's plan. At all cost, one of us has to get free."

## Once Again

It was 7:00pm Eastern Time, Saturday night June 13th when embedded Islamic State cells across America received a notice from numerous social media sites they monitored that a message awaited them. This night, Twitter carried the deadly instructions.

@SmallTalk09099 So many have so little to say #LIFEISGOOD

@WinterWonders89898 The joys of winter are never ending #STAYWARM

@RelaxandEnjoy 7728Don't forget to take time to exercise #TAKEYOURTIME

## Blow to Net Neutrality – June 17

Stan Dodge, Google's Data Center Security Chief, arrived to work having spent the weekend preparing for his weekly security briefing. Stan flashed his badge at the door, emptied his pockets and deposited the contents into the tray along with his briefcase, iPhone and tablet PC. More slowly than he preferred, he made his way through the metal detector then gathered his property and reloaded his pockets. Stan knew his staff groaned about these arduous procedures but, it's always better to be safe than sorry.

It was a quick walk to the kitchen for his daily cappuccino with a double espresso. Afterward he shot across the lobby to the imposing security door where a member of his security team sat at his disk maintaining a constant vigilance. Stan swiped his ID card then stared into the retinal scanner. The red light turned green and he heard the familiar whine and click of the door unlocking. With a gentle pull, the massive security door broke free with a puff of air and Stan entered Google's secure Network Operations Center. Then, it was a short walk down the sterile hallway and two quick steps up to his lofty perch from where he observed one of the most powerful hubs of the Internet in the world— The Dalles Google Data Center.

Google's $1.2 billion data center resided in an understated structure with water vapor rising from its cooling towers. Located in beautiful The Dalles Oregon, on the Columbia River, the Google Data Center was strategically located between the Bonneville and John Day hydroelectric dams ensuring constant access to its life's blood—electricity.

While Stan anticipated "just another day," eight unassuming figures, each transporting four drones, approach their assigned launch sites from all points of the compass. Each dutifully followed navigation instructions, ironically provided by cheerful and friendly voices on their smartphones, approached within two miles of The Dalles Google Data Center and maneuvered their nondescript minivans and SUVs into positions shielded from view.

Once settled in, sunroofs opened and each drone commander awaited his launch authorization as the smartphones began their countdown.

T-minus three minutes. Each operator flips the power switches on his four drones to the on position awakening their deadly armada. Blue and red LEDs flickered confirming the drones had awakened, were active and the programmed pre-launch diagnostics had begun.

T-minus one minute. The drones' LEDs flickered one last time and then glowed steady blue indicating all systems were go.

T-minus 5, 4, 3, 2, 1…the attack squadron of thirty-two drones rose up slowly, gently guided through the sunroofs by their commanders. Once free of the vehicle, the drones ascended to three hundred feet and began the short, momentous two-mile journey toward Stan's Data Center. At thirty-five miles per hour, the drone armada began their brief five-minute trek to changing both Stan's and Google's lives forever. As in previous attacks, these simple vehicles of doom, buzzing toward The Dalles, chronicled their mission by broadcasting real-time video to social media around the world. To make matters worse, the video was passing through Stan's Data Center…The ultimate irony.

Barely settled in, with his cappuccino resting on his desk untouched, Stan was startled by the sound of alarms and sudden chaos. As he scanned the dozen plus security video feeds strategically positioned in front of his desk Stan heard explosions and saw smoke, fire, sparks and carnage as his Data Center tried vainly to stay alive. This day, one hundred Google employees joined the ranks of victims of the Islamic State as Google's services went dark for millions of users.

### Busch Stadium—the Threat Escalates

As Stan Dodge reeled from the attack on Google's Data Center. The long-arm of Al Qaida reached deeply into the American heartland. Citizens coast-to-coast were on the edge of their seats listening to the news of the most recent drone attacks. Fortunately, one's peace-of-mind was easily established by the age-old and time-tested adage; *this couldn't happen to me*. Unfortunately, how we think about something has little or no effect on another's actions. At 3:00pm Wednesday afternoon, eight of Barakat's drone operatives began preparing their individual drones for a scheduled attack the evening of the following day.

This day Islam has decided to change its attack plan ever so slightly. The assigned operators made their way through the well proven process of programing their drones. The difference this day, however, was the payload. Yes, C4 would be used, yet in much smaller quantity than the amount used against Google. Two hundred fifty grams of C4 was carefully formed into a ball. Each operator, wearing protective clothing and a breathing respirator, gingerly inserted the C4 and detonator wired to the drone into a two quart Tupperware container half-filled with a white powder—RICIN. Once the C4 charge was in place, the operator gently poured more of the deadly powder into the Tupperware container fully covering the C4. Each drone was carrying a payload of five hundred grams of RICIN poison each lethal enough to infect two hundred thousand people.

Click! The lid to the container was fastened into place followed by a couple of strips of duct tape methodically placed to assure the lid would not come off. As with all previous deadly payloads, this benign looking Tupperware container was affixed under the drone with a few strategically located plastic tie-wraps.

With the payloads securely in place, the eight operatives powered-up their personal fleet of terror. The LEDs blinked green then red as the onboard computer went through its diagnostics. Once the green LEDs stopped blinking and glowed steadily, the operators tapped the screen on their iPhones and within moments a datalink was established and each drone was programed with navigation and attack profiles. Once completed, the progress icon on the iPhone stopped spinning and was replaced with the words "Programming Complete." All that was left for these covert soldiers of Islam was to carefully place their drones under a blanket in the vehicles.

At 7:00 PM the following day eight unassuming individuals left the confines of their suburban garages and made their way toward Busch Stadium where the game between the St. Louis Cardinals and the Cincinnati Reds just began. It was a typical beautiful St. Louis evening and capacity crowds gathered to see their beloved Cardinals defeat the Reds.

At 8:15 PM, at the bottom of the fifth inning, Cardinals led the Reds 6 to 3 as each of the eight delivery vehicles pulled into their assigned launch points two miles from Busch Stadium. As many times before, the operators flipped the power switches on each of their four drones to the on position and the pre-programmed self-diagnostics began. The six rotors on each drone began spinning and the LEDs flickered from red to blue confirming all was ok.

At 8:20 PM, diagnostics were complete and thirty-two drones came to life beginning the pre-launch process. Sunroofs in the eight transportation vehicles opened and within moments, one-by-one, the drones began rising up through the sunroofs, gently guided by their operators. Once clear of their vehicles, each group of four drones quickly rose up to their pre-assigned five-hundred-foot cruising altitude and began the short two-mile journey toward Busch Stadium. Just as quickly and seamlessly, sunroofs closed and eight vehicles invisibly began their journeys back to their suburban strongholds. Barakat's agents' responsibilities were complete. It was now up to Barakat's autonomous creations to complete their missions.

It had been a quick couple of innings and the Cardinals still led the Reds 6 to 3. Thirty-two thousand fans, entrenched in the pitching battle, cheered their favorite team. Unfortunately, joy was soon to be brought to an abrupt halt. The moonless sky made for an eerie black backdrop for the daylight brightness of Busch Stadium's lights—blinding everyone who dared to look toward the sky. Just as Busch Stadium's night-lights overwhelmed one's vision, the din of the crowd made it difficult to hear the friend in the adjacent seat and impossible to hear the high-pitched buzzing of the electric motors and propellers of the Jihadist's attack drones. Swooping in from eight different directions, the drone armada came together over second base. At first, the hopeful thought was that this was simply a demonstration of the latest toy drones. Unfortunately, curious interest was replaced by panic and overshadowed passion for the game as thousands of fans began a mad dash toward the exits. Unfortunately, recognition of the threat was one step too late as the thirty-two drones moved apart and into position strategically covering all seating from the outfield bleachers to home plate.

The fans continued their panic stricken effort to flee, stepping on one another and elbowing young and old to the ground. The fear and panic was palpable with no sign of abating as the lead-drone broadcast the armada's effect on thirty thousand baseball fans throughout social media and across the world.

T-minus 5, 4, 3, 2, 1…As before, the video feed went black, but the brilliance of thirty-two strategically placed explosions overwhelmed the stadium's lighting for just a moment and filled Busch Stadium in a cloud of white powder. But wait. Unlike Lincoln, New York and The Dalles, something was different. No one was injured. Was it possible this attack was a dud? Thirty-two duds? Within moments after the explosions, the tone of the crowd changed from outright panic to curiosity. What happened?

Curiosity aside, fans continued exiting Busch Stadium, however, much more calmly as the stadium announcer encouraged everyone to take their time and exit the stadium in an orderly fashion. Of course, one would need to be a fool to think nothing happened. The panic of the moment, paired with the deep black sky and bright stadium lights camouflaged what had been perceived as dust. But, it was nothing of the kind as the deadly RICIN poison fell like snow on tens of thousands of Cardinals and Reds fans. Life in America had changed once again as the aftertaste of terror permeated tens of thousands of citizens in a new and frightening way.

### The White House

"What in hell just happened?" demanded President Bennett. "What are we going to do to defend against this onslaught?"

"Mr. President."

Bennett turned to David Charmer, Director of the CDC "What Dave?"

"Mr. President, as yet we don't know the immediate health impact from yesterday's attack on Busch Stadium. People are flooding into local ERs and HAZMAT teams have secured the stadium. Our best guess is it will take months to clean up this mess. Assuming we can clean it up at all. Mr. President, the bottom line is simple. Busch Stadium may be under a state of quarantine for a very long time."

"You mean….Busch is off limits indefinitely?"

"Yes Mr. President. The level of contamination is unprecedented. After reviewing the recovered debris from the drones, we estimate that upwards of thirty-six pounds of RICIN poison was spread across the stadium."

"I don't have a sense of what thirty-six pounds of RICIN is. Explain it to me."

Charmer, shuffled through is notes to retrieve the answer the President wanted. "Well Mr. President, according to our experts, two milligrams of RICIN is considered deadly. The frightening fact is there is over four hundred and fifty thousand milligrams of RICIN per pound. In a worst case scenario, thirty-six pounds of RICIN is equivalent to sixteen million milligrams. Hmmm....Roughly, this is potentially lethal to seven million people. Mr. President, this is a catastrophe of epic proportions!"

The quiet in the Oval Office was thick and weighted heavy on everyone's shoulders. Bennett stood leaning against his desk surveying the eyes of the eight attendees. "Mr. President." Bennett snapped his head in the direction of Harold Simpson, Director of Homeland Security. "Harry! Now what?"

"Well, Mr. President, it's obvious to me that we must take serious and unprecedented measures to protect our citizens."

"And Harry, what do you suggest?" asked Bennett sarcastically.

Glancing around the room, uncomfortable about what he was about to say, Simpson's lips parted "Mr. President, we need to minimize the ability for these attacks to hurt our citizens. To do that we may need to limit gatherings and crowds. Perhaps we need to impose curfews."

"Curfews! That's just CYA for imposing martial law" blurted Bennett. "I am not going to be the first U.S. President since Lincoln, to impose martial law! It is not going to happen on my watch. There has to be a better way than curbing our citizens' rights."

"Mr. President," said Thomas Gomez, Director of the Federal Aviation Administration.

Turning to Director Gomez, "Yes Tom. What are you thinking?"

"Mr. President, it's obvious these devices are navigating U.S. airspace either autonomously or under remote control. Regardless of the controlling mechanism, their size and operating altitude makes them impossible for our radar systems to detect."

"Ok Tom, cut to the chase."

"Well Mr. President, if these devices are being controlled remotely we could jam their radios. Unfortunately, we don't know when and where an attack will occur nor do we know their operating frequency or frequencies. Or, if they are even controlled by radio at all. Our guess is they are operating and navigating autonomously via GPS which leaves us very few options. If we knew an attack was in progress, we could spoof the GPS signal, which is equivalent to shutting down our GPS satellites for all uses during that time."

"Tom, I've heard that suggestion already. It's impossible. GPS is critical for transportation on every level from cars to airplanes. Shutting down GPS would be catastrophic and result in economic suicide."

Roger Kerns, Bennett's Chief of Staff interrupted, "Mr. President, as important as this is you have a meeting with the Chinese Ambassador in five minutes."

"OK Roger. Gentlemen. We are screwed if we don't get our arms around this matter immediately. As you all know, I expect to hear from Congress this evening as well as receiving a game plan from the Joint Chiefs. Put your damn heads together and work this problem. I want answers and I want them immediately."

"Until then, gentlemen," glared Bennett, "Today I am signing Executive Order 432 authorizing deployment of a shotgun toting state militia. We will be appointing Sheriff Johnson of Lincoln, Nebraska as the National Director. We served together in the Teams. He is an exceptional man and a true patriot. Roger has already broached the idea with him and I will confirm with him in the morning."

### The Sheriff Steps Up

Sheriff Johnson sat at Turner's bar drowning his sorrows. "It's hard to believe Bonnie and Karen are gone. Joe, give me another."

"Sheriff, how are you holding up?" asked Joe, the proprietor of Turners. "As good as one can expect. Basically, shitty!" snapped Johnson. "They say time heals all wounds. I say bullshit! It's been two months since those bastards attacked Lincoln and killed my wife and daughter and I'm not feeling any better!"

"It's going to take time Sheriff. Believe me. I lost my Susan three years ago to cancer. I never thought I would get through it. But, instead of drowning my sorrows, I decided to honor her, and now I volunteer with Lincoln's cancer foundation. I know it won't bring my Susan back, but I know she would be happy that I am doing something."

Johnson threw back his shot of Jack Daniels and slapped the glass down on the bar and turned his attention to his cold beer. Wiping his damp lips on his right sleeve, he stared into Joe's eyes long enough to make Joe a little uncomfortable. "You Joe! You have a point. Bonnie has always supported me throughout my career. Back at the Teams she always understood when I had to go on a mission and was always there for me when I returned."

"What are you getting at Sheriff?" asked Joe.

"Isn't it obvious? I have to honor Bonnie just as she honored me. I have to do something about this situation," said Johnson.

"What are you going to do Sheriff?" asked Joe,

Speaking more loudly than usual, Johnson announced his intention. "I don't believe we can count on our government to deal with these assholes. Islam has us all by the balls and they are going to destroy this country. There is only one answer, we have to take this battle to the streets. We need to fight them where they stand."

Joe, looking confused asked, "Sheriff, how are you going to do that?"

"I got a call this afternoon from President Bennett. He asked me to head up the National Militia. I am going to recruit every shotgun toting patriot and former Special Forces team member I can to lay siege to these bastards and protect America. These lone wolf Jihadists think they have us by the balls. They will soon learn what it means to have their balls in my hands."

### A Different Reunion

Fifteen days after Johnson's call from President Bennett, he found himself on stage at the Washington D.C. Hilton ballroom watching more than five hundred citizen-warrior patriots find seats. The sense of patriotism was palpable as concerned citizens, law enforcement, military and former Special Forces members filed into the ballroom.

Tapping the microphone a few times, more out of nervousness than purpose, Sheriff Johnson spoke loudly, barely needing the PA system. "Ladies and Gentlemen. Ladies and Gentlemen. Please take your seats so we can get this meeting underway."

"As you know, President Bennett signed Executive Order 432 authorizing activation of a national militia as America's first line of defense against the Islamic State's drone attacks. According to the President's order, it is my responsibility to establish and recruit armed citizens, we call Militia Responders, in communities across the county to maintain vigilance and provide a swift and destructive response in the event a drone attack is detected."

Johnson turned to his assistant, "Put up the slide please."

"Each Militia Responder will be required to receive clearance from their local law enforcement agency necessitating an abbreviated Department of Justice background check. Once approved, permits will be issued along with yellow Militia Responder Vests. As shown in this slide. Militia Responders will be authorized to carry twelve gauge shotguns with a maximum of three rounds of double-aught buck cartridges in the magazine. Any questions?"

"Yes. Sheriff Johnson, I'm Rich Stockton, Chief of Ferris County Police. So, what you are suggesting is we're going to have hundreds of shotgun toting citizens roaming the streets? I don't know about you Sheriff, but that makes me more than a little nervous."

"Well, Chief Stockton," snapped Johnson, "what would you suggest?"

"Sheriff, I really don't know. It just seems crazy. Why can't our sworn officers take on this responsibility?"

"Chief. First, it's what the President wants and second, there simply aren't enough sworn law enforcement professionals in America to scan the skies and enforce the law at the same time. The bottom line is simple. As long as an applicant passes the DOJ background check, you will issue their permit and support their efforts. If you don't, you will be in violation of the President's Executive Order."

Pausing for a moment, Johnson took a sip of water and said, "Folks, these savages have technology that can and will rain down death and destruction on this county. Until the government comes up with a better solution or finds a way to end this threat, it is our job to disable as many of these contraptions as possible, minimizing the impact on our citizens."

"Good luck and may God bless us."

# Chapter 6

———————◆———————

### *Back Room of Autonomous Systems*

The aroma of coffee filled Autonomous Systems' conference room as David Kramer, the new CEO, settled into his seat at the head of the grand conference table with only two other seats occupied.

Kramer took a sip from his cup and broke the silence. "Over the past few months, all of us have come to the same conclusion. The capabilities and actions of the recent drone attacks mirror our technology. Our suspicions have been confirmed by the call I received three days ago. Roger Kerns, the President's Chief of Staff, invited me to attend a White House meeting the day after tomorrow. I need to be prepared to address the obvious questions."

"Over the past month," continued Kramer, "I've had a team of our brightest engineers reviewing the information provided by the FBI."

"Other than the fact we're leaders in autonomous drone systems, is there another reason they called you?" asked Carl Summers, Autonomous' Chief Technology Officer.

"Yes. Roger Kerns told me that recent covert imaging and facial recognition identified that Richard Chambers was standing with the Islamic State leader during a demonstration of their drone capability. In fact, they don't believe our team was lost in the disappearance of our company jet, but was abducted."

Ron Parsons, Autonomous Systems' Project Manager, with his coffee cup dangling in mid-air stared at Kramer, "You mean Chambers and the others are alive?"

"They have no evidence other than pictures of a man they believe to be Chambers. Nothing was said about the others. But they do suspect that if Chambers was alive, it was likely others were as well. If this is the case, they believe it very likely that Chambers and the others incorporated our technology into the Islamic State's attack drones. Whether their involvement was voluntary or forced I don't know. I presume I'll learn more in a couple of days."

"Is there more evidence other than their belief that some guy looks like Chambers?" asked Summers.

"Actually, yes. As you would expect, some components of the attack drones have been recovered. The FBI has identified some PROMs with firmware which they hoped we could help unravel. More importantly, based on Chamber's apparent involvement they were hopeful we could help in their investigation."

"Do they think we had anything to do with it?" asked Parsons.

"Currently, their working theory is only Chambers and his team are working for the Islamic State. At this moment, they don't suspect anyone at Autonomous. They hope, however, that there is something we can do to help neutralize this growing threat. So, today, we need to put our heads together and come up with a plan. I cannot go into a meeting with the President of the United States empty-handed."

"Well, we better assemble our team and work this problem. If they're correct about the drones employing Autonomous code, then we are the best ones to devise a countermeasure," conceded Summers.

"I couldn't agree more Carl. We better be prepared to take on this challenge. I need a solution in my pocket in two days. My flight leaves for Washington at 9:00am the day after tomorrow. Don't expect to get any sleep until then."

### Back at the White House

As Kramer made his way down the stairs of Autonomous Systems' replacement jet, he was met by three imposing gentlemen in black suites, wearing sunglasses, and sporting ear phones with a motorcade of three black Chevrolet Suburbans positioned near the jet.

One of his greeters, held up his identification. "Mr. Kramer, I'm Special Agent Terry Spence. I'm here to escort you to the White House. Please board the middle vehicle. My people will get your bags."

Nervously, Kramer boarded the suburban, swiftly followed by the three gentlemen that greeted him on the ramp. The vehicle was dead quiet except for the hum of the engine followed by the choreographed sound of seat belts clicking. Agent Spence snapped his finger forward directing the driver to move out and the motorcade accelerated quickly, passing through the airport gates without slowing down.

Twelve minutes later the ominous motorcade pulled into the White House driveway where Roger Kerns stood, awaiting their arrival. "Good morning Mr. Kramer, I'm Roger Kerns. We spoke a few days ago. Welcome to the White House. Please follow me."

Kerns and Kramer swiftly navigated the White House hallways and security arriving at the President's conference room. "President Bennett will join us shortly."

Kramer paused, glancing around the room. He estimated a dozen people occupied seats around the conference table. A young lady gently grasped Kramer's arm and asked, "Mr. Kramer, can I get you a cup of coffee or something? Allow me to show you to your seat."

"Yes. Yes, I would appreciate a cup of coffee," uttered Kramer nervously as he made his way around the conference table to a seat identified by a name card inscribed 'David Kramer, CEO Autonomous Systems.'

"Ladies and gentlemen, the President of the United States," announced Kerns.

In unison, the sound of chairs against the carpeted floor broke the silence as a dozen plus men and women rose to their feet as President Bennett, followed by three aids, entered the room.

"Good morning everyone, thank you for joining us today. We have a serious problem to solve," said Bennett. "According to our intelligence, Moktar Barakat is leading the drone attacks on U.S. territory and citizens. The most recent of these attacks was on Google's data center in Oregon along with the biologic attack on Busch Stadium. We need a solution and we need it now. I would like to turn this discussion over to Harold Simpson, the Head of Homeland Security. Harold."

"Thank you Mr. President. As everyone is aware, we are falling prey to a most insidious attack strategy. To date, the Islamic State has taken credit for these attacks, and for all practical purposes, they appear to be the action of disparate lone wolf jihadists embedded in America. As President Bennett stated, our intelligence agencies believe these efforts are led by Moktar Barakat, shown here on the screen. Barakat is an electrical engineer educated at Edinburgh University. His education aside, we don't believe he possesses the technological resources to create such sophisticated autonomous systems. It is our belief, however, that the man shown here, Richard Chambers, does have the technological know-how and is most likely the mastermind behind this development effort."

Jennifer Palmer, Senate Majority Leader raised her hand, "Mr. Simpson, are you telling us that one man is the source of this technology?"

"Not exactly Senator," replied Simpson. "Eighteen months ago a private jet operated by Autonomous Systems was en route from San Francisco to Mumbai then on to Kuala Lumpur with Mr. Chambers and his leading technology team comprised of five engineers and their autonomous drone systems project manager. Seen here are Kent Anders, Gary Sasaski, Akio Chan, Jeff Chaplain, Will Schmidt and Liz Collins. Along with Mr. Chambers, all were presumed lost when their Falcon Jet disappeared over the Bay of Bengal after departing from Mumbai. Last communication with the aircraft was from its captain declaring an emergency. Shortly thereafter, radar contact was lost. A situation reminiscent of Malaysian Air Flight MH370. Like MH370, after exhaustive searching no sign of wreckage was found. We believe, however, that the aircraft diverted from its course to Kuala Lumpur and flew under the radar arriving in Islamabad, Pakistan at which time Mr. Chambers and his team were removed from the plane and the aircraft likely destroyed. Supporting this theory are these images of people we believe to be members of the Autonomous team and the burning hulk of what appears to be a Falcon Jet."

"So," said Senator Palmer "You're telling us that this Barakat guy abducted a team of our leading drone engineers and forced them to develop this technology?"

"In a nutshell Senator, that's our operating theory," responded Simpson, "What we don't know is whether their collaboration with Barakat was voluntary or they were forced to do so. It does appear, however, by Mr. Chambers' close proximity to Barakat in this picture and his clothing, that he is a willful participant."

Palmer snapped, "A traitor? What are we going to do about it?"

President Bennett stood up. "Senator, this is why we are here today. Everyone in this room was invited because they each have a unique and potentially valuable contribution to make. Please, let's move past this and get to the problem at hand. We are dealing with a proven threat to the security of America. Today's objective is to develop an effective game plan and response to this threat as soon as possible. We don't know if, when, or where another attack will occur. But, based on the recent events, Barakat and his followers are bold and committed to harming U.S. citizens. We need a plan to put a stop to it now!"

President Bennett sat down and turned the meeting over to Harold Simpson. "Ladies and gentlemen, today we have with us Mr. David Kramer, the current CEO of Autonomous Systems who replaced Richard Chambers. We believe Mr. Kramer and his team are best equipped to help us develop a response to Barakat's attacks. Mr. Kramer, the floor is yours."

Making every effort to not show how truly nervous he was, Kramer slid his chair back, picked up his folio and made his way to the front of the room. "Mr. President, distinguished colleagues. It's truly unfortunate that our meeting today is the result of such regrettable and unpropitious circumstances. Normally I find myself speaking to the press, engineers and marketing professionals about the opportunities autonomous drone technology offers. It's truly disturbing to think that our technology may have been co-opted for such evil purposes.

"Unfortunately, aside from the pictures suggesting Richard Chambers is aiding Barakat in developing this terrible weapon, the FBI has retrieved incriminating evidence that is simply undeniable."

Kramer, paused for a moment then pressed the button on the remote control bringing up his PowerPoint presentation showing some computer chips. "What you see here are computer chips known as PROMs, which stands for Programmable Read Only Memory. Recently, the FBI recovered a few PROMs from some of the drone wreckage.

"For those unfamiliar with what PROMs are, allow me to explain. PROMs are used by software engineers to store basic software programming to control fundamental functions of a computer system. Fortunately, the FBI successfully extracted the code programmed into this particular PROM. Unfortunately, the FBI was unable to uncover any relevant information. Since we are the clear leaders in drone technology, they contacted us and asked us to look at the code."

Kramer advanced the slide and a screen of computer gibberish was displayed.

**Code Sample 1:**

#if CONFIG _HAL_BOARD==HAL_R@UD_TR_AMP1

#if CONFIG _HAL_BOARD==HAL **_SAVE US_** AMP1

**Code Sample 2:**

#if CONFIG_GPS_BOARD==GPS_BOARD_ZR_HMB

## #if CONFIG_GPS_BOARD==GPS_BOARD *AS INC*

"The FBI shared their theory that Chambers may have had a role in development of the attack drones. At the FBI's request, our engineers reviewed the recovered code and confirmed their suspicions. The recovered computer code was clearly from operating system software Autonomous Systems developed prior to the loss of Chambers and his team.

"After our programmers reviewed the code, one of our team members recalled that Will Schmidt was a SCI-FI fan and his favorite movie was 2001: A Space Odyssey. If there are any SCI-FI fans in the room, you may recall that the computer on the Discovery spaceship in the movie was the HAL-9000. Many believe that Arthur Clarke, the author of 2001, hid something in the computer's name. If you increase each letter of HAL by one character, it translates to IBM—the leader of the computer industry at the time. As such, we ran the code through an algorithm and are confident we discovered a clue we believe hidden by Schmidt. As you can see here, the characters in Code Sample 1, R@UD_TR and ZR_HMB, when each character is increased by one translates into SAVE_US and in Code Sample 2, the code translates to AS_INC. Hopefully, as we continue to scrub the code we will discover additional messages from Schmidt."

"So, can you turn these godforsaken things off?" asked Senator Palmer.

"I'm sorry Senator. Not exactly. However, knowing the underlying logic employed certainly gives us a distinct advantage in creating an effective response," replied Kramer. "More importantly, we believe the existence of the SAVE US and AS INC messages in the code were not random events. We believe they are clues left by someone as to the possible existence of a mechanism for neutralizing or counteracting this threat—a backdoor if you will. My team is feverishly exploring this possibility back at Autonomous Systems. My hope is our efforts will reveal additional messages providing us the key to taking control of these drones. I assure you, our engineers will continue, unrelentingly, exploring this possibility."

"Currently, we believe an effective response system can be implemented. Unfortunately, Autonomous Systems would have to scale up its development and manufacturing well beyond its current capacity. We at Autonomous are confident we can develop a system of sentinel and defensive drones that would work together as drone armadas equipped to guard America and neutralize any threat."

"How much is this going to cost us?" asked Palmer.

President Bennett, stepped to the podium. "Senator, we're not here today to discuss money. Our duty today is to consider Mr. Kramer's plan. If it has merit, which I believe it does, I want to see if we can achieve a consensus to commit the entire resources of the United States government behind more than a response but an effective deterrent to this dastardly threat."

"Mr. Kramer, please share your plan."

"Thank you Mr. President," replied Kramer. "The good news is a viable and effective response to this threat is within our reach. Since much of the technology is readily available, my proposal will require a modest commitment, nothing like the effort required for the Manhattan Project or Apollo. Our vision is simple. We simply have to quickly implement Autonomous Systems' core technology to meet this threat. Toward this end, we propose the development of two types of autonomous drones. The first being Sentinel drones that will orbit communities autonomously monitoring the skies for intruders. Our Sentinel drones will be able to remain airborne for four to six hours at a time and monitor the electromagnetic spectrum for signatures indicative of these assault vehicles. Once detected, the Sentinel drones will broadcast the position of the attacking drones and command deployment of Defensive drones. All of this will be computer controlled and fully autonomous. Basically, we must fight fire with fire. Once deployed, each of the Defensive drones will be equipped with two response mechanisms. The first will be a grappling system with which the Defensive drone literally ensnares the attacking drone, disrupting its ability to fly and forcing it to the ground. The second modality will be a focused Electromagnetic Pulse transmitter, known as EMP. This device will allow us to target an attack drone with a debilitating surge of energy which will disrupt or damage the attacking drone's electronics."

Senator Palmer raised her hand, "Mr. Kramer. Excuse me. How many of these devices will we need?"

"Well, Senator, we will need hundreds of Sentinel drones orbiting every populated area and targets of interest. Based on our calculations, we estimate that hundreds of thousands of these devices will be needed to create an effective defensive shield. As for Defensive drones, we estimate we'll need approximately five Defense drone for every one Sentinel drone."

"So, what do you believe these devices will cost?" asked Palmer.

"Senator, our current estimate is five thousand dollars per Sentinel drone and ten thousand dollars for each Defense drone," replied Kramer. "In order to establish an effective drone shield capable of monitoring one thousand to two thousand targets, we would need at least two hundred thousand Sentinel drones and one million Defensive drones. The cost for this system would be roughly eleven billion dollars."

"Eleven billion dollars," exclaimed Senator Palmer. "Are you kidding?"

Once again President Bennett moved to the podium. "Senator, we believe this cost can be shared with communities and private enterprise. Considering the alternatives, eleven billion dollars to deploy this system to protect two thousand geographic areas is not outlandish. It's roughly five million dollars per area. I'll be executing an executive order authorizing emergency funding for Mr. Kramer's plan today. We cannot wait any longer."

### The Militia Steps Up

Peter Barnes, wearing his florescent yellow Militia vest, cradled his Remington 870 Tactical shotgun loaded with three three-inch twelve gauge cartridges in the magazine and one in the chamber. Peter scanned the Orlando skies ready to respond. Peter Barnes, sixty-two years old, served two tours in Iraq and was proud to continue protecting his beloved country. With loaded weapon in hand and twenty-four additional rounds in the case clipped to his belt, Peter joked with his companion, "Jack. I am locked and loaded!"

"Pete, what do you think are the odds that we will ever see a drone?" asked Jack.

"I don't know buddy, but let one of those sons-of-bitches get in range and it's a goner," grinned Peter.

The warm ocean breeze, paired with the red cast of the waning sun, was just the beginning of another peaceful Orlando evening. Pete and Jack patrolled the beach-front community along with hundreds of locals and tourists enjoying the summer evening. Pete's eyes, ever skyward, maintained a diligent scan for a potential intruder.

All of a sudden, Pete's attention piqued as the silence is broken by the familiar click of Jack's safety. "Pete! Pete! I've got one," shouts Jack as he shouldered his weapon and swung up and eastward toward a swiftly moving object buzzing low and erratically. Bang! Bang! The quiet night is broken as Jack discharged two quick rounds towards his target.

Loud screams created a cacophony of chaos as hundreds of startled beach goers ran in every direction in response Jack's shotgun fire.

Jack's first round struck his target and the quadcopter began to spin wildly crashing to the ground twenty yards away.

Pete and Jack, secured their weapons and sprinted toward the downed vehicle finding a mass of debris with one propeller futilely trying to lift the craft.

"Dad, they shot my drone!" wailed a little boy twenty yards away.

Pete, picking up the battered toy-drone shook his head. "Jack, this isn't good."

### The Sheriff Reports

It's the rare citizen that wasn't aware of the Second Amendment. For many, the right to bear arms paired with a well-regulated Militia is fundamental to preserving freedom. Unfortunately, in response to the Islamic State's drone attacks, many Americans found themselves caught between the potential benefit of an armed Militia and the all-too-frightening unintended consequences resulting from thousands of shotgun-toting citizens watching the skies.

A year ago Sheriff Johnson was content keeping the peace in the mid-west slow Lincoln Nebraska. Today, through a stroke of fate he found himself burdened with the responsibility of being the leader of a national Militia.

"Mr. President, over the past four months thirty-five thousand citizens have been inducted into the Militia," reported Johnson. "These are great people committed to defending America."

"I understand Sheriff," responded Bennett, "but yesterday a Militia member in Orlando shot down a nine-year old boy's toy drone. Graham, this is not good."

"Mr. President, I understand. But, we all knew this was a possibility," replied Johnson. "People are going to make mistakes. They are going to over react. Regardless, I believe we need to move forward for this program is a good solution for protecting America."

"Graham, I agree with you. I am counting on you to let these valiant volunteers know that they need to be careful," said Bennett.

"Mr. President. You have my commitment that Militia members will be properly trained and informed," replied Johnson.

# Chapter 7

———————◆———————

### *Once Again*

As the clock struck 7:00pm Eastern Time, Saturday June 27th embedded Islamic State cells across America received another notice through social media calling them to action. This evening's benign yet deadly message set the terror wheel in motion.

@ASimpleThought Summer is our time to relax #SUMMERFUN

@SomeVacationthoughts I Can't wait to go RVing #ROADTRIP

@HappyFourth Patriotism is alive and well #GODBLESSAMERICA

### *Just a Quiet Summer Night*

For Carl and Brandy Anders it was just a quiet summer evening they planned to spend with their children, and ten thousand locals, watching fireworks at Crew Stadium in their home town of Columbus Ohio. Since sunset in Columbus happens at 9:04pm, Carl and his family pulled into Crew Stadium at 7:45pm to ensure they got good seats. At sixty-eight degrees it was a brisk summer evening as the Anders family nestled into their seats draped in light blankets on the fifty-yard line in Section 126. "Wow!" Exclaimed Brandy to her three children, "Your father got great seats. This is going to be an amazing show."

After devouring the traditional summer fare of hotdogs and Cokes, the Anders family relaxed in their seats savoring hot cocoa when they were called to attention as the National Anthem began and the massive American flag was unfolded covering the field by hundreds of U.S. Marines. "I just love being an American," whispered Carl into Brandy's ear.

"Daddy! Look!" shouted eight-year old Carl junior pointing toward the sky as an approaching flight of vintage airplanes began their pass over the stadium in the missing-man formation honoring fallen military personnel. "Yes, Carl," responded his father, "tonight we honor the many men and women who have fought and died for our freedom. The fourth of July is a very special day."

Moments later Carl junior, once again pointed skyward while tugging on his father's sleeve. "Look daddy, more airplanes." Carl, looked in the direction his son was pointing and immediately became alarmed.

"Brandy, we have to get out of here. Now!" as he pulled his family from their premier seats and began scurrying up the long flight of stairs toward the exit. "What's wrong Carl?" resisted Bandy. "I don't know" whispered Carl, "this just doesn't look right to me. Let's go!"

With fireworks booming and filling the sky with smoke, a squadron of miniature aircraft began what is now the all too familiar attack pattern that fuels panic for every American. The eight menacing craft swooped into Crew stadium and began orbiting the field descending closer and closer toward the unsuspecting crowd. Simultaneously, more than one hundred men and women, positioned throughout the stadium, raised their shotguns toward the approaching drones. The sound of one hundred shotgun cartridges being racked into their chambers was unmistakable. More frightening, however, was the concussion of deafening muzzle blasts filling the stadium. The din of hundreds of rounds of ammunition discharges filled Crew. Each smoky discharge added to the growing remains and sweet acrid aroma of fireworks.

Simultaneously, thousands of screaming spectators became aware of the aerial threat and scrambled with abandon toward the exits, pushing the less formidable to the ground as the drone attack squadron maneuvered over the seats.

Blam! "I got one!" exclaimed one Militia member as a drone spiraled and exploded near the fifty-yard line. The downed drone dispersed its deadly shrapnel wounding five fireworks operators that futilely tried to flee the chaos yet were now on the ground in a bloody mess.

In spite of the armed Militia, the seven remaining drones made their way to their targets and in a well synchronized ballet exploded in unison delivering their deadly payloads into thousands of scared and confused onlookers.

Just as quickly as it began, the attack ended leaving more than two thousand Columbus citizens dead and thousands more injured.

Unfortunately, the drones were not the only cause of the mayhem. It will be discovered afterwards that fifteen innocent bystanders fell victim to Militia 'friendly' fire.

### Back at the White House

Sunday morning, President Bennett, Chief of Staff Kerns and Vice President Colby sat somberly on the couch in the center of the Oval Office. The silence was thick and oppressive.

Kerns broke the silence, "Mr. President, the Speaker, Majority Leader and the Attorney General are on their way. General James just entered the building."

"Wonderful. Just wonderful," Bennett uttered sarcastically. "What the hell are we going to do?"

"Mr. President," said Kerns "the numbers are in from Columbus as well as Oakland and Fort Worth. In all, seven thousand three hundred and forty-three people have been killed and more than ten thousand sustained mild to serious injuries. I can't begin to express how this feels."

"How it feels? Hell! It feels like Armageddon!" blustered Bennett as he rose to his feet and moved over to his desk. "It feels like the end of the world. We need answers. And we need answers now. But it seems like none are coming."

Ruth Holcomb, Bennett's secretary entered the Oval Office and announced that General James, the Speaker, Majority Leader and Attorney General had arrived.

"Show them in, Mrs. Holcomb," said Bennett.

Bennett approached the door and greeted each as they enter the Oval Office. "Thank you for coming over so quickly. We have work to do."

Bennett's advisors made their way into the Oval Office, choosing their seats strategically with aplomb and feigned humility consistent with Washington DC power play.

"Well people, suffice it to say we don't need to review yesterday's events. We are in the midst of an all-out attack on U.S. soil. What we need is a bi-partisan solution. A solution I intend to share with America this evening in a nationally televised speech," proclaimed Bennett.

Well, Mr. President," began Attorney General Sanitch, "clearly our citizens are not safe anywhere. As we've discussed before, there are benefits to ordering curfews. However, since the Islamic State's targets have not been limited to sports arenas and such, I don't believe imposing a curfew will yield the results we seek."

Bennett, paused for a moment then began to speak "Cur…" as the door to the Oval Office swung open. Just as quickly, a dozen men in suits swarmed in moving swiftly toward President Bennett. "What the hell?" exclaimed Bennett.

In a loud and forceful tone the man leading the swarm announced, "Mr. President. You need to come with us. Now!" By now, the gravity of the situation began to set in as three Secret Service Agents manhandled Bennett from his chair and whisked him out the door with Colby, Santich, James, Palmer, Teasdale and Kerns following close behind.

"What's going on?" demanded Bennett.

"Mr. President. Keep moving. The White House is under attack."

Within minutes, Bennett and his entourage were literally thrown into the Deep Underground Command Center (DUCC) as the vault-like door slammed shut and secured by the armed Marine on duty.

Bennett stumbled over to his seat at the conference table and settled in as Agent in Charge Kennedy directed the group's attention to the main screen.

"Mr. President, we've detected a swarm of drones en route to the White House from all points of the compass," explained Kennedy. The group scanned the video screens encircling the room searching for signs of the attacking drones.

"There! There's one," shouted Colby. Kerns pointed out another. Within a minute more than a dozen drones were seen on every screen in the room streaking toward the White House maneuvering into the all-too-familiar coordinated attack pattern.

"Mr. President," stated Kennedy. "This screen shows the LaWs, Laser Weapon System tracking the swarm approaching Constitution Avenue." The group turned their attention to the black and white LaWs display as the cross hairs narrowed on the swarm as the LaWs Weapons Commander issued the firing command. The room was eerily silent while everyone watched in anticipation of the swarm's destruction.

As the swarm crossed Constitution a puff of grey/white smoke billowed followed by an incredible explosion as the LaWs inflicted damage on the swarm.

Beyond the billowing smoke cloud, the LaWs energy beam continued depositing its force on an unsuspecting target. Without warning, a tanker truck hauling gasoline traveling East on Constitution exploded in a ball of fire as the LaWs energy beam burned a hole through the tank.

"Did we get...?" Bennett's words trailed off.

Before Bennett could finish his sentence the remaining swarm of eight drones were seen continuing their trek toward the White House. The video display showed the LaWs system adjusting to take another shot. "Fire!"

Almost immediately, there was another puff of smoke followed by an explosion. Unfortunately, like before a half dozen drones continued moving toward the White House crossing E Street and descended low hugging the ground as they moved in for the attack.

Before the LaWs Commander could issue another firing order, the swarm moved into a tight spinning attack formation tracking North with the West Wing clearly its target. Before another shot from the LaWs system could be ordered, the swarm moved in close to the White House. Reducing their speed to an almost dreamlike slowness, the drones sidled up close to the West Wing and without warning exploded in unison. Smoke filled the video displays shielding the devastation of the attack. Regardless of the tens of feet of concrete and steel that protected the DUCC, the President and his entourage felt the ground shake. A sickening deep thud resonated in the pit of everyone's stomach.

The silence was palpable as the people glared at the screen.

After what seemed like an eternity, Bennett finally broke the silence. "Does anyone have a cigarette?" In spite of Bennett's commitment to quit smoking, Kerns always kept his favorite brand on hand, just for situations like this. Kerns approached Bennett removing a cigarette from the pack. "Yes Mr. President," as he offered a cigarette with his left hand while withdrawing a lighter from his pocket with his right in one seamless motion.

"Just when we thought things couldn't get worse," exclaimed Bennett. "Answers! We need answers now!"

### The President's Speech

The stage manager initiated the countdown with his right hand held out then folded down a finger for each passing second, "Mr. President, you are on the air in 4, 3, 2 " he silently mouthed the number one then pointed his single finger toward President Bennett.

*"My fellow Americans. No President in the history of this great nation looks forward to this topic. Certainly there have been periods in America's modern history that my predecessors have had to come before this country's citizens and share horrific news. From the attack on Pearl Harbor on December 7th to the heinous September 11th attack on the*

*World Trade Center. And now, what is clearly an all-out and concerted assault against the United States and its citizens. To date, there have been no less than twenty drone attacks resulting in the death of more than thirty thousand innocent citizens. And this morning, America was struck at its core with an attack on the White House resulting in the deaths of eighteen brave men and women dedicated to protecting this great country."*

Americans everywhere were mesmerized by President Bennett's speech. Hanging on every word. Anticipating an answer. An answer that would provide them the assurance and peace they so desperately desire. Unfortunately, the reality of 9/11, like so many unsavory memories tempered over time. But no longer. The Islamic State has not only awakened these memories, they have forged new and more frightening visions of an America that is no longer safe. An America where its citizens can no longer lead a peaceful existence free of the threat of violence and mayhem. America, the world's technology leader is not only the recipient of the Islamic State's wrath, it is being pummeled by its own technological innovations.

*"My fellow American's," continued Bennett. "What appears to be our darkest hour is actually our greatest opportunity. An opportunity to pull together and protect and defend all that is valuable and righteous to us. Until we can subdue the perpetrators, beginning this evening, I am instituting a curfew limiting the gathering of large numbers of our citizens. The governors of each state have been directed to activate their state's national guard to enforce this curfew and assist law enforcement in monitoring suspicious activity that may be associated with planning or executing further drone attacks.*

*"My friends, it pains me to take this action, but in order to ensure the safety of our friends and families, there is no other course. Immediately following this speech, the Director of Homeland Security, Harold Simpson, will hold a press conference outlining the details of the curfew. Good night and God bless us all."*

## Progress at Autonomous Systems

"This is simply getting out of control. Innocent people are being killed and nothing is being done," proclaimed Kramer. "Now yesterday, the White House was attacked."

"Mr. Kramer," said Carl Summers, Autonomous Systems CIO, "we have been working feverishly, night and day, programming the surveillance and defense drones."

"When can we expect to see a demonstration?" asked Kramer.

"Actually Mr. Kramer," uttered Summers cautiously. "I believe we will be ready for a demonstration as early as tomorrow."

"Great!" exclaimed Kramer. "Schedule it and I will ask General James to fly in from Washington."

The morning sun broke through the low overcast blanketing the test range. The Autonomous team was in position and the spectators were safely seated and secured a safe distance away.

Carl Summers announced over the public address system, "T-Minus 3 minutes for system test."

System engineers and technicians performed last minute adjustments along with checks and cross-checks.

"T-Minus 5, 4, 3, 2, 1...begin demonstration," ordered Summers.

On cue, the roof of the Autonomous Systems deployment cargo container began opening lengthwise. Once opened, twenty-five surveillance drones began their ascent from the container to their 400 foot loitering altitude while tracking to their assigned surveillance stations. Within three minutes the hum of the surveillance drones could be heard from all points around the test range.

"Initiate invasion," commanded Summers.

A new sound was heard, emanating from all around, as the invading fleet of enemy drones moved toward the test range's ground zero. Everyone sat in anticipation waiting to see if this system worked.

"Surveillance drones have identified twelve targets," announced Summers. "Response orders have being issued to the Defense drones."

Almost immediately, until now unnoticed and innocuous, low plastic dome shaped enclosures distributed randomly around the test range each emitted a puff of smoke as their half-round covers flew fifty feet into the air. Once the covers cleared their enclosures, the unmistakable sound of powerful electric motors filled the air as massive six rotor drones rose quickly into the sky coordinated and directed by the constellation of surveillance drones orbiting high overhead calling the shots.

The enemy drones began forming into the familiar attack formation as they aligned themselves and tracked toward ground zero. The Defense drones moved quickly. No longer guided by the Surveillance drones, the Defense drones, each operating autonomously, calculated and tracked direct intercepts toward the attacking swarm. The enemy drones, clearly employing their own sensory system, became aware of the flight of Defense drones and broke from formation and began evasive maneuvers. Just as quickly, the Defense drones broke as well and locked onto their network-assigned targets. High overhead was an incredible aerial ballet of twenty-four autonomous drones engaged in combat while twenty-five Surveillance drones monitored the activity.

Like a swarm of bees on a random mission, the dozen enemy drones turned, banked and flipped in response to the oncoming Defense drones, yet they continued to make progress toward ground zero. The engagement, now only seven minutes since the demonstration began, continued as the spectators sat with their mouths open.

Clack! The sound of spinning propellers clashing was heard as a Defense drone connected with its target. Both drones began to spiral away from each other corkscrewing to the ground. In half a rotation, the damaged enemy drone exploded spraying its shrapnel across the test range as the damaged Defense drone crashed into the desert floor.

"Target neutralized. Eleven remaining," announced Summers.

The swarm of enemy and Defense drones continued their chaotic engagement as they moved closer and closer to ground zero. Once again, another loud clack was heard and the damaged Defense and its targeted enemy drone spiraled toward the desert floor. Like before, the enemy drone exploded delivering its deadly shrapnel while the Defense drone crashed nearby.

The ten remaining enemy drones move toward ground zero as their man-on-man Defense drones feverishly struggled to intercept and neutralize its assigned enemy. The adaptive intelligence of the enemy drones demonstrated a unique ability to both evade interception and make progress toward their assigned targets.

"Ground zero attained," called Summers.

The enemy drones form up into a spinning circular pattern over ground zero. Clack as a Defense drone neutralized its target. Unfortunately, the neutralized enemy drone exploded and delivered its deadly payload into ground zero wreaking devastation. Moments later, the remaining nine enemy drones exploded in unison and destroyed the small building that resided alone at ground zero and the ensuing blast and concussion destroyed five remaining Defense drones orbiting nearby.

"Demonstration complete," announced Summers.

Upon completion of the demonstration, the remaining four Defense drones each returned to their launch pads as the twenty-five surveillance drones, orbiting overhead, returned to the Autonomous Systems' trailer ending their mission and demonstration.

The spectators sat in awe. Clearly the surveillance and defense technology has promise. Unfortunately, the neutralized enemy drones were only diverted from their intended target and delivered their deadly payload someplace else. Today, the deadly payload of neutralized attack drones was delivered into the desert floor, but in the real world, the shrapnel or even biologics of intercepted and neutralized drones would very likely result in devastation. Perhaps, as feared, the drone threat is indefensible.

"It has become appallingly obvious that
our technology has exceeded
humanity," Albert Einstein

# Chapter 8

◆

### Return to Islamabad

Hungry, Akio Chan rose early and walked into the break room, only to find Jeff Chaplain and Will Schmidt already sitting at the table, savoring cups of tea.

"Good morning Akio. Ready for another day in paradise?" quipped Chaplain.

"Stop it Jeff! You know it isn't funny," chided Will.

"Screw you Will! You cope in your way and I'll cope in mine," snapped Chaplain.

Liz and Chambers arrived at the same time, long since having given up any attempt to conceal the fact they were a couple.

"Any port in a storm," Chan mumbled to himself as Liz prepared a cup of tea for Chambers.

Chambers moved alongside Akio, "Excuse me Akio. What did you say?"

"Nothing Richard. Just mumbling to myself," replied Akio.

Chambers leaned into Akio and whispered, "Well, my friend, I suggest you keep your opinions to yourself. OK?"

"I'm sorry. I will," replied Akio as he turned and sheepishly retreated to his customary seat next to Jeff Chaplain.

Liz handed Chambers his tea and slid into her seat next to him. Pausing for a moment to savor the sweet, dark aroma of his hot cup of tea, Chambers then turned to his team and asked, "So, what's the status?"

"Gary uploaded the latest build last night. New PROMs have been burned and are ready for final integration. Testing is scheduled for today," reported Liz.

"Good," proclaimed Chambers. "Like you, I hate what we're doing, but even if our chances for release are remote, we need to survive. I'm certain our friends know we're alive and well."

"Little does he know," Schmidt thought to himself. "Little does he know."

"Liz, what time do we depart for the test range," asked Chambers. Turning her attention to her ever present clipboard, Liz flipped through a few pages and paused. "Richard, we're scheduled to depart at 8:30. Ninety minutes from now."

Chambers and his team, dressed in orange jumpsuits, were almost indistinguishable from one another—with the obvious exception of Liz wearing the traditional hijab. The crew shuffled toward the bus with all but its windshield painted black.

Regardless of the reason, it had become a unique treat for the team to be allowed outside their underground bunker which had been their world since their capture.

Once seated, the bus began moving toward the massive door as it slowly retracted overhead making way for the bus. Breaking into the open, the searing glare from the sun poured in through the windshield. Sasaki raised his right hand, shielding his eyes, alleviated momentarily the discomfort while waiting to adjust to the bright morning sun.

The driver maneuvered his vehicle into position in the six vehicle motorcade as they accelerated away from the compound.

Long since being relieved of their watches, Chambers estimated that they had been on the road for almost three hours and expected to arrive at the test range very soon.

### SEAL Team Six

"Frontline to Mother Goose, over."

"Frontline, this is Mother Goose, go ahead."

"Frontline is in position. Convoy comprised of six vehicles including bus, two SUVs, cargo van and two pickup trucks equipped with thirty-caliber machine guns arrived on scene. Over."

"Roger Frontline. Video link live. Continue monitoring. Over."

Commander Mark Johnson, the Team's leader, turned his attention to the arriving convoy and the gathering of hundreds of Islamic State warriors sporting the ever-present AK-47's, gathered in the open area. The warriors cheered as the convoy arrived and came to a stop before the waiting throng.

"Frontline, Mother Goose, Over."

"Mother Goose, Frontline, go ahead."

"Maintain focus on the bus and obtain imaging of the personnel. Over."

"Roger Mother Goose. Image personnel on bus. Over."

Johnson directed Chief Zane to image the personnel emerging from the bus. "Roger Commander." Zane focused her high-powered telescope equipped video camera on the front of the bus as the door opened. Narrowing her focus on the first two to emerge, Zane bracketed their faces between crosshairs. The real-time images made their way up to the Predator drone orbiting at 60,000 feet which in turn relayed the information to the communication satellite positioned just above the horizon. Traveling half way around the world, at the speed of light, the images arrived at Langley and were run through facial recognition then displayed on the front screen of the situation room. "No ID" flashed on the screen with lines pointing to each of the figures exiting the bus.

Six orange-suited hooded figures exited the bus and lined up outside. The door closed quickly and the bus moved off heading back the way it came.

Futilely, Zane focused her attention on each of the figures, uploading the images to the Predator loitering high overhead as the bus moved away into the distance. The Langley computer feverishly tried to identify the orange-suited figures. But to no avail. Six separate video images were displayed on the Situation Room screen as the facial recognition system feverishly flickered through images placing characteristic markers across each of the hooded targets. One-by-one, the Langley computer posted its results.

Target 1: NO ID

Target 2: NO ID

Target 3: NO ID

Target 4: NO ID

Target 5: NO ID

Target 6: NO ID

"Frontline, Mother Goose. No ID. Over."

"Roger Mother Goose. Over."

"What now, Commander?" asked Chief Bruce Walker.

"We wait."

"Roger Commander," replied Walker.

President Bennett, sat with his elbows on his knees and his head resting on his hands turned and looked at General James. "General, we need to do something."

"Mr. President, I agree. The intel supports that these are the Autonomous Systems' team members. It's truly unfortunate that they are being forced to serve the Islamic State. However, if there is even a remote chance that these are the drone engineers, they need to be stopped. And stopped now!"

Bennett, shook his head and sat up straight while rubbing his eyes. Adjusting his tie, Bennett turned to General James, "Give the order General."

"Roger Mr. President. Fire control. You are go to launch."

"*Five, four, three, two, one. Fire!*"

High above, the loitering Predator acknowledged receipt of its command as its deadly Hellfire missile came to life in a plume of white smoke and flame and headed down. Down toward the target painted by Seal Team Six from the safety of their hillside encampment.

Half the main screen in the Situation Room displayed the real-time video from the nose of the Hellfire with its crosshairs aligned dead center on its target. The other half of the screen showed the image from Zane's point-of-view. Almost as quickly as the command was given, the Hellfire's camera closed in on its target. Closer and closer as the target filled the screen and suddenly the image went black.

Zane's video, however, captured a much different scene. Her video showed the swift arrival of the Hellfire missile then, in the blink of an eye the trail of smoke from the rocket quickly turned into a blinding explosion that decimated everyone and everything in the kill zone.

"Mother Goose, Frontline. Target destroyed."

"Direct hit Mr. President," reported General James.

"Frontline, Mother Goose. Roger. You are cleared to extract. Over"

"Mother Goose, Frontline. Roger. Frontline Out."

Johnson, turned to his team. "Let's pack up and head to the extraction point."

### Barakat's Shell Game

Chambers was initially confused by the six orange garbed and hooded individuals seated quietly on the bus. But, their purpose became obvious as the bus was shaken by the blast from the Hellfire's arrival. Barakat turned to his people in the bus and declared, "They are heroes dying for Allah. Let us move on to the weapons test site. Americans are fools and we will wipe them from the face of the earth."

As the bus made its way, Barakat read a prayer from the Qur'an, Sura 9 At-Tawba, Ayah 111 for the martyrs struck dead by the Hellfire missile.

"Allah hath purchased of the believers their persons and their goods; for theirs in return is the garden of Paradise: they fight in His cause, and slay and are slain: a promise binding on Him in truth, through the Law, the Gospel, and the Qur'an: and who is more faithful to his covenant than Allah? Then rejoice in the bargain which ye have concluded: that is the achievement supreme."

"Oh my God!" declared Will Schmidt. "Our country just tried to kill us."

"You can't be sure of that," replied Chan.

"Bullshit. You felt it. That site was blown to smithereens," asserted Schmidt.

"I guess that answers any question about a rescue mission," declared Schmidt. "Screw President Bennett. Screw America. I'm done with them. Let's make this technology indefensible."

### The Sheriff's Militia

Sheriff Johnson stood in the wings just off stage of the Dallas Hilton Doubletree ballroom, quietly reviewing his speech notes. Rene Fellows, Johnson's aid, tapped Johnson's shoulder. "Sheriff, President Bennett is on the phone for you."

Looking around for a quiet and secure place to speak with President Bennett, Johnson noticed the ballroom's sound booth. "Thank you, I'll take it in the sound booth."

Graham slipped into the quiet and secure solitude of the sound booth and closed the door behind him as he placed the cell phone to his ear. "Mr. President. Good evening. What can I do for you?"

"Graham, I know you're preparing to address the Militia Leadership this evening. I just wanted to remind you that I am truly concerned about the merits of this strategy. The citizens recently killed and injured by Militia fire is simply unacceptable. I know you agree that this cannot continue to happen."

"Mr. President, I couldn't agree more. In response to this past week's unfortunate events, we will be establishing enhanced guidelines regarding procedures and more importantly, the characteristics of the shotgun loads being used. I believe that lighter loads paired with our new engagement policy will minimize the possibility of repeating such events," said Johnson.

"Thank you Sheriff. I know you and I are on the same page regarding the use of Militia to protect our citizens. Regardless, any further injury of citizens will put this program in jeopardy and force me to rescind my order. Understand?"

"Yes Mr. President. I understand. Rest assured my leadership understands and the district representatives attending tonight's meeting will agree wholeheartedly with our changes."

"Very well Sheriff. I am counting on you and the Militia to protect Americans from this evil menace."

"You have my commitment Mr. President."

"Thank you Sheriff. Good night."

Johnson emerged from the sound booth and handed the cell phone back to Fellows. "When does the program start?" asked Johnson.

"You have fifteen minutes before Vice President Colby introduces you," replied Rene.

The Hilton Doubletree Ballroom adequately accommodates one thousand attendees. Tonight, it was standing room only with fifteen hundred plus in attendance. Fifteen hundred sworn Militia District Leaders from every state and major city in the country. Men and women committed to leading their local Militia members in protecting the lives of Americans going about their everyday activities.

"Ladies and gentlemen," boomed the loud voice over the public address system. "Please stand for the National Anthem and presentation of the colors."

A local teenager of some repute began singing the Star Spangled Banner a cappella accompanied by fifteen hundred patriotic voices desperately trying to carry the historically difficult tune. The color guard made its way from the back of the room carrying the flags of the United States of America, the State of Texas and the recently introduced United States Militia. As the National Anthem came to its end, the color guard stood at attention on stage, then placed each of the flags in their respective stands.

As the applause subsided, the voice over the Public Address system announced that the Honorable Jeffrey Baker, the Mayor of Dallas, would lead the Pledge of Allegiance.

Mayor Baker approached the podium and turned to face the flags and placed his right hand over his heart and began, "I pledge allegiance to the flag of the United States of America." Johnson was overwhelmed by the thousands of patriots vowing and reaffirming their allegiance to America.

Once again, the Public Address system came alive, "Ladies and gentlemen, the Vice President of the United States."

Vice President Colby made his way across the stage to deafening applause. Like so many politicians, the Vice President had a way of waiving and smiling that made each person in attendance feel as if he was waving and smiling just for him.

"Thank you. Thank you. Please be seated. Thank you," smiled Colby as the crowd settled down and took their seats.

"Ladies and gentlemen, today America is faced with the worse challenge since the Revolution. The sanctity of our borders has been breached and innocent citizens are being killed. But thanks to dedicated patriots like yourselves and tens of thousands more, President Bennett and I believe we can defeat this threat."

The crowd broke into a wave of applause. Yet, once settled down, Colby continued pandering to the crowd. Before leaving the stage, he announced. "Ladies and gentlemen, your leader and tonight's speaker, Sheriff Graham Johnson."

Johnson humbly approached the podium, pausing for a moment as he gazed over the ebullient crowd that applauded feverishly.

*"Thank you. Thank you. Please be seated.*

*"Thank you Vice President Colby, distinguished guests and Militia Leaders from across this great country. There isn't a single person in this room that isn't intimately aware of the threat posed by the Islamic State and their automated attack drones. To date, there have been twenty-two attacks against our country, the most audacious being the recent attack against the White House. Thanks to God and the swift response of the Secret Service, President Bennett was not injured. Tonight, our agenda is simple. We, as the duly chartered and authorized Militia of the United States, are the first line of defense to protect our citizens. More importantly, we must ensure the safety of these same citizens. Unfortunately, recent engagements have resulted in loss of life or injury of these same citizens we're charged to protect. As such, in a few minutes Ronald Jett, the Militia's Policy Director, will bring you up to speed on new engagement and response procedures. My friends, I know each and every one of you share my passion and love of this country. Thank you for your commitment to join us in protecting this great land. God bless you all and God bless America. I am happy to turn the meeting over to Ron."*

# Chapter 9

◆

### *Executive Order*

"Good morning, Tom. Please join us," as President Bennett shook FAA Director Thomas Gomez's hand. "My pleasure Mr. President. I'm sorry we are meeting under the shadow of the current situation," replied Gomez.

Gomez, took a seat on the couch next to Vice President Colby, along with Homeland Security Director Harold Simpson, Attorney General Grant Santich and Link Farnsworth, the White House Press Secretary.

Bennett, savoring the aroma of his favorite Turkish blend, took a sip. "Gentlemen, this onslaught is out of control. Our defenses are lacking and the random nature of the attacks makes preparation impossible. We need to step up our efforts and find a solution to containing this threat," declared Bennett. "Tom, what can we expect from the FAA?"

Before Gomez could take a sip of his much needed coffee, he exchanged the cup for his iPad. "Mr. President, as you know detecting these small agile aircraft maneuvering at low altitude is difficult at best. Unfortunately, further complicating detection is the fact that the skies are riddled with thousands of hobbyist and commercial remote controlled drones. These drones complicate radar detection and identification of real threats. We at the FAA believe that these activities should be curtailed immediately if not eliminated altogether."

"Harold, what's Homeland's position on domestic drones?" asked Bennett.

"Mr. President. Clearly these drones add to the confusion. I agree with Tom. Private done activities needs to be discontinued as soon as possible."

Bennett turned to Attorney General Santich, "Grant, do we need to take this to Congress or can I issue an Executive Order?"

"Mr. President," replied Santich, "Banning drone activities can either be effected by a ruling from the FAA or an Executive Order. I believe an order from you is the most efficient and less likely to be disputed by Congress."

"Ok Grant, we'll prepare the order and it will be signed immediately. Link, let's schedule a press conference this afternoon and make the announcement."

"No problem Mr. President. I'll call a briefing for 2:00pm," replied Farnsworth.

## Press Conference

Reporters from around the world filled every seat of the White House press room as Farnsworth approached the podium. "Good afternoon everybody. Thank you for joining us for this impromptu White House briefing. Joining me today is Homeland Security Director Harold Simpson and FAA Director Thomas Gomez. As you know, the effects of the Islamic State's current drone attacks have been devastating. Early detection and immediate response is our highest priority. Unfortunately, our efforts have been hindered by the growing popularity of civilian drone use. These benign and albeit friendly drones interfere with our defense systems' ability to differentiate between enemy and friendly drones. As such, the President decided, through executive order, to institute a ban on both hobby and commercial civilian drone use until such time that our strategic defense systems can reliably detect, differentiate, and respond to these aerial threats. Both Homeland and the FAA along with federal and local law enforcement will enforce this order. As you can appreciate, our schedule is hectic and I need to cut this briefing short. I believe the press kit will answer your questions. Regardless, I will take one question. Terrance, fire away."

"Thank you Link. Terrance Gamble, Associated Press. First, clearly people are frightened by current events, however, doesn't the curtailment of legitimate drone operations infringe on civil rights? Second, is there any evidence that legally operated drones have interfered with enemy drone detection and response?"

"Thank you Terrance. The President has the utmost respect for our citizens' civil rights. Just as importantly, he is concerned about their safety. Rest assured, he did not come to this decision lightly. Until this morning, he has made every effort to avoid this decision. After conferring with Congress, his Cabinet and the Attorney General, President Bennett believes this executive action is an appropriate and acceptable response to the current threat. As for your second question, I will ask Director Gomez to respond."

Gomez moved to the podium. "Thank you ladies and gentlemen. As discussed with President Bennett, we don't have any clear-cut evidence that legal personal drone operations have interfered with enemy drone detection. What we do know, however, is every day our low level approach and departure surveillance radar detects hundreds of targets. And the number of targets is growing daily. Unlike birds, the flightpaths of these aircraft indicate intelligent control. To date, legal drone operators have done a commendable job of keeping clear of airport operations. The issue, however, is the clutter illustrated by this radar image from the Chicago attack. As you can see, the drones that formed up into their final attack pattern are obvious. However, if we look at earlier radar tracks, these drones are interspersed with numerous other targets we believe to be friendly drones. Because of this confusion, our ability to respond before the enemy drones formed up into their final attack pattern was impossible. Here is the bottom line. With the proliferation of friendly drones, it is simply impossible to ensure early detection of enemy drones. This inability to positively identify a target makes it impossible to swiftly deploy an effective response."

Farnsworth returned to the podium. "Ladies and gentlemen. Thank you for your patience and understanding. This is a critical issue, and the President believes we owe it to our citizens to do everything we can to protect them. The President believes this executive order moves us a step in the right direction, and it complements the administration's efforts to improve national security. Thanks, everybody. Have a good afternoon."

### A Fearful Populace

"Good evening. I'm Jeff Stoddard and this is my co-anchor Gretchen Chen. Welcome to United News Network Evening Edition. Drones are banned. That's the news from the White House this afternoon. According to Press Secretary Link Farnsworth in a White House Briefing this afternoon, President Bennett has signed an Executive Order banning both commercial and hobby use of drones. Joining us tonight is Janet Randall, Enforcement Officer with the Federal Aviation Administration and Connor Sterns, Executive Director of the Free Skies Alliance. First, Ms. Randall, like it or not, drone operations in the United States is now illegal. What are the consequences for violating the President's Executive Order?"

"Jeff, thank you for having me on this evening. We at the FAA fully support President Bennett's Executive Order. Historically, the Director has been a supporter of both personal and commercial use of drones.

Unfortunately, as the sky becomes filled with 'friendly' drones, both the FAA's and the Military's ability to detect, identify and respond becomes dramatically impaired. Evidenced by the numerous drone attacks to date, we must maximize the effectiveness of our surveillance techniques and response capabilities. Eliminating the confusion presented by 'friendly' drone activity is a logical and immediate solution. Jeff, as for the consequences, violating the ban will subject the operator to confiscation of the drone, a ten thousand dollar fine and six months in jail for each violation."

"Thank you Janet, let's hear what Connor Sterns of the Free Skies Alliance has to say. Connor."

"Thank you Jeff. I understand what Janet is saying, however, we at the Free Skies Alliance couldn't disagree more. Banning legitimate use of personal and commercial drones is uncalled for, and a scary slippery slope. I know I sound like a broken record, but, if history has taught us anything, banning one right only leads to the abolishment of others. We at Free Skies believe the FAA and the U.S. Military has more than adequate capability to distinguish between legitimate drone use and that of the Islamic State."

"Well folks, our time is running short. So, from our news room in New York, Gretchen and I to want thank Connor Sterns and Janet Randall for joining us to discuss this change in America's drone policy."

"I'm Jeff Stoddard. Good night."

"And I'm Gretchen Chen. Good night."

### Barakat's Response

"Emir," whispered Abdul to Barakat, as the two men strode down the hallway with Richard Chambers a few steps behind, to meet with Kang Ko, the Chief Executive Officer of North Korea's leading drone manufacturer, Korea Navigation Company. "Abdul, I share your anger toward the west's attack as well as your grief for the death of our brothers. But remember my friend, our brothers died a glorious death. Allah Akbar!"

Ko, sitting quietly in the humble conference room of Barakat's secret complex rose to his feet as Barakat and his two colleagues entered the room. "Mr. Ko! It's a pleasure to finally meet you," exclaimed Barakat. Moktar, sporting an all too friendly smile took Ko's hand in his and pumped it vigorously. Ko, forcing a smile to mask his discomfort, bowed slightly from the waist. "Emir, the pleasure is all mine."

"Mr. Ko, the work you and your people have been doing for us in your North Korean and Malaysian factories has been nothing short of remarkable," exclaimed Barakat. "However, today, I want to discuss expanding your production to meet our growing needs."

"Emir, I assure you both KNC and our supreme leader are committed to do whatever is necessary to meet your needs."

"Very good. Very good!" proclaimed Barakat. "Allow me to introduce you to Richard Chambers, the leader of our technology team. While you're here, he will work with you regarding our technology and production requirements. Richard."

Chambers stepped forward with his hand extended, "Mr. Ko, it is a pleasure to finally meet. Your organization has been doing a wonderful job."

The four men moved around the makeshift conference table strategically positioning themselves. "Mr. Ko, beginning immediately we need to increase production to ten thousand drones monthly. I presume this isn't going to be a problem," asked Barakat.

"Not at all Emir. We can expand our production to meet any requirements you have," replied Ko.

"Wonderful," exclaimed Barakat. "More importantly, as Mr. Chambers will explain, we need the units delivered to our strategic staging areas under the guise of humanitarian relief or benign cargo. Mr. Chambers."

Richard rose from his seat, "Gentlemen, as outlined in the package provided last month, the shipping containers are to be modified with false ceilings providing storage for one hundred fully charged and deployable Mark-1 drones. As noted, each container's roof will be remotely operated allowing both land and sea deployment. Mr. Ko, are there any questions or problems?"

"Mr. Chambers, our partner headquartered in Pyongyang, Ocean Shipping Management Company Limited, has already modified two hundred shipping containers per your specifications. Assuming one hundred containers will be in transit back to North Korea or Malaysia at any given time, the remaining one hundred outbound containers will provide adequate capacity to deliver ten thousand Mark-1s monthly. Of course, we and OSMC have the capacity to increase production and shipping at any time."

Barakat slipped in a question: "Mr. Ko, what is the delivery window for the first ten thousand Mark-1s?"

"Emir, containers are being loaded as we speak and should be on their way by July twenty-fourth. Shipping time from Pyongyang to Mexico's Acapulco Terminal is nineteen days. According to OSMC, transit time from Acapulco to Acuna Mexico across from Del Rio, Texas, for example, is approximately nineteen hours. In our first phase, twenty containers will be delivered to their destinations across Mexico's northern border between August twenty-fifth and thirtieth. I hope this meets your needs."

Barakat, rose from his seat and extended his hand to Ko. "Mr. Ko, absolutely. You are doing a fine job. Unfortunately, gentlemen, I must excuse myself. Mr. Ko, I will leave you in Mr. Chamber's capable hands. We are making great progress. Allah Akbar!"

Pausing for a moment, Barakat looked Abdul in the eyes and announced, "Today my brother, we take our mission to a new level. The West will pay. Don't take your eyes off of Chambers."

### Call to Action

As Jeff Stoddard and Gretchen Chen signed off for the evening, hundreds of thousands of smartphones across America chirp wildly grabbing the attention of their Twitter following owners. With the exception of a few hundred, the balance of these Twitter followers are clueless social media junkies awaiting receipt of every insignificant tweet fearing they will miss something, anything important that will enhance their feckless lives. For many, the messages are meaningless, yet for a few hundred smartphone owners the tweets carried a deadly message that will again rain terror and destruction upon America.

Hundreds of Islamic State operators, dispersed across America, dropped what they were doing to read the incoming social media feeds. As before, this night Twitter unwittingly carried the deadly encoded instructions.

@SergeantPepper May I introduce to you #BILLYSHEARS

@RockyRacoon Only to find Gideon's bible
#ROCKYREVIVAL

@LucyInTheSkies Waiting to take you away
#BOATONARIVER

The clock started ticking.

### Angry Autonomous Team

Sitting in the break room, Chamber's team was provided a rare treat. Video from Fox News. Breaking news flashed across the bottom of the screen. "Good evening, I'm Sandra Wilson. Today, American forces struck a deadly blow against the Islamic State's drone capability in Pakistan. As seen in this video from the nose of the Hellfire missile, intelligence agencies believe they destroyed not only the Islamic State's drone test range but also killed the development team behind the technology. Let's go to the White House where Press Secretary Link Farnsworth is holding a press conference."

Farnsworth, already at the podium. "Good evening everybody. Thank you for joining us for this briefing. Last night, at 7:45PM Eastern Time, U.S. Special Forces and the United States Air Force struck a dramatic blow against the Islamic State's drone capability. U.S. Intelligence and international agencies identified what we believed to be the Islamic State's drone test range outside of Islamabad. As shown in this video, we believe the six orange jumpsuit-clad individuals, who recently exited a bus, to be the drone engineering team. Based on credible multi-national intelligence, President Bennett issued the order to deploy a single Hellfire missile from the U.S. drone orbiting overhead. As can be seeing on the screen, both ground and missile video feeds showed a direct hit on the target killing all the personnel in the immediate area. Post attack intelligence confirmed the suspected drone engineering team was killed in the attack. Jim, do you want to get us started today?"

"Sure. Thanks, Link. Jim Ranger, Washington Post. How long has intelligence surveillance been going on prior to the attack? Also, rumor has it that the drone engineers were the U.S. team from Autonomous Systems believed to have been lost in a private plane crash last year. If this is the case, why didn't we try to rescue them? Can you clear up this question?"

"Thank you Jim. To answer your first question, multi-national intelligence assets on the ground and electronic surveillance have been collecting data for over six months. It was determined that the highest chance for a successful operation would be to focus on the test range which proved effective as shown in both the ground and missile based video feeds. Jim, as for your second question, I can't get caught up in outlandish theories and speculation about the lost employees of Autonomous Systems. All evidence points to the fact that these people were lost in an unfortunate plane crash. Since there was no one to rescue, a rescue attempt was not warranted. Becky, do you have a question?

"Yes Link. Becky Yen, TMZ. Regardless of the White House's position on the lost Autonomous personnel, it seems eerily reminiscent of Malaysia Air Flight MH370 that a team of expert drone engineers and their airplane mysteriously disappear never to be found. More importantly, however, further fueling speculation about the Autonomous Team is information we recently received that components from recovered attack drones contained a message from the lost Autonomous team. Do you have any comments?"

"Thank you Becky. Unfortunately, as I said to Jim, the White House cannot and will not engage in conspiracy theory speculation. Candidly, it is a shame that you brought up MH370. We don't believe that these two events are interconnected in any way and to dredge up MH370 just seems cruel to the families that lost loved ones on that plane. Finally, I've heard this speculation before about messages embedded in the attack drones. I assure you, no such messages have been uncovered. I'm sorry we have to bring this conference to such an abrupt end, but we have a very pressing schedule. Thanks, everybody. Have a good evening."

Barakat walked over to the television and flipped off the power and stood quietly looking each of the Autonomous team members in the eye. "I hope this puts to rest any question you have about your importance to America and hopes of being rescued. If they believed you were working for the Islamic State, they decided you were expendable! And now, in their opinion you don't exist. I assure you, no rescue attempt will be made."

"More disturbing to me is the rumor that messages from you have been embedded in our technology. If you think you can subvert our efforts I assure you, you are wasting your time. Your long-term wellbeing is under my control and I will not stand for any effort to sabotage my mission. So, I will ask only once. Have any messages been hidden by you?"

Chambers and his team, sat quietly, anticipating Barakat's next move.

"This is your chance to atone for violating my trust and good treatment."

Barakat and the team, played a very dangerous game of chicken. A game where the first to blink loses. "You people disappoint me. I am the only friend you have. America has abandoned you and as of today, you are all dead. If you want to see another day, you will answer my question."

Jeff Chaplain, fearing for his life, shifted nervously in his chair feeling each bead of sweat run down the back of his neck. Jeff pondered to himself, "I'm a lowly test engineer and the most replaceable member of the team."

"Mr. Barakat, I'm just a test engineer and had nothing to do with any messages. It isn't something I could or would do," said Chaplain.

"Jeff, thank you for your honesty. And I believe you had nothing to do with placing messages in the drone's PROMs," replied Barakat as he glanced over to Abdul. In a fraction of a second Chaplain was pulled from his chair and forced to his knees by Abdul as one of Barakat's soldiers placed the muzzle of his AK-47 against the back of his head.

Crying, Jeff wailed, "Wait! Wait! I didn't do anything. Chan and Gary did it. Not me. I told them not to do it."

Chambers, rose to his feet, "Emir. Please. I believe there is a misunderstanding."

Jeff, struggled futilely against the frightening cold metal of the weapon's muzzle pressing hard against the back of his head, "Please. Please. Ple…"

CrraaccK! The single shot ended Jeff's pleading and sprayed blood and brains across the floor leaving none of Chambers' remaining four team members unscathed.

Liz, almost leaped from her chair as the concussion from the AK-47 penetrated deep to her core. "Oh my God! No!" as Liz dropped her head sobbing into her hands.

"Let this be a lesson and your last warning," declared Barakat, "I will not tolerate any further attempts to undermine this program. If you think you are not expendable keep in mind the images of America killing whom they believed to be you and poor Mr. Chaplain laying here before you. Get back to work. We are on a tight schedule."

### *Autonomous Systems Deploys Drones*

"Did you see last night's White House Press Conference," Ron Parsons asked Carl Summers. "These guys are killing Americans. They killed them right on TV."

"Yes Ron. I saw it. We really don't know who those people were. All we know is they were wearing orange jump suits and hoods. That's it. Nothing more," replied Summers.

"Sure. Go sell crazy someplace else. You and I know that Chambers and our friends were kidnapped by those the Islamic State. We've all seen the messages and so has the White House! There is no way those messages were random noise. They were intentionally placed in the code. You know that and I know that. Something only Chambers' team could have done. And what is the President's answer? Blow up their asses. This is bullshit," ranted Ron.

David Kramer walked into the conference room and was confronted by the tension between Parsons and Summers. "What's bullshit, Ron?"

"Did you see the killing of our friends on TV last night? I can't believe it. We all know that they were our friends. We know who put those messages in the PROMs. It couldn't be anyone else. These bastards killed our friends. Cold blooded murder! And we are working with them. I can't believe it. How can we support this crap?" asked Ron.

"Ron, what choice do we have? This is a real threat. If we don't get our system deployed, more innocent people will die. And that's not bullshit. Unfortunately, it's about the greater good. The Islamic State is unscrupulous. If it was Chambers and his team that died in the drone attack, that will seriously impair their ability to advance their technology."

"More importantly, how is it that the reporters knew about the embedded messages? The FBI will be arriving shortly to talk with us about the possibility of a leak. Only the three of us, and a couple of engineers knew of the existence of the embedded messages. Trust me, disclosure of the existence of the messages is treason. Rest assured, I'm not going to fall on this sword. Do either of you know anything about who leaked the information to the press?"

Ron, recoiled striking a defensive posture. "Hey! Don't look at me. I didn't tell anyone anything. Period! I am not going to take the fall over this."

"Ron, I'm not blaming anyone. All I know is the source of the leak can only be from Autonomous or someone in government. According to Bennett's Chief of Staff, they don't believe the leak came from the government. All fingers are pointing at us. I suggest we get this under control. According to our attorney, it's already a federal offense. And lying to the FBI will exacerbate the situation."

"David, all I know is I didn't do it," replied Carl. "My hands are clean."

"Ron….is there anything you want to tell me?"

"No," Ron snapped back. "I didn't talk with anyone. Not a soul. It has to be one of the programmers. My bet it's that asshole Deeb. I have never trusted that bastard."

"Ok. Ok. Let's get the programmers in here immediately before the FBI is scheduled to arrive. We are better off if we uncover the leak rather than letting the Feds do so. Call them in now! Put them in conference room 3."

"I'll have them here in five minutes," replied Carl.

Knock. Knock. Rebecca Richards tapped on the door carefully poking in her head. "Excuse me Mr. Kramer."

"Yes Rebecca?"

"Hmmm…there are two agents from the FBI at the front desk. They want to speak with you."

"Thank you Rebecca. Please tell them I'll be right there."

Rebecca eased back out through the door as smoothly as she arrived. Pausing for a moment, Kramer glanced back over his shoulder at Parsons and Summers. "We're going to get to the bottom of this leak."

ID in hand, "Mr. Kramer, I'm Special Agent Lane and this is Special Agent Richards. Thank you for meeting with us today."

"Welcome to Autonomous Systems. It's not a problem. As requested, I've assembled relevant team members in conference room 3. Shall we move over there?

"Sounds great Mr. Kramer. Thank you."

Kramer pivoted on his heels and moved swiftly to conference room 3 with the FBI agents in tow.

Through the smoked-glass of conference room 3 Kramer saw Summers and Parsons looking out over the parking lot and two people seated at the table.

Kramer walked into the conference room with agents Lane and Richards, "Good morning everyone. This is Special Agent Ralph Lane and Special Agent…let me see, yes. Special Agent Janet Richards from the FBI." Lane and Richards moved in close to Carl and Ron, "Good morning gentlemen."

"Good morning Agent Lane. I'm Carl Summers. I'm Autonomous Systems' Chief Technology Officer. This is our Project Manager, Ron Parsons," said Summers.

"Good to meet you," replied Agent Lane. "Who do we have here?"

Carl turned his attention to Christopher Samuels and David Sams seated at the conference table. "This is David Sams and Christopher Samuels. They are two of our software engineers that participated in evaluating the PROMs from the recovered drones."

As Agent Lane approached, Sams and Samuels jump to their feet as if called to attention by their drill sergeant. Lane extended his hand, "Relax gentlemen. Nice to meet both of you. Please relax. By the way, job well done on uncovering the embedded messages in the drone's programming."

Sams replied nervously, "Not a problem. It wasn't that complicated."

Lane and Richards took seats at the head of the conference table. Lane pulled a file folder from his briefcase. "Hmm….According to our records, Mr. Summers. Um…may I call you Carl?"

"Yes, please do."

"Well, Carl, according to our records there were three members of the engineering team that uncovered the message. Let me see. Yes, here it is. A Mr. Arman Deeb. Will he be joining us today?"

"Yes, you are correct. Mr. Deeb is a member of the engineering team. Unfortunately, Arman didn't show up for work this morning," replied Carl.

"That's unfortunate. Carl, was this a planned day off for Mr. Deeb?"

"No. It wasn't. Arman just didn't show up."

Agent Lane leaned over to Agent Richards and exchanged whispers while pointing at the file folder. "Well gentlemen, we have a simple question. Do either of you have any information about disclosure of the existence of the embedded messages to the press?"

Almost in unison, Samuels and Sams shook their heads and replied, "No!"

"That's what we figured. And as for you Carl, Mr. Parsons and Mr. Kramer, do you have any knowledge how this information was released to the press?"

Kramer, took the lead, "I assure you neither I, Carl or Ron have any knowledge of the leak beyond that which was reported in last night's press conference."

"OK, gentlemen. That's pretty much what we assumed. Unfortunately, Mr. Deeb's absence is disturbing. I assume, Carl, you can provide Special Agent Richards with Mr. Deeb's contact information?"

"Yes. Yes of course. Right away."

Getting up from the table, Special Agent Lane gathered his files and stowed them efficiently into his briefcase. "Gentlemen. Thank you for your time and cooperation. Here are our cards. If you remember anything, please don't hesitate to call either Special Agent Richards or me."

Kramer shook Agent Lane's hand, "let me show out."

"Don't worry about it Mr. Kramer, Agent Richards and I can find our way. Good bye."

### Meeting Mr. Deeb

Agents Lane and Richards approached the unassuming condominium home of Arman Deeb. Rapping forcefully on the door. "Mr. Deeb! FBI. Open up!" announced Special Agent Lane.

Within moments, Lane heard the click of the deadbolt as the door was unlocked and cracked open ever so slightly.

"Mr. Deeb?" asked Lane.

"Yes. How can I help you?"

Lane held his ID up so Deeb could verify his authority, "Mr. Deeb, I'm Special Agent Lane and this is Special Agent Richards. May we come in?"

"Is there a problem?"

"Mr. Deeb, may we come in? We need to speak with you."

Deeb hesitated for a moment then opened the door and invited these two menacing souls into his humble home.

"Mr. Deeb, we just met with your fellow team members at Autonomous Systems. It was our understanding you were instructed to be available for that meeting. But alas, you were not present. Why?" asked Lane.

"I know. But I didn't feel well this morning and decided to take a sick day," Deeb responded timidly.

"Well Mr. Deeb, I hope you're feeling better. It is, however, important that we speak with you."

Following Deeb into the living room, Lane and Richards instructed Arman to sit down and strategically and menacingly positioned themselves in chairs to his right and left.

"Mr. Deeb, it is our understanding that you are an engineer at Autonomous Systems. More specifically, you are responsible for system security. Am I correct?"

"Yes. That's correct. What's going on?"

"Well Mr. Deeb, as you know, we believe that Richard Chambers and his team are alive and working with the Islamic State. Do you have any information that you can share with us?'

Looking more than a little nervous, Deeb responded "I thought that the team was killed when the company jet was lost. Why would I know anything about that?"

"Mr. Deeb. I need to caution you. This is an official investigation and it is a felony to lie to a Federal Agent."

"I don't know anything. I'm not lying."

"Mr. Deeb, we have evidence to the contrary. Please stand up."

Hesitating for a moment, Arman stood up. Simultaneously, Special Agent Richards moved in behind Arman and grasped his left arm as she pulled hand cuffs from her belt and deftly secured Arman's arms behind his back.

"Mr. Deeb," said Agent Lane. "You are under arrest. You have the right to remain silent. Anything you say can and will be used against you in a court of law. You have the right to an attorney. If you cannot afford an attorney, one will be provided for you. Do you understand the rights I have just read to you?"

His head hung low, "Yes I do. But, I haven't done anything wrong."

"Come with us Mr. Deeb," insisted Agent Lane.

Once Deeb was secured in the back seat, the ominous black SUV swiftly departed for the airport where their government jet waited at the ready to deliver Arman to FBI headquarters in Washington D.C.

### Deeb's Interrogation

From Deeb's perspective, the flight to D.C. seemed to take forever as he sat in the FBI's Gulfstream with his hands cuffed in his lap. Agent's Lane and Richards sat quietly in the front of the jet talking casually.

"We are preparing for final approach into Andrews. Please take your seats and fasten your seat belts," announced the pilot.

Agent Lane, rose from his seat and walked toward Deeb. "Mr. Deeb, I need to confirm your seatbelt is secure." He reached down toward Deeb's lap and drew his seatbelt snug across his lap. Convinced Deeb was secure, Lane returned to his seat to prepare for the landing.

The big Gulfstream taxied up to a non-descript hanger where three black SUVs awaited their arrival. While Lane and Richards waited with Deeb in front of the airplane, the flight attendant unlocked the door and extended the plane's air stair. Deeb was swiftly escorted down the stairs and into the middle SUV. Once secure in his seat the caravan of SUVs began their trek toward FBI headquarters.

With lights flashing, the SUVs covered the thirteen miles from Andrews in ten minutes rolling through the guard gate up to the garage door of the FBI's intake center. As quickly as he was placed in the SUV,

Deeb was extracted and marched into FBI headquarters escorted by Lane, Richards and six rifle toting agents.

Deeb has never been so frightened in his life. Regardless of his questions and protestations, Lane and Richards remained quiet and simply moved him toward the interrogation room.

The dark institutional green of the interrogation room door swung open and Deeb was placed firmly into a seat and his handcuffs were effortlessly secured to the table. Just as quickly, Lane and Richards left the room and allowed Deeb time to sweat.

Richards, turned to Lane, "what's next?"

"I have a call into the Director. He wants to personally witness the interrogation," replied Lane.

A commanding Chirp….Chirp…emanated from Lane's cellphone.

"Lane here. Yes Director. Mr. Deeb is in interrogation room seven sir. We are ready to begin upon your arrival. Yes sir. We'll await your arrival," spoke Lane.

"The Director will be here in fifteen minutes," said Lane. "Let's go to the observation room and await his arrival."

Lane and Richards watched, through the one-way mirror, as Deeb fidgeted and struggled to get comfortable.

"I don't think he's going to be a challenge," said Lane.

"I agree. Fifteen minutes," replied Richards.

"Twenty dollars that he breaks in eight minutes," offered Lane.

"You're on!" responded Richards.

The observation room door swung open and Director Teich swooped in accompanied by two agents.

"Good afternoon Director. I'm Special Agent Lane and this is my Partner Special Agent Richards," offered Lane.

"Nice meeting both of you. Great job on securing Mr. Deeb. What do we know?" asked the Director.

"Mr. Director, over the past few months, we have been monitoring numerous communications between Autonomous Systems and some unknown correspondents in Pakistan. We presumed it was someone from Chambers' team. As our people scrubbed the messages, it became clear that Mr. Deeb had been corresponding with Akio Chan and Will Schmidt. Both presumed lost in the Autonomous Systems' jet incident and now believed held in Pakistan along with Chambers. What we know is Mr. Deeb has been feeding Chan and Schmidt technical information and providing them access to software code libraries. Additionally, it was determined that he informed them of the Drone On initiative."

"Okay, continue," said Teich.

"We scheduled interviews at Autonomous as a ruse to flush out Mr. Deeb. Per our request, he was expected to participate in an interview at Autonomous Systems today. But, when we arrived, he was a no show. Apparently, he called in sick. With Mr. Deeb being a no-show, we concluded our interview at Autonomous, and Agent Richards and I proceeded to Mr. Deeb's residence where he was placed under arrest and subsequently transported here. Since initial questioning at his residence, we have not spoken with Mr. Deeb. Our plan is to begin the interrogation shortly," explained Lane.

"This is great. I look forward to seeing if he explains himself," commented Director Teich.

"As a matter of fact Mr. Director," commented Lane. "How far are we going to be allowed to go in interrogating Deeb? Basically, are our hands tied?" asked Lane.

"Agent Lane. Regardless of what Mr. Deeb may or may not have done, we are not barbarians. I serve at the pleasure of the President and he has been very specific that we do not torture prisoners or enemies of the state. We follow the rule of law. As such, you can go as far as you desire. Just be careful. Understand?" asked Teich.

"Yes Mr. Director. I believe I do," replied Lane. "Shall we begin?"

"Please do," replied Teich.

Lane and Richards excused themselves as they exited the observation room heading for interview room seven.

Beep…beep…beep…beep, went the familiar sound of a security access keypad followed by the undeniable 'clack' of a solenoid controlled digital lock releasing its hold on the door and its jam. Lane swung the door wide as he and Richards strolled into the interview room closing the door forcefully behind them followed by the sound of the door locking securely.

"Mr. Deeb. Can we get you something to drink?" asked Richards.

"No. Umm..No. I'm not thirsty."

"Fine. Then, we shall begin," said Lane.

"Mr. Deeb, tell me what you told Chambers' people," demanded Lane.

Looking more than a little shaken, Deeb responded, "I don't know what you're talking about."

"Mr. Deeb, believe me when I tell you that this is going to go much easier on you if you are honest and cooperative. Lies and evasion will only worsen your already desperate situation," asserted Lane. "I am only going to ask you one more time. What have you told Akio Chan and Will Schmidt?"

"I thought they were dead. Killed when the Autonomous jet was lost," said Deeb.

"Mr. Deeb. We know that you have been communicating with Chan and Schmidt somewhere in Pakistan. Rest assured that we have instructions from the highest level to extract the information we need from you at all cost."

Deeb, struggled to maintain his composure, "I don't know why you people are harassing me. I know my rights. I want a lawyer."

Fed up with the lack of progress being made with Deeb's interview, Director Teich exited the comfort of the observation room and burst into the interview room. "Mr. Deeb. I'm FBI Director Teich. I'm here for one purpose. Under the direction of the President of the United States, I'm here to ensure, at all cost, any and all necessary and relevant information is extracted from you. Trust me when I say at all costs! Whether you know it or not, we are in a state of war with the Islamic State. As such, you're a prisoner of war. A combatant. As such, you don't have any rights other than those we provide you. I'm only going to say this once. Either you provide Agents Lane and Richards what they seek or you will find yourself sweating in a hole in Guantanamo for the rest of your life. Do you understand me?" proclaimed Teich.

Director Teich paused for only a moment on his way out of the interrogation room and leaned in close to whisper in Lane's ear, "Agent Lane, carry on. Do whatever is necessary to extract the information we need. I'm done here and I expect your report shortly."

"Yes sir," snapped Lane. "You can count on us."

As the door closed behind Director Teich, Lane turned to Deeb. "Mr. Deeb. We want to know everything you shared with Chambers' team. Trust me. There isn't anything we won't do to extract the truth! You don't want to test my limits."

"Yes, I communicated with Will and Akio. But not directly. I left them messages on the server and they responded the same way," explained Deeb, sweating under the pressure.

"So, you freely admit to consorting with the enemy. Correct?"

"I really don't know what you mean by consorting. All I did was answer some of their questions and provided them access to some of the Autonomous Systems source code. They said they needed it or they would be killed. I was only trying to save their lives."

"Is there any other information you provided Chambers' people?"

"None that I can think of. I did tell them that Autonomous Systems was working on a mobile game. What does that have to do with anything?"

"Mr. Deeb. What exactly did you tell them about mobile gaming?" asked Lane.

"Nothing more than I just told you. I was not involved with the game developers. I just told them that it looked like Autonomous was getting into a new line of business. What could be wrong with that? Why are you so interested?" asked Deeb.

"Well Mr. Deeb, it is clear to us you have broken a number of laws. You will be remanded over to the U.S. Marshall and transported to Guantanamo in the morning. Perhaps while there, your memory will improve," said Lane.

"But…But..I didn't do anything wrong.

"Unfortunately Mr. Deeb, that's a matter of perception. We believe you did quite a bit wrong and contributed to the death of hundreds of thousands of innocent citizens. Agents will be here soon to escort you to your holding cell."

# Chapter 10

◆

*WMD*

Unfortunately, intermittent drone attacks have somehow found their way, like so many frightening realities, into the American psyche giving rise to the mindset—it only happens to someone else. Today, however, the paradigm has shifted. The state of Islam has chosen to step up its presence by broadening its attack profile across a wider and more diverse footprint, casting its hideous and painful shadow upon every quiet soul.

Over the past two days, twenty semi-trailer trucks made their way from the port of Acapulco to destinations along Mexico's northern border. Each cargo container carried harmless yet much needed goods and materials to every imaginable and logical destination ranging from Walmart to manufacturers. Unbeknownst to the dedicated long-haul truckers, nestled invisibly beneath the roof of each container towed north, were one hundred attack drones awaiting their wakeup call and ultimate journey across the U.S. border to the waiting hands of nondescript agents of doom. Like a well-choreographed production, two hundred Islamic State technology-jihadists, followed the GPS guidance of their iPhones, trekked toward the U.S. Mexican border. Within hours of one another, each arrived at their pre-assigned destination awaiting arrival of their charges—hundreds of drones resting patiently in steel cocoons awaiting the command to emerge and slip across the border. Two thousand attack drones will soon arrive, unseen, ready to be retrieved by their operators who will ultimately transport them to their respective launch points. Unlike prior attacks, these drones have come pre-loaded with their deadly cargo—two pounds of C4, two pounds of stainless steel ball bearings and a pound of RICIN.

At 12:30am Central Time, electrons coursed through the arteries of the international cellular system. Unless you knew what you were listening for, this stream of energy, the subtle cell phone signal carrying the group text message, appeared benign and uninteresting—Breakfast downtown at 8:30am. OK? Chris. But, to the twenty steel-cocoons it was their long-awaited wake-up call. Following the bright friendly chirp of the incoming text message, the sequence began with the click of the roof latch retracting followed by the steady whirring and struggling of a single electric motor as the roof sections pivoted lengthwise exposing one thousand drones to the cool night air.

Once the sequence had started, there was no turning back. The green power lights of two thousand drones glowed brightly as twelve thousand rotor blades spun up to speed. One-by-one the drones ascended into the darkness, swirled skyward in a helix until the last drone cleared its hanger. Just as quickly and quietly as it all began, the cargo containers' motors reversed their direction, and retracted each container's roof followed by the deliberate click of the locking latch sliding into position. Soon, these containers will begin their journey south then across the sea to meet their new cargo.

Two hundred feet above the transport containers, two thousand drones aligned themselves into flights of ten and navigated their short trip north to their assigned destinations in the United States.

### WMD August 21: Arrival

Adib Touma, like one hundred and ninety-nine of his fellow Islamic State brothers, followed his iPhone to his assigned destination. In Adib's case, he made his way from Phoenix to the sleepy desert town of Naco, Arizona and sat quietly in his van in the parking lot on Newel Street, across from the oldest golf course in Arizona—Turquoise Valley. More importantly, Adib was less than a mile from Naco Mexico in Sonora where his drones were deployed.

At 1:00am, Adib's iPhone chirped apprising him of the imminent arrival of his assigned drones. Adib slipped from the warmth and comfort of his mini-van and opened the side door and waited like a shepherd for the arrival of his flock of drones. Looking up into the moonless southwest sky, Adib futilely strained to make out his ten drones. All he saw was the pitch black sky decorated by the bright band of the Milky Way. Try as he might, Adib never saw the arrival of his ten drones. He did, however, hear the familiar high-pitch whirr of sixty electric motors spinning six rotors on each drone. He tracked the sound of the arriving drones as they began orbiting above the treetops of Naco Arizona. Once again, like clockwork, Adib's iPhone chirped announcing their arrival. In response to the chirp, he tapped the screen of his iPhone and his precise location was relayed to the lead drone. Immediately, the flight of ten drones swirled overhead and one-by-one they landed. Thanks to the amazing ultrasound and imaging systems, they aligned themselves in a tight formation in front of Adib. Just as quickly as they landed, their motors turned off and the glowing green power lights extinguished. "Amazing," Adib muttered to himself.

Driven by paranoia, before retrieving his precious cargo, Adib glanced over both shoulders fearing intruders. Fortunately for Adib, most, if not all of the one thousand and forty-six citizens of Naco were either fast asleep or distracted by another activity providing uninterrupted opportunity to complete his mission. One-by-one Adib picked up each drone and placed it carefully into his mini-van. In less than ten minutes all ten drones were safely packed away and Adib returned to the driver's seat and started the engine. As invisibly as he arrived, Adib turned left out of the parking lot and headed west on Newel having begun his two hundred and twenty-mile journey north back to Phoenix.

### WMD August 23: Preparation

Under the cover of darkness, Joseph Thompson, whom too many was a nice kid, but a loner, returned to his basement garage in the sleepy Austin, Texas suburb of Pflugerville. Earlier that morning, like one hundred and ninety-nine other Islamic State Jihadists on the same mission, Joseph followed the GPS guidance on his iPhone to retrieve his fleet of drones. In Joseph's case, his destination was Laredo, Texas, across the border from Nuevo, Mexico. Unlike the previous drone attacks on American soil, these agents of doom are only charged with the responsibility to recover their drones at their rendezvous points then, when ordered to do so, then deliver them to their assigned attack launch destinations.

Joseph's first job was simple enough. Replenish the batteries of each drone by plugging one of the ten battery chargers he purchased at Best Buy earlier in the week into each drone's micro-USB jack. As he connected each battery charger, each drone enthusiastically responded to the flow of current by blinking its LED red and green verifying its batteries were being charged.

Joseph's second task, albeit highly technical, thanks to Chambers' team was no more challenging than charging his drone's batteries. After a few taps on his iPhone the process of programing his fleet of drones began automatically. Concealed from Joseph and his counterparts, each drone received navigation and attack profiles for one of two targets. When Joseph deployed his drones from his mini-van, they will divide into two five drone flights and head to their programed destinations. All Joseph needed to do was follow the turn-by-turn navigation directions from his iPhone then await his launch orders. Thanks to the brilliance of Chambers' team of engineers, once activated, Barakat's squadron of attack drones will navigate and execute their missions flawlessly, effectively and autonomously.

### WMD September 7: Delivery

Labor Day is a special national holiday celebrating the American labor movement and dedicated to social and economic achievements of the nation's workers. Today, Barakat's insidious plan will once simultaneously again rain terror down upon hundreds of thousands of Americans across four hundred targets. This Labor Day, not only will Barakat disrupt the day's festivities, all American's will intimately know his vision to fundamentally change America once and for all.

The sequence began at 6:00am Eastern Time when two hundred iPhones awakened and chirped their call-to-action for these patient and loyal technology-Jihadists to carry out Barakat's plan.

Young Joseph Thompson was awakened by his iPhone at 5:00am Central Time, like all his cohorts. Joseph rubbed the sleep from his eyes and slowly rose from the warmth of his bed. Joseph then turned his attention to his iPhone and tapped the screen beginning the process that will change the lives of hundreds of thousands of innocent Americans, forever!

As he stood fighting the lure of his warm bed, Joseph leisurely pulled on his pants. In the dimly lit room, he swept his foot under the bed in quest of his other Nike. Moving quietly through the house to avoid awakening his parents, he made his way to the kitchen for breakfast and a cup of herbal tea. According to the iPhone's display, he needed to begin transporting his fleet no later than 3:00pm to ensure more than enough time to complete the three-hour drive to Houston. Joseph was confident nine hours gave him more than enough time to prepare his fleet, take care of his daily activities and complete the drive to Houston.

Like the good son he was, upon finishing his bowl of cereal and toast, Joseph washed the dishes and wiped down the counter so his mother wouldn't be burdened with having to clean up after him. Before continuing his mission, with his tea and iPad in hand, Joseph slid into the warm and so very comfortable overstuffed chair in the family room to spend some quality time on Facebook reading his friends' posts and make a few posts to his wall. Joseph tapped the Twitter icon and tweeted out "Today will be a great day!" Pausing for a moment, Joseph glanced at his wristwatch and noted that it was 6:45am as he logged out of Facebook and Twitter then climbed out of his favorite chair. As he shuffled through the house toward the basement garage, Joseph fought the lure of his warm and comfortable bed. As he opened the basement door, he was struck by the brisk morning air wafting up from the basement garage. First, things first. In ten minutes the sun will rise over San Antonio and he must prepare for his daily prayers. At the base of the stairs he placed his cup of tea on the counter and reached into the cabinet retrieving his hidden prayer rug and carefully rolled it out onto the garage floor. Kneeling respectfully on the rug, Joseph quietly began the ritualistic salat so not to awaken his mother. As he rose from his prayers, Joseph stood straight and exclaimed Allah Hoo Akbar. After pausing for a moment to revel in his peace, Joseph carefully rolled up his prayer rug and returned it to the security of the garage cabinet.

At 8:00am Joseph began loading the mini-van with his fleet of ten fully charged, armed and programmed drones. Once his fleet was stowed and secured, he covered them with a gray drop cloth he retrieved from another cabinet. Picking up his now tepid cup of tea, Joseph took a sip and contemplated his mission.

Out of respect for his mother, Joseph returned to the kitchen to rinse his teacup and place it in the dishwasher. For a moment, he sat at the kitchen table enjoying the view and early morning quiet of his family home. "Now what?" he thought to himself, fighting the niggling doubt in the back of his mind. It didn't take long for Joseph to come to the conclusion that waiting around the house would be unsettling and decided to begin his journey to Houston early. He rose from the kitchen table and returned to the basement garage. In the quiet of the morning, Joseph slipped into the driver's seat of the family mini-van and turned the key slightly bringing the van to life. Joseph reached up and pressed the button on the garage door opener and the door obediently moved upward flooding the garage with the bright morning sun. Joseph slowly backed out carefully and commanded the garage door to close before him. Unknown to Joseph, as he maneuvered his van into the street, one hundred ninety-nine followers of the Islamic State also began their fateful journey to change America forever.

### *It's Time*

Through the day, the Islamic State's covert agents of doom emerged from the safety of their innocuous suburban abodes and followed their iPhone's turn-by-turn directions until the 'too friendly' voice announced *"you have reached your destination"* indicated by a little checkered flag on the map. Upon arrival, vehicles strategically parked hoping to avoid prying eyes. Now they waited. How long? No one knew. For some, they sat in quiet prayer. Others sought entertainment on their iPhones playing games, listening to music or scanning social media. Yet others, reclined their seats and fell asleep.

At 7:00 pm Eastern Time, two hundred smartphones across the country once again came to life chirping, beeping, ringing, buzzing, shaking or playing music calling for their owners' attention. It's time muttered Adib

Touma, perched in a secluded park overlooking downtown Phoenix. Joseph Thompson, who has been in Houston most of the day, shook himself awake and prepared for what was to come.

First retracting the vans' sunroofs then slipping out of drivers' seats, Adib, Joseph and one hundred ninety-eight others crawled into the cramped quarters of their soccer-mom vehicles and began the process of launching their fleets of drones. Each drone operator quickly flipped ten switches, one after the other, powering up their fleets. As the drones' electric motors whirred, the operators tapped the screens on their iPhones which initiated the attack sequence.

The drones came alive, each executing self-diagnostics. Within moments, two hundred iPhones displayed the same message: "Pairing complete. Tap to launch." Each operator raised his whirring drones, one-by-one, up through their sunroof. Upon clearing the roof, each craft strained for release then rose into the air a few hundred feet and loitered awaiting arrival of its partners. Every operator repeated the process nine more times as the ten drones automatically divided into two groups of five. The groups of five drones paused momentarily as if they were thinking about their next step. Actually, thanks to the genius of Chamber's team, the drones were communicating with one another through infrared and ultrasonic transmitters and receivers which, in addition to exchanging data enabled the drones to be aware of each other's physical proximity. The fully autonomous capability of Barakat's drones was simply brilliant and elegant. Not only does ultrasound provide each drone proximity information about its counterparts, it also enabled them to navigate around objects as well as provide a proximity detonation backup mechanism. It seems the co-opted Autonomous Team thought of everything.

On cue, four hundred five-drone-squadrons began a spiraling dance in the morning sky and quickly dashed off in the direction of their assigned targets. Targets unknown to the Islamic State's high-technology-jihadists. Once again, in unison two hundred iPhones came alive and displayed the same message *"Mission Complete. Allahu Akbar!"* The iPhone screens returned to their home pages as the operators slipped into their drivers' seats. Barakat's domestic agents of doom closed their sunroofs and headed home. Home to vanilla lives awaiting what was next to come.

### The White House and North Korea
David Haydon, CIA Director, joined President Bennett, Vice President Colby and Chief of Staff Kerns and Homeland Security Director Harold Simpson in the Oval Office.

"Mr. President," began Haydon, "earlier this week our assets in Pyongyang secured intelligence that North Korea is cooperating with the Islamic State in production and delivery of their drones. Unfortunately all we have is thin proof. We'll continue to investigate every lead to narrow our focus."

Sitting, a little befuddled, Bennett pondered Haydon's short yet disturbing report. "You must be kidding. North Korea is collaborating with the Islamic State? This changes everything."

"Yes Mr. President. We're certain they are collaborating. What we don't know, however, is specifically to what degree and how. Based on the information we've gathered so far, we suspect there is a facility, approximately thirty kilometers northeast of Pyongyang in P'yŏngsŏng, the capital city of the province of South Pyongan in western North Korea."

"Do you believe that Barakat and his people have relocated to North Korea?" asked Bennett.

"No Mr. President. According to our sources, we believe that Chambers and his people are in Islamabad," said Haydon.

"Well David, your people are doing a great job," responded Bennett, "Keep up the good work. We need to know exactly what is going on in North Korea. This certainly complicates everything. Our mission is simple, we need to protect American lives."

"Yes Mr. President. I understand and will continue to collect as much intelligence as possible," replied Haydon.

"Well Gentlemen, our lives have grown more complex. We will meet again as soon as the CIA has more information."

"Our world faces a crisis as yet unperceived by those possessing power to make great decisions for good or evil. The unleashed power of the atom has changed everything save our modes of thinking and we thus drift toward unparalleled catastrophe," Albert Einstein

# Chapter 11

———————◆———————

### Breaking News

"Good evening, this is United News Network. We are interrupting this program to report live on numerous drone attacks across America. I'm Jeff Stoddard and this is my co-anchor, Gretchen Chen."

"Beginning 7:00pm Eastern Time reports of hundreds of drone attacks have been coming in. Our lines are flooded with calls from our affiliates from Florida to California each reporting attacks in their communities. Let's go to Lisa Ortiz in Los Angeles California. Lisa."

The screen split with Stoddard on the left and the right filled with the image of a young and frightened Latino woman. "Thank you Jeff, I'm reporting live from Los Angeles International Airport. What we have here is pandemonium. As you can see behind me, there are numerous fires on the airport as well as a fire in the distance. So far, what we know is the attacks against LAX began around 4:00pm. Similar to the attack at Chicago O'Hare earlier in the year, Air China Flight 334, a Boeing 747, on final approach was attacked by a swarm of drones. The plane was seriously damaged in flight and crashed into a community just east of LAX. We have some GoPro footage shot from two cars on the San Diego freeway. As you can see in the video, a swarm of drones approached Air China Flight 334 from the west and impacted the airliner bringing about its destruction. At the moment, we have no information about survivors. What we do know is at least four additional drone attacks occurred on the airport property. From what we have been able to learn, three attacks took place against Terminal 2, Terminal 4 and the Thomas Bradley International Terminal. The fourth attack was reported to have occurred on the field destroying at least three airliners loaded with passengers awaiting takeoff. Emergency personnel are working feverishly to reach everyone in need."

Stoddard, looked shocked "Lisa, is there any information about casualties?"

"Jeff, not at the moment. Los Angeles Mayor Rowlands and Police Chief Anderson have scheduled a press conference for an hour from now. I'm certain we will get more information at that time."

"Lisa, thank you. Keep us updated with any breaking news," said Stoddard.

"As we stated at the beginning of this broadcast, reports of attacks have been coming in from across America. Now from our affiliate in Las Vegas, Nevada Kevin Kerns. Kevin."

The right screen filled with a young and clearly inexperienced looking reporter. "Jeff and Gretchen," reported Kerns. "I am here on the strip in Las Vegas, where at least four casinos have been attacked. This evening at 7:15, it was reported that the Bellagio, the Wynn, MGM and the Luxor fell victim to drone attacks. So far, fires are raging at the Wynn and the Luxor and emergency personnel are feverishly struggling to rescue literally hundreds if not thousands of injured people. According to reports, at least fifteen hundred people are dead. More frightening is the report that along with the explosions, HAZMAT teams have detected RICIN. Thousands of people are flooding Las Vegas emergency rooms with injuries and fearing RICIN poisoning. So far, we don't know the numbers but reports are coming in that many people have been contaminated with the deadly RICIN poison. Emergency services have asked that anyone who was present at any of the attack scenes or have been in contact with a victim to immediately go to your nearest emergency room to see a doctor."

"Kevin, thank you. We'll continue to report on the events in Las Vegas. Right now, we're going to join a news conference with David Charmer, the Director of the CDC."

David Charmer was speaking to the press at the Centers for Disease Control. "This evening, beginning around 4:00pm Eastern Time, we received reports of hundreds of drone attacks across the country. Unfortunately, similar to the Busch stadium attack this past June, along with explosives and shrapnel, these drones carried the deadly poison RICIN. We at the CDC are certainly concerned about the devastation explosive equipped drones can cause. However, the fact that hundreds of thousands of people are being exposed to RICIN is of grave concern to the CDC and President Bennett. We, along with local emergency services are responding to this threat."

"Mr. Charmers, Howard Zimmer, AP. Can you please share with us how serious RICIN exposure is?"

"Mr. Zimmer, as you may know, RICIN is a deadly poison which, unfortunately is fairly easy to make from castor beans. When purified, it can be lethal and difficult to trace. According to bioterror experts, RICIN is a crude and clumsy weapon. However, within a few hours of inhaling significant amounts of RICIN, a victim may display respiratory distress, coughing, fever, nausea, and tightness in the chest followed by heavy fluid buildup in the lungs making breathing difficult. Additionally, victims' skin may begin to turn blue. Over several days, liver, spleen and kidney failure could result in death. Whether inhaled, injected or ingested, an extremely small dose of RICIN can quickly produce symptoms and result in death within 36 to 48 hours due to respiratory or circulatory system failure. Unfortunately, there isn't a cure."

"How much RICIN must a person be exposed to for it to be deadly? Also, is there an antidote?" asked Zimmer.

"Mr. Zimmer, the sad fact is inhaled RICIN is about a thousand times more deadly than if it is ingested and can be deadly in very small doses. In fact, an average adult need only inhale two milligrams of RICIN, equal to thirty grains of salt, for it to be deadly. Unfortunately, there isn't an antidote for RICIN. We at the CDC advise that anyone who believes he or she has been exposed to RICIN to wash as quickly as possible, breathe fresh air and seek medical care immediately. The standard treatment is intravenous fluids. In the event RICIN has been ingested, a doctor may administer fluids as well as charcoal to promote vomiting. I cannot over emphasize that anyone believing they have been exposed to RICIN seek medical attention immediately."

"So Gretchen, it's clear that today's attacks have far-reaching implications. As Mr. Charmers of the CDC said, anyone who believes they may have been exposed to RICIN should see a doctor immediately."

### Got One

For no apparent reason, at 5:00 pm Richard Young, a Militia member, on regular patrol turned into Town Lake Park along the Colorado River in Austin, Texas. The simple fact is, Richard expects this evening's patrol will be like every other; quiet and boring. The disappointing reality is Richard expects to end his patrol empty-handed. The good news was so far Austin has been free of drone attacks. Perhaps, thanks in some small part by the efforts of the Militia and people like Richard.

Thanks to his Militia training and six years as a Marine, Richard felt more than prepared to handle any challenge being a Militia member presented. Unknown to Richard, however, his evening's patrol will be far from boring.

For no particular reason, Richard turned left onto West Riverside Drive off South Lamar Boulevard, and made his way toward the most desolate area of the park. Visitors to Austin's parks typically subside in the evening and this Labor Day was no different. As Richard navigated Riverside Drive, the park was empty with the exception of a green mini-van parked out of the way in a clearing off the road. Having nothing more to occupy his time, Richard decided to break up the monotony and investigate the lone vehicle. Rolling up in his nondescript "Militia-mobile" as he liked to call it, Richard stopped twenty yards from the suspicious vehicle and stepped out with his trusty Remington 870 pump-action shotgun in hand.

Squeezing the button on the microphone clipped to his shoulder, "Militia Control, Militia 22. Over."

"Go ahead Militia 22."

"Militia 22 is in Town Lake Park. Approaching suspicious green Chrysler mini-van License Plate S923 99."

"Roger Militia 22. Keep us advised. Over."

"Roger. Militia 22."

Carefully, Richard approached the lone mini-van when he observed a young mid-eastern looking gentleman sleeping in the driver's seat. *Tap...Tap...Tap* against the window with his MagLite flashlight Richard awakened the lone sleeper. Raising his left hand against the intrusion of the bright MagLite, the driver squinted to allow his eyes to adjust. To Richard, the driver appeared more than startled, he looked downright edgy. During the few moments while the driver collected his wits, Richard swept his flashlight across the interior when the hairs on the back of his neck began to stir. Thanks to his Militia training and the drone videos constantly played on every television and internet channel, Richard was skilled in target identification. "Holy shit!" muttered Richard. In one fluid movement, he jacked a round into the chamber of his Remington and leveled both the weapon and MagLite on the driver "Put your hands up! Get out of the van!" For Richard, the driver paused just a little too long. "I said out of the van! Now!" Clearly the driver was not enthusiastic about Richard's request and had other plans as he quickly reached for the key already in the ignition. Just as quickly, Richard grabbed the handle with his left hand threw open the door before the driver could turn the key. In a snap, Richard lunged forward placing the muzzle of his Remington squarely against the driver's ribs "Hands up! Get out of the van. NOW!"

As the driver slowly raised his hands, Richard gave him just enough room to slide down from the driver's seat. "On the ground!" said Richard firmly.

Now, face-down and spread eagle, Richard placed his right knee against the driver's back. Retrieved his handcuffs and secured the driver's hands in one fluid motion. Now Richard made the most important radio call in his life.

"Militia Control, Militia 22. Terror suspect in custody. Need backup immediately."

After what seemed to Richard like an eternity, three Austin PD cruisers screeched to a halt pouring out six energized souls in the blink-of-an-eye. "Put down the weapon and step back!"

"I'm Richard Young, badge number 2234."

"I don't care who you are. Put the weapon down and step back," ordered the officer.

Richard complied and carefully laid his Remington on the ground and stepped back with his hands high above his head. One of the responding policeman, with the name Sanchez over his right pocket, came alongside Richard and asked for his ID. Upon confirming Richard's identity Sanchez apologized. "Mr. Young. Sorry for seeming distrustful. But, I know you appreciate that we must be careful."

"No problem officer Sanchez. I understand. Let me show you what I found."

Young, Sanchez and two other officers approached the van and peered inside. "Son of a bitch!" exclaimed Sergeant Garber. "Control. Patrol 32. On scene. We need HAZMAT, bomb squad and FBI immediately. Over."

"Roger Patrol 32. HAZMAT, Bomb Squad and FBI en route. Over."

While Young described the events leading up to his infamous radio call, Town Lake Park was alive with every emergency service and helicopter Austin had to offer in addition to FBI Special Agents, who upon their arrival immediately took command of the situation and moved the driver into one of their black SUV.

### Situation Room

The White House Situation Room was awash in the surreal glow from the video screens that encircled the room streaming live video from across the country. Raging fires, smoke and chaos filled the screens providing the backdrop for America's leadership to address the Islamic State threat. President Bennett, fixated on the display directly behind his seat, shook his head and turned to his advisors. "Our worst fears have been realized. America is the victim of an all-out attack. How bad is it Harold?"

Harold Simpson, Director of Homeland Security, "Mr. President. According to preliminary reports, there are at least three hundred, if not more, attacks in forty states. So far, more than one hundred thousand deaths have been reported. Keep in mind, this is preliminary and I fear the numbers will get worse."

Bennett, threw his paper-coffee cup against the wall out of unbridled frustration, "Jesus Christ! This is Armageddon! How the hell did we miss this?"

"Excuse me Mr. President," said General Garland James, "I don't know if this is Armageddon. What I do know is that we have been caught with our pants down. The Islamic State has successfully brought its mission en masse to the United States. As we have discussed before, this attack strategy is indefensible. We don't have adequate nor effective defenses as proven in the Washington attack. It is time that we take the offensive. The Joint Chiefs believe we need to escalate our efforts against the Islamic State as well as addressing North Korea's involvement."

"What in hell are we going to tell the country? *'Caught with our pants down'* isn't going to fly. We need a plan and we need one now!" exclaimed Bennett.

"General, we need the Joint Chiefs to come up with a response immediately."

"Mr. President, we have a plan. We believe we must immediately deploy one hundred thousand troops into the Middle East and at least fifty thousand into South Korea. We need to make it clear that we will not sit idly by. We need to put the pressure on them. Diplomacy isn't going to work. We need to call it what it is. WAR!!"

"I am not happy doing so, but I don't see any alternatives. Anthony, you need to get the State Department off its ass now and speak with our allies in the Middle East as well as allies around the world. We need a coalition. The cost of this effort must be shared by all. Mark my words, this threat is not going to be limited to the U.S. These god damn terrorists are going to involve everyone. And I mean everyone!" declared Bennett.

Everyone in the room turned their attention to Anthony Umberg, Secretary of State, seated at the far end of the conference table. "Mr. President, I've already spoken with the Prime Ministers of Britain, Israel, Japan, Canada and Australia. Preliminarily, they are prepared to commit whatever resources are necessary to combat this threat. You and I have calls scheduled over the next two hours with Jordan, Turkey and the Saudis. Tomorrow morning I'm meeting with the U.N. Security Council."

Bennett turned to Speaker Teasdale and Senate Majority Leader Palmer, "Robert, Jennifer, can I presume that Congress is not going to hold up approving a declaration of war against the Islamic State and potentially North Korea? We don't need any partisan bullshit here."

Almost as if orchestrated, Teasdale and Palmer responded together, "Yes Mr. President."

"There is some good news Mr. President," said FBI Director Mitchell Teich. "We have a drone terrorist in custody along with ten drones."

"When? Where?"

"This evening, 1700 hours Central Time in Austin, Texas. A local Militia member, a Mr. Richard Young, observed a suspicious mini-van in a park in Austin. Upon approaching the van, Mr. Young observed what he believed to be drones and took one Mr. Abdul Neifeh into custody and called local and federal law enforcement. Mr. Neifeh is currently being transported to Washington and his home has been secured."

"This is great news. So, our Militia averted an attack and saved untold lives! Great news. Get Sheriff Johnson and Young to Washington immediately. We need them for a press conference."

"Will do Mr. President," replied Kerns.

Bennett, stood up, pushing his chair deliberately against the conference table. "Unlike Churchill, I am not certain history will look back and see this as 'Our finest hour.'" Bowing his head, Bennett offered a prayer, "Dear God…You are my refuge and my shield; I have put my hope in your word. Folks, that's Psalm 119:114. If we ever needed Devine intervention, it is now. Amen!"

"Offense is the essence of air power,"
General H. H. 'Hap' Arnold

# Chapter 12

◆

### *The Revolution 'Will' be Televised*

Nations around the world recoiled in disgust upon hearing the news of the death and carnage the Islamic State inflicted on America. Not since America's dropping of the atomic bombs on Hiroshima and Nagasaki has there been such tremendous and focused devastation. Now, only twenty-four hours since the Labor Day attacks began, upwards of two hundred thousand men, women and children lost their lives in these brutal and savage attacks. More insidious, however, was the Islamic State's decision to include the poison RICIN contaminating hundreds of thousands more. It will be years before anyone can truly assess the ultimate degree of damage the Islamic State visited upon America.

In this age of social media, networks and online channels, media was replete with unlimited videos documenting the Labor Day attacks. From smartphones to GoPro cameras, there was no shortage of videos immortalizing every imaginable aspect of the Islamic State's blow to America. If third-party videos chronicling the Labor Day events weren't chilling enough, as in previous drone attacks real-time video was broadcast from every flight of drones across America from coast to coast. So much for Gill Scott-Heron's '70's counter-culture poem *The Revolution Will Not be Televised*. Clearly his vision of the future didn't include ubiquitous video recording devices in the hands of millions of citizen-reporters. Maybe in Scott-Heron's view, the revolution would not be televised but, it is clearly being documented vicariously, touching every soul across the globe. But something was about to change. The sympathy of distant observers reeling from the events in America is about to go global. Barakat's league of technology-jihadists are preparing their next blow. Barakat's plan to expand the Islamic State's footprint of terror against infidels across the globe will undermine the frail fabric of humanity that keeps the world from sliding into a new Dark Age.

### *Presidential Message*

The morning after Labor Day America sat stunned in disbelief that such devastation could be rained down upon the mightiest nation in the world. Such devastation that the carnage of 9/11 pales in comparison.

President Bennett stood behind his desk in the Oval Office, prepared to give the speech of his presidency. Every presidency has a defining moment. Unfortunately for President Bennett, his had begun.

The Stage Manager pointed to President Bennett, held up five fingers and began his countdown. "Five…Four…Three…Two…" He silently mouthed the word One as he pointed to President Bennett. The camera's red light blinked on.

*"My fellow Americans. Like you, I am deeply disturbed and saddened by the drone attacks that have been occurring in our county. Certainly, the limited number of attacks prior to yesterday have been horrific. Yesterday, however, the Islamic State escalated its assault against America to a new and diabolical level. According to our reports, three hundred and ninety-eight locations across forty states were targeted by the Islamic State's robotic drones. From civic centers to sports arenas, the Islamic State struck a devastating blow against America. Current estimates put the death toll at one hundred eight-four thousand men, women and children and hundreds of thousands more injured. Even more insidious and cruel, hundreds of thousands of our brothers and sisters have been exposed to the deadly poison RICIN. Fortunately, our medical and emergency services, the finest in the world, have responded to this threat saving untold thousands of lives. If you believe you were exposed to this deadly poison, I and the CDC urge you to see a doctor immediately.*

*"Until now, we have worked closely with the leaders of the free world and the United Nations to find a peaceful solution. Unfortunately, this is not to be. Today, I am invoking my war powers with the consent of the United States Congress and support of the United Nations. Prior to ordering our forces into battle, I have consulted with our military commanders to take every necessary step to prevail as quickly as possible and ensure the safe return of American and allied service men and women. As presidents before me, I am committed to ensure that this will not be a long and protracted endeavor. I am committed to providing our troops with the best possible support and to bring them home quickly and safely.*

*"As your president, I recognize this is an historic moment. I also understand that America is weary from the long and costly actions we have endured in the Middle East. Unfortunately, the Islamic State has chosen to bring their violence to our country. Today, I am committed to ensure us all and for future generations a new world order of peace. A world committed to the rule of law, not the rule of terror as demonstrated by these*

*aggressors. I assure you, we will be successful and together we can forge a new world order grounded in peace.*

*"America, along with the leadership of our allies, hoped the use of force could be avoided. Unfortunately, in the shadow of Labor Day, we now believe force is necessary. Today, over twenty nations have committed forces against the Islamic State, establishing an unprecedented and unified international coalition against terror.*

*"Beginning immediately, one hundred thousand U.S. and Allied troops will be strategically deployed throughout the Middle East in the most forceful, quick and effective manner possible.*

*May God bless American and the coalition forces at our side as we stand up to the tyranny of the Islamic State. God bless the United States of America."*

President Bennett's image was replaced by talking heads and commentators across every broadcast and Internet news channel.

### Opinions and the News

"Well ladies and gentlemen. You just heard the news. The day after the horrendous Labor Day attacks, President Bennett has invoked the War Powers Act and is preparing an all-out offensive against the Islamic State in the Middle East. As he mentioned in his speech, this will be a unified effort between America and over twenty allied countries. This is certainly an unprecedented moment in President Bennett's term of office. To help us better understand what just happened, we have with us this morning retired General Gary Arnold, a UNN contributor."

The screen splits, with Jeff Stoddard on the left and General Arnold on the right seated at a desk, framed between the United States and Marine Corps flags.

"Good morning General. Thank you for joining us following President Bennett's historic speech," said Stoddard.

"You're welcome Jeff. It is truly an unfortunate and a sad state of affairs. I understand the President's decision and I whole-heartedly support him. My only wish is that he would have come to this decision sooner and perhaps the devastation on Labor Day could have been averted or at least minimized," said Arnold.

"How do you mean General?" asked Stoddard.

"Well Jeff, I had advised the President that I believed the drone attacks would continue and likely escalate. And escalate they did. Three months ago, at a meeting with President Bennett and the Joint Chiefs, I recommended a preemptive strike, which would not only inflict serious damage on the Islamic State, it would help avert any subsequent attacks. Unfortunately, the President did not heed my advice. So here we sit, the day after the worst and most devastating attack on American soil in history. And now the President is acting? It's a shame he didn't decide to place our troops in the Middle East six weeks ago," ranted Arnold.

"General. Aren't you being a little harsh on President Bennett? This has been a tough time for everyone. It seems to me you are doing a little Monday morning quarterbacking. Wouldn't you agree?"

"Jeff. I am not a Monday morning quarterback. I am a retired three-star General of the United States Marine Corps. This has been my profession for my entire adult life. What we have here is an all-out attack on America and our way of life. We need to act swiftly and decisively. I fear President Bennett may be a little late to the party," retorted Arnold.

"Well General. I certainly respect your opinion and thank you for your years of sacrificial service to our country. We will just have to sit by and watch as the President's plan unfolds and hope for the best. Thank you for joining us this morning," replied Stoddard.

"Thank you, Jeff. Have a great day," said Arnold.

### The Interrogation

Regardless of his intent to murder untold thousands of Austin citizens, luckily for Abdul Neifeh, America is governed by the Rule of Law and respect for human rights. Since his delivery to the FBI's Washington D.C. headquarters, Abdul has been left to sweat out his fate for the past twenty hours in a dark and sterile interrogation room chained to a table.

Abdul, praying silently, tried to subdue his fears and, more importantly, his urgent need to urinate. Suddenly, Abdul's concentration is broken by computer beeps as the room's electronic access control buttons are pressed. Click! The electronic locking mechanism released its hold on the door and two clean-cut and strident looking individuals entered the room.

"Mr. Neifeh, I am Special Agent in Charge Lane and this is Special Agent Richards. I presume you know that you are in FBI headquarters and are being held under suspicion of conspiracy to commit terrorist acts against America, possession of illegal explosives, and possession of biological weapons."

"I want a lawyer. I know my rights. I'm an American," asserted Neifeh confidently.

"I am sorry Mr. Neifeh. That's just not going to happen. Since the United States declared a state of war against the Islamic State, you are being held as a war criminal. You have no rights. What you do have Neifeh, is the opportunity to make things a lot easier on you. Cooperate with us, answer our questions and it will bode well for you during your sentencing," explained Lane. "First, who are you working for?"

"I didn't do anything. I was just waiting to deliver some toys to a swap meet. That's all. I'm not a terrorist," protested Abdul.

"Mr. Neifeh, lying to me does not give me the impression that you are willing to cooperate. In fact, it feels like you are just being defiant. Are you willing to work with us in resolving this problem?" asked Lane.

Abdul sat defiantly, staring straight ahead. "I have nothing to say and I have to go to the bathroom," muttered Abdul.

"Where and how did you get possession of the drones found in the back of your vehicle?" asked Lane.

"Who do you work for?"

"How do you receive your orders?"

"Listen Neifeh!" asked Lane sternly "This is a game you cannot win. We are under orders to do whatever is necessary to extract from you answers to our questions. Do you understand?"

Abdul, continued his overt defiance, "I told you, I have nothing to say."

Lane turned to Richards. "Let's let him sweat a little longer."

Click! The electronic lock secured the door behind as Lane and Richards left Abdul alone to ponder his future.

Standing outside the interrogation room, Richards turns to Lane "How far are we expected to go to get him to talk?"

"Listen, I lost my brother in the Busch Stadium attack. I am willing to go as far as necessary. If you aren't comfortable with this, then you can remove yourself from my detail. Do you understand?" stressed Lane.

"No. I'm not interested in leaving your detail. I want answers and will do whatever is necessary," answered Richards.

"Even torture?" queried Lane.

"I hadn't thought of it. But, they just killed almost two hundred thousand Americans. We have to stop this," replied Richards.

"Ok. I have a meeting with the Director in an hour. We'll let Neifeh sweat."

### The President

Worldwide sympathy for America after the Labor Day attack was amassing. President Bennett, sat somberly at his desk, staring down at the pile of condolence messages from leaders across the globe.

Roger Kerns stood in front of Bennett's desk, "Mr. President" as he patiently awaited his reply. "Mr. President?"

"Oh. I'm sorry Roger. I was lost in thought," replied Bennett.

"I understand Mr. President. None of us imagined when you took the oath of office that we would be facing such a crisis. Of course, we knew terrorism was not going to go away anytime soon. But, terror based mass destruction and devastation. Who could have guessed?" shared Kerns.

"It's our job to expect the unexpected Roger! Who else is going to do it?" rumbled Bennett.

"We missed the signs. Like 9/11, we missed the signs. The loss of the drone engineers from Autonomous Systems. The attacks prior to Labor Day. The bold nature of the Islamic State. We focused more on doing the right thing than doing what I was elected to do...protect our citizens," exclaimed Bennett. "Now we have to do whatever is necessary."

"Whatever, Mr. President?"

"Yes! Whatever. What's the status on the terrorist that was arrested in Texas?" asked Bennett.

"He is in custody at FBI Headquarters here in DC. So far, interrogation has yet to yield any information. The Director wants to know how far to go to extract information?" asked Kerns.

"As far as we have to. As far as we have to," said Bennett.

## Labor Day Plus 2: September 9

The death toll continues to grow hourly as bodies are discovered and individuals succumb to their wounds and RICIN poisoning. Everyone knows that America has changed and is facing a new and very dark future. Whether this is the beginning of Armageddon or not, for certain it is proof that Barakat's mission has struck America at its core, creating a frightened populace.

For so many Americans, the fallout of the Labor Day attack was difficult to comprehend. Millions of citizens followed civil defense suggestions to stay home and shelter in place and avoid large crowds, fundamentally bringing America to a standstill.

Two days after the Labor Day attack, as so many times before, embedded Islamic State cells not just across America but in Canada, England and Australia have acknowledged the chirping of their iPhones as Twitter called them to execute their deadly plan.

## Labor Day Plus 3: September 10

Before anyone had a chance to recover from the nightmare of September 7th, Barakat awakened his lone wolf technology-jihadists who have, until now been patiently awaiting 'their' message. Once again, smartphones chirped the all-too-familiar sound of a message routed though social media capturing the attention of the Twitter followers.

@WaterBoy Eight glasses a day is all you need #REFRESHING

@SunSet What a beautiful evening #REDSKYATNIGHT

@Aurora The sky is ablaze #NORTHERNLIGHTS

As done many times before, the hashtags were diligently entered into the coupon code fields of hundreds of innocuous e-commerce websites. For many, the hashtags resulted in a ten percent discount off their purchase. However, two hundred of Barakat's diligent followers in Oregon and Washington as well as Vancouver, British Columbia, England and Australia, got something more. They received their deadly instructions that were seamlessly downloaded into their waiting iPhones. After a few spins of the download progress icon, two hundred iPhones were programmed with navigation information and instructions for these enemies of America, Canada, Australia and England. Saturday, five days after Labor Day, Barakat will once again strike a fatal blow in the name of Islam.

Thousands of technology-jihadists across the globe viewed the tweets and once again began the process of discovering if they were the ones called to serve the Islamic State. Long before receipt of the day's Social Media messages, hundreds of the Islam State's embedded agents of destruction had already retrieved their ten-drone fleet and squirreled them safely away in their garages, basements and storage lockers. Today, thousands of drones are being readied by their operators to once again strike America along with five hundred drones being prepared in Canada, England, and Australia. Today, Barakat extends the hand of Islamic State to strike blows against English-speaking infidels across the world.

# Chapter 13

———————◆———————

### *Labor Day Plus 4: September 11*

Except for the few onlookers that admired the two sleek three hundred foot plus yachts, carrying members of the Saudi Royal Family, framed by the setting sun, the passing of the *Princess Star* off the Oregon coast and the *Desert Star* motoring through the Strait of Georgia, the body of water separating Vancouver Island and Vancouver British Columbia, went markedly unnoticed. As quickly as it began, the setting sun slipped below the horizon, filling the sky with a deep radiant crimson as darkness and the glorious night sky encroached upon the setting sun. Like its sister ship the *Desert Star*, the *Princess Star* continued motoring north for more than an hour after sunset when two nondescript souls on each of the luxury yachts pulled back a tarp revealing a covey of Barakat's attack drones destined for Canada and America.

The container ships *Deliverer* and *Eastern Star* glided just off the ports of Sydney in New South Wales, Australia and Southampton in England. Like other cargo ships, they waited their turn to dock and disgorge themselves of their tightly packed cargo into the waiting hands of port crane operators, for the precious cargo to begin its journey to their destinations. Darkness had become Barakat's best friend and protector. Since the drones developed by Chambers and his team navigated autonomously, they had little need for daylight and the veil of darkness made these small dark automatons almost invisible.

An hour after sunset, five containers stored topside on both *Deliverer* and *Eastern Star* received their telephonic instructions and one-by-one their roofs opened to reveal one hundred armed drones slumbering quietly in the darkness. As so many times before, the drones awakened and spiraled upward, beginning their journey to the waiting hands of Barakat's agents in England and Australia. As one container closed its doors, another began the process of releasing its cargo of terror into the cool night air.

### *The White House: September 10*

The gathering of Bennett's advisors in the Oval Office began to grow tiresome. Meeting after meeting, but no solution to the drone attacks was forthcoming.

Three days after Labor Day Bennett entered the Oval Office as seven perfectly groomed and somber gentlemen rose from the couches in respect. Scanning the room quickly, Bennett took attendance and began shaking hands.

"Good Morning David, how are things at the CIA?"

"We feel the pressure Mr. President," replied Director Haydon,

"Terrance, I can't tell you how happy I am to have you as my Vice President."

"Thank you Mr. President. The pleasure is all mine."

"Mitch. How is it going with the suspect in FBI custody?"

"Slowly Mr. President. He wants to lawyer up," replied FBI Director Mitchell Teich. "Rest assured Mr. President, that isn't going to happen. He isn't a criminal suspect. He is a war criminal. Period!"

"General James, thank you for joining us today. We have much to discuss."

"The military is at the ready Mr. President," snapped General James.

"Harold, I presume things are busy at Homeland," queried Bennett.

"Beyond imagination Mr. President. Beyond imagination," responded Director Harold Simpson.

Bennett noticed a new attendee. Certainly familiar, a friend from his distant past. "Mr. President, this is Sheriff Graham Johnson from Lincoln Nebraska and the head of the Militia."

"Thanks Roger. I know the Sheriff."

"Graham, it's good to see you again my friend. The work you're doing with the Militia is nothing short of magnificent. Especially the capture of the drone agent in Austin, Texas. Good job. Very good job indeed. I look forward to the ceremony with Mr. Young this afternoon."

Johnson, stood at attention in perfect SEAL fashion, shook Bennett's hand, "Thank you Mr. President. I am honored for the opportunity to serve our country."

"Please gentlemen. Sit down." Bennett took his customary seat at the top of the u-shaped seating area.

"General, what is the status of the deployment in the Middle East?" asked Bennett

"Mr. President, we're making progress and will have one hundred thousand troops on the ground in the next five days. Our advisors are already on the ground and the Gerald R. Ford Task Force is on station in the Persian Gulf," replied General James.

"Outstanding. We need to put the pressure on these guys and stop this chaos," announced Bennett.

"Roger, what's next on the agenda?" asked Bennett.

"Mr. President. Sheriff Johnson wants to brief us on the progress of the Militia and discuss a plan he would like to present for your consideration."

Bennett turned his attention to Johnson, "Sheriff Johnson, you have the floor."

"Mr. President, as you know, the Militia has faced a number of challenges, the most significant of which was deploying enough members to cover every possible target. What I want to propose today is for me to change my focus. I want to assemble my former SEAL team and track down Barakat and the Autonomous Team to cut the head off the serpent."

President Bennett took a sip from his coffee. He paused for a moment then turned to Johnson. "What do you need and what can you achieve?"

"Mr. President, I am certain that my team can disrupt Barakat's ability to continue his development and manufacturing efforts. We need to kill these guys and do whatever is necessary to disrupt their manufacturing and delivery mechanism."

"General James, David, what is the Joint Chief's and the CIA's position on Sheriff Johnson's plan?" asked Bennett.

"Mr. President, the CIA is in favor of a covert action against Barakat. We are prepared to provide Sheriff Johnson whatever support and intel he needs," replied David Haydon.

"Great! General. Your thoughts?"

"Mr. President. I don't know why we need to activate Sheriff Johnson when we have SEAL teams trained and at the ready," replied General James.

Johnson leaned forward. "Mr. President. I respect every member of the Teams. As you know, I have a vested interest in this fight. I lost my wife and daughter. My team is motivated and at the ready. We can be in-country as quickly as General James can drop us in. As far as I'm concerned, we need to bring all our assets to bear against this menace. I promise you, my team will not fail you," said Johnson.

"Gentlemen, as far as I'm concerned we need to play every card we have. Sheriff, if you take on this responsibility, what happens to the Militia?" asked Bennett.

"Mr. President, the Militia is doing a great job. Anyone can take over my responsibility as Director. I can be more effective in ending this chaos at its source rather than simply trying to defend against it stateside," announced Johnson. "I beg you to give me a chance."

Bennett pondered his request for a moment, reflecting on his time with Johnson in the Teams. "Roger, prepare whatever order is necessary to authorize the Sheriff. I will sign it immediately. Good luck Sheriff. I believe in you and respect that you deserve this opportunity," said Bennett shaking Johnson's hand. "General, I assume I have your support?"

"Yes Mr. President. Always!" snapped James.

"Thank you Mr. President. We will be ready for deployment in ten days," promised Johnson.

"Ok. We have a proactive plan thanks to Sheriff Johnson. Gentlemen, we still need a solution to defend against any further attacks. What's the status?" asked Bennett.

Harold Simpson picks up a folder, "Mr. President, we at Homeland have a number of plans. As you know, Autonomous Systems is deploying its sentinel and attack drone technology. Unfortunately, it will take the better part of a year and billions of dollars to deploy this strategy around primary targets such as Washington D.C.—which is being installed as we speak." Simpson flipped through his folder, "Mr. President, we have an additional plan that we believe in."

"What is it?" asked Bennett.

"We believe there is merit in the CHAMPS technology from Boeing."

"What is CHAMPS?" asked Bennett

"Sorry Mr. President. CHAMPS stands for Counter-electronic High-energy Advanced Magnetic-electro Pulse System. It is a stationary version of Boeing's missile based technology. It's designed to respond to any technology assault with a focused Electro-Magnetic Pulse, EMP, which will disrupt the attacking drones' electronics and bring them down."

"Are there are consequences we need to consider?" asks Bennett.

"Certainly Mr. President," replied Simpson. "We believe any CHAMPS response to a drone attack will be effective. It will, unfortunately, disrupt other electronic systems as well. Any vehicle or system that employs electronics including cars, cell phones and airplanes will be disrupted. Our tests, however, show that CHAMPS can be focused to minimize collateral damage," replied Simpson.

"What will happen when the drones are disrupted by CHAMPS? Are they vaporized or something?" asked Bennett.

"No Mr. President. They will lose their ability to navigate and crash to the ground. The sad fact is they will likely explode on impact. The good news is we hope they can be brought down before they reach their destinations thus minimizing the loss of lives by keeping the drones away from populated targets," replied Simpson.

"Ok. We have to step up our defense capability. If you guys at Homeland believe in, uh...CHAMPS, let's get it going. Roger, inform Boeing that they need to deliver," announced Bennett.

"Already done Mr. President. CHAMPS is currently being installed around potential D.C. targets including the White House, Capital, Supreme Court, etc." explained Kerns.

Bennett stood up. "Gentlemen, we cannot allow another attack like that which took us by surprise on Labor Day. My presidency is committed to finding a solution to protect America and its citizens. Thank you for meeting today. Good luck Sheriff. My prayers are with you."

Kerns guided President Bennett out of the Oval Office to Marine One waiting on the White House lawn.

### Back with Barakat

Barakat sat quietly in his room when Abdul Fadel tapped gently on the door jamb. "Emir, have you seen the news from America?"

"Yes Abdul. We have struck America at its core. I am pleased that they know what it is like to be attacked from the sky," replied Barakat. "I am certain they don't like the taste of their own medicine."

"Emir, Chambers is requesting a meeting with you. He wants to discuss his future."

"Well Abdul, I am happy to speak with Mr. Chambers. But not right now. Unfortunately for Chambers, he is not my priority. We are about to launch another attack on America as well as England, Canada and Australia. Finally, the long-arm of Islam will be felt by infidels worldwide," Barakat stated boldly. "Let Chambers sit for a while. I will speak with him in a few days."

Chambers and his remaining team sat in the meeting room enjoying their humble yet satisfying meal of lamb, rice and vegetables provided by Barakat.

"I would give anything for a hamburger," announced Will.

Liz, who normally sat quietly, couldn't help but agree with Will Schmidt. "Really. I'd kill for a Big Mac and fries. Unfortunately, I don't believe they are anytime soon in my future."

"For sure!" agreed Gary Sasaki. "Personally, I'm amazed we're still alive. At some point they won't need us. Just like America's attack on us at the test range, we are simply disposable. The more mature the technology becomes, the more likely it is Barakat will simply throw us away."

Chambers, trying to be a voice of reason, said "Look guys, clearly Barakat needs us. All of us. If he didn't he would have done away with us a long time ago."

"Richard," asked Akio "where do you go when they take you out of here?"

Trying to cover up his discomfort, "No place special Akio. Barakat just pulls me into a meeting. Does some sabre rattling and demands more from us," replied Chambers. "I believe I have done a good job of ensuring that all of us are relevant. Every one of us! We need to keep the faith and be hopeful that America will charge in and free us."

Akio, throwing down his meager piece of lamb, "Sell crazy someplace else Dick. America doesn't give a damn about us. Have you forgotten they tried to kill us?"

"No Akio, I haven't forgotten. We must make every effort to communicate with the outside world so they know we're still alive. Hell, they can't just leave us here to rot," exclaimed Chambers.

"Dick, we don't need CEO Rah-Rah. You may have been our boss back at Autonomous, but here, Akio, Will and I are the key players. I think we should speak with Barakat. Not just you!" asserted Gary. "He has to understand that the three of us are doing the heavy lifting on this project, not you or Liz."

"If you want to speak with Barakat, nothing is stopping you. Take your best shot," replied Chambers, looking disgusted.

Akio, unhappy with Chambers arrogance, returned to his meal.

"Ok...Ok...Let's get past the bitching. What's the status of the shielding for the electronics?" asked Chambers.

Liz, as project manager, took the lead. "Richard, so far the shielding seems to be working against the small amount of EMP we are able to produce. Unfortunately, we don't have a high-energy EMP generator with which to test. Regardless, Akio believes the shielding should be effective against any low-energy EMP that is thrown at the drones. I presume, if and when the drones encounter a military grade EMP, we will find out how effective the shielding really is."

"Great. As you know, Barakat is an engineer and sees EMP shielding as an important defensive mechanism for the drones," replied Chambers. "Barakat wants to see a demonstration of the shielding tomorrow. Are we ready?"

Akio mumbled, "We're always ready Dick. Always!"

### Labor Day Plus 5: September 12

For many, five days after Labor Day may be of little significant historical value. On the lighter side, John F. Kennedy married Jacqueline Bouvier in 1953 and in 1990 Australia banned Bungee Jumping. However, September 12th resonated with the nation of Islam for this is the day in 2001 that President George W. Bush declared war against terrorism and the Consulate in Benghazi, Libya was attacked eleven years later. Today,

Barakat intends to mark September 12th as a memorable day in history as he spreads his new age aerial terror across the globe.

Unknown to the congenial residents of Sydney, Australia, fifty of Barakat's technology-jihadists were called to attention promptly at 2:00pm beginning the first of Barakat's worldwide September 12th assaults against the enemies of the Islamic State. Like clockwork, fifty of Barakat's devoted followers began the process of freshening batteries and programming each of their ten drones. Flickering LEDs and spinning icons on iPhones were the only indications that Barakat's mission was underway. As time progressed, each of Barakat's lone wolf technology-jihadists began preparing themselves for the evening's mission. Only pawns in a well-orchestrated plan, the drone commanders diligently loaded their squadron of ten finely tuned implements of destruction into their run-of-the-mill mini-vans and carefully covered them with blankets and sheets shielding them from curious eyes.

As the Australian sun sank slowly toward the western horizon and shadows grew longer, these followers of Islam began the process by quietly unrolling their sacred prayer rugs upon the ground. Kneeling respectfully, each bowed deeply and dutifully paying homage to Muhammad. Allah Akbar.

Ironically, fifty iPhones chirp happily signaling the beginning of their fateful journey. Almost in unison, fifty vans-of-destruction slipped quietly from the security of their garages as Siri emotionlessly and diligently provided turn-by-turn directions to their prescribed launch points.

Per Barakat's plan, Australia will become the newest member of a unique family. A family where terror became close and personal. A family, that come sunrise will mourn loss and forever wear the permanent scars inflicted by the jihadist soldiers of the Islam State.

Promptly at 6:00pm, and unknown to one another, Barakat's agents arrived at their destinations; Kumba Point, Blue Point Reserve and Cremorne Point. Each strategically positioned to easily and quickly reach their pre-set targets. Sitting quietly, the men waited patiently, overlooking Sydney harbor, watching the screens of their iPhones for the order to power up their fleets and launch their deadly assault against the tranquility of Sydney, Australia.

At 6:30pm fifty iPhones came alive displaying the simple go order "*BEGIN.*" Slipping from the warmth of their seats, each drone commander opened his sun roof and slipped into the back of his van to begin the launch sequence. In one smooth motion, each drone was lifted carefully toward the sun roof as the power switch is slipped to the on position. Immediately, six high speed electric motors whirred as the drones strained to be released. One-by-one, each drone majestically rose from the commander's hands and zoomed smoothly up and away loitering at two hundred feet awaiting the arrival of the rest of the fleet. Almost as quickly as the drones were carefully placed in the vans, ten drones orbited leisurely high above awaiting the go command as their human partners quietly drove away to the seclusion of their suburban life.

Almost as one, five hundred drones skimmed across Sydney Harbour as each diligently tracked their predefined course. Without warning, two hundred drones made their way to the Sydney Opera House where two thousand plus Aussies and tourists eagerly awaited the 7:30 show time and overture for what has been called a saucy and splendid production of Cole Porter's *Anything Goes*. Unfortunately, tonight anything goes will forever have a new meaning.

Promptly, Barakat's drones arrived, orbiting a couple of hundred feet above the majestic arching shells of the Sydney Opera House's roof. After completing four leisurely orbits over the Opera House, the lead drone's computer, broadcasting its live video feed into social media, processed the ultrasonic feedback from its sensors confirming its target and initiated the attack sequence for the entire squadron. In unison, two hundred C4 laden drones swirled downward in a sweeping arch as the lead drone loitered up high capturing the event for all to see. The first drone struck the high arching roof of the opera house spraying thousands of stainless steel projectiles and RICIN down upon the crowd that unwittingly milled below. Before anyone could even grasp what just occurred, drone after drone plunged into the opera house delivering death and destruction. The sinister lead drone captured every deadly moment of their mission for all the world to see then plunged into the opera house for the glory of Allah.

The iconic shells of the magnificent Sydney Opera House were gone. The building that famed American architect Louis Kahn once proclaimed '*The sun did not know how beautiful its light was, until it was reflected off this building*' today laid in rubble and devastation changing forever lives of thousands of theatre goers and Sydney residents as well as Sydney's beautiful skyline. Unfortunately, the beautiful Sydney Harbor Bridge too was part of Barakat's plan.

The final flight of one hundred drones, launched from Blue Point Reserve, had a more insidious target–Kirribilli House the home of Prime

Minister Ronald Grimes. As the flight of one hundred drones arrived on station, again the lead drone, broadcast its video for all to see, confirmed its target and delivered the attack command. Almost silently, each drone swooped down from its perch high above Kirribilli House wreaking havoc and destruction. Kirribilli House, strained diligently to suffer through each attack, but to no avail. Drone after drone assaulted the structure with hundreds of pounds of C4 explosives, deadly stainless steel ball bearings and RICIN killing hundreds and contaminating many more in attendance of a formal state dinner. The Prime Minister and his wife became the latest victims of Barakat's agenda.

Over the years, England had experienced its share of trials and tribulations punctuated by the subway bombing of 2005 killing fifty-two and injuring many more. Today, England's terror death toll will ratchet up to a new and unprecedented level. As in Australia, fifty of Barakat's operatives were called to action at 2:00pm on September 12th and began their diligent and ritualistic preparations. As the sun moved toward the western horizon, these focused and determined jihadists loaded their vehicles and began their pilgrimage of terror. Guided by Siri, each technology-jihadist followed her directions arriving at numerous launch points in secluded parks across London. One-by-one, they positon their vehicles in open areas away from prying eyes quietly awaiting their call to action.

At 6:45pm, forty-five minutes before sunset, fifty iPhones awakened and chirped the call to action to the waiting drone operatives. Nervously, yet committed, they opened their sun roofs then slip into the back of their min-vans and began activating their fleets. As has happened across the globe, each operator lifted the first drone sliding the power switch to the on position. Fifty drones came to life as the operators tapped the screens of their iPhones. Blinking and whirring, each drone strained to be released into the air. Five…four…three…two…one…The fifty lead drones were lifted up through sun roofs then smoothly ascend upward two hundred feet awaiting arrival of their comrades. In less than five minutes, each operator successfully deployed his ten drones gazing upward admiring his handiwork as the fleets of drones came together in orderly and geometric formation. Chirp…Chirp. The iPhones announced completion of the operators' responsibilities and signaled their departure and ultimate return to their homes.

As they loitered for only a few minutes, the drones began following their programming and navigated quietly toward their assigned targets.

Once again, Barakat's arrogance was personified as the lead drones of each of the attack squadrons began broadcasting their progress toward destruction.

Tonight, Barakat's intent was to change the peaceful London community by bringing a level of devastation not seen since Hitler's Blitz started on September 7$^{th}$, 1940. A period when forty thousand Londoners were killed over fifty-seven days. Not just intending to kill the infidels, Barakat intended to mar London forever, destroying seven prominent landmarks.

With pinpoint accuracy, one hundred drones arrived over Buckingham Palace as the lead drone diligently broadcast the macabre scene into social media. As quickly as they arrived on station, the attack squadron began their descent toward the palace and in a blink of the eye, the swarm crashed into the majestic structure, deploying over one hundred pounds of C4, stainless steel ball bearings, and RICIN everywhere. As if satisfied that the attack was successful, the lead drone initiated its sacrificial plunge transmitting vivid video of fire and destruction as it plummeted from its station high above. The image of devastation loomed larger filling video screens across the globe then went black as the final blow to Buckingham Palace was inflicted.

Barakat's vision for his blow to London was not limited to Buckingham Palace. While the palace became the newest victim of terror, three hundred companion drones turned toward their targets destroying London's Eye, Westminster Abby, Big Ben, and the Hammersmith Apollo Theater which brought to an end the careers of the classic rock band Turner James and Company. In one final blow, one hundred of Barakat's drones dropped their hammer of destruction on Heathrow Airport destroying twenty airliners on the ground as well as the main terminal building, which ended the lives of thousands of innocent travelers.

For Barakat, Labor Day plus 5 wasn't limited to Australia and England. Fifty agents in Canada and an equal number in America were scheduled to carry out his plan to ensure the long-arm of terror was felt across the globe.

"Air power may either end war or end civilization," Winston Churchill

# Chapter 14

———————◆———————

### News Report

"Good evening. I'm Jeff Stoddard and we interrupt this evening's program to cover the news of the Islamic State's latest drone attacks. Today, the Islamic State's diabolical reign of terror from the sky has gone beyond America. Now, five days after the devastation of the Labor Day attacks on America, our allies around the world including Australia, England and Canada have fallen victim to the Islamic State's latest assault on innocent citizens. Today, thousands of Islamic State drones savagely attacked and laid to waste national treasures and landmarks throughout these countries, killing thousands and injuring tens of thousands more," announced Jeff Stoddard.

"What we see here is broadcast footage via social media from drones that attacked Sydney, Australia, which totally destroyed the Sydney Opera House, the Prime Minister's residence and numerous prominent landmarks.

"I am now joined by United News Network's military advisor, retired three-star General Gary Arnold. "General Arnold, thank you for joining us on such short notice."

"My pleasure Jeff. I am, however, sorry that we are on the air as a result of the utterly brutal attacks on America and our allies."

"Yes General. This is a very sad time for us all. Before we begin, let's take a look at some of the drone video footage from England, Canada and America."

The image on the screen faded into two video feeds. On the right were drones laying to waste Rogers Arena in Vancouver, British Colombia, killing over two thousand fans during the Charlie Boyz concert and devastating the entire structure. On the left, another drone video feed showed the most famous landmark in all of British Columbia—Canada Place, with its beautiful sails enveloped in flames and two cruise ships; one on fire and the other listing away from the dock, slowly sinking into the harbor. What was once a beautiful tourist destination for visitors from across the globe, has become damaged beyond recognition and is a tomb for thousands who lost their lives in this evening's attack.

Once again the screen faded now into a montage of terror and devastation as footage from England, Australia and America showed death, destruction and chaos wielded by the Islamic State's new age, devastating and indefensible assault initiative. The montage ended as the Grand Coulee Dam on the Columbia River, tried to withstand the assault. But alas, America's largest hydroelectric dam was no match for hundreds of C4 laden attack drones. The fleet inflected unimaginable damage which in a short time brought to a halt this grand facility as millions of gallons of water from Lake Roosevelt spilled forth and a shroud of darkness fell upon five hundred thousand of homes from Washington to California.

"General, the devastation inflected by these attacks is incomprehensible. What are we going to do?" asked Jeff.

"Jeff, certainly America's security and intelligence agencies have historically done a commendable job at detecting and disrupting many terrorist activities. Unfortunately, and I have said this before, I believe we were lulled into complacency during the years following 9/11. As the State of Islam grew in strength and sophistication, they've successfully developed advanced technology supported by legions of invisible lone-wolf terrorists giving them the capability to project terror wherever they please— evidenced by the earlier attacks this summer, the Labor Day attacks, and today. As for your question, I am certain our military and technology leaders are making progress at deploying defenses that can and will thwart this threat. More importantly, we need to project our military might into the mid-east and cut the head off this demon. Which is exactly what President Bennett has ordered with one hundred thousand American troops being deployed in the mid-east. The good news from today's events is I believe we can now depend on more Allied support in this mission."

"Thank you General. Ladies and gentlemen, please stay tuned as we cover breaking news as it develops. Good night and God bless America and the rest of the free world."

### Breakfast at the White House

Sunday morning dawned in the White House with President Bennett, FBI Director Mitchell Teich and Chief of Staff Kerns gathered over coffee in the private residence. Bennett sipped his coffee and paused for a moment, then spoke. "I can't believe it. These third-world pains-in-the-asses are wreaking havoc with impunity. Have we found anything from the Islamic State operative that was captured in…where was it? Austin?"

"That's correct Mr. President. Austin, Texas" responded Teich, "We've tried everything in the book short of torture to extract information from the suspect. He has simply clammed up. The ten drones recovered from the scene have been divvied up among a number of agencies—CIA, Homeland, FBI, Military and of course, Autonomous Systems."

"Anything new?"

"Mr. President, basically the drones are similar to other drones we've observed or recovered. Each is loaded with approximately two pounds of C4 explosives, thousands of stainless steel ball bearings and two pounds of RICIN. There were, however, a couple of things worth noting. First, these drones appear to be equipped with some kind of shielding. It looks as if the electronics are enclosed in a copper screen." Pausing to thumb through a folder, "One of our engineers called it a Faraday Cage."

"What is the purpose of the shielding?" asked Bennett.

"Well Mr. President, we suspect it is a counter measure to defend against an Electro-Magnetic Pulse weapon. You know. Like Boeing's CHAMP weapon we are deploying around D.C."

Bennett pondered the scope of what Teich just said. "Will the shielding be effective against CHAMP?"

"At the moment Mr. President, the drone's shielding is being tested and we should have a sense of its capacity to counter CHAMP's EMP. We are hopeful that the shielding will be ineffective against the massive energy level delivered by CHAMP. We should have test results tomorrow," replied Teich.

"Mitch, you said a couple of things. What else is there?" asked Bennett.

"Well Mr. President, Autonomous Systems found another embedded message in the firmware. As before, it appeared to be a message from the missing Autonomous Systems' team."

"Are you joking? I thought they were killed in that drone attack in Islamabad a couple of months ago," responded Bennett.

"It seems, Mr. President, the Autonomous team is still alive. Embedded in the firmware was this message." Teich slid over a page of computer code highlighted in yellow. "If you connect the highlighted code segments, the message reads. *We are alive. Please rescue us. GS.* We believe

'GS' stands for Gary Sasaki. An engineer on the Autonomous Systems jet lost over the Bay of Bengal."

"Son of a bitch. Who the hell did we kill in that attack?"

"We don't know, Mr. President. Since the people were in orange jump suits with hoods over their heads, we presumed they were the Autonomous team. Of course there was no way to confirm that. Based on the new message, we suspect they were decoys and the Autonomous team is still alive."

Once again, Bennett returned to his coffee. "Well, perhaps Sheriff Johnson's team will find what we are looking for."

### Johnson's Team Assembles

Monday 1800, 14 September, Johnson's team has assembled in D.C.'s Fusion Cell. "HOOYAH!!"

In unison, Johnson's entire team of former SEALs responded, "HOOYAH!!"

"Gentlemen, thank you for getting here so quickly. As you know, each of us has been reactivated by Presidential Order along with rank and privileges thereto. As commander, I'll be leading this expedition to respond to and neutralize the drone threat that has been spreading like wildfire. Toward this end, the President has authorized us to execute operations in Islamabad to locate and neutralize Barakat's drone capability. Just as important, we are tasked to find and extract the seven members of the Autonomous System's team believed to be alive and in captivity. It's believed these people are the brain trust behind the Islamic State's drone technology led by Moktar Barakat. Barakat's picture and profile along with his subordinates and the entire Autonomous team is provided in your briefing package."

"The list in front of your briefing package contains the names and roles of each team member. I trust you will spend this evening reacquainting yourselves. We will reconvene here tomorrow at 0800 and begin our mission briefing."

## Johnson's Teams

### BLUE TEAM
**Graham Johnson** — Leader
**Randy Summers** — Corpsman
**Grant Walker** — Interrogator

**J.P. Smith** — Small Arms Specialist
**Willie Miller** — Heavy Weapons Operator
**Garland Truman** — Navigator/Jumpmaster

## RED TEAM
**Richard Hernandez** — Ordnance
**Bob Davis** — Sniper
**Albert Gonzalez** — Breacher
**Fred Torres** — Communicator
**Peter Gray** — Surveillance
**Brad Davis** — Small Arms/Jumpmaster

Tuesday, 0800, 15 September.

"HOOYAH!!"

In unison, HOOYAH!!"

"Good morning gentlemen! I hope you had a relaxing evening because today we will be upping the tempo in preparation for insertion into theater. We depart Andrews Friday 18 September at 2000 and arrive over our jump point at 2200 on 19 September. We will HALO in from thirty thousand feet. We'll deploy chutes at three thousand five hundred feet, approximately three minutes after exiting the aircraft and stack-up six deep with Master Chief Davis, our jumpmaster, guiding Red Team and Chief Truman guiding Blue Team. Master Chief."

Master Chief Davis stepped to the podium and yells, "HOOYAH!!"

"HOOYAH!!" responded the team.

"Good morning gentlemen! I have very little to say. We will form up at 0600 tomorrow for HALO orientation then execute a practice jump promptly at 1100 hours. If you have any issues making your participation impossible, speak with me after this meeting and Captain Johnson and I will make adjustments. Captain."

"Thank you Master Chief. Gentlemen. In your briefing package, and displayed on the screen, is our target located at 33.731 Latitude by 72.937 Longitude. Satellite and high-altitude reconnaissance imaging shows what appears to be a protected area believed to be the entry to Barakat's underground facility. Intel from local assets have identified two ventilation shafts, indicated by the yellow arrows, that lead down in to the facility which we believe to be thirty meters below the surface. Gentlemen, our mission is simple. First, we will breach the facility in two teams. Blue Team will gain access through the northern ventilation shaft and locate command and control with your mission objective being capture Barakat and neutralization of his leadership. Red Team will gain access through the southern ventilation shaft. Your mission objective is to locate and retrieve the Autonomous Team. Rules of engagement are simple. Shoot to kill. For the next three days, you will be divided into your teams for detailed briefings, equipment checks and preparation. Gentlemen. We will succeed. HOOYAH!!"

"HOOYAH!!"

### Slap in the Face

As the Sun peeked over the eastern horizon on the crisp Fall Wednesday morning, New York City and the rest of the world was still reeling from the heinous and brutal attacks against America on Labor Day and the global assaults five days later. Like the attacks on 9/11, people found it difficult to reconcile the reality with the surreal nature of such events. Over the past year, the very real nature of the Islamic State's ability to strike at will against any target anywhere with impunity was simply beyond imagination. Across America, defensive systems were being deployed. Unfortunately, apart from obvious vulnerable and important targets, such as Washington D.C., there were simply too many places to protect.

The United News Network morning show, like so many media outlets, focused its attention on the events of the previous week. Interview after interview repeated the same message—the Islamic State's drone terrorism is indefensible. While the pundits pontificated on President Bennett's mistakes and the impotence of the United Nations, the attention of thousands of people milling through the streets of Manhattan was drawn upwards. The Big Apple's vertical nature has always been the perfect setting for pranking with those around you. The simple act of looking up, albeit a cliché, can act like a contagion causing hundreds of heads to snap back wondering what was going on high above. Was it a suicide jumper, an alien invasion or an unfortunate window washer hanging on for dear life? Today, the events high above the crowd would prove to be not so benign. Today, people throughout the city were looking up, drawn by the multi-sensory and unmistakable buzzing sound paired with glimpses of low-flying black drones navigating a hundred feet above the streets and between the buildings. Today, New Yorkers were not just curious, they were overwhelmed with dread.

A red band appeared across the bottom of the United News Network screen reading 'BREAKING NEWS.' The host listened intently to the audio feed in his right ear. "Ladies and gentlemen, we interrupt this morning's program to bring you breaking news. Reports are coming in from all across New York City of drones, apparently hundreds of them converging from all directions. Air raid sirens are wailing across the city. Here we have a video feed from atop the United News Network building. The scene is simply unbelievable. In fact, surreal. Our cameras are tracking numerous drones making their way between the buildings. At the moment, we do not know their destination."

"Oh my God. Here we have video feeds via social media which is obviously coming from the attacking drones."

"We just received word that a number of drones have been shot down by Militia members. Unfortunately, witnesses say the drones weren't being destroyed but rather crashing into buildings and exploding. There is pandemonium everywhere.

"Once again, here we have the video from the attacking drones. It looks like we have five different feeds, each showing what appears to be targeting cross-hairs. As yet, we cannot make out the target. Wait! It appears that the target is the Freedom Tower. It seems that hundreds of drones are making their way through Manhattan directly for the World Trade Center's Freedom Tower."

The Militia's efforts to take down the attacking drones was almost ineffective. Even after destroying a few dozen drones, hundreds continued on course directly toward the Freedom Tower.

As the image of the Freedom Tower grew larger, a subtle sign of activity became visible. Three rings of bright lights, evenly dividing and encircling the structure, began to throb and pulsate faster and faster. As the drone squadrons came closer, the lights grew brighter creating a blinding visual effect accompanied by an almost imperceptible yet deafening series of tones. Almost immediately, one-by-one drones fell out of the sky crashing into nearby buildings, spraying the streets with flames, smoke, shrapnel, and RICIN. Coincidentally, cars, trucks and busses within five hundred yards of the Freedom Tower came to a sudden stop as their electrical systems shut down. Hundreds of thousands of New Yorkers' cell phones went dark as they feverishly tried to make calls and capture the chaos on their smartphones.

The drone video feeds suddenly went black immediately replaced by reporters around the city capturing for history the Islamic State's heinous and brutal assault on America. Drone after drone crashed short of the Freedom Tower in a futile attempt to lay waste to the memorial to 9/11.

"Ladies and gentlemen. Reports came in from across the city. The Freedom Tower was under attack. Explosions were being observed all around the area encircling the tallest building in America. As yet, no one knew how many casualties there would be. But, if these attacks are like those before, one can expect the impact of this assault will be devastating. As you can see from the cameras atop the United News Network building, amazingly the Freedom Tower has been left somewhat unscathed. It appears only a few drones impacted the structure. Regardless, the Freedom Tower has been damaged and is on fire. At the moment, we don't know what happened. It appears that some defensive weapon has been installed on the Freedom Tower which successfully staved off the attack. Unfortunately, there is substantial damage to surrounding buildings and people below as hundreds of drones fell from the sky exploding on impact."

Almost as quickly as it began, the attack was over and the bright lights encircling the Freedom Tower went dark as flames and smoke engulfed the surrounding area. A review of video footage showed that the attack against 1 World Trade Center was thwarted, yet one hundred and fifty drones crashing out of control killed more than three thousand people in the surrounding area.

### Presidential Press Conference

The White House press room was filled to capacity as Press Secretary Farnsworth approached the podium. "Good afternoon everybody. Thank you for joining us for this White House briefing. Please stand for the President of the United States."

President Bennett made his way up the two steps to the podium that was emblazoned with the Presidential Seal.

*My fellow Americans, it is with great pain and sorrow that I am here today to discuss this morning's brutal attack against the Freedom Tower in New York City. Once again, Islam attempted to attack America at its core by trying to assault sacred ground — the 9/11 Memorial. However, I am pleased to announce that thanks to our technology prowess, the CHAMPS defensive weapon recently installed on the Freedom Tower successfully averted most of their evil intent.*

*Over the past week and a half, the Islamic State has escalated its assault against America and our Allies to a new and diabolical level, killing thousands of innocent citizens in America, England, Australia and Canada. Today, the death toll continues to climb with estimates in excess of three thousand men, women and children and hundreds of thousands more injured. Again, the evil nature of Islam has been clearly exposed by its use of these drones and deadly poison, RICIN.*

*As I have said many times before, our medical and emergency services are the finest in the world and are responding as we speak to meet the needs of those affected by this morning's attack. As before, if you believe you have been exposed to RICIN, go to your doctor or an emergency room immediately.*

*I am here to assure you that my administration is doing everything in its power to quash any further attacks and bring the perpetrators to justice. As we speak, over one hundred thousand U.S. and Allied forces are being deployed in the mid-East with the sole objective of bringing an end to this crisis.*

*Just as importantly, America has been and will continue to be a technology leader evidenced by the deployment of CHAMPS, which stands for Counter-electronic High-energy Advanced Magnetic-electro Pulse System. Basically, a force field that disables the electronics at the core of the attacking drone technology. Fortunately damage to the Freedom Tower was minimal, but the surrounding area took substantial damage.*

The image of President Bennett slipped into the upper right corner of the video image as Jeff Stoddard, anchor for United News Network returned. "As President Bennett's press conference continues, joining us is United News Network's military advisor retired General Gary Arnold. General, what is President Bennett going to do to achieve his stated objective?"

"Jeff, at the very least we need to keep up the pressure on Islam. Clearly we need to locate its drone facilities and stop production. Unfortunately, I suspect that by now the technology is being manufactured by rogue allies of Islam."

"General, what do you think about the CHAMPS defense system?"

"Jeff, CHAMPS is representative of our technology leadership. We have a variety of energy weapons in the U.S. arsenal. Deployed in aircraft, ships, satellite, mobile, and stationary configurations. It represents the most flexible and effective deterrent against technology-based weapons."

"General, unfortunately there appears to be substantial risk for collateral damage. How substantial is the risk and how will the risk be managed?"

"Well Jeff, every weapon has the risk of collateral damage. In the case of CHAMPS, *all* local electronics will be affected. Yet, if the attack is neutralized, I believe, as this technology evolves, we will be able to deploy what science fiction writers characterize as *force fields* capable of protecting valuable assets. CHAMPS represents a genuine paradigm shift in defensive weaponry."

"On a different note, General, who do you suspect the Islamic State's partners are?"

"Jeff, my best guess is North Korea. They have technological expertise and are committed to opposing the U.S."

"Are you suggesting that the U.S. needs to face-off with North Korea?"

"Jeff. The fact is simple. The Islamic State doesn't have manufacturing capability. Connect the dots. It doesn't take a genius to figure out who their technology partner is."

# Chapter 15

———————◆———————

## *HALO*
### *Wednesday 0600, 16 September*

Certainly 6:00 AM comes early, but, given the previous night's activities, Johnson's team was just a little groggier than usual. In classic military fashion, there's nothing like too much alcohol and storytelling to prepare a man for combat. Now assembled in Andrews Air Force Base's Hanger 3, Johnson's team sat patiently with the massive C-17, the same aircraft that will take them half way around the world, providing the backdrop for their mission briefing. Johnson, along with Master Chief Davis entered through the tall hanger doors and onto a small stage set-up below the giant Boeing's left wing.

"HOOYAH!! Gentlemen"

"HOOYAH!!"

"We are two days and counting from our departure Friday at 2000 hours. The aircraft behind me will be taking us and our gear direct to our jump point at which time we will depart the aircraft at thirty thousand feet. According to Master Chief Davis, our practice jump went well and we are ready to HALO into Islamabad. Great work. Today, we'll continue our mission review and Thursday we execute equipment checks, load the aircraft and complete final readiness procedures. By the way, I know we don't like to think about it, but do not forget to sign your DFAS 2984 form designating your death beneficiary."

For the better part of the day, the team reviewed every minute detail of the mission plan. Every man, all proven professionals, knew his job and could be depended on to perform professionally and expertly. At the end of the day, the team dispersed and headed for dinner then off to their racks. Johnson couldn't help but revel in his team's commitment, professionalism and most of all, patriotism. Like many leaders before him, he knew these men would follow him into the depths of hell. Johnson, however, couldn't help but wax a little sentimental thinking about his team. Past missions, losses and wins. Now much older, he questioned his sanity about what lay ahead. "What in hell are all these old farts doing?" But, just as quickly as the thought pushed its way into his consciousness, Johnson returned it where it belonged. Deep down and out of sight.

### _Friday 1930, 18 September_

The massive C-17 lumbered across the tarmac on taxiway "Whiskey" making its way to Andrews' Runway 1 Left. Each man, in his own way, prepared himself for what lay ahead. No one expected this to be an easy mission. Worse yet, if history is truly the best predictor, everyone to a man was a little skeptical about the dependability of the intelligence provided by '_Government_' sources. Some analyst back at Langley may believe he provided good intel, however, in reality, it wasn't his ass on the line. Even though no one mentioned it, the memory of the CIA's bad intelligence about Saddam Hussein's Weapons of Mass Destruction proved disastrous for President Bush as well as the bad intel on Benghazi. Covert or not, every successful military mission depended on good intelligence and no one wants a mission to blow up in his face. Embarrassment aside, every man, including Johnson, wanted this mission to succeed. For Johnson, success was defined very simply: find Barakat and neutralize his drone capability. Retrieving the Autonomous team was secondary.

For some, the hours slid by unnoticed as they slept throughout the flight. Others, however, couldn't push the mission out of their minds. Now, at 2000 hours on Saturday 19 September, just two hours from the drop zone, Master Chief Davis awakened Johnson and his team to ready themselves for the real beginning of the mission.

"Gentlemen. We depart the aircraft in one hour forty-five minutes. Please use this time to don your gear and check equipment."

Each man rose from the comfort of the C-17's less than luxurious seating and moved in two lines toward the aircraft's pressurized jump bay where they promptly performed final weapons checks then donned their jump gear. Like a finely tuned machine, each man checked his teammate's parachute, weapon, oxygen and mask then raised their right arms high above with thumps up indicating they were ready. Before they knew it, the ten-minute warning was issued and Johnson's team and jump support personnel switched over to their own oxygen bottles then double and triple checked equipment, connections and oxygen pressure. A dozen thumbs pointed skyward indicating everyone was ready.

"HOOYAH!!"

Some stood quietly awaiting their fate. Others prayed for the Lord's blessing and protection as the red ready light illuminated at t-minus five minutes. The depressurization warning horn sounded as the jump bay's life sustaining atmosphere was vented out into the near vacuum of thirty thousand feet. As the massive rear cargo door began cycling downward, each team member looked intently at their jump buddy watching for signs of hypoxia for there is only one to two minutes of Time of Useful Consciousness at thirty thousand feet. Slowly and deliberately the massive cargo door of the C-17 finished its journey revealing the ominous pitch-black sky over Islamabad.

Blue and Red teams stood in two clusters anticipating the go order. T-minus 5, 4, 3, 2, 1....The jump light changed from red to green indicating arrival over the drop zone and the jumpmaster issued the go order. Two-by-two, Blue and Red team members plunged into the darkness. Almost as quickly as it began, the last four men departed the aircraft and the massive C-17 banked hard left heading west as the cargo door retracted and the jump bay was pressurized. In a surreal series of events, the C-17's captain guided his massive steed on its long trip back to Andrews after completing his small but critical role in defeating this indefensible threat.

Each man plummeted through the darkness head first, quickly reaching terminal velocity as the C-17 disappeared overhead. At one hundred twenty miles per hour the two teams would reach three thousand five hundred feet in a little more than two minutes, at which time they would slow their descent by flattening out from the head-first position then deploy their life saving parachutes. On time, chutes were deployed. Like an aerial ballet, and with the aid of night vision goggles, each team member stacked up with his jumpmaster, ensuring everyone arrived on the ground close together. Garland Truman led the Blue Team stack and Master Chief Davis led the Red Team as both men deftly guided this elite force to a pinpoint landing two miles from Barakat's stronghold.

Successfully inserted into the Pakistani desert, these invisible men blended into their surroundings, yet fully visible to one another thanks to SEAL Night Vision Goggles. Quickly and silently they shed their parachutes and jump gear, as each man stripped himself of unnecessary burdens and readied himself for the mission at hand. Clad in desert camouflage, the team was fully equipped with high-powered satellite communications gear, GPS, explosives, and carrying fully suppressed MP5s, MK-13 grenade launchers, M-60's, M82 50 caliber sniper rifles and a Benelli M4 shotgun for good measure. Pulling his MP5 in close, Johnson felt right at home. Tonight, this mission called for speed and concealment. Seamlessly, these men, oblivious to the chill of the desert night, worked silently and efficiently knowing America's security hung in the balance.

The two teams formed up around Johnson. "Gentlemen, glad we're all here. Torres, make contact with mission command."

Torres pressed the key on the transmitter, "Freedom Team, calling Command."

"Command. Go Freedom Team."

Torres handed Johnson the headphone. Johnson slipped the device over his right ear and keyed the transmitter button, "Command, Freedom Team is on station and ready to go."

"Freedom Team, you are go!"

"Roger! Freedom Team is go."

Like so many missions before, Johnson raised his right hand and signaled for his two teams to move out.

The hills west of Islamabad were a desolate and godforsaken place. Like the rest of Pakistan, poverty reigned supreme and there was filth everywhere. Johnson and his team made great time thanks to the cover of the moonless dark night. If it weren't for GPS navigation, locating Barakat's complex would have been more difficult.

Garland Truman, team navigator, peered over the edge of the embrasure and carefully compared what he saw through his binoculars with his maps. "Captain. Bingo! Target one klick dead ahead."

"Good job Chief. Torres, get Command on the line."

"Roger Captain. Command. Command. This is Freedom Team. Over."

"Freedom Team, this is Command. Go ahead."

As before, Torres handed the headset over to Johnson. "Command, Freedom Team has target in sight. One kilometer. Are we clear to go? Over."

"Freedom Team. This is Command. We understand you are one kilometer from target. You are cleared to go. Godspeed, gentlemen. Over."

"Roger Command. Freedom Team cleared to go. Out."

Johnson signaled for his team to draw near. As he knelt down, huddled close to the best men he had ever known, "Gentlemen. We have received the go order from Command. You all know your jobs and our priorities. Remember, neutralizing Barakat's capabilities is first and foremost. Recovery of the Autonomous team is secondary. Salem, you will position yourself with the M82 in the water tower at our three o'clock. We are counting on you to cover our backs."

"Captain. What are our rules of engagement?" asked Master Chief Davis.

"Gentlemen, this is a high priority mission. Shoot to kill," responded Johnson.

"Gentlemen, before we proceed, I want to thank you for your bravery and patriotism. We have been through much together and I know each of you to be my brother. I pray that our Lord will protect us and return us home to our loved ones. God bless you all and God bless America. Amen."

In sync, like the warriors they were, they responded quietly together. "Amen"

Charged and ready for action, Johnson looked at his men and stirred them up. "Freedom Team! Are we ready?"

In a hushed tone, "HOOYAH!!"

"Blue Team North. Red Team South. Good luck gentlemen. See you inside. HOOYAH!!"

Salem slid over the edge, breaking right, heading for the water tower. Blue and Red teams moved out, with Johnson joining Blue team. Normally, one klick doesn't present much of a challenge. But, Johnson's experience has taught him a very important lesson—*Don't take any chances!* As such, they progressed cautiously across the remote hillside.

"Captain. Bird's Nest in place," radioed Salem over the intercom.

"Roger Bird's Nest," replied Johnson.

Surveilling the area through his Night Vision binoculars, Salem identified a guard. "Blue Team. Bird's Nest. Single armed hostile at your two o'clock."

"Roger Bird's Nest. You are go to neutralize," replied Johnson.

"Roger Blue Team," replied Salem. As he released the microphone button, Salem turned his attention to the armed target glowing bright green against the darkness. He adjusted the range on his M82, then took a breath and held it for a heartbeat. Smoothly he squeezed the trigger and was rewarded by the reassuring kick from the M82 then fwoop, as his bullet headed downrange. Before he could exhale, and long before the muffled sound from his weapon could reach his target, he watched his prey fall face down into the brush.

"Blue Team. Bird's Nest. Target neutralized."

"Roger Bird's Nest. Out."

Red and Blue teams made a break for their intended entry points. Like swarms of silent marauders, both teams arrived at the edge of the encampment stalled by primitive fencing. Without saying a word, Gary Walker of Red team and Albert Gonzales of Blue withdrew bolt cutters from their packs. Quickly and surgically, each man made his way through the fencing like a hot knife through butter. Like magic, the fencing curled right and left providing clear entry for the two teams.

The two teams made short work of covering the fifty yards from the fence to their respective ventilation shafts. Fortunately, the shafts were primitive at best. With little more than a quick pull, the tops were on the ground revealing thirty-six-inch-wide shafts from the desert floor to the concrete thirty meters below.

Again Gonzales and Walker went into action and secured the repelling gear around the base of each shaft. Once secured, Gonzales and Walker took the lead and fast-roped down to the underground compound. One-by-one, as adrenalin surged through their bodies and hearts pounded, each man descended into the darkness. As they dropped onto the floor below, each man assumed a defensive positon awaiting the arrival of each team's members.

Johnson, the last man to enter Barakat's compound, surveilled the area, then signaled for Blue Team to move out. At the same time, Brad Davis moved Red Team in quest of the Autonomous Team. The facility was dark. Much darker than one expected for night time. It was pitch dark.

Johnson jumped on the radio, "Red Team Leader. Blue Team. Over"

"Roger Red Team. Go ahead," replied Davis.

Johnson, looked around as each man swept the area with their E1D Surefire Defender flashlights. "Red Team, there is something very wrong here. No joy. Over."

"Roger Blue Team. Same here. This place is empty and quiet as a tomb. All we see is evidence that people lived here, but, no people. Over."

"OK Red Team. Continue your sweep and meet us topside in thirty minutes. Over."

"Roger Blue Team. Top side in thirty minutes. Over."

Calling upon all his will, Johnson could barely contain his anger. "Damn shitty intelligence," he muttered to himself.

"Skip?" asked Garland. "What do you want to do?"

"There isn't anything we can do. Sweep the area for any useful information then let's get topside in thirty minutes so we can call command," ordered Johnson.

"Roger Skipper," replied Garland.

Thirty minutes was more than enough time to search Barakat's abandoned compound for it was literally picked clean. Other than garbage and crappy office furniture, there wasn't a single shred of useful information to be gleaned from this fiasco.

Once topside, the two teams formed up. "Torres, get Command on the horn," barked Johnson.

"Affirmative Skipper." Keying his microphone, Torres made the call. "Command. Freedom Team. Over."

"Freedom Team. Command. Go ahead."

Johnson swiftly took the headset fully prepared to lay into Command. "Command. Freedom Team. Over."

"Freedom Team. Command. Go ahead."

"Command. Target is empty. I repeat. Target is empty. Request extraction. Over" barked Johnson.

"Freedom Team. Confirm that compound is empty. Over," replied Command.

"Roger Command. Facility is completely abandoned. No sign of life. Request extraction immediately," seethed Johnson.

"Roger Freedom Team. You are cleared for extraction. Choppers will be at extraction point Lima X-ray in sixty minutes. Over."

"Roger. Lima X-ray in sixty minutes. Freedom Team out." As Johnson handed the headset back to Torres.

### President's Office

"What in hell are you talking about?" yelled Bennett.

"Johnson just reported in. Barakat's facility was abandoned. One hostile was neutralized," said Chief of Staff Kerns.

"How in hell is this possible?" demanded Bennett.

"I don't know Mr. President. Based on the most current intelligence, that facility should have been swarming with people," replied Kerns.

"What kind of an operation is the Agency running over at Langley? How could they be this wrong? It was my understanding that the latest intel wasn't more than a week old," insisted Bennett.

"I know Mr. President. The CIA Director is on his way to brief you."

"Great. More damn briefings and no damn results," complained Bennett. "Let me know when he gets here. We have to put an end to this ineffectual bullshit. And I mean now!"

Bennett slid into his desk chair and changed topics. "What is the status of the jihadist captured in Austin? Has the FBI made any progress?"

"I spoke with Director Teich this morning," replied Kerns. "So far, he isn't talking. Short of torture, interrogators have tried everything. These fundamentalists are tough cookies. Candidly, I think he is hoping we kill him so he can go out in a blaze of glory."

"Screw him. We are not going to expedite his path to seventy virgins. Let him sweat it out in Guantanamo for the next fifty years as far as I'm concerned. No fast-pass to paradise for him," snapped Bennett.

"Mr. President, don't forget you have a meeting with your cabinet, congressional leadership and General James tomorrow morning at nine AM."

# Chapter 16

◆

*Changing America*
*Daily News*

"Good evening, this is United News Network Evening Edition. I'm Jeff Stoddard and this is my co-anchor Gretchen Chen. Tonight, like so many nights before, we are sad to report that the chaos continues with random drone attacks occurring daily across America. Today alone, America suffered six separate attacks which appear to have no rhyme or reason. Just random. Making matters even worse, this week international attacks continued in England and now France, Israel and Russia have become the newest targets of the Islamic State's drone agenda with dozens of attacks on London, Paris, Jerusalem and Moscow. It is clear Islam intends to spread its long and indefensible arm of automated terror across the globe. Unfortunately, it is obvious no one is immune.

"In some cases, America's CHAMP system and our National Militia successfully responded to and repelled some of the attacking drones, minimizing the armadas' deadly impact. Unfortunately, once again our defenses seemed inadequate to halt this onslaught," said Gretchen Chen.

The broadcast image split into two with Stoddard on the left and the right filled by a bald strident looking gentlemen. "Joining us this evening is United News Network's military advisor, retired General Gary Arnold. General, what can you share with us regarding America's inability to quell this crisis and the growing expansion of the Islamic State's worldwide reach?" asked Stoddard.

"Jeff and Gretchen, thank you for having me on this evening. Like you, the feeling of impotence and despair is overwhelming. Personally, I am very concerned. America, and now the world have never faced a more frightening, insidious and formidable challenge than these autonomous drones. The leadership commanding these deadly armadas clearly has the ability to strike wherever and whenever they please. Unfortunately, the obvious randomness and disregard for civilian life makes deployment of an effective defensive strategy difficult, if not impossible."

"General," says Gretchen Chen. "How, may I ask, can a defensive response be impossible?"

"Well Gretchen. It's like killing ants attacking your home. Try as you might to kill the ants, they will simply find their way into your house through another crack or crevice. Each time these drones are confronted by CHAMPS, the commanders of this initiative simply pivot and attack another random target. The reality is simple. We cannot deploy CHAMPS on every building, sports arena or facility in America. The task would be overwhelming and astronomically expensive. Nor can we deploy an infinite number of Militia members. It is physically and financially impossible to deploy CHAMPS and the Militia everywhere. Since our enemy demonstrates such heinous disregard for life, even if all significant structures were protected by CHAMPS, once encountered they could simply turn their attention to another target or even individual homes. Basically, I don't believe a viable defensive solution exists," offered Arnold.

"General, and your thoughts on the Islamic State's international expansion," reminded Stoddard.

"Oh yes. Thank you for reminding me Jeff. The international issue is significant for the only countries being targeted by Islam are clearly non-sympathizers. Basically, infidels. What this expansion tells me is that the Islamic State has far more capacity and commitment to spread its terror across the globe with impunity than we suspected. This Jeff, I fear, is the foundation for a true world conflagration. One, however, without any fronts or battle lines. Just robotic heartless drones killing people in cold blood."

Responding to the ever present teleprompter and director, Jeff changes directions. "Thank you General."

"You're welcome Jeff. Thank you for having me," replied General Arnold.

### The President's Decision

The Directors of Homeland, FBI, and the FAA along with the Secretary of State, Attorney General, and Secretary of Commerce sat quietly in the Oval Office as they waited President Bennett's arrival. An overwhelming sense of futility and foreboding hung over the room as cups of coffee were quietly swirled and sipped. After weeks of analysis and brainstorming, it was clear among those present that their collective recommendation would have far-reaching and devastating social and economic impact on both the American and international communities. None were pleased with their alternative, yet, no other solution had been devised to defend against the Islamic State's robotic warriors. Everyone recognized the consequences of the group's suggestion, but, no one wanted to take ownership of the proposal.

Like a whirlwind, the door to the Oval Office swung open and President Bennett, Vice President Colby and Chief of Staff Kerns swarmed in.

Bennett assumed his customary seat and turned to the attendees, "Gentlemen. Time is up. We need a solution and we need it now. This is simply out of control."

The men sat quietly, awaiting someone to speak.

"Guys, somebody has to begin," demanded Bennett.

"Mr. President," said FBI Director Mitch Teich. "As you know, our team has been evaluating the drones we secured from the arrest in Austin Texas. Now, we have a clear understanding of the technology and control modalities they employ. As you probably know, they are highly dependent on GPS navigation which is augmented by what appears to be ground imaging and map based control as a backup. We believe if they lose GPS signal, they can navigate via their integrated imaging system. Basically, these units are truly autonomous."

"OK Mitch. Yes, I have been fully briefed on their autonomous capabilities. So, what is our answer?" asked Bennett.

"Well Mr. President, we believe the only immediate and most effective solution we can employ in the near-term is to shut down America's and Russia's civilian GPS satellites," offered Harold Simpson, Director of Homeland Security.

"Holy shit Harold, this seems a little extreme. What are the consequences of doing so? Is there an effect on our military?" asked Bennett.

Thomas Gomez, FAA Director decided he needed to express his concerns. "Mr. President, as you know, the U.S. Airspace system is heavily dependent upon GPS technology. Fortunately, the military doesn't depend on the civilian GPS constellation of satellites. However, shutting down GPS will have far-reaching civilian impact. First, shutting down our GPS Constellation immediately eliminates over three thousand instrument approaches to airports across the country. More specifically, doing so will have devastating economic effects on the airlines. Operationally, GPS provides billions of dollars in fuel savings by enabling the airlines to fly more economical and efficient routes. Without GPS, the cost of air travel will rise dramatically. Literally billions of dollars annually. For the airlines, this is a financial catastrophe. For the FAA, we've invested billions of dollars on engineering and deployment of Next Gen ADS-B services which are planned to go into full implementation in 2020."

"Thomas, refresh my memory. What is ADS-B?" asked Bennett.

"Well Mr. President, ADS-B stands for Automatic Dependent Surveillance and Broadcast which is fully dependent on GPS for aircraft positioning, separation and reporting. ADS-B was designed to replace aging and archaic conventional radar facilities by literally networking all aircraft in U.S. airspace with air traffic control," replied Gomez. "From any perspective, shutting down GPS will be devastating. Not only will the billions invested in ADS-B be lost, the cost to revamp conventional radar facilities would be horrific and take time."

"Jerome. Any thoughts from Commerce," asked Bennett.

Jerome Price, Secretary of Commerce shuffled through his papers, taking a moment to think through his reply. "Mr. President, I agree with Harold. The economic impact on aviation will be horrendous. Unfortunately, the economic damage does not end there. My office believes that every business dependent on GPS will be effected. Aviation related companies that manufacture GPS navigation technology such as Garmin, Bendix and Honeywell will be devastated. Furthermore, businesses across America including shippers, farmers, maritime, rail and even personal and business transportation depend on GPS in unimaginable and valuable ways. Without GPS services, all businesses will suffer incalculable financial consequences."

"Holy crap," exclaimed Bennett.

"Mr. President, I hate to throw more wood into the fire, but there are even more consequences," offered Director Teich. "Currently, we have more than three hundred thousand parolees, probationers, sex offenders and even people awaiting trial tracked and monitored by GPS. Without GPS, these threats to society will have free reign to move about unmonitored and with impunity. Prior to shutting down GPS, I believe we must incarcerate the highest risk individuals under house arrest monitored by GPS, or else we can expect a significant spike in crime rates across the spectrum."

Turning to Attorney General Santich, "Grant, I presume you agree with Mitch. What can we do with these monitored criminals?" asked Bennett.

"Mr. President. Yes. I agree with Director Teich. He and I have discussed this matter in great detail. I believe, before shutting down GPS we need to incarcerate the most dangerous and high risk individuals currently monitored by GPS. Specifically those having committed violent crimes, those with gang relationships and, of course, sex offenders. Particularly pedophiles. This effort will be truly formidable, expensive and, to say the least, constitutionally challenging."

"Guys, this is devastating. But, it's my understanding that the Russians have a worldwide GPS solution. What's it called?" asked Bennett.

"It's called GLONASS, which stands for GLObal NAvigation Satellite System," explained Director Gomez. "And yes, it is supported by all major commercial technology providers including aviation, transportation and telecommunications."

"Okay. It's obvious we need Russian buy-in. Anthony, where are we and the State Department with the Russians?" asked Bennett.

"Mr. President," replied Secretary of State Anthony Umberg. "Prior to this week's attacks on Moscow, the Russian's were indifferent. Now, I can assure you they are more motivated. When it comes to drone terror, America and Russia are allies."

"Anthony, let's schedule a call with President Volkov as soon as possible and get on the same page."

"Already done Mr. President. You have a conference call with President Volkov scheduled for three today, which is one am in Moscow," replied Umberg.

"Ok. Great. He's a reasonable man and I expect he'll support our plan."

"Rich, arrange for an executive order to shut down GPS. Every day we delay, thousands die. We need to do it immediately. Is seventy-two hours too soon?"

Bennett polled the men in attendance seeking support for shutting down GPS.

Thomas Gomez raised his hand. "Mr. President. Before we move forward, I still want to emphasize the importance of GPS on all aspects of aviation. I think we need to give the private sector, specifically aviation GPS-technology companies, the opportunity to come up with a solution. I propose that we plan a temporary six month GPS shut down in hopes that GPS security can be enhanced."

"Gentlemen. I tend to agree with Tom. In this room we will plan for a six-month shut down of the GPS satellites. At the same time, Tom, meet with the manufactures and get them working on a solution."

"Yes sir Mr. President," replied Gomez with a sigh of relief.

"Gentlemen. We move forward. We need to marginalize these attacks anyway we can."

### Bennett Drops the GPS Bomb

The sun hung low over Washington D.C., casting long purple shadows across the Rose Garden as the press awaited President Bennett to speak to America.

Link Farnsworth, Bennett's Press Secretary accompanied him to the Rose Garden and quickly reviewed the major talking points. "Mr. President, your speech is on the teleprompter and we are ready to go whenever you are."

"Thank you Link. I'm ready."

Farnsworth walked to the podium in the Rose Garden. "Good evening everybody. Just a reminder, I will address any of your questions after the President's speech. Ladies and gentlemen, The President of the United States."

The attendees stood out of respect as President Bennett, FAA Director Gomez, Speaker Teasdale, Senate Majority Leader Palmer and Richard Young approached the podium.

Gazing upon the attendees, Bennett took a deep breath and turned to the camera awaiting the go signal from the stage director.

*"Good evening. Before we begin this evening, I have a special ceremony I am honored to perform.*

*"We are fortunate to have many dedicated Militia members who selflessly patrol and protect our communities daily. Today I am joined by*

*Richard Young, a proud member of our National Militia in Austin Texas. Welcome Richard.*

*"Operating alone, Richard detected, subdued and took into custody an Islamic State terrorist who was prepared to launch ten explosive and RICIN laden drones on Austin Texas. Richard is a true American hero who personally saved thousands of lives. Richard, on behalf of every American, and specifically the citizens of Austin, I want to thank you and congratulate you for a job well done. Today, we are celebrating Richard's accomplishment with America's Medal of Freedom, the highest honor that can be bestowed upon a non-military citizen.*

*"Thank you Richard for your service to America."*

Bennett placed the beautiful Medal of Freedom around Richard's neck then shook his hand vigorously, pausing for the obligatory photo op. Without notice Richard was whisked away by Link Farnsworth.

*"My fellow Americans, we are truly lucky to have citizens like Richard committed to protecting our way of life. Unfortunately, all of us are weary of the ongoing attacks on our country. I want to assure everyone that leaders across the globe whose countries have fallen victim to these acts of war feel as I do. Something needs to be done.*

*"Since the first attack on Lincoln, Nebraska on April nineteenth, these acts of terror have successfully impacted the American way of life in unimaginable ways. The good news is, citizens of this great county have come together to help those devastated by these random and horrific attacks. From Joe Plumber to our great military, we are pulling together as never before, standing up for our way of life. This evening, I am here to share with you that we are willing to do whatever is necessary to impede the Islamic State's ability to strike another blow.*

*"As you know, these drones clearly operate autonomously and are supported by lone-wolf jihadists invisibly embedded within our borders. Like the one subdued by Richard Young, these cowards hide among us. I assure you, they can hide, but we will be relentless in ferreting them out and bringing them to justice.*

*"Since these attacks began, hundreds of thousands of our friends and family have been killed and many more injured. More alarming is the recent report from the CDC that over three thousand Americans are dying monthly from RICIN poisoning. This enemy knows no boundaries and is committed to damaging our way of life at any cost.*

*"Over the past months, our friends in Australia, England, Canada and now France, Israel and Russia became targets of Islam. Since the Lincoln attack, I, along with my cabinet, the Joint Chiefs and Congress, have worked around the clock to develop viable responses to this onslaught.*

*"The CHAMPS technological defense is working, but will take time to deploy nationwide. Our Militia, though dedicated, can only do so much. Today, we and our allies are in agreement that we need to implement extreme measures to protect all our citizens.*

*"As you know, our forces are amassing in the Middle East, forming the largest allied military coalition since World War II to take the battle to the Islamic State's front door, in an operation we call Freedom Resolve. Until the mission of Freedom Resolve is realized, we still need to take immediate action to protect our citizens here at home and in every country affected by these attacks.*

*"As such, effective seventy-two hours from now, United States and Russian Global Positioning Satellite Systems will be shut down. We believe doing so will impede these drones' ability to navigate and find their targets. I understand that in doing so there will be far-reaching and unforeseen consequences. But I assure you, we prospered before the introduction of GPS and will do so now. I am confident this will only be temporary until we are victorious over the Islamic State's agenda against America and our allies.*

*"God bless you all and God bless these United States. Good Night."*

### The Morning News

"Good Morning. I'm Phillip Carlson, along with my co-anchor Trudy Sloan. Welcome to UNN's Early Edition. Well Trudy, we heard the news. Both American and Russian Global Positioning Satellite Systems will be shut down in seventy-two hours."

Trudy deftly took the handoff from Carlson, "Yes, I did Phillip. Last evening, in a speech given in the Rose Garden of the White House, President Bennett announced that GPS satellites will be shut down in seventy-two hours…three days from now. I don't know about you Phillip, but GPS has become part of my everyday life."

"Trudy, I couldn't agree more. GPS is almost a way-of-life. We all have a sense of the importance of GPS on the American economy, but this morning it was made evident when the stock market opened to a record loss of three thousand points. Specifically, airline stocks are down over twenty percent as well as GPS manufacturers such as Garmin, Bendix, and Honeywell who are all suffering as a result of President Bennett's announcement."

"Yes Phillip. In order to appreciate the overall impact of this monumental decision, let's welcome Howard Crist, former Secretary of Commerce. Mr. Crist. Welcome."

Occupying the right half of the screen was Howard Crist, a stoic mature gentleman exuding confidence and quality breeding. "Thank you Phillip and Trudy. It is always a pleasure to join you."

"Mr. Crist, what immediate impact will this decision have on everyday Americans?" asked Trudy.

"Trudy, it is almost incomprehensible the breadth and reach of this decision. GPS is integral in just about every aspect of the American economy from shipping to maritime navigation. You may not be aware of this, but in many cities the opening and closing of bus doors is controlled by GPS."

"Bus doors? Who would have guessed?" commented Trudy.

"Certainly," continued Crist, "the loss of control of bus doors is a minor inconvenience. I only mention it to illustrate how integral GPS has become to Americans. The best indicator of this landmark decision is the response by Wall Street. Today's three-thousand-point drop is a clear statement that losing access to GPS will be disastrous for business."

"Mr. Crist. Disastrous in what way?" asked Carlson.

"Well Phillip, the airline industry alone saves billions of dollars annually in fuel costs by being able to navigate more direct routes compared to conventional navigation. This increase will be devastating to ticket prices and airline profits."

"What other consequences are we to expect Mr. Secretary?" asked Trudy.

"Personally Trudy, I am concerned about this decision on many levels. The most subtle consequence is GPS tracking of parolees and sexual predators. Today, we have over three hundred thousand perpetrators of violent or sexual crimes under house arrest and closely monitored by GPS ankle bracelets. The moment GPS is shut down, it is reasonable to expect tens of thousands of these individuals will begin roaming freely and commit crimes. Why? Because, that's what they do. Aside from crime, which is very costly, if President Bennett elected to re-incarcerate these people we are looking at a cost to do so1. Very likely in excess of one hundred billion dollars annually. Honestly, I understand the President's decision in response to these horrendous drone attacks, but the trillions of dollars in direct economic cost to America will be very devastating. Either way, the Islamic State strikes a devastating blow against America."

"Thank you Mr. Crist. As always, your thoughts and opinions are truly welcome," said Phillip.

"Thank you Phillip and Trudy. My pleasure."

"Trudy. There you have it. President Bennett's decision to shut down GPS is a real double edged sword. Hopefully his decision will dramatically reduce the drone attacks, but we are going to be confronted by the potential for increased crime and devastating economic consequences. I pray the pluses outweigh the negatives."

"Phillip, I agree. Wait one moment. Ladies and gentlemen, we are getting breaking news that drone attacks are being reported in Houston, Los Angeles, Chicago, Denver and more. Reports are coming in that hundreds of drones have been sighted moving low above the ground in cities across America. As yet, no explosions have been reported. Let's go to Ronald James, reporting from Los Angeles. Ronald, what can you tell us?"

"Phillip and Trudy, I am on top of the U.S. Bank tower about a half mile from Century City Plaza which is the location of Westfield Mall. As you can see in the video, it appears that numerous drones are heading toward Century City. How many drones? I don't know. But it looks like dozens and dozens. Air raid sirens are blaring across the city and there is pandemonium everywhere. According to reports, people are trying futilely to evacuate the Century City Plaza Towers, Westfield Mall and surrounding buildings. Literally, thousands are struggling to get out of buildings everywhere. Thousands of people are trying to escape this attack."

"Ronald. Trudy here. Are you certain the attack is targeting Century City?"

"Trudy. I can't say for certain. But based on the direction they are headed, I fear Century City is their target. As you can see, our cameraman is tracking dozens of drones coming together from numerous directions in their all-too-familiar attack pattern. We can see Militia members and law enforcement firing into the air at the oncoming drones. Oh my goodness. Look. Right over Santa Monica Boulevard two drones were shot down and crashed and exploded onto the street. Chaos is everywhere. Oh my! Trudy, dozens of drones just passed by me just above street level. I am certain, they are heading for Century City."

"Ronald. We are streaming the video that is being broadcast through social media that clearly is coming from these drones. Based on the images we're watching, it's obvious their target is Century City," reported Trudy.

"Yes Trudy. Century City is the target. Dozens of drones have grouped up and are now orbiting Century City. The image is surreal. They look like predators waiting to leap upon their prey. Oh no! It's happening. Can you see it? One-by-one drones are diving into Century City continuing their reign of devastation. There are explosions everywhere. More people than I can count are falling to the ground."

The camera zoomed in on the ground around Century Plaza obtaining a close up view of the devastation.

"Trudy. This is very sad and disturbing. According to our video, it looks like people are either dead or injured. This is the most horrific scene I have ever witnessed. This is just terrible," groaned Ronald.

Just as quickly as it started, the attack was over as the last drone broadcasting the video dove into the smoking remains of Century City.

"Trudy and Phillip. As you can see the attack is over and emergency personnel are swarming into the area. Unfortunately, I fear they will find death and destruction."

"Ronald," said Phillip. "Thank you for reporting on this tragedy. Keep us updated with any new information."

"Thank you Phillip," said Ronald, clearly trying to contain his emotions. "Will do."

"Technological progress has merely provided us with more efficient means for going backwards," Aldous Huxley

# Chapter 17

————————◆————————

### *Drone On (Taking Virtual Control)*

It went barely noticed. Just another mobile game app slid into position among the millions of others available in Apple, Google, Amazon and Microsoft mobile app stores. For some, it was just a game promoting violence for people with too much time on their hands, willing to while away hours flying virtual Islamic State drones and crashing them into various targets. Each successful attack by a player's drone earned him points with the opportunity to level-up and receive badges of accomplishment and cash rewards paid on their Starbuck's cards. More than just a shoot 'em up game, Drone On was integrated into social media, broadcasting each mission's outcome, bolstering the often weak egos of these solitary isolated gamers with their heads buried deep in their smartphones and tablets. Media was awash with pundits accusing Banger Mobile Games as being opportunists and profiteers making millions of dollars with their Drone On mobile game. For many, Banger was simply exploiting the misfortune of hundreds of thousands of victims of the Islamic State's drone attacks.

Psychologists, however, have a different opinion. Appearing nightly on network television, many mental health professionals believed Drone On likely provided some catharsis helping people cope with the utter frustration and sense of impotency fueled by the indefensible chaos going on in the real-world.

For many, the idea of Drone On was reprehensible and exploited the pain and suffering caused by the Islamic State's drone terrorism. The idea of encouraging people to play a game grounded in real-world suffering was simply macabre, unsavory and opportunistic. But, the marketing geniuses at Banger Mobile Games figured providing a game that was relevant to events in the real-world would be appealing. And appealing it was. Within the first week Drone On was downloaded one hundred million times worldwide making it the most successfully mobile game app in history.

### *Daily News*

"Good evening, I'm Jeff Stoddard and this is my co-anchor Gretchen Chen. Like so many nights before, once again we are so very sad to report that America along with England, Australia, Canada, France, Israel and Russia continue to fall victim to daily drone attacks. Yesterday, Century

City Plaza and the Westfield Mall in Los Angeles were laid to waste by massive drone attacks. According to Los Angeles Mayor Thomas Rowlands, the death toll from yesterday's attacks reached thirty-five hundred, with thousands more injured and untold numbers exposed to RICIN. Gretchen, this is simply horrific."

"Jeff, I agree. In my entire career as a journalist these ongoing attacks are the most disturbing news I have ever covered."

"Also disturbing are the consequences resulting from the announcement that America and Russia are shutting down their Global Positioning satellites. Again, Wall Street responded losing twenty-five hundred points for a total loss of twenty percent in two days. Literally, two of the worst days in the stock market's history," reported Stoddard.

"Jeff, on a lighter note, the mobile game Drone On just set the record for the most downloaded game in history with one hundred million downloads in the first week."

"Gretchen, I suppose anything that takes our attention away from the pain and suffering happening daily is good. Although it seems exploitive. Let's have Dr. Tina Johnson, a United News Network contributor, weigh in on this phenomenon. Dr. Johnson, thank you for joining us this evening."

As usual, the screen divided into two with Jeff Stoddard on the left as a beautiful blond came into view with the Capital Dome as her backdrop.

"Thank you Jeff and Gretchen. I'm happy to join you."

"Dr. Johnson, as a psychiatrist, how do you explain the interest in this new mobile game? Is it a symptom of some underlying frustration?"

"Jeff and Gretchen., thank you for having me on tonight. Personally, I believe the massive success and engagement with this mobile game is a normal response to a truly frustrating situation. I believe it's simply a coping mechanism in response to the impotence we all feel about these drone attacks. Candidly, a little diversion is probably a good thing."

"So, Dr. Johnson, you don't believe this is a problem?" asked Gretchen.

"No Gretchen. I don't see playing a game as causing any problems. People are frustrated and need to channel that frustration somewhere.

Perhaps playing a game gives them a sense of hope and allows them to channel their inner pain," replied Johnson.

"Thank you Dr. Johnson. We'll have David Banger, the creator of Drone On joining us shortly. I am certain we will be talking with you again soon," said Jeff.

"Thanks Jeff. As always, it's my pleasure."

The image of Dr. Johnson faded to black and was soon replaced by a studious looking gentleman who was likely a geek in an earlier stage of his life.

"Now, joining us from Palo Alto, California is the President and CEO of Banger Mobile Games, the creator of the hit mobile game; Drone On. Welcome Mr. Banger."

"Thank you Jeff. It is a pleasure to be with you this evening," replied Banger in an upbeat tone.

"Mr. Banger…"

"Jeff. Please call me Dave," suggested Banger.

"Thank you…err Dave. As I was about to say, what brought you to create Drone On?" asked Stoddard.

"Well Jeff, first, at Banger, we're just game developers. Not social engineers. Developing fun and engaging games is what we do. Six months ago, we were discussing a new game and the idea for Drone On was right in front of us in our own skies. To some, it might appear that we are being coldhearted and opportunistic. But in fact, our motivation was truly altruistic. Playing Drone On is kind of like hitting a wall with your fist or kicking the dog when you're angry, however, without any of the negative consequences. It just lets our players blow off some steam. What could possibly be wrong with that?"

"Dave, you hit a home run with Drone On. It is the most successful mobile game in history. It's difficult to imagine that one hundred million people across the globe are really playing Drone On. I have intimate experience because my own son is an avid Drone On player," said Stoddard.

"Yes Jeff, we are so very proud of the success we're experiencing with Drone On. It's true. Millions of people are playing Drone On. In fact, they are playing Drone On a lot. The average player spends in excess of an hour a day playing Drone On. Not only are our players enjoying the challenge of the game, we get feedback every day telling us that Drone On makes them just feel better. We are so very pleased," replied Banger.

"Dave, all of us at UNN wish you continued success. Hopefully some good will come to your players who are clearly avid Drone On devotees. Thank you for joining us this evening."

"Thank you Jeff. The pleasure was all mine. Drone On!" responded Banger.

### Six Months Earlier

Knock! Knock! "Mr. Kramer. Do you have a few minutes?" asked Christopher Samuels, software engineer for Autonomous Systems.

"Sure Chris. Come in. Sit down. What's on your mind?" asked Kramer.

Nervously, "Well Mr. Kramer, I've been chatting with David Sams about our problem. You know him. He's on my development team. We have an 'out of the box' idea I want to float past you," said Chris.

"Sure Chris. What is it?"

"Well. It's kind of weird. But, I think it has merit."

"OK. I'm listening."

"Based on the field demonstration of the Surveillance and Defense drones, it's pretty obvious that not only was it not as effective as we had hoped, it's a very expensive solution. As a result, we've been running some laboratory tests on one of the captured drones. I believe we can take control."

"Really? That's great news."

"Taking control is just part of our idea. We believe we can inexpensively piggy-back a new technology—we call Control Nodes—on the existing nationwide cell tower networks. Each Control Node would have multi-spectrum sensors capable of detecting drones based on a number of dimensions: Motor energy signatures, sound signatures, cell video broadcasts, infrared and ultrasound. Once detected, I believe we can take control by co-opting inter-drone communications channels."

"Ok. I see the detection capability. How do we take control?" asked Kramer.

"Well, our idea is to route this information via the cloud to tens of thousands of mobile devices running an app allowing users to directly take control and redirect the attacking drones to some safe area, we call False Targets, for retrieval or detonation."

"Holy shit! You're suggesting that some 'Joe Citizen' will be controlling these drones?"

"Well. Yes. Kind of. In fact, our idea is to publish a game app. In doing so, the players won't actually know they're really controlling the drones. From their perspective, they're controlling virtual drones in a game. As real drones are detected they will simply be injected into the game and assigned to a player. In fact, we can assign real-drones to the best players assuring the best outcomes."

"Ok. I see it. How do we keep them from crashing real drones into real buildings?" asked Kramer.

"Actually Mr. Kramer, that's the easy part of the problem. We simply define a virtual world based loosely on the geographic area where the drones are operating. The underlying mapping in the app ensures a one hundred percent safe maneuvering area for the players' targets are pre-defined, remote and safe areas—the False Targets. Trust me Mr. Kramer, we can do this." assured Chris.

"Chris. This is weird…but I get it," replied Kramer.

"Mr. Kramer, imagine millions of people playing this drone game where they are unwittingly guiding actual drones against False Targets. Since they would be controlled locally by players communicating via any number of Control Nodes near them, we can minimize communication delays and reliance on some centralized technology. In fact, I believe people make the process fully and dynamically adaptive. The people and the Control Notes provide incredible redundancy. If one Control Node fails, control simply fails over to another Control Node or even a new player making the entire system fail-safe. All we need is a mobile game developer," said Chris.

"Getting the game created isn't a problem. A college buddy of mine is David Banger, the CEO of Banger Mobile Games. They are perfect for creating this app. I will put a call into President Bennett's Chief of Staff immediately and have David fly in for a meeting. How quickly can you have an agenda and specification ready?" asked Kramer.

"Mr. Kramer. The specification is already written and I can have a meeting agenda ready by morning," replied Chris.

"Set the meeting. I'll send the Autonomous jet to pick up David immediately," said Kramer. "Great job! Simply amazing!"

Chris rose from his chair. "Thank you Mr. Kramer. I just want to help."

"You're doing a great job Chris. Great job indeed."

As Chris left, Kramer tapped the button on his intercom, "Becky, get Roger Kerns on the phone immediately."

### Game Strategy

"David, thanks for flying in on such short notice and not asking any questions. I understand you have a company to run. But, I'm certain you'll soon appreciate the importance of joining us today and the need for secrecy," said Kramer.

"Not a problem David. Thanks for sending the jet. That was a real treat. My company needs a jet," he said sporting his typical smile.

Beep. "Mr. Kramer, Roger Kerns and FBI Director Teich are here," announced Kramer's secretary.

"Thank you Becky. Please take them to Conference Room 3. I'll be there momentarily."

"FBI Director? Roger Kerns? Isn't he President Bennett's Chief of Staff? Kramer, what am I getting into?" asked Banger.

"Yes David. Please bear with me, you'll understand very shortly. Trust me, this will probably be the most important meeting of your life," replied Kramer.

Kramer and Banger walked into Conference Room 3 and joined Kerns, Teich and Sams, while Chris Samuels readied his presentation and laptop.

"Gentlemen. Let me introduce David Banger, CEO of Banger Mobile Games. Mr. Kerns, please express my appreciation to President Bennett for being receptive to our idea."

"My pleasure David. Nice to meet you Mr. Banger. As odd as the idea struck us, the President believes it has merit. Shall we get started?" suggested Kerns.

As the meeting began, David Banger was overwhelmed by what was expected of him. Never in his wildest imagination did he envision that he had a part to play in countering the Islamic State's devastating terror strategy. He couldn't help but reflect back on his college philosophy class, which at the time he thought was a waste, and recognize the truth in Plato's position on art mimicking nature. Banger mused to himself, "Plato would be pleased his view of reality was playing out fifteen hundred years later."

It only took twenty minutes for Chris Samuels to walk through his presentation. As the last PowerPoint slide dissolved, Kramer took control of the meeting.

"Gentlemen. This is our plan. I recognize it's unconventional, but in light of the overwhelming success of mobile gaming, paired with our ability to deploy Control Nodes, I believe this can be done. David, what do you think?" asked Kramer.

"Well, creating a mobile drone war-game isn't a problem. We have a number of first-person shooter and adventure games that we can easily re-task to this project. Additionally, our current server farm is more than adequate to handle the immediate load and it can be expanded as needed. All we need is to tie the data streamed to and from the Control Nodes to our servers. This is a classic Cloud computing problem. It's nothing we can't handle," said Banger.

"How long will this take?" asked Kerns.

"Mr. Kerns. We can have a prototype up and running in sixty days. The final version should be deployable shortly thereafter. Bottom-line. If we do an 'all-hands-on-deck' effort, I believe we can have this game app up and running in ninety-days or less," replied Banger.

"Well gentlemen. The President wants a solution. You have my authorization to move forward. Cost is no object. Get it done and get it done quickly. Actually, the only bottleneck is going to be getting security clearances. Director Teich, can we expedite the background checks?" asked Kerns.

"Not a problem," replied Teich. "We can do the background checks concurrent with roll-out of the project. I presume in the early stage, your programmers won't need to know they are working on a Top Secret project. Once we clear your team, you can then fill them in on the details. Mr. Banger, will this work?"

"Absolutely. Not a problem. All my team needs to know is they're creating a new mobile war-game about drone attacks. That's it. Nothing more. When it comes to tying into the Control Nodes, our team will be limited to a few people on a-need-to-know basis. How cool. Never in my life did I imagine I would ever utter those words," replied Banger smiling.

Kerns and Teich stood up and collected their briefcases. "Gentlemen. Let's get this done. I will report to the President that he can expect your game in ninety days," said Kerns.

Mitch Teich, paused for a moment. "Don't we need a name for this game?"

"Yes Director Teich. We do," replied Banger.

"How does Drone On sound?" suggested Teich.

Pausing for a moment to digest Director Teich's suggestion. Suddenly Banger had that rare feeling in the pit of his stomach that overwhelms marketers when a great idea falls in their laps…Drone On is a great name. "Sounds great to me," said Banger. "I think Drone On is the perfect name and is marketable. Great idea."

"Thank you Mr. Banger. I am honored," replied Director Teich.

"You're welcome. Gentlemen, please convey to President Bennett that Banger Mobile Games won't let him down," pledged Banger as he shook Kerns' and Teich's hands vigorously.

Kramer, not wanting to be left out, "Drone On works for me. My team will have the Control Nodes ready to go in forty-five days. Chris, can you make that happen?"

"Yes Mr. Kramer," responded Chris nervously. "We'll get it done."

As Kerns and Teich left Conference Room 3, Kramer, wearing his CEO hat, looked at Banger and the Autonomous team, "Gentlemen, this is an historic moment. I feel a little like Robert Oppenheimer must have felt when he was charged with the Manhattan Project. This is a tremendous responsibility. We will not fail."

# Chapter 18

◆

## *Three Days Later…A World without GPS*

"Good evening, welcome to the evening edition of United News Network. I'm Jeff Stoddard and this is my co-anchor Gretchen Chen. Once again, like so many days before, the world is under attack. However, there is a difference. Today, we are three days since President Bennett's announcement that U.S. and Russian Global Positioning System satellites would be shut down. And, shut down it is. There is, however, a difference. According to the military and civilian observations, the attacks seem less accurate. Less focused. Perhaps due to the lack of GPS navigation."

"Yes," says Gretchen. "Reports are coming in from all over the world that attack drones are certainly making their way toward targets, but in a less precise pattern. More interesting is that in some cases, drones are flying off into the distance and crashing in fields far away from populated areas. Hopefully this is good news. Let's chat with General Arnold, United News Network's military contributor. General Arnold, welcome."

Adjusting his microphone, "Thank you Gretchen and Jeff. Thank you for having me on this evening."

"General Arnold," asked Jeff. "What are your thoughts about the recent drone attacks?"

Glaring sternly into the camera, "Jeff, what we are seeing is a plan that is working. Now that President Bennett has taken definitive action against this threat we are seeing results."

"So, General, you're crediting the shutting down of America's GPS satellites for the reduced effectiveness of today's drone attacks?"

"Absolutely Jeff. These contraptions can't navigate if they don't know where they are. Clearly they depend on GPS. And now, they are flying blind," explained Arnold.

"But General! How do you explain the drones that just went and crashed into vacant fields far away from populated areas?" asked Gretchen.

"Gretchen, I really don't know. It could be a fluke. Or, perhaps we have the capacity to co-opt the drones and take navigational control and fly them to a safe area where their munitions will have little to no effect. Personally, I'm a believer in this theory," responded Arnold.

"But," asked Stoddard. "If we are taking control, how is it being done? Why aren't all the drones crashing in safe areas? There seems to be more to this story than meets the eye."

"There may be. But, as far as I'm concerned, Islam was smacked down today. America finally has responded to the Islamic State's egregious attacks on America and it looks effective. Hopefully, Jeff, if they find that their drones are not getting through, they will cease their relentless attacks," suggested Arnold.

"We can only hope," agreed Stoddard. "General Arnold, thank you for joining us this evening and thank you for your service to this great country."

"Thank you Jeff and Gretchen. It has been my honor. Good night," replied Arnold.

"Well Gretchen, perhaps reduced effectiveness of the Islamic State's drone attacks is a positive consequence of President Bennett's decision to shut down the Global Positioning satellite system. But, as everyone expected, there are negative consequences. Let's go to UNN's financial reporter, Rebecca Saunders from New York. Rebecca, good evening."

"Good evening Jeff and Gretchen. Yes, shutting down America's GPS is truly a double-edged sword. As many predicted, after President Bennett's announcement there have been far-reaching implications. Today, once again Wall Street responded. Airline stocks dropped a record thirty percent as ticket prices soared due the costlier routes that must be flown, not to mention modifications to instrument approach procedures. I spoke with FAA Director Thomas Gomez today. He said that the loss of GPS is devastating to aviation as a whole. More specifically, the multi-billion-dollar investment and transition into what is called ADS-B, or NextGen will be delayed indefinitely. In doing so, Director Gomez said that billions of dollars will have to be invested in maintenance of antiquated technology which ADS-B was designed to replace. But, without GPS, the FAA's next generation of air traffic control cannot be implemented. This is another example of the effect the Islamic State's drone agenda has had on America."

"Rebecca, for our viewers who are not familiar with the importance of GPS in aviation, can you explain what ADS-B is?" asked Jeff.

"Certainly Jeff. ADS-B, which seems to be yet another cryptic aviation abbreviation is actually quite fascinating. ADS-B stands for Automatic Dependent Surveillance and Broadcast. Basically, by 2020 all commercial and general aviation aircraft were to have installed specialized radio receivers and transmitters that communicate with GPS satellites. In turn, the technology automatically *BROADCASTS* each airplane's identifier, position, speed, direction and altitude. These broadcasts are received, which is the *SURVEILLANCE* part of ADS-B, by airplanes in the area as well as air traffic control facilities and airport towers. Each airplane would have a display in its cockpit that showed all nearby aircraft. NextGen technology is so advanced, ADS-B equipped airplanes can automatically identify and predict possible conflicts between aircraft and enable air traffic controllers to direct all activities. Very simply, ADS-B is similar to networking airplanes together much like computers are networked together. Unfortunately, without GPS, ADS-B is impossible to implement."

"Thank you Rebecca. I know I speak for many of our viewers in expressing my appreciation for your explanation of the importance of GPS in aviation. I hope there are solutions on the horizon," expressed Gretchen.

"You're welcome Gretchen. And yes, there is a solution. Unfortunately it is costly and takes time to implement," commented Rebecca.

Not wanting to be left out of the discussion, Jeff Stoddard asked, "What solution Rebecca?"

"Jeff, today I spoke with representatives of Honeywell, Bendix and Garmin corporations. Each provide GPS technology to aviation. They shared with me that they believe secured communications between aircraft and GPS satellites can be established. As they explained it to me, GPS navigation systems can employ security technology similar to that used when we connect to an online store or bank with our computers, smartphones or tablets. In doing so, only authorized and registered GPS users would be allowed to use our Global Positioning Satellite System," explained Rebecca.

"All that sounds great Rebecca. But, rarely a day goes by that we don't report on security breaches and hackers. Wouldn't a 'secure' GPS solution be subject to the same security threats and hackers?" asked Jeff.

"Jeff, everyone I've spoken with is confident that effective security technology can be deployed. This is only possible because the number of secure GPS users is infinitely small compared to the number of computer users in the world. Experts believe they can efficiently and affordably implement extremely complex security protocols for the aviation GPS user base. A solution that's impossible to do for hundreds of millions of computers around the world," replied Rebecca.

"Well Rebecca. Once again, thank you for a job well done. Good Night," said Gretchen.

"My pleasure Jeff and Gretchen. Good night."

### The President is Ecstatic

"Who would have believed it? And who in their right mind would have approved it?" said Bennett as he shook his head in disbelief.

"Well Mr. President," said Chief of Staff Kerns. "These guys at Autonomous Systems and Banger Mobile Games came through. Think of it, a great many of today's drone attacks were thwarted by thousands of gamers unwittingly saving America. Amazing! Simply amazing!"

"Once again, American ingenuity comes through. It's almost laughable. We're on the verge of World War III and the answer is hordes of mobile phone-toting gamers. Holy crap. Who in their right mind would have believed this was going to be our answer? Who indeed?" chuckled President Bennett. "Who indeed?"

"Regardless Mr. President. We did it!" declared Kerns. "In light of the effectiveness of Drone On, it might be worthwhile reconsidering your position on shutting down the GPS satellites."

"I know. Gomez over at FAA, Teich at the FBI and Attorney General Santich are all lobbying like hell for me to reconsider my decision. I realize we're dealing with serious consequences, but, I think we need to monitor the effectiveness of Drone On a while longer before we switch the satellites back on. After all, it has only been one 'real' day," declared Bennett. "Let me think about it."

"Either way Mr. President, Drone On is working. And working very well."

### Barakat's Game Response

"Mr. Chambers, how did this happen? You assured me your technology was flawless. Today, we find that our drones are losing their way and missing their assigned targets. What is going on?" demanded Barakat.

"Well Emir, as we have discussed many times, the shutting down of U.S. and Russian GPS was inevitable. Why it took so long was anybody's guess. Regardless, that's why we implemented the image-based navigation capability as a backup. Based on our computer simulations and real-world testing, our image-based backup navigation accuracy shouldn't be more than five percent off. An error factor that doesn't explain how so many of our drones completely missed their targets. Clearly there is more going on than the lack of GPS signals," said Chambers.

"Mr. Chambers. What 'more' is going on?" asked Barakat.

"Did you actually expect the U.S. to just sit idly by doing nothing? Implementation of a technological countermeasure was inevitable," said Chambers.

"What kind of countermeasure?" asked Barakat.

"All I have is a theory and an idea," replied Chambers.

"Ok Mr. Chambers. Talk to me," demanded Barakat.

"I don't believe the drones are just wandering off course due to loss of navigation signals. To me, this massive diversion of the attack drones is clear evidence of intelligent control. I believe there is some coordinated process in place. More importantly, I believe the worldwide success of the Drone On game is not a coincidence," said Chambers.

"Why do you believe this game has anything to do with our problem?" asked Barakat.

"Emir, I happen to know that David Kramer, Autonomous System's current CEO, is personal friends with the Founder and CEO of Banger Mobile Games, the creator of Drone On. This just can't be a coincidence. In fact, you may recall a number of months ago our contact at Autonomous, Arman Deeb, alluded to a game that was being developed by Autonomous Systems. I believe the game Deeb referred to was Drone On," said Chambers.

"Mr. Chambers, are you telling me that our drones are being controlled by a game? Is this even possible?" asked Barakat.

"Yes Emir. It isn't only possible, I believe that is exactly what's happening. We have downloaded copies of the Drone On game and installed them on a number of smartphones. Based on our decompilation of the underlying software, and our real-world testing, I believe Drone On is being fed information about our attack drones through a distributed network of multi-spectrum sensors and transmitters. Our working theory is that they are piggybacking this array of sensors and transmitters on cell towers throughout America. In doing so, they can have wide area coverage and redundancy. Once one or a group of our drones is detected, control information can be collected then delivered through the Cloud into Banger Mobile's gaming servers. From there, our drones are simply incorporated into the game. From a player's perspective, they don't know whether they're controlling a virtual drone or actually controlling and navigating one of our drones. In reality, unbeknownst to the game player, he is simply flying a virtual drone to some target in a game. If the gamer is flying one of our drones, we believe they are provided targeting coordinates which cause our drones to be flown to some benign destination such as the empty fields we have heard about in the news reports. The brilliance of this strategy is that the game logic allows our real drones to be assigned to the best Drone On gamers maximizing the desired outcome," explained Chambers.

Looking stunned, Barakat stared Chambers in the eye, "This is unbelievable."

"Emir. You know I've pledged my commitment to the cause of Islam and to being your loyal servant. I assure you, I have a plan to counter any interference by Drone On and neutralize this response by America," assured Chambers.

"What is that plan Mr. Chambers?" asked Barakat.

"Very simply, we need to deploy a counter game to Drone On that allows game players to re-target our drones," explained Chambers. "In fact, I believe my team can deploy an update or enhancement, if you will, to the Drone On game, literally taking over the game like a virus takes over a computer. In doing so, we ensure these same Drone On gamers navigate our drones where we want them. Additionally, we can deploy our own game that connects to the Banger game servers thus empowering our local operators to either regain control or to simply interfere with another player's control of one of our drones. In the least we need to inject some chaos. In doing so, I believe this will result in loss of control by the gamers. As you know, once direct control is lost, our drones' internal programming will reassert itself taking back control and continue on their mission profile, autonomously. In essence, we can either allow the gamers to fly our drones on our behalf, or simply inject enough chaos that causes our drones to reassert their autonomy," explained Chambers.

"Outstanding Mr. Chambers. This is wonderful news. How long will it take to implement your plan?" asked Barakat.

"Not very long. We have been working on this for the past couple of months in anticipation of just such a scenario," said Chambers.

"What about your team members suspected of communicating with Autonomous Systems?" asked Barakat.

"Actually Emir. Since we relocated to the new facilities, I don't think we need to do anything. As long as they are communicating with Autonomous Systems, we have free access to their servers and code libraries. In fact, it was the information received from the contact at Autonomous that made us aware of the United States' game strategy. Unfortunately, our contact at Autonomous Systems has been unresponsive for the past thirty days or so. Regardless, we still seem to have limited access to their servers. Unfortunately, I am growing suspect as to the reliability of the information we are accessing. I believe we should continue as we have for the time being and monitor the situation," suggested Chambers.

"Ok Mr. Chambers. Continue with your plan. Allah Akbar!" exclaimed Barakat as he embraced Chambers.

"Allah Akbar my Emir," replied Chambers.

### Financial News

"Good morning. I'm Grant Underwood. Welcome to United News Network's Business Report. This morning the Dow, once again, opened to a two-thousand-point loss. With us today is Carrie Connors, UNN's business correspondent reporting from the floor of the New York Stock Exchange. Carrie, thank you for joining us this morning."

"Thank you Grant. This morning I'm on the floor of the New York Stock Exchange. Like citizens coast-to-coast, people here are battle weary. Aside from the daily drone attacks wreaking havoc, President Bennett's decision to turn off America's Global Positioning Satellite system has had far-reaching negative effects on literally every business sector. The obvious victim being the airlines, who once again found their shares opening twenty percent below yesterday's close," reported Carrie.

"Yes Carrie. We understand the airlines are suffering badly without GPS. But, you mentioned other businesses. Who else is impacted by President Bennett's decision?" asked Grant.

"Grant, companies being effected by the loss of GPS signals are truly far-reaching. Today, the publicly traded company RideMe, the largest ride-sharing company, just filed for Chapter 11 bankruptcy protection. According to a release by RideMe, GPS positioning capability was fundamental to its business model. Without GPS, it's impossible to geographically connect drivers with their customers. According to RideMe, since President Bennett's announcement, utilization is down seventy-five percent. With no belief that America's GPS services will be restored anytime soon, RideMe's stock has lost over fifty percent of its value. Being left with no alternative, RideMe's management elected to seek protection in bankruptcy," said Connors.

"This is truly devastating. RideMe was one of the largest IPO's in U.S. history. Didn't they support a thirty-billion-dollar valuation on their IPO six months ago?" asked Underwood.

"Yes Grant. RideMe was a true darling of Wall Street and one of the largest IPO's in history. Now, the future of the company is in question," replied Carrie.

"Carrie, you mentioned other businesses. What other business sectors are struggling under the loss of GPS?" asked Grant.

"Obviously many businesses rely on GPS. Stocks are down across the entire transportation sector. Certainly the airlines are a big part of this sector. However, freight and logistic companies have grown to depend on GPS for efficient tracking of trillions of dollars in assets on the road, rail, sea, air and even in warehouses. Without GPS, the ability to know where inventory is has become impossible. No one anticipated this occurrence and as such, manual methodologies were abandoned years ago. Now these companies are scrambling to find alternatives to GPS," replied Carrie. "Grant, the loss of GPS is devastating to the financial community."

"Carrie, as always, it's a pleasure having you join us on the Business Report. It is sad, however, that the news you have to share is so disturbing. Keep us posted with any breaking news," said Grant.

"Yes Grant. These are very difficult times. I will stay on top of this story," replied Connors.

The television broadcast now exclusively showed Grant Underwood. "The loss of GPS has truly been devastating for many companies. Today, however, for some companies all news is not bad. Banger Mobile Games' stock is up five hundred points for the week, now commanding a twelve-billion-dollar market cap. Joining us from Palo Alto is the CEO of Banger Mobile Games, David Banger. Good morning, Mr. Banger."

David Banger's image faded into view as he paused due to the lag in communication between New York and Palo Alto, California.

"Good morning Grant. It's a pleasure to be with you this morning. Please, call me Dave," replied Banger.

"Certainly Dave. This must be a bittersweet time for you and Banger. Stocks across the market are plummeting, yet Banger Mobile is flying high," said Grant.

"Yes Grant. My heart goes out to the CEOs and investors of companies being negatively affected by the loss of GPS. I'm certain President Bennett never wanted anyone to suffer from his decision. But, he had to weigh the lives of millions of Americans against corporate profits. No matter how one looks at it, people are truly more important," responded Banger.

"How is it going at Banger?" asked Grant.

"As you can see by our stock performance, things couldn't be better. In fact, the number of people playing our flagship game, Drone On, has soared past one hundred fifty million worldwide. The game is successful beyond our wildest expectations," answered Banger.

"This is truly good news for Banger and wonderful news for your shareholders. Is this a 'one-trick-pony' for Banger, or is there more to come?" asked Grant.

"Well Grant, we are a creative development company. Rest assured Drone On is not our only product. Nor will it be our last. We have a very aggressive development and growth strategy and intend to be the dominant gaming company in the world," replied David.

"David. Err. Dave, all of us at UNN want to congratulate you and wish you continued success. Thank you for taking the time to join us this morning," said Grant.

"Grant, the pleasure is all mine. Thank you for having me," replied Banger as his image faded from view.

"With the monstrous weapons man already has, humanity is in danger of being trapped in this world by its moral adolescents," General Omar Bradley

★ ★ ★ ★ ★

# Chapter 19

$\blacklozenge$

*The News*
*Embattled America*

"Good evening, I'm Jeff Stoddard and this is my co-anchor Gretchen Chen. Welcome to the evening edition of United News Network. As another day drew to a close, America continued to fall prey to the Islamic State's unrelenting drone attacks. Fortunately, for some unknown reason, many of the attacking drones were reported crashing into open fields away from populated areas. One can only suspect why this is happening. In order to acquire some insight into this change of events, we have Dr. Janet Grey, Chairman of the Department of Artificial Intelligence and Robotics at MIT."

Sitting in her office at MIT, Dr. Grey waited patiently as Richard Thomas, UNN's remote cameraman awaited the signal from the network. "Dr. Grey," said Thomas. "You are on the air in ten seconds." Grey primped and readied herself as Richard quietly counted down to zero. Three...two...one...The camera's red light blinked on brightly.

"Dr. Grey," said Stoddard, "Thank you for joining us this evening."

"My pleasure."

"Well, Dr. Grey, as an engineer and the chairman of MIT's Department of Artificial Intelligence and Robotics, you must have a unique perspective on what's happening with these drones. How is it, even after shutting down our Global Positioning Satellites that the attacks are able to continue?" asked Stoddard.

"Based on my observations, it's my guess that these drones do not rely solely on GPS for navigation and guidance. With access to powerful, portable and truly low-cost technology, I'm certain these drones employ supplemental navigation capabilities," replied Dr. Grey.

"Such as what doctor?" asked Stoddard.

"Jeff, like many military attack systems in the U.S. arsenal, these drones likely employ multiple navigation capabilities. For example, our Tomahawk missiles use GPS for primary navigation. However, they also have the capability to navigate by Inertial Navigation, Terrain Contour Matching, as well as imaging-based Digital Scene Matching and Area

Correlation technologies. These technologies can work together or independently to enhance GPS navigation and accuracy. In the event of GPS signal loss, any of these systems can provide navigation and guidance to accurately locate and identify the assigned targets," replied Grey.

"So, you believe the attacking drones have such capability?" asked Stoddard.

"Yes. That is the only explanation for the successful attacks since President Bennett ordered the GPS shutdown."

"But, Dr. Grey. It seems like a number of drones are not finding their targets and are crashing in vacant fields or deserted buildings. How do you explain this?"

"No technology is perfect. Either there are navigation weaknesses within these drones, or another technology is being employed by our government that is interfering with their navigation capabilities," commented Grey.

"Do you believe our government has technology that is capable of redirecting drones to unpopulated areas?" asked Stoddard.

"If such technology exists," replied Grey. "I'm unaware of it. It does seem odd, however, that so many drones appear to be finding their targets which supports my belief that they are not totally dependent upon GPS. Yet, since a significant number of drones are ending up in unpopulated areas, I believe there is a very high likelihood some technology is being successfully employed that diverts them from their targets. If this is the case, I am very pleased," replied Grey.

"Dr. Grey, thank you for joining us tonight and sharing your technological and operational insights. We too are hopeful that our government has technology that is successful against these persistent attacks. We look forward to having you on again in the future," said Jeff.

"You are very welcome. It was my pleasure," replied Grey.

### A Taste of a New Dark Age

Like water flowing over the ground, the effects of nature's persistent forces are subtle yet substantial over time. Just as the Grand Canyon wasn't carved out in a day, the influence of technology on society proved to be a slow yet constant pressure, forging over time a new and very different existence. Just weeks ago, the average citizen couldn't conceive of the American way of life without automobiles, airplanes, cell phones and

GPS. But a life without GPS was now a reality. To the average citizen, the role GPS played in his or her life, like the trickle of water that coursed through the southwest carving out the Grand Canyon, was barely noticeable. That is, until President Bennett took it away on a moment's notice.

Overnight, availability and benefits of GPS services took millions upon millions of mobile Americans by storm when GPS-empowered services and technology slipped into their hands like a comfortable glove or familiar tool. Always at the ready, and more often than not, working flawlessly. Whether an iPhone precariously perched on a car's dashboard, or an extravagant two thousand dollar in-dash unit rationalized as a much needed accessory, GPS and its friendly yet persistent turn-by-turn spoken navigation instructions became as fundamental to driving as gasoline. But now, things have changed. Today, these same millions of travelers gaze upon their trusty GPS technology, only seventy-two hours after President Bennett's announcement, confronted by a rarely seen message—Satellite Error. An ever-present reminder that something at the core of their way-of-life had changed. Like so many things that go underappreciated, GPS-powered services were just an integral and barely noticeable part of our daily lives. Just another of the many things we took for granted in our advanced high-tech culture.

Drivers who earned their licenses more than twenty years ago have faint memories of paper road-maps. Large, unwieldy pulp-monstrosities difficult to fold and often strewn about inside the car. Talk to someone old enough, and they'll likely dredge up a fond memory about dad pulling into a Texaco gas station to pick up a *free* map to plan a road-trip, or allow dad to retain his manhood by proving to mom he wasn't lost. But alas, paper road-maps, whether from the Auto Club, Michelin or the brilliant brothers Thomas of 1915, lost their battle with GPS and slipped into our anachronistic past, taking up their well-earned position as just another topic for 'remember when' conversations. That is, until now.

As GPS manufacturers struggled to find a way to extract the dagger President Bennett plunged deep into their backs, management of dormant, hibernating map publishers, like Rand McNally and Michelin, were beside themselves and giddy as school girls by the opportunity before them as America slipped back in time to the Dark Age before GPS. Feverishly these CEO's of the printed map world, who long since relinquished their standing in personal navigation, issued commands to dust off drafting tables, hire cartographers and roll the presses to fill demand for paper maps. Demand they hoped would revitalize their long forgotten businesses and once again, fill their coffers with profits. In contrast to the business challenges GPS technology vendors confronted, paper map publishers stood on the verge of a renaissance. How long would it last? No one knew. But, today a hard and cold lesson has been learned: Nothing is guaranteed.

President Bennett's drastic decision to shut down GPS was rife with consequences. GPS-enhanced navigation, albeit the loss of which is just an inconvenience for many, proved to be a nightmare for tens of thousands of employees laid off from businesses dependent upon GPS. From Apple iOS software developers to leading-edge aerospace manufacturers, management teams didn't miss a heartbeat to pull the trigger eliminating jobs in an effort to stop the bleeding as the viability of their businesses came into question.

Overnight, shipping and logistics companies scrambled to operate in a world without GPS. Just a few days prior, trucks and shipping containers diligently announced their locations providing manufacturers, distributors and retailers real-time intelligence as to the whereabouts and expected delivery of much-needed goods and supplies. This backslide into a realm without GPS brought the economic benefits of just-in-time inventory control to a screeching halt with consequences rippling all the way down to Joe-consumer.

Commerce aside, hundreds of thousands of criminals under house-arrest and monitored by GPS ankle bracelets were literally 'nowhere to be found.' In an instant, they had fallen off law enforcement's GPS-powered tracking system. Probation and parole officers coast-to-coast feverishly struggled to ensure that those now unmonitored-and-unaccounted-for-threats-to-peace didn't slip into their old ways. Unfortunately, this was not to be. Within twenty-four hours of the President's announcement, 911 calls soared twenty percent, swamping the capability of even the most prepared law enforcement agencies. The chilling wind of change had cut deep into society's core as drug dealers, thieves, sexual predators and heaven forbid, child molesters freely combed America's streets seeking opportunity. The growing sense of a burgeoning post-apocalyptic America permeated one's consciousness reinforced by 24/7 news reports. With or without drones, the Islamic State had torn the fabric of America.

### The President

Along with Roger Kerns, Speaker Teasdale, Senate Majority Leader Palmer, FBI Director Mitch Teich, FAA Director Tom Gomez and

Commerce Secretary Jerome Price sat pensively in the Oval Office awaiting President Bennett's arrival.

"Gentlemen, Senator Palmer, the President understands the consequences of his decision to shut down GPS. This morning, it is his hope that a solution to stop the bleeding from the loss of GPS can be uncovered and remedy this terrible situation," shared Kerns. "The President will be here momentarily."

As Kerns uttered his last syllable, the door to the Oval Office swung open almost crashing against the wall when President Bennett swooped in. "Gentlemen, Senator Palmer, thank you for coming over this morning. We have work to do."

Bennett slipped into his chair, encircled by his advisors as Tyron Garner, the President's butler, placed a cup of coffee on the table before him. "Mr. President, is there anything else you need?" asked Garner.

"No Tyron. Thank you. I'm fine. By the way, how is your son doing at Stanford?"

"Thank you for asking Mr. President. He just started his second year and is having the time of his life."

"Very good Tyron. That is good news indeed."

As Tyron left the office, Bennett picked up his cup and momentarily savored the aroma. This moment always pleased him.

"Gentlemen. Senator. I fear shutting down GPS may have been a big mistake," uttered Bennett. "I'm not sure if the financial destruction caused by this decision isn't worse than the attacks. For sure, lives are being saved. But, we are in the midst of an economic meltdown. Talk to me."

Thomas Gomez, putting down his cup of coffee, took the lead. "Mr. President, as you know, aviation GPS manufacturers have enthusiastically signed on to modifying their technology to comply with the new Secure-GPS protocols. Unfortunately, this is going to cost billions in development and retrofitting aircraft. Neither manufacturers, airlines or the general aviation community can afford to shoulder the cost of doing so."

"Thomas, what are you implying? A bailout?" asked Bennett.

"Candidly Mr. President, I don't see any other way. Tens of thousands of jobs have been lost in aviation, compounded by the economic burden imposed on the airlines. The sooner you announce financial support for the airlines, general aviation and manufacturers, the quicker we can fix this problem," answered Gomez.

"What do you estimate the cost will be?" asked Bennett.

"Approximately thirty thousand dollars per airliner and, two thousand per general aviation airplane. At forty-five hundred aircraft in the air carrier fleet and two hundred thousand GA aircraft, we estimate roughly five hundred million," shared Gomez.

Bennett precariously placed his cup of coffee on his knee, "I get the problem in aviation. Mitch, what about monitoring criminals? They are running amuck," declared Bennett.

Teich paused for a moment, "Mr. President. The reports are staggering. Coast-to-coast, 911 calls are up dramatically since we have no way to keep track of these people who were under house arrest. There just aren't enough probation and parole officers to handle the work load. I agree with FAA Director Gomez that deployment of Secure-GPS is a good answer. Unfortunately, we estimate the cost to refit three hundred thousand criminals and parolees with Secure-GPS monitors will cost approximately seven hundred fifty million dollars."

"Holy crap. That's just another way of saying a billion dollars," replied Bennett.

"Okay. Okay. I can only presume that the Commerce department has something to add," quipped Bennett.

"The consequences of losing GPS has been far-reaching," said Jerome Price. "I believe we need to enable Secure-GPS forthwith. In doing so, we can very quickly get products and materials moving again. But..."

"I know. I know. There is always a but...In this case, what's it going to cost?" asked Bennett.

"Mr. President," offered Price "we will need to provide subsidies to GPS manufacturers to implement secure services. Unfortunately, like in aviation, it will be necessary to subsidize GPS users to help them upgrade their technology. Fortunately, the technology is less costly than that used in aviation. But, the number of users is measured in millions. Unfortunately, we estimate the subsidies will cost upwards of three billion dollars."

Shaking his head, Bennett turned to Speaker Teasdale and Senator Palmer. "Jennifer, Robert, my quick estimate is we will need to appropriate at least four billion to implement this plan. Can I count on you?" asked Bennett.

"Mr. President, the House will not let you down," replied Teasdale.

"The Senate is behind you one hundred percent Mr. President," added Palmer.

Leaning forward in his chair, Bennett extended his hand to the congressional leadership, shaking Palmer's and Teasdale's hands. "Thank you Jennifer. Thank you Bob."

Bennett stood and arched his back to relieve months of accumulated stress. "People. Good work. The appropriations will be allocated and approved. Speak with your GPS constituents and get them rolling. We need to climb out of this hell-hole immediately. How long will it take to deploy this Secure-GPS strategy?"

"We estimate at the FAA that satellite re-programming and retrofit of both commercial and general aviation fleets will take six months or less," offered Gomez.

"The FBI and Justice can be ready as soon as the secure protocols are available," declared Teich.

Bennett, turned to Price. "I presume Commerce can implement quickly?" asked Bennett.

"Absolutely!" declared Price.

"Well gentlemen, Senator, let's move forward. Thank you for joining me this morning and offering a viable strategy," said Bennett. "Mitch. Please stay for a few minutes, will you?"

"Yes Mr. President. Happy too." said Teich as the rest of Bennett's advisors made their way out of the Oval Office.

Sinking back into his chair, Bennett motioned for Teich to join him. "Mitch. How long have we known each other?" asked Bennett.

Pondering for a moment, "thirty-one…ummm…thirty-two years? A long time. The years just roll together Mr. President," replied Teich.

"Carl, Mitch. You were the best-man at my wedding. Why can't you call me Carl?" cajoled Bennett.

Smirking slightly, "Well, Mr. President, as long as you occupy this office, I will accord you the courtesy and respect you deserve. So, until such time, it will be Mr. President. But for now, Mr. President, what can I do for you?"

"Okay….I get it," conceded Bennett. "I want to know about the status of the interrogations of the terrorist that was captured in Texas and the Autonomous System's programmer.

"Ah. Mr. Neifeh and Mr. Deeb. Well Mr. President, as you know, Mr. Abdul Neifeh was apprehended by Mr. Richard Young, a Militia member, in the midst of the Labor Day attacks. Mr. Young successfully disrupted Mr. Neifeh's attempt to deploy ten bomb and RICIN laden drones from a park in Austin, Texas. The arrest went off without any difficulty and Neifeh was transported to FBI headquarters for interrogation. Since Neifeh was taken into custody, he has not been cooperative and no valuable information was secured from him or his residence. We have employed every legal interrogation procedure available to us to no avail," explained Teich.

"That's too bad. What about the Autonomous programmer?" asked Bennett.

"Mr. Deeb. Truly an interesting character." responded Teich. "The good news is, Mr. Deeb seems truly harmless. Yes, it's true he provided Chambers' team access to Autonomous software, but, as you know it worked out to our advantage. It was the information we gleaned from his interrogations and knowledge of the software Chambers' people used that provided us the building blocks for creating Drone On. Which, by-the-way Mr. President was a brilliant decision on your part. Simply brilliant."

"Come on Mitch. You know I had little to do with it," said Bennett.

"Mr. President, I know you didn't invent Drone On. You did, however, recognize its potential and gave it the go-ahead. I'm certain neither of us believe FDR or General Groves provided Oppenheimer any meaningful technical guidance on the Manhattan Project. Do you? But, without Roosevelt and Groves, Oppenheimer would never have developed the atomicbomb. I assure you, Roosevelt was just as instrumental in developing the Atom bomb used to end World War II as you are in developing Drone On and beating the Islamic State's drone threat. Mr. President, this is an historic time for your presidency. Simply historic. Enjoy it." exclaimed Teich.

"Mitch, you are too kind and a great friend. I don't know how I would get through this mess without you. Thanks," smiled Bennett.

"The pleasure is all mine Mr. President. All mine."

### Strange Bedfellows

Abdul Fadel walked into Chambers' quarters. "Mr. Chambers, the Emir wishes to see you. Please come with me."

"Yes. Of course," replied Chambers as he gathered his iPad and notebook. "Where are we going?"

"The Emir wants you to meet someone."

"Who is it?" asked Chambers.

"You will know soon enough. Please. Get into the truck."

It had been months since Chambers and his team left the underground compound in Islamabad. No one was really surprised since moving around was a good strategy if you wish not to be found by the enemy. But, never in Chambers' wildest imagination did he expect to wind up here. Squirreled away deep in North Korea. "Certainly the Islamic State's war strategy was broader than the average American could have imagined," pondered Chambers.

Chambers and Fadel trundled along through the streets of Pyongyang for thirty or forty minutes before pulling up to a guard gate. The driver, speaking Korean, soon secured access and Chambers and Fadel continued up to what clearly was the formal entrance to the facility where awaiting their arrival was an entourage of western-dressed gentlemen proudly displaying their iPhones and iPads.

As Chambers exited the vehicle, he was greeted by a gregarious westernized young man. "Mr. Chambers. I am Seong Sun. It is a pleasure to meet you. I will be your escort within the palace and act as your translator if you should need one," explained Sun.

"Thank you," responded Chambers.

Chambers leaned near Fadel and whispered, "The palace? Where are we? Who are we meeting?"

"In due time Mr. Chambers. In due time," replied Fadel.

Following on the heels of Sun and the entourage, Chambers and Fadel were kept close together as they were swept along at a pace just short of a trot. Before long, Chambers and Fadel were escorted into an ornate meeting room where Barakat was seated savoring his traditional coffee.

Placing down his cup, Barakat rose to his feet with a grand smile with hand extended. "Mr. Chambers. It has been too long. Too long."

"Emir, you have piqued my curiosity," said Chambers.

"I am certain I have. I assure you, you will not be disappointed," quipped Barakat.

"Please. Be seated and join me. Would you like some coffee? It is excellent," declared Barakat.

"Yes. Thank you," said Chambers as he took a seat at the table next to Moktar.

"Mr. Chambers. As you know, since we first met with Korea Navigation Company, we've developed a unique relationship with North Korea's leadership. Today, we are meeting with the Supreme Leader of the Democratic People's Republic of Korea. He should be here shortly," said Barakat.

"Kim Jung-Un? I am meeting the Supreme Leader? Emir, what do you expect from me?" asked Chambers.

"Mr. Chambers, we are expanding our alliance with North Korea on many levels. Today, I want you to share with the Supreme Leader the progress you have made with our drones and acknowledge the important role and leadership they have played in executing our plan," explained Barakat. "This meeting is a formality. He simply wishes to meet our technology leader."

"I am surprised Emir. I will do my best. Is there anything I need to know prior to his arrival?" asked Chambers.

"You will be fine Mr. Chambers. I will lead the meeting," said Moktar.

Chambers and Barakat sat quietly enjoying their coffee, as the entourage hovered nearby, anticipating the Supreme Leader's arrival. In a whirlwind, the main door to the meeting room swung open as the room filled with the Supreme Leader's attendants creating a path for him to the meeting table. With determination and presence, Kim Jung-Un sauntered into the room glaring at Chambers, creating a situation that made him more than a little uncomfortable.

Seong leaned forward, placing his hand on Chambers' right shoulder and whispered into his ear. "Mr. Chambers, please rise and bow at the waist until greeted by the Supreme Leader. When he speaks to you, just say, it's my honor Your Excellency. Once he acknowledges you, you may stand up. Any questions?" asked Seong.

Chambers, nervous and speechless simply shook his head.

Barakat and Chambers, bowing at the waist waited patiently to be acknowledged by the leader of North Korea.

"Emir Barakat. It is always a pleasure to greet you in my home," spoke Kim Jung-Un. "Who is this with you today?"

Barakat, rose up. "Your Excellency. The honor is all mine. Allow me to introduce you to the leader of our drone technology team, Mr. Richard Chambers."

Turning to Chambers, Kim Jung-Un spoke. "Mr. Chambers, it is good to finally meet you. The Emir has told me much about the wonderful work you have been doing."

"The pleasure is all mine Your Excellency. I am honored to work for the Islamic State and the Democratic Republic of North Korea," said Chambers.

The Supreme Leader took his seat at the head of the table. "Gentlemen, please sit and tell me of your accomplishments and how we can continue our wonderful work together."

"The combination of hatred and technology
is the greatest danger threatening
mankind," Simon Wiesenthal

★ ★ ★ ★ ★

# Chapter 20

———————◆———————

### *Gaming*

Ricky Granger, cloistered in his bedroom in Springfield, Illinois required no excuse to avoid his homework. Instead, he tapped the Drone On icon on his iPad. With a frosty cold energy drink at the ready, Ricky positioned his microphone carefully in front of his mouth, barely touching his lips. After tapping Drone On's team button, he saw his buddy, Pete Zell, was online. "Outstanding," Ricky muttered to himself. After a glancing tap on his name, Pete's live video feed appeared in the upper left-hand corner of Ricky's iPad and Drone On popped up the communication controller. As he has done hundreds of times before, Ricky's left thumb deftly tapped the black talk button. "Hey Pete. How do you read?"

"Loud and clear Ricky," replied Pete.

"Great," responded Ricky. "Hey! Did you see that I leveled up last night? I achieved Warrior Level Three and received a Gold Commander Badge."

"Yep. I saw the Facebook post. Awesome! You're a Drone On god. Doesn't that put you in the top five percent of all Drone On commanders?" asked Pete.

"Yeah! Way cool! I even received twenty-five dollars on my Starbucks card from Banger Mobile. Wanna hook up in the morning and spend some of these Drone On bucks?" asked Ricky.

"Works for me. How about seven at Monroe and Bruns?" suggested Pete.

"I'll be there. Right now, let's combine our fleets and attack New York. I want to try and level up again tonight. Maybe we'll earn more cash. You up for it?"

"Let's rock and roll buddy," replied Pete.

Within moments, Zell's and Granger's two flights of ten attack drones maneuvered into view on their iPads. Their target, prominently displayed in the center of their iPads, was the Bank of America building. "Pete, you head east over 34th street and I'll track north on 8th. This should easily be worth ten thousand points each," noted Ricky.

"Roger Commander."

Within minutes Ricky's drones arrived at the corner of 8$^{th}$ and 34$^{th}$ then he turned them east on 34$^{th}$ joining Pete's flight of ten drones. Pete and Ricky deftly maneuvered their drones as their crosshairs centered on the Bank of America building.

"Ready?" asked Ricky.

"Ready commander," responded Pete.

"Commence attack pattern Delta," commanded Ricky as each boy tapped the Attack Pattern Delta button on their iPads. The twenty drones joined in a well-choreographed dance orbiting a few hundred feet above Manhattan. Convinced the fleet was in position, Ricky tapped the attack button and the twenty animated drones, heavily laden with eighty pounds of virtual C4 explosives, began attacking the Bank of America building as the Drone On app animated the utter destruction of the target followed by the words 'Mission Accomplished' as ten thousand bonus points were added to each of the boy's Drone On accounts.

"Bingo! That was awesome Pete," declared Ricky. "Bummer!"

"What's the matter Ricky?" asked Pete.

"My mom just called me for dinner. I have to go buddy. See you at Starbucks in the morning. Good mission buddy."

### The News - America Fights Back

"Yes Gretchen, today has been amazing," said Stoddard as his makeup artist quickly patted perspiration from his forehead and touched up his makeup.

"Gretchen! Jeff! You're back on the air in fifteen," announced the director into Stoddard's and Chen's earphones. UNN Evening Edition's Stage Director held up his right hand in front of the teleprompter and started the five second countdown folding one finger with each passing second. "Five...four...three," followed silently by folding each of the remaining two fingers. As he reached one, he pointed swiftly at the anxious news anchors.

"Welcome back. I'm Jeff Stoddard and this is Gretchen Chen. Unfortunately, Gretchen, like so many days before, America and our allies around the world have once again suffered unrelenting drone attacks causing grave destruction and killing thousands."

Gretchen, nodding in agreement, "Yes Jeff, it's truly sad, but, there is good news. Again yesterday, for some unknown reason, hundreds of the Islamic State's drones fortunately failed to reach their intended targets, crashing harmlessly in vacant fields, lakes and into abandoned buildings. In fact, last evening, here in New York, upwards of twenty drones were observed over Manhattan. But, for some unknown reason, only a dozen crashed into the Bank of America building with the remaining drones harmlessly meeting their demise in the Hudson River."

"Yes Gretchen, this is truly bewildering, yet good news. Over the past few months, the accuracy of the drone attacks seems to have diminished. My hope is our military has developed some reliable defenses against these drone raids," commented Stoddard. "Hopefully UNN's military consultant, General Gary Arnold will be able to shed some light on this positive change of events. Good Evening General Arnold. What are your thoughts behind the decreasing accuracy of the attacking drones?"

"Good evening Jeff and Gretchen. Yes, the crashing of the attack drones into empty fields, abandoned buildings and last night into the Hudson River is puzzling. From my perspective, these events are too consistent to be random failures of the attacking drones' technology. According to my sources, upwards of twenty percent of detected drones have failed to reach their targets. From reports, these drones appear to be operating in a coordinated fashion, yet seem to wander off to their ultimate destruction. My guess is our military has developed a technology that confuses or reprograms the navigation profile of the attacking drones. If this is the case, it is wonderful news. Each drone that fails to reach its target dramatically raises the Islamic State's cost to execute these attacks and, more importantly, reduces the damage they can inflict on America and our allies," reported General Arnold.

"Well General, let's hope our military is behind this turn of events. Personally, this would be most comforting. General, on a more conventional note, what are your thoughts on the ground mission, Freedom Resolve, in the Middle East?" asked Stoddard.

"Jeff, President Bennett's mission, Freedom Resolve, is making tremendous progress. Only today, fifteen thousand U.S. and Allied forces in Iraq recaptured Baghdad, killing fifteen hundred ISIS members and driving the remaining enemy forces into the foothills northwest of Baghdad toward the city of Nebai, ultimately driving them into Syria. Fortunately, our forces took few casualties and are now occupying Baghdad. As illustrated on the map, supporting this effort are three additional divisions, totaling forty-five thousand troops. One moving south from Turkey, another moving north into Syria from Jordan and the third division moving north into Iraq from Saudi Arabia. This is a classic pincer movement intended to drive ISIS into Syria and ultimately blocking any escape route by the sea."

"General, the mission of Freedom Resolve is obvious from the map. My question is, what's going to happen to Lebanon? It seems to be right in ISIS's exit path," asked Gretchen.

"Well Gretchen, as part of Freedom Resolve, an additional division has been strategically positioned along the Syria/Lebanon border in order to ensure Lebanon's security," replied Arnold. "In all, this is an effective ground strategy. Let us not forget that U.S. and allied air forces are pounding ISIS daily which hopefully will disrupt their command and control," added General Arnold.

"General Arnold. Thank you for joining us this evening. As always, thank you for your years of selfless service to this country and, I pray God protects our men and women on the frontlines. Good night General," closed Stoddard.

"Good night Jeff and Gretchen. The honor has been all mine," replied Arnold.

### The Sheriff Returns

As they savored their first cups of morning coffee, Sheriff Johnson and Chief of Staff Kerns sat in the Oval Office awaiting President Bennett's arrival.

"Sheriff, President Bennett will be here momentarily. I urge you to stay focused and offer positive suggestions. As you know, he doesn't take well to complaining and finger pointing."

"Mr. Kerns. I don't intend to point fingers at anyone. The intelligence was just flawed. Just plain flawed. I dropped my team into hostile territory only to find the cupboard was bare. How is it the CIA wasn't aware that Barakat's team had moved out?"

"I don't know Sheriff. It's unfortunate that the ball was dropped and the mission wasn't successful. We have, however, new intelligence I believe you will find very interesting."

"What's that, Mr. Kerns?"

"Let's wait for the President. I'm certain he'll want to share it with you. Care for more coffee?"

"Yes, thank you."

Roger Kerns tipped the coffee pot forward, pouring the hot steamy liquid into Johnson's cup.

"Thank you."

"My pleasure Sheriff."

Without warning, President Bennett stood framed in the open doorway of the Oval Office. "Enjoying yourselves gentlemen?" Bennett asked smiling.

Kerns and Johnson, startled like schoolboys caught in some nefarious mischief, deposited their coffee cups on the table and rose quickly. Kerns spoke first. "Not at all Mr. President. Sheriff Johnson and I were just reviewing the Islamabad mission."

"Islamabad. What an abomination. Graham, I cannot adequately express my regret for this situation. Heads will roll at Langley. I promise you that," assured Bennett.

"Not a problem Mr. President. As you know, we are accustomed to dealing with fluid situations. I assure you my team isn't upset with the poor intelligence but rather with the fact they couldn't complete their mission. I promise you sir, my team is at the ready to deploy on your command," declared Johnson.

"Very good Sheriff. I'm happy to hear that because we have need for your team's talents," said Bennett.

"Mr. President, FBI Director Teich, CIA Director Haydon and Special Agent Lane will be here momentarily to brief us on the status of Barakat and the Autonomous Team. I believe you will be intrigued by their latest intelligence," said Kerns.

"Is this intel we can depend on? I have no desire to ask the good Sheriff to go off on another wild-goose chase."

"Absolutely Mr. President. It's compelling, reliable and terribly disturbing."

President Bennett's secretary, Ruth Holcomb, entered the office with Director Teich, Director Haydon and Special Agent Lane. "Mr. President, Directors Teich and Haydon are here."

"Thank you Mrs. Holcomb." Rising from behind his desk, Bennett walked toward the two gentlemen with his hand extended. "David, Mitch, good to see you my friends. Whom do we have here?"

Teich grasped and shook the President's hand vigorously, "Good to see you Mr. President. Allow me to introduce you to FBI Special Agent Lane, who has been conducting the interrogations with the drone jihadist apprehended in Austin and the Autonomous Systems engineer that has been consorting with Chambers' team."

"Good to meet you Agent Lane. Have you met Sheriff Johnson and Chief of Staff Kerns?" asked Bennett.

Lane extended his right hand to Sheriff Johnson. "It has not been my pleasure sir. Good to meet you Sheriff Johnson. Thank you for your service. Also, I'm so very sorry for the loss of your wife and daughter. That was truly a tragedy."

"Thank you, a pleasure to meet you Agent Lane," acknowledged Johnson, as their hands met.

Haydon reached out and grasped Johnson's hand with both his hands. "Yes Sheriff," said Haydon. "I too am so very sorry for your loss. And, I want to apologize that the Agency dropped the ball on Islamabad. I promise you, this will not happen again."

"Sheriff, we've met before," said Teich as he reached out to shake Johnson's hand.

"Yes Director. Good to see you again," replied Johnson.

With the pleasantries behind them, Bennett decided to move the meeting along. "Gentlemen, let's get down to business. Please have a seat," pointing to the Oval Office's over-stuffed couches and chairs.

"Agent Lane, let's begin briefing President Bennett," instructed Teich.

"Yes sir," acknowledged Agent Lane. "Mr. President, Sheriff Johnson, a Mister Arman Deeb, the Autonomous Systems' engineer, and Mr. Abdul Neifeh, the drone jihadist apprehended in Austin Texas, have been our primary focus over the past couple of months. As expected, neither man is aware of the other. Over the past year, Mr. Deeb has had periodic and regular contact with the Autonomous Team members believed held by Moktar Barakat in Islamabad. And, Mr. Neifeh, an isolated lone-wolf operative embedded in America, is believed to receive his direction via social media and some as yet unknown technology."

Savoring his coffee, Bennett paused for a moment to absorb Agent Lane's report, "Thank you Agent Lane. Good job."

CIA Director Haydon shuffled a couple of pieces of paper. "Mr. President, as a result of the information we've been able to gather from sources in Islamabad, drone surveillance and internet traffic from the Autonomous Team, it's clear that Chambers and his people have been moved. Unfortunately, this information came too late to update Sheriff Johnson. We are sorry to have risked your lives for nothing Sheriff."

Sheriff Johnson nodded in appreciation. "I understand Director. These things happen."

"Well, Mr. President, Sheriff Johnson, I can assure you that we now have solid intel on the whereabouts of Barakat, Chambers and his remaining team members. They have been relocated to North Korea and are the guests of the Supreme Leader," explained Haydon.

"What!?! North Korea," exclaimed Bennett. "Are you joking?"

"No Mr. President. I assure you this is not a joke." replied Haydon. "They are, shall we say, guests of Kim Jung-Un."

"Do we know precisely where they are?" asked Bennett.

"Yes sir. In fact, our assets on the ground captured this photographic evidence of a person believed to be Mr. Chambers visiting Kumsusan Palace of the Sun. The Supreme Leader's residence."

"This is simply amazing. What else do we know?" asked Bennett.

"Mr. President," said Haydon, "we know a lot. In fact, we successfully tracked Chambers' return to his compound upon leaving Kunsusan Palace via satellite. We believe, with high confidence, Chambers and his team are being held in a remote and secure facility thirty-two kilometers northeast of Pyongyang in P'yŏngsŏng, the capital city of the province of South Pyongan in western North Korea."

"Okay. It's good news that we know where in hell they are. What are our options gentlemen?" asked Bennett.

"Mr. President. Dependent upon your opinion as to the status between the U.S. and North Korea, we have a few options including, military invasion, missile attack, or, if Sheriff Johnson and his team are up to the challenge, a covert insertion," replied Haydon.

"Sheriff, what do you think?" asked Bennett.

"Mr. President, my team is ready to go on your order. We can be ready for insertion into North Korea in seventy-two hours," snapped Johnson.

Chief of Staff Kerns could no longer hold his tongue. "Mr. President, any of these options is an overt act of war and has significant consequences."

"Roger, I understand. The fact is, these drone attacks continue daily and North Korea is clearly providing support, manufacturing and delivery capability. We need to take action, and do so now. Call in Congressman Teasdale, Senator Palmer and Secretary of State Umberg. I want to make a decision by the end of the day. Sheriff Johnson, prepare your team to be inserted into North Korea as soon as possible. We need to put a stop to this chaos."

"Yes sir. You can count on me and my team," responded Johnson.

"Mr. President. Inserting Sheriff Johnson's team will be tricky. The fact is, conventional methods will not work," offered Haydon.

"What are you suggesting?" asked Bennett.

"Well Mr. President, we at the Agency believe the most viable insertion strategy will be a HALO but not by typical aircraft. Our analysts have reviewed every scenario and the most viable option is a V-HALO, or very high altitude low opening parachute maneuver, using the X-37D space plane," suggested Haydon.

"How is this going to work?" asked Bennett.

"Mr. President, we can launch Sheriff Johnson and his team from Vandenberg in seventy-two hours. The X-37D will begin its reentry and pass over North Korea at approximately one hundred fifty thousand feet, at which time Sheriff Johnson's team will deploy. The X-37D will continue descending and ultimately land in Alaska," explained Haydon.

Haydon looked at President Bennett and Johnson, pausing for comment. "Once on the ground, Sheriff Johnson and his team will breach the compound. Our computer simulations suggest that the best course of action is to dispatch Barakat and his people if present. On an uncomfortable note Mr. President, we believe that the Autonomous Team should be dispatched with extreme prejudice. Any attempt to recover them will substantially complicate the mission and reduce the likelihood of Sheriff Johnson's team making it to the extraction point. Unfortunately, it is very likely they will have to fight their way to the extraction point which is Sunan International Airport, 18 kilometers northeast of P'yŏngsŏng where they will be met by a C-17 accompanied by a flight of F-35s."

"Are you up for this Sheriff?" asked Bennett.

"Yes sir! We're ready," snapped Johnson. "Mr. President, we will follow your orders to the letter, but I suggest you give us a chance to recover the Autonomous Team. I'm certain my team can handle this."

"Thank you Sheriff. I too want to recover the Autonomous Team. I believe we owe them that. But if they won't come, you'll have to liquidate them Sheriff, work with Director Haydon on formulating your plan. At this point, I need to speak privately with Director Teich. Thank you for joining us this morning gentlemen," said Bennett.

Johnson rose to attention, "thank you for including me in this meeting Mr. President. I'll work closely with Director Haydon and his people," as he snapped a salute to his Commander-in-Chief.

Bennett deftly returned the salute. "Thank you Sheriff. God bless you and your team. Good luck."

"Thank you Mr. President," replied Johnson, as he, Haydon and Lane left the Oval Office.

"Mitch, let's chat a little about Drone On," suggested Bennett.

"Certainly Mr. President. It's my pleasure," responded Teich.

"This Drone On strategy is the craziest plan I've ever heard. Is it still working?" asked Bennett.

"Mr. President, as crazy and unconventional as it sounded, the plan is working. According to our numbers, twenty to thirty percent of the attacking drones are being diverted by the gamers. Banger's engineers have created an amazing piece of software that is being played across the globe," explained Teich.

"How many people are actually involved in diverting attacking drones?" asked Bennett.

"Well Mr. President, to date over one hundred million copies of the Drone On app have been installed on mobile devices worldwide. According to our numbers, upwards of twenty-five thousand users in the U.S. have actually participated in controlling 'real' drones as well as their virtual drones," explained Teich. "As unconventional as this strategy appeared, the damn strategy was working. Hopefully, more players will achieve higher levels of proficiency which should raise their effective rate even higher. Hopefully, if Sheriff Johnson is successful, we can anticipate a decrease in attacks. Additionally, Mr. President, we believe a number of Islamic State terrorists are even playing the game!"

"Well, as crazy as this strategy is, I am committed to supporting it. Keep up the good work. Roger, please express my appreciation to Mr. Banger as well as David Kramer at Autonomous Systems for a job well done. At some point we need to give these guys medals. In secret of course. They won't be able to wear them in public for a long time, I fear"

"Yes Mr. President. I'll pass your message on to them. They both have done an incredible job," replied Kerns.

Once again, Mrs. Holcomb appeared at the door of the Oval Office. "Mr. President, Attorney General Santich is here as requested."

Bennett placed his coffee on the table. "Thank you Mrs. Holcomb. Please show him in."

As he stepped away from his desk, Bennett met Grant Santich half way as he strode across the Oval Office. "Good morning Grant. It's good to see you."

"My pleasure Mr. President," as he shook Bennett's hand.

Santich stepped to his right to shake Mitch Teich's hand, "Good morning, Mitch. It's always a pleasure."

"Mine as well Grant. How is Becky? Recovering well from surgery I hope."

"She's doing fine Mitch. Thanks for asking."

"That's great news."

With pleasantries complete, Santich waved to Chief of Staff Kerns standing behind the couch, "Good morning, Roger."

"And to you Mr. Attorney General," acknowledged Kerns.

Bennett gestured for the men to sit down. "Gentlemen, we need to talk about the problem with house arrests. Grant, what can you tell us?"

While Grant poured a cup of coffee, "Mr. President, the news isn't good. Since the GPS shutdown, law enforcement across the country has reported that forty percent of those under house arrest, or approximately one hundred twenty thousand felons, are unaccounted for. Literally nowhere to be found. The simple fact is criminals are roaming the streets which we believe are contributing to the significant spike in crime rates nationwide."

Bennett shifted uncomfortably in his chair. "What about the remaining, uh…hundred fifty thousand formerly GPS monitored?"

"They too are problematic. According to reports from local parole and probation departments, over one hundred thousand have been apprehended on probation or parole violations and are either under arrest in local facilities or, in some cases, returned to prison. Mr. President, the economic consequences of the GPS shutdown to the criminal justice system has been staggering. Current estimates put the cost in excess of one billion dollars. And, that's just an estimate of the cost to apprehend and incarcerate. Crime statistics are currently immeasurable."

"Grant, Mitch, it's my understanding that the upgrade to the new secure-GPS will be deployed in the next ninety days. What's being done to implement this new technology for home monitoring?" asked Bennett.

"Mr. President, I believe Director Teich can best address this question," replied Grant.

"Okay. Mitch, what do we know?" queried Bennett.

"Mr. President, as of reports I received yesterday all the approved vendors are feverishly implementing the new technology. Unfortunately, this has been a costly endeavor. The cost to deploy the new technology will be in excess of four hundred million dollars in equipment alone. Of course, there's the added cost of locating these people and attaching the new monitors. In all, we estimate the total cost will exceed one billion," explained Teich.

"This whole situation is untenable," offered Bennett. "But what choice do we have? A billion to incarcerate or a billion to monitor. Either way, it's costing us a boatload!" exclaimed the President.

"It certainly is Mr. President. I agree, what choice do we have?" offered Teich.

"None at all. None at all," muttered Bennett.

"I have a meeting with the Joint Chiefs and have to excuse myself. Thanks for your unrelenting commitment to the security of this great country. Keep up the good work."

# Chapter 21

◆

### *Autonomous Team in North Korea*

The sun barely peeked through the window of Chambers' room, glistened off Liz's wet body as she emerged from the shower. "Come here Liz," whispered Chambers.

Reluctantly, Liz sauntered over to Chambers propped up on his pillow with his naked body partially covered by the sheet. "Richard, what's going to happen to us?" she asked.

Reaching up, Chambers gently grasped Liz's hand and coaxed her into bed. "Who knows? Who really knows what the future has in store for anyone? We're alive, somewhat comfortable and you and I are together. What else can we ask for?" as he drew her in close pressing himself against her back, enjoying the full length of her supple body against his.

"I know. But I so want to go home and have a life with you. I want everything I ever dreamed of with you," she sighed.

Chambers pulled her gently toward him, and kissed whispering "We will—I promise."

As a single tear made its way down her cheek, Liz buried her face in Richard's chest and quietly murmured, "I love you, Richard."

As their passion grew stronger, Liz's doubts and fears melted away for just a fleeting moment. Resting in the afterglow, Chambers comforted Liz and assured her, "you know I love you. Right now we're safe. I'm doing everything in my power to keep us that way. I'll find a way out of this mess. I promise."

"I know Richard. I know," as Liz rose from their bed and pulled on her robe.

Gary, Akio and Will had finished their breakfast when Chambers and Liz walked into the kitchen. "Good morning guys. How are you doing this morning?" asked Chambers.

"Shitty," mumbled Gary. "How do you expect us to be? We're prisoners in North Korea. Guests of a psychotic despot. What's there to feel good about?"

"At least we're still alive," exclaimed Chambers.

"Well, at least we have one thing to be thankful for," mumbled Will Schmidt.

Standing at the counter, their backs toward the boys, Liz poured two cups of coffee. One for herself and one for Chambers. Akio, who shared Gary's frustration, jutted out his tongue and crossed his eyes at the loving couple. Having caught Akio in the act, Gary and Will struggled to suppress their laughter over his utter contempt for the couple.

Fortunately, Akio sucked in his tongue just in time as Chambers glanced over his shoulder. Chambers returned his attention to the steaming cup of coffee, "Did I miss something gentlemen?" asked Chambers.

"Uh…No. Nothing at all," replied Gary. "Nothing at all. My coffee went down the wrong pipe."

"I hope you're ok," replied Chambers. Pulling out a chair for Liz, Chambers slid into his seat and began the morning's discussion. "Let's discuss the transfer of technology to the manufacturing group. Shall we?" asked Chambers. "What's the status Liz?"

Liz opened her calendar and turned to today. "This afternoon we have our final orientation meeting with Ko and his engineering team from Korea Navigation Company. So far, they've implemented version six-dot-three-dot-two of the firmware as well as fabricating six pre-production samples of version three-dot-four of the hex-rotor drone. Testing of these units is scheduled for tomorrow. Assuming successful completion of the field test, the new model will go into full production," explained Liz.

"Akio, how has the lab testing of the units gone so far?" asked Chambers

"Richard, our code and technology always works. That's what made Autonomous Systems so successful. Not your BS marketing hype," snapped Akio.

"Akio, I'm weary of your continued hostility. All of us are victims here."

"Yeah. We're all victims. Right! But you're the only one that gets to leave this godforsaken dungeon. By the way, where do you go?" asked Akio.

"Akio, I'm tired of justifying myself to you. I'm doing my job. You just do yours. Or don't. I really don't care. The only one you'll hurt is yourself. You want one of Barakat's henchmen to put a bullet in the back of your head? That's your call," glared Chambers.

"But...But...," stuttered Akio.

"There aren't any buts. Do your damn job and shut the hell up!" suggested Chambers.

"Liz, what time is the meeting with Ko and his people?" asked Chambers.

"Two PM."

Chambers pushed back from the table, "I'm going to my room to work. I'll be back at one thirty."

As Chambers disappeared from the kitchen, Akio, pissed off and struggling to veil his disgust, continued his tirade. "Who the hell does he think he is?"

"He's the boss," said Will. "More importantly, he's buddy-buddy with Barakat. I for one want to stay alive. So, knock this crap off Akio, or you'll get us all killed."

Liz, sat quietly shifting nervously in her seat.

"But they need us!" exclaimed Akio. "Chambers doesn't do dick!"

"That may be true, but Barakat seems to like him and we don't have any choice. I just want to stay alive," snapped Will.

"Me too," added Gary. "Quit screwing with him or I'll kick your ass."

Sipping her coffee, Liz paused for a moment waiting for the tension to abate. "Guys, shall we prepare for this afternoon's meeting?"

## Gaming

Ricky Granger sat quietly at his favorite Starbucks while he waited for Pete to show up. Not unlike a typical modern teenager, Ricky was content to nurse his six dollar Double Venti Espresso Mocha, generously provided by Banger Mobile. In anticipation of Pete's arrival, he casually tapped the screen of his iPad and perused the available Drone On campaigns. Pride got the best of Ricky, as he broke into a smile and reveled in the joy of his Drone On Gold Commander Badge prominently displayed on the home page. "This is just too much fun," he muttered between sips.

"Hey Pete!" called Ricky, as he waved at Pete Zell walking through the door of the crowded Starbucks. "I've got your Venti Cappuccino here."

"Thanks Ricky. Or should I thank Banger?" laughed Pete sporting a sardonic grin.

"Yep. Drone On...the app that pays us to blow crap up. It's just way too cool," exclaimed Ricky.

Throwing his leg over the comfy leather chair, Pete plopped down and snatched up his foamy Cappuccino, spilling a little on his pants.

"Ricky, did you see I leveled up after our attack last night?" asked Pete.

"Yeah. Very cool. Way to go, Warrior Level 2. Good luck trying to catch up with me. I'm a Drone On god!" laughed Ricky. Want to execute a mission before class?"

"Sure. Let's do it."

"Pete, I've been monitoring a number of campaigns. Check this out. I've been given the assignment to attack Los Angeles Airport," announced Ricky.

"That sounds cool Ricky. Let's do it!" agreed Pete.

"Okay. Quick, log into LAX Siege before anyone grabs your spot," commanded Ricky. "Let's combine our fleets and join the attack. I want to level up again and earn more cash!"

"You got it. Let's rock and roll buddy," as Pete retrieved his iPad from his backpack and mashed the home key. "Crap, I wish Apple would make these things boot faster."

"Yeah. They're slow as hell. I hope Starbucks' WiFi isn't bogged down. There are too many people in here," complained Pete. "Okay, I'm online," After a couple of quick taps, "Okay, I'm in the LAX Siege campaign."

Pete's and Ricky's fleets of attack drones maneuvered into view on their iPads. Pete's from the west and Ricky's from the south accompanied by two other fleets that joined the mission.

"Wow, this is going to be epic," exclaimed Pete.

"Really! LAX is going to be devastated," replied Ricky. "Let's do it."

Drone On displayed LAX in the center of each boy's iPad as the four attack squadrons moved in for the kill.

"Pete, I am going to swing west and come over the top of the airport, drop down to two hundred feet and fly my drones along runway two four left and take out the United 747 on final," declared Ricky.

"Outstanding! I'm going for the control tower," replied Pete as he maneuvered his drones between the four parallel runways.

"Where do you think the other squadrons are going?" wondered Pete.

"Don't know. I'm too busy with my own drones," said Ricky.

"Roger Commander."

As quickly as it began, the four attacking drone squadrons maneuvered into position, with their destinations dead center in the cross hairs of their targeting windows as Drone On displayed the countdown to impact in the upper right-hand corner of each boy's iPad.

Ten...Nine...Eight...Seven...Six...

"I'm on track with my target centered," declared Pete.

"Me too," acknowledged Ricky head down with Starbucks' patrons moving to and fro oblivious to the boys activities.

Three...Two...One...

"Bingo!" declared Pete.

"Watch me. I'm going head-to-head with the jumbo jet," shouted Ricky as his drones exploded on contact.

Each boy's iPad was awash in chaos and animated carnage as the four squadrons decimated Los Angeles International Airport. The words Mission Accomplished flash across their screens followed by the estimated total killed.

"Holy crap," exclaimed Ricky. "Four hundred dead."

The chaos on the iPads was quickly wiped clean and replaced by their ten thousand point bonus award.

"Hey Ricky," called Pete. "I just got ten bucks on my Starbucks card. Tomorrow it's my treat."

"Great job! Look Pete, I got twenty-five bucks. I guess a Jumbo Jet's worth more than a control tower," laughed Ricky. "We have bank!"

### The Evening News

As the commercial fades, United News Network Evening Edition returns with Jeff Stoddard and Gretchen Chan. "Welcome back to our report on drone attacks in America and around the world," said Jeff Stoddard.

"Yes Jeff, the sad fact is the attacks continue and are increasing in numbers around the world. However, as we've reported over the past few months, for some unknown reason the attacking drones are proving to be somewhat less effective."

"So true Gretchen. This morning, approximately forty drones were observed in the vicinity of Los Angeles International Airport. And as so many times before, upward of twenty percent of the drones ended up crashing harmlessly. In the case of the LAX attack, many drones crashed offshore into the Pacific Ocean. Fortunately, according to reports, only twenty of the forty reported drones detonated their explosive payloads on the airport. Unfortunately, there were still nearly three hundred killed, and many more people injured or contaminate by RICIN"

### Johnson and the X-37D Team

As before, Johnson's team huddled in a sterile military hanger with its floors clean and shiny beyond compare. This time, however, they gathered at Vandenberg Air Force Base in California. Like before, the wing of the C-17 that rose high above them is the craft that will pick them up and return them home after they complete their mission. Not deliver them.

Once again Johnson, followed close behind by Master Chief Davis, strode toward his team, dwarfed by the hanger's monstrous doors. "HOOYAH!! Gentlemen."

"HOOYAH!!" replied eleven pumped up special operators.

"Well gentlemen, our President has once again called upon us. I assured him that we stood ready to do our best to honor this country. Are you with me?"

"HOOYAH!!" replied his team.

"Gentlemen, by now you've reviewed your briefing packets. As before, our mission is to neutralize Moktar Barakat who is now believed to be a guest of North Korea's Supreme Leader, Kim Jung-Un. We will make every effort to destroy any and all engineering and manufacturing capability, collect intelligence and, if possible, recover the captured Autonomous Team. We believe there are upwards of ten souls held by Barakat including Richard Chambers, six Autonomous Systems engineers and the Falcon Jet's flight crew. As before, pictures and bios of each are in your briefing packets. This isn't going to be an easy mission. I anticipate we'll have to fight our way out of P'yŏngsŏng to our extraction point 18 kilometers northeast at Sunan International Airport, where our friendly C-17 will meet us along with a flight of six F-35's providing close air support. Any questions so far?"

Satisfied his team was on board, Johnson continued his briefing. "Gentlemen, as outlined, we'll V-HALO into North Korea from the X-37D space vehicle which is being fueled and made ready for launch at Space Launch Complex-6, affectionately called 'Slick Six' by the locals. Tomorrow morning, we board the X-37D at 0100 hours with a planned launch time of 0300 hours. After liftoff, the X-37D will enter into a northwest polar orbit and sixty minutes later we'll begin our reentry over Antarctica. Upon initiating reentry, the X-37D will descend to one hundred thousand feet tracking toward North Korea and reduce its speed to three hundred knots. Upon arriving over P'yŏngsŏng, approximately 2100 hours local time, the X-37D will open its rear door at which point we'll depart the craft and execute a V-HALO maneuver. As before, Master Chief Davis will review the procedure. However, he assures me, other than altitude—only a mere additional sixty thousand feet—the jump will be the same as the one we performed into Islamabad. Gentlemen, Master Chief Davis will continue the briefing. See you in the morning gentlemen. HOOYAH!!"

"HOOYAH!!"

### Chamber's Counter Game — Drone Assault

Barakat, clearly unsettled by the recent failures of his drone assaults, quietly awaited Chambers arrival.

Barakat's aid, Abdul, gently knocked on his door, "Emir, Mr. Chambers is here as requested."

"Thank you Abdul, bring him in."

Barakat rose from his chair and approached Chambers as he entered. Moktar took Richard's hand and shook it forcefully. "Good morning Richard. We have much to talk about. Please sit down."

"Thank you Emir. Like you, I am acutely aware that the apparent cyberattacks on our drones demands our immediate attention. Rest assured, my team has not been idle. More importantly, I am pleased to inform you that they've implemented a solution I believe will please you," offered Chambers.

"That's wonderful news Mr. Chambers. I have grown terribly concerned."

"Well Emir, as you know, over the past few months my team has worked diligently reverse-engineering the Drone On game application. I'm pleased to tell you that we have complete understanding of the technology and have implemented a counter-response which, at the very least, will inject enough chaos to neutralize the effectiveness of Drone On and hopefully dramatically improve our drones' effectiveness," explained Chambers.

"Tell me about it."

Chambers tapped the home button on his iPad activating the Drone Assault application created by his team. "Emir, as I've shared with you before, we believe Banger Mobile Games' Drone On app is communicating with our drones through a network of communication nodes they likely piggy-back with America's cell towers. I'm pleased to inform you that we've successfully hacked into Banger's game servers enabling our Drone Assault app to be seen as just another gamer controlling both virtual and real drones. With our new onboard firmware, we believe more than eighty percent of our drones will reject Drone On control and take guidance orders from Drone Assault players. As you know, Drone Assault, published by our business partner Millennial Games, was made available on both Apple IOS and Android a week ago. Since its introduction, more than fifty million copies of our application have been downloaded by gamers across the globe making Millennial Games one of the most successful game developers in America. Truly ironic. Not only is Millennial a good technology partner, the economic rewards for our cause will be dramatic. Your holdings in Millennial has appreciated more than five hundred million dollars."

Smiling, "this is truly wonderful news. Praise Allah."

"Allah Akbar," replied Chambers as he bowed to Barakat.

### Step Up Cyber Warfare

"Emir, I have one additional thought regarding Drone Assault," said Chambers.

"I'm listening."

"Well Emir, as you know Millennial Games has distributed more than fifty million copies of Drone Assault. Unfortunately, the game is not being played as much as we would hope. The simple fact is most people are playing Drone On. Rather than just hope for more active players, I believe we should make every effort to engage allies of Islam to be committed active Drone Assault players," suggested Chambers.

"In what way?"

"Of the thousands of your embedded operatives around the world few if any are playing Drone Assault. More importantly, on any given day very few are actively involved in deploying the attack drones and the remainder are patiently waiting idly by. I believe we can significantly counter the effect Drone On is having on our drones if we engage dedicated Drone Assault players. Especially players that share your vision. Toward this end, I believe you should call upon your agents to actively play Drone Assault daily. In fact, it would be helpful if they played Drone Assault as often as possible. As such, I suggest we reach out to supporters of the Islamic State across the world and enroll them as Drone Assault players," explained Chambers.

"What needs to be done in order to implement this plan?"

"Emir, our communication mechanism via Social Media provides us immediate access to do so. We have already set up the game to be downloaded just as we do with the attack profiles. All that needs to be done now is tweet out the hashtag my team has alt the ready."

Without missing a beat, "That's a great idea. Let's do so immediately," replied Barakat.

### Game On

At 4:00pm Eastern Time cell phones across the globe emitted the all-too-recognizable tones and captured the attention of their owners to notify them that a new message awaited. This evening, Twitter carried the call to action.

@SmallTalk Feel competitive? #PLAYFAIR.

Once received, thousands of Barakat's followers entered the hashtag into the coupon fields of the now-familiar e-commerce websites maintained by Barakat's supporters. Within moments, these responsive warriors of Islam were prompted to tap the download button and install the Drone Assault app. Within thirty minutes, over ten thousand committed followers of Islam became the newest Drone Assault Cyber Warriors dedicated to ensuring that every one of Barakat's drones would be assured the greatest chance of reaching their intended targets.

While waiting for his water to boil, Adnan Boulos took a few moments to scan his Facebook pages, catching up on recent activities and photos posted by his friends and family when his iPhone chirped the arrival of new tweet. Praying he has once again been called to serve Allah, Adnan eagerly tapped the Twitter link.

As Adnan had done hundreds of times before, his iPhone quickly switched from Facebook to Twitter where he gazed upon the latest message from @SmallTalk. With his teapot whistling for his attention, Adnan highlighted the hashtag and wasted no time copying the characters to the clipboard. He exited Twitter and launched Safari where he entered the URL for one of the many e-commerce websites he had been previously provided. Adnan quickly clicked the 'Coupon Redemption' button in the upper right hand corner of the web page and deftly pasted the hashtag into the coupon field then tapped the Redeem button. The screen paused for only a moment after which Adnan was presented Drone Assault's secret download page. Chambers' people understood the importance of creating user-friendly software. Consistent with this design objective, the download progress icon spun determinedly as millions of ones and zeros were transferred over the Internet into Adnan's iPhone. Almost as quickly as it began, Adnan's new software was installed, as evidenced by a new icon on his home page—Drone Assault—accompanied by a simple message: *'Click to Join Campaign.'* Seamlessly, Adnan Boulos had become the newest member of Moktar Barakat's legion of Cyber Warriors advancing the cause of Islam and leveling the mobile gaming playing field. Drone On was being challenged head-on.

"As technology advances, it reverses the characteristics of every situation again and again. The age of automation is going to be the age of 'do it yourself',"
Marshall McLuhan

✖ ✖ ✖ ✖ ✖

# Chapter 22

◆

### The Launch and Arrival

At zero one thirty hours, twelve heroic souls quietly rode the elevator up the two hundred thirty-five foot gantry to board the tried, but not yet proven X-37D spaceplane. "The average man," pondered Johnson, "would have to be stark raving mad to climb into this contraption. But not my men. They are not your average men. They are the bravest men I have ever known." It was, however, unnerving climbing into an experimental spacecraft, sitting on top of one hundred and fifty thousand pounds of solid and liquid rocket fuel waiting to be hurtled half-way around the globe to parachute into the darkness from a hundred thousand feet. And then there's the task at hand upon arrival: Save the world.

Having secured the crew and payload, the launch support team of Slick Six rode the gantry's elevator down to the safety of the bunker buried deep below Space Launch Complex-6.

The time turned zero two thirty and Vandenberg's Mission Communications Officer (MCO) began the formal countdown; "*T-minus thirty minutes.*"

Sheriff Johnson and his team waited quietly, flat on their backs in their snug acceleration couches. As the Atlas 5 sat ready on the launch pad, the sensation of fuel coursing through the big rocket's arteries, sounds of valves opening and closing, the ubiquitous and ongoing controller communications and even now, in the 21st century, the ever present hum of electronics intruded upon everyone's thoughts.

This Atlas 5. This morning. This launch system created by the geniuses at Lockheed Martin may have the appearance of your run-of-the-mill rocket ready to deliver a generic communication satellite into orbit, but not today. Perhaps yesterday, or the day before. But most certainly not today. Today, the United States Air Force's super-secret X-37D spaceplane sat snuggly in the cocoon-like payload fairing atop the mighty Atlas 5 booster. This pointed graceful fairing will do its duty to smooth airflow and reduce the effects of drag as the Atlas made its way through the Earth's thick lower atmosphere. Aerodynamics aside, today the fairing's main purpose was more about camouflage than airflow. Johnson and his team were not just going to strike a blow against America's enemy, they were going to infiltrate a sovereign country in an outright act of war. Keeping the real nature of the Atlas 5's mission a secret was of the utmost importance. Important because deniability was fundamental to all covert operations—both successes and failures.

Inside the X37D, the crew lay on their backs, blindly facing skyward as each second arduously ticked away syncopating with twelve separate heart beats, marching toward the launch.

Johnson glanced at his wristwatch and noted the time: 0259 hours. He slid his thumb to the right and pressed the intercom button, "Gentlemen. It's an honor to serve with you. May God bless us and our mission," offered Johnson.

As if on cue, his men responded in traditional SEAL fashion, "HOOYAH!! Commander."

The MCO broke the quiet and continued the countdown, "*T-minus five...four...three. Main engine start.*" As the mighty Atlas 5's engines surged to life, the MCO offered the traditional blessing of manned spaceflight which echoed throughout time since the first U.S. manned space launch in the sixties, "*Godspeed.*"

Accompanied by a tremendous roar, the booster's engines built to full thrust as the Atlas shuttered and strained against the firm grip of Earth's gravity, until finally breaking free at T-plus one second as it struggled to lift Johnson, his men and one hundred fifty thousand pounds of rocket fuel.

Just moments into the ascent, the rocket's autonomous onboard computer executed a precise pitch and yaw maneuver to position the craft in the correct attitude for its sub-orbital polar trajectory. Shaking violently, Johnson was amazed their vehicle wasn't coming apart at the seams. Amid the overwhelming chaos, the Atlas 5 climbed upward struggling to pull away from the Earth's unrelenting hold.

"*T-plus forty-six seconds, altitude thirty-thousand feet, max Q,*" announced the MCO as Johnson's team experienced peak aerodynamic forces that resisted their craft's acceleration through the atmosphere.

"*T-plus ninety-nine seconds, SRB separation, altitude one hundred twenty thousand feet,*" called out the MCO. The sudden vibration of the Atlas' solid rocket boosters being shed reverberated through the entire spacecraft. "One hundred twenty thousand feet, my God, we're officially in outer space," exclaimed Johnson.

Moments before receiving the call from the MCO, Johnson and his men wondered when the excitement was going to end. Then the crew was suddenly surprised by the palpable silence as the chaos of the launch came to an end when the Atlas' booster engines cut off accompanied by distant vibrations announcing that things were changing.

"*T-plus two hundred and twelve seconds, altitude three hundred thousand feet, we have MECO and successful payload fairing jettison,*" announced the MCO as the Atlas 5's computers issued the Main Engine Cutoff command and fired the explosive charges separating the payload fairing encasing the X-37D. Splitting in two, the payload fairing unfolded like a flower blossoming, exposing the X-37D to space, then the two halves of the fairing dutifully followed the spent booster tumbling earthward as the second-stage Centaur began its pre-start sequence.

Johnson and his men enjoyed the short silence as the X-37D and the Centaur coasted upward, carried only by momentum provided by the now spent powerful Atlas 5 launch vehicle.

"*T-plus two hundred fifty-one seconds, altitude five hundred thousand feet, Centaur Main Engine Start, t-minus five...four...three...two...one...Main Engine Start,*" declared the MCO. Once again the men were slammed into their seats with six Gs of force as the Centaur's engine ignited. For seventeen minutes the Centaur continued accelerating, violently shaking and straining skyward toward its one hundred sixty-two-mile maximum altitude.

"*T-plus one thousand and one seconds, altitude one hundred twenty-one miles, Centaur Main Engine-Cutoff, t-minus five...four...three...two...one...Main Engine Cutoff,*" declared the MCO as the Centaur ceased its battle against gravity.

"*Orbiter Separation, t-minus five...four...three...two...one...Orbiter separation,*" announced the MCO over the headphones as the Centaur fell away and tumbled majestically, following the same fate as the Atlas booster and the payload fairing. Tumbling back to earth, unseen by Johnson and his men.

Forty minutes into the flight, the spaceplane fired its retro-rockets and began its descent toward the earth, slowing in anticipation of Johnson's team leaping from the exit door at the back of the vehicle. The MCO, per the detailed flight plan, issued his pre-jump command. "*Prepare to jump, t-minus 20 minutes.*"

Johnson depressed his microphone button, "Roger, prepare to jump."

Johnson then depressed his intercom button issuing the command to prepare for the upcoming departure from the now proven X-37D. As quickly as he issued his order, the men dutifully slapped their belt-buckles releasing their restraints. A dozen floating belts were gently pushed toward the floor of the cabin as the men quickly clambered to their feet and struggled against the forces of nature that impeded their way toward the back of the X-37D to don their backpacks, parachutes, oxygen and weapons.

"*T-minus ten minutes*," announced the MCO.

"Roger. T-minus ten minutes" snapped Johnson.

Gathered in the jump area, Master Chief Davis issued his pre-jump instructions. Each man, in a finely-tuned manner, turned to his jump buddy and diligently checked harnesses and gear. One-by-one, Davis heard each man report equipment ready and secure.

"Oxygen check, initiate depressurization," commanded Davis as Johnson grasped the pressurization lever and turned it right to vent the vital life sustaining oxygen into space. Each man once again turned to his jump buddy and scanned his face looking for signs of hypoxia, and dutifully tapped oxygen gauges strapped to their wrists confirming flow of the precious gas. One-by-one the men declared they were ready.

"*T-minus five minutes*," announced the MCO.

"Roger. T-minus five minutes, ready to deploy," replied Johnson as he raised his right hand high above his head with his thumb up, readying his men for deployment. "Gentlemen, prepare to exit. Freefall to five thousand feet. Blue team stack up on Chief Truman. Red team, stack up on Master Chief Davis. Roger?" commanded Johnson.

"HOOYAH!!

"*T-minus thirty seconds*," declared the MCO. "Roger, T-minus thirty seconds," replied Johnson.

Satisfied his men were ready, Johnson reached forward and grasped the bright red t-shaped handle recessed deep into the bulkhead and rotated it upward. As he positioned the handle, the rear door began its slow, yet deliberate journey downward, creating an inviting platform from which he and his men would leap into the void.

"*T-minus ten seconds*," announced the MCO. "*Prepare to jump.*"

"Roger," acknowledged Johnson. "Ready to jump."

"*T-minus five...four...three...two...one...Jump!*" commanded the MCO. "*Good luck gentlemen.*" Two-by-two the twelve men leapt into the darkness toward the unknown far below.

As Johnson and his team plummeted toward Earth, the X-37D's autonomous systems ignited its engines and steered the craft northeast toward Alaska, where it would land in a remote and secure area.

### President's Situation Room

Deep in the Pentagon's situation and command center, along with CIA Director Haydon, Station Chief Grant and General James, President Bennett sipped his coffee, bathed in the bluish glow of video screens encircling the entire room while they waited patiently, listening to the radio chatter as the X-37D approached its target.

General James leaned forward, "Mr. President, as you can see on the main display, the X-37D is approaching the jump point. Freedom Team is in position and ready to deploy."

"General, this is just insane," declared Bennett.

"Yes sir, I agree. But it's necessary. You have taken a bold step toward putting an end to these attacks," assured James. As they listened intently as Johnson's team deployed.

"Mr. President, the screen on the right is infrared imaging from the two jumpmasters' body-cams. Note the different blinking patterns of the infrared beacons identifying Red and Blue team members. As they descend, the two teams will begin to assemble. Pyongsong is five hundred forty-seven meters above sea level, or approximately seventeen hundred feet. Once they reach five thousand feet, they'll deploy their parachutes and execute a stacking maneuver allowing each team to be guided by their respective jumpmaster, ensuring the teams land in close proximity to one another," explained James.

"Yes General, I'm familiar with this maneuver. Once they're on the ground, how long will the mission take?" asked Bennett.

"*Freedom Red, form up. Freedom Blue, form up,*" commanded Master Chief Davis.

"Mr. President, that depends on the amount of resistance they encounter. We believe this assault is unexpected and will likely go mostly unnoticed. But, Johnson and his team are prepared for whatever they encounter. Also, as you can see on the screen to your left, we have four MQ-9 Reaper UAVs loitering at fifty thousand feet one hundred fifty miles west of Pyongyang offshore over the Bay of Korea in the Yellow Sea, armed with Hellfire missiles in the event they need air support. There is also a squadron of F-35s ready to launch from CVN-77, the George H. W. Bush."

"*Freedom, altitude sixty-five thousand feet,*" reported Chief Davis.

"How long will it take them to be on station if needed?" asked Bennett.

"Fifteen minutes for the Reapers and six minutes for the F-35s Mr. President."

"Okay. I just want Johnson and his team kept safe. Do you understand?"

"Yes Mr. President. So do I."

"*Freedom Team, altitude six thousand,*" called Davis.

"They're almost ready to deploy Mr. President. They're approaching five thousand feet right now," explained General James.

"*Freedom Team, altitude five thousand five hundred, deploy chutes! Deploy chutes!*" commanded Davis.

The twelve members of Freedom Team, hurtling toward the ground deployed their chutes, arresting their descent as they majestically began maneuvering into the stacked formation. Quietly and expertly, one-by-one each team member seamlessly docked with the parachute below him, assembling into two six-man stacks, deftly guided by their jumpmasters for a pinpoint landing within twenty meters of each other. Passing through two thousand feet Master Chief Davis issued the order to break-off and lower dingleberries. As Red team swung right and Blue left, each man released his equipment packs which were now suspended below and held secure by the ten foot lowering lines.

"Mr. President, they're orbiting the landing zone and have deployed their equipment packs. The next few minutes will be swift and chaotic," explained General James.

As each man touched down, one-by-one chutes were collapsed, pressure helmets removed, harnesses shed and each man extracted himself from the life preserving pressure suit that made V-HALO possible. Once free of the burden of the pressure suit, they gathered their equipment packs.

"Mission command, Freedom Team is on the ground," announced Johnson.

"Roger Freedom Team. We have you on satellite," replied Command.

Without uttering a word, each team gathered into two tight circles. Down on one knee with weapons at the ready, they scanned the area a mere five hundred yards from their objective.

"Humanity is acquiring all the right
technology for all the wrong reasons,"
R. Buckminster Fuller

✖ ✖ ✖ ✖ ✖

# Chapter 23

◆

### The Mission

The two teams, positioned and ready for anything, scanned the area. Johnson leaned in close and quietly began issuing orders. Short deliberate gestures. Orders no one really needed to hear because every man knew his job. And knew it well. With barely a glance, Petty Officer Bob Salem, Freedom Team's sniper, along with Petty Officer Peter Gray, leaped into action and moved undetected along a shallow culvert making their way to a water tower seventy-five yards from their objective. Hunkered down at the base of the tower, Gray peered intently through his Night Vision Goggles and scoured the area for threats as Salem made his way up the rusty rungs on the leg nearest the men.

Bob Salem was born to be a sniper. Every action, every movement completely under control and non-reactive. Petty Officer Salem was truly the most deliberate member of Johnson's team. He could be depended upon to respond to any threat quickly and efficiently. Squeezing life and death decisions into the short, imperceptible time between breaths and heartbeats. Deliberate difficult decisions. The kind of decisions that years later wake a man up in a cold sweat from a deep sleep. Decisions that truly mean the difference between life and death. Salem wasn't a cold blooded killer, he was a first rate professional and patriot.

Once Salem was settled into his high perch, Gray made his way up the tower to provide targeting support and communications. Gray wasn't a tall man, five nine at best, but he was agile and powerful. Bench pressing three twenty and running ten miles was an everyday way of life for Peter Gray. Albeit short in stature, Gray was a stand-up man respected by all.

Depressing the button strategically positioned over his left index finger, Salem reported to Johnson, "Freedom One. Eagle's Nest in position."

"Roger Eagle's Nest. Report," replied Johnson.

Both Salem and Gray surveilled the facility through high-powered night vision binoculars. Pausing for a moment, Gray tapped Salem's shoulder and directed his attention north to two guards leaning against a light post huddling close together grabbing a quick smoke. Salem made a mental note of their location and height of each man. Continuing their scan, they were amazed at just how little security this facility had. Perhaps it was ignorance or the more likely fact that it was buried deep in the center of North Korea and no one in their right mind could or would show up here. Breaking a slight smile, Salem thought to himself, "These assholes don't know Johnson and his team."

"Freedom One. Eagle's Nest. Area clear. Only two locals twenty yards from main entrance," reported Salem.

"Roger Eagle's Nest. Stand by."

Red and Blue teams moved quietly, positioning themselves within fifty yards north and south of the objective. It was a simple one story structure secured behind a ten-foot concrete wall with the obligatory and always annoying barbed wire.

"Gonzales, what do you think?" asked Johnson of Albert Gonzales, Freedom Team's breacher.

"It looks like a cinch Skipper. We can go over the wall, but if Salem neutralizes the guards, the front door looks pretty darn inviting," replied Gonzales.

"I agree. The front door it is," nodded Johnson.

"Eagle's Nest, Freedom One. Neutralize hostiles on my order. Standby," commanded Johnson.

"Roger Freedom One," snapped Salem as he jacked a round into the chamber of his sniper rifle. "Gray, give me range and wind."

"Roger. Seventy-five yards. Wind steady at five knots from the northwest," announced Gray.

Johnson, quickly gestured with his right hand pointing at Red Team then directed their attention to a line of vehicles left of the main entrance. Once acknowledged, Johnson raised his right arm, making a fist. Once assured his men were ready he issues the go signal for the two teams to move out.

"Eagle's Nest," called Johnson. "Moving out. Neutralize."

"Roger," responded Salem.

The two guards were still huddled over their cigarette, oblivious to what was about to happen. In a moment of irony, Salem pondered, he was about to free these two souls from the bondage of tyranny from their country's Supreme Leader.

Gray, ever vigilant, knew Salem's question before was going to ask it. "Wind three knots and steady."

Salem, lying prone, his rifle firmly propped up against the water tower's rail slipped into his zone as the world around him fell silent and his vision narrowed to the field of view offered by his scope. A zone of silence and tunnel vision, seeing only his two targets and hearing nothing other than the sound of his blood coursing across his eardrums. For just a moment, in the barely perceptible time between heart beats, Salem's breathing stopped momentarily, as the index finger of his right hand smoothly squeezed the trigger becoming one with his weapon as the muffled fwoop of the fully suppressed M82 goes unnoticed by his targets. Just as quickly as it began, the fifty caliber round penetrated the face of the man on the left just as he offered the cigarette to this compatriot. Before he could accept the smoldering cigarette, he felt the splash of warm blood against his face. Even through the sterile view of his sniper scope, Salem could see that target number two sensed something was wrong. Very wrong as he glared at his headless buddy. But, before the poor schlub could make sense of what just happened, Salem released the next round, fwoop, and target number two's head similarly exploded, his body falling almost simultaneously on top of his pal as the cigarette smoldered nearby.

Once again, Salem depressed his mic button, "Freedom One, targets neutralized."

"Roger Eagle's Nest. Maintain surveillance," ordered Johnson as he gave Red and Blue teams the go order.

General James leaned over to President Bennett, "Mr. President the guards have been neutralized. Johnson's men will soon breach the facility."

"I can see that General. Thank you," muttered Bennett.

The ten men made short work of the twenty yards from their holding position to the steel gate guarding the complex Chief Albert Gonzales inspected the formidable gate closely. Without missing a beat, he retrieved a shiny square packet and slipped it through the gate, strategically positioning it just behind the lock. In one quick motion, he grasped and pulled the small ring which quickly transformed the small packet into a four foot square reflective Mylar shield he fastened to the gate. With the reflective shield secured, Gonzales shaped a small ball of nano-thermite and pressed it firmly into the gate's latching mechanism, followed by the magnesium detonator and remote trigger. Joining his team huddled alongside the gate, he quietly called, "Fire in the hole." As they've done a hundred times before, the men shielded their eyes as Gonzales pressed the trigger. In a swift violent moment, the nano-thermite ignited in a blinding swoosh lighting up the darkness, yet hidden from view of anyone in the compound thanks to the Mylar shield. Just as quickly as it began, the blinding flash subsided, leaving only a smoky trail and a small puddle of melted steel on the ground as evidence of Gonzales' handiwork. Pressing gently, Gonzales swung the massive teel gates open, giving way for the next phase of the mission. Smiling, "Skipper, after you."

"Eagle's Nest, Freedom Team, over" called Johnson.

"Eagle's Nest, go ahead," replied Gray.

"Ready to breach. Are we clear?"

"Roger Freedom Team. The area is clear," responded Gray.

"Roger Eagle's Nest."

Johnson and his men gathered around the open gate low to the ground and scanned the area awaiting Johnson's order to penetrate.

"Command, Freedom Team ready to penetrate objective," called Johnson.

"Freedom Team, Command. You are free to go," responded command.

Johnson and his team leaned into a huddle and grasped hands. "Gentlemen, let's put an end to the chaos. Our mission is clear. Disrupt their ability to create their technology, recover intelligence, and at all costs, we will recover the Autonomous people. However, if any of the Autonomous team puts up any resistance, we have direct orders from the President to terminate with extreme prejudice. Everyone knows his jobs. Hernandez, you and Walker reconnoiter outside and find transportation for evacuation. Preferably something with weapons. Okay?"

"Roger Skip. We all want out of here," replied Hernandez

"Well gentlemen, are we ready?" asked Johnson

"HOOYAH!!" whispered Johnson's team.

"Let's go," commanded Johnson.

Pressing forward, the men moved into the complex and spread out securing the area. Hernandez and Walker broke left to protect their flank as they sought transportation, while the remaining eight men made their way to the main entrance of the single-story building which appeared unguarded.

"Skip, do we just knock?" quipped Chief Davis.

"Nothing is ever that easy Master Chief," replied Johnson. "Let me check in with Command."

"Command, Freedom Team. Ready to breach the building," called Johnson.

"Roger Freedom Team. You are cleared to go," responded Command.

The men huddled in the moonless darkness along both sides of the building's door as Davis, crouched low, reached over to try the handle. "Looks unlocked Skipper."

"Let's go!" ordered Johnson.

Chief Davis opened the door just a crack and inserted his fiber-optic infrared camera. He quickly scanned the area behind the door, "Skipper, the room looks clear. Seems to be about five by ten meters with a hallway directly opposite the door."

"Seems simple enough. Let's go in."

Davis, with his weapon at the ready, crouched even lower and slowly pushed the door open accompanied by the screeching sound of rusty hinges breaking the silence to reveal an empty room. Without another word, the eight men swarmed into the room and took up defensive positions opposite the hallway. Miller and Torres moved swiftly to assume positions on each side of the opening with their weapons pointed into the hallway. Confident the hallway was clear, the remainder of the team advanced as Torres and Miller stood firm providing cover.

Swiftly and silently Johnson and his men advanced into the hallway toward a corridor as Torres and Miller brought up the rear. Raising his right arm with a clinched fist Freedom Team stopped dead in its tracks as Johnson and Davis surveilled the intersecting corridor. Looking to the right, Davis pointed out a guard dressed in Arab garb. With a single nod from Johnson, Davis raised his silenced weapon and deftly squeezed the trigger releasing a single round. As with the guards outside, the fwoop of the suppressed weapon was immediately followed by the sound of his target falling to the ground. Without another word, Johnson's Blue team broke right down the corridor as Davis' Red team moved left.

"Skipper," whispered Davis into his ear mounted microphone. "All clear. Advancing down the corridor."

"Roger Red Team. We are advancing down our corridor," replied Johnson.

Both teams swiftly advanced through the building stopping short as they both arrived at a large dark open area filled with humming computers and dormant drones.

"Torres and Miller," called Johnson in a hushed tone. "Search the room and set the explosives as we check out what's behind the door at the far end."

"Roger Skipper."

Without another word, Torres and Miller moved into the room and silently began cracking open computers and extracting hard drives as the remaining six men advanced toward the closed door.

"Skipper," whispered Davis as he swung open the door. "This is eerily quiet and seems too easy."

"I agree. Let's count our blessings."

As Johnson peered into the room, they saw what appeared to be a community room and kitchen surrounded by six smaller rooms which Johnson assumed, hoped, were the Autonomous Team's sleeping quarters.

"Hold," whispered Johnson as one of the doors began to open. The six men, invisible in the darkness, planted themselves against the walls and crouched low with their weapons pointed at the door. The shadowy outline of a single male slowly emerged rubbing his eyes, unaware of Chief Walker crouched low against the wall with his dark yet shiny Ka-Bar knife at the ready. Without a sound Walker rose up slowly behind the man. In one smooth move, Walker grabbed him, clasped his hand across his mouth and placed the cold sharp steel of his Ka-Bar against the intruder's ribs. The man, struggled in terror, clawed futilely at Walker's arm as he tried to make sense of what was happening.

"Quiet," whispered Walker as Johnson emerged from the darkness.

Standing before the intruder, Johnson leaned in close and whispered, "we're U.S. Special Forces. Make one sound and Chief Walker will end it right here and now. Understand?"

The man's arms collapsed to his side as Walker sensed a sigh of relief.

"Chief Walker is going to release you. Do not make a move or utter a sound. Understand?" cautioned Johnson.

As the man nodded in understanding, Walker relaxed his grasp across the man's mouth yet firmly grabbed his shoulder with his Ka-Bar still in position.

Holding his finger to his mouth, Johnson reminded the man to be quiet. "I'm SEAL Team Commander Johnson. Who are you?  Quietly."

Fighting for air and shaking from adrenaline the man stuttered, "Uh…I'm Will Smith of Autonomous Systems."

"Okay Mr. Smith. How many Autonomous personnel are here?" asked Johnson.

"There are only five of us. The rest have been killed," explained Smith.

"Who are they?"

"The killed people?" asked Smith.

"No. Who's still alive?"

Still frazzled and fighting the adrenalin surge, "Richard Chambers, Liz Collins, Gary Sasaki, Akio Chan and me. The rest are dead. They were killed either in the jet or shortly after our arrival."

"Okay Mr. Smith. Are they here in the building?  Are there any guards?"

"Yes, they're asleep in their rooms. No. No. There's usually only one guard in the building at night and, I believe, there are guards outside," offered Smith.

"Okay Mr. Smith. Stand over there with Chief Walker. And don't make a sound. I assure you, Chief Walker is a patient man but will not hesitate to silence you. Permanently! Understand?"

Smith nodded vigorously as Walker took him by the arm and shuttled him back near the entry way.

"We're going to get you out of here," assured Johnson.

Slowly opening the door next to Smith's room, Davis peered inside and saw someone asleep. Swiftly Johnson and Davis entered the room and quietly approached the bed. In one fluid motion Davis placed his hand over the man's mouth and pinned him to the bed. Startled, the man awakened with his eyes bulging in fear as Davis held him firmly against the bed in spite of his protestations.

"Shush! Be quiet. We're U.S. Special Forces here to rescue you. Are you going to be quiet?" asked Davis.

Like Smith, the man nodded reassuringly immediately ceasing his resistance.

"I'm Commander Johnson. Who are you? Quietly!"

As Davis slowly removed his hand from the man's mouth he began blathering on. "Oh my God. Is it really you? Are we saved?"

Davis quickly slipped his hand back over the man's mouth, "shut up. Just tell me quietly who you are," commanded Johnson.

Fumbling for words, "I'm Sasaki. Gary Sasaki."

"Nice to meet you Mr. Sasaki. Are you ok?" asked Johnson.

"Yes. Yes. Now I am," replied Gary. "I can't believe it. Is this really happening?"

"Yes Mr. Sasaki. It is really happening. We have much to do and it will be a challenge to get you out of here safely. This is Petty Officer Summers, please follow him. I shouldn't have to remind you to be quiet and cooperative. He will not hesitate to silence you. Do you understand?"

"Yes sir. Yes! I understand," as Sommers escorted Gary Sasaki over to Walker and Smith.

As Johnson exited Sasaki's room, he observed Smith and Truman exiting the adjacent room with a man in tow.

"Skipper, this is Akio Chan. He's been extremely cooperative," explained Truman.

"Great, take him over to Walker. Keep him quiet."

Davis continued to explore the remaining rooms finding all but one empty which was clearly occupied by two people. He and Smith slipped into the room followed by Johnson. The three men silently crept up and approached the sleeping occupants. In one fluid motion, Davis and Smith pinned the two sleepers to the bed and placed their hands across their mouths. Awakened and overwhelmed by terror, the man and woman struggled in vain against the two strong men that held them firmly to the bed.

"Please be quiet. I am Commander Johnson with U.S. Special Forces. This is a rescue mission. Do you understand?"

Liz Collins' eyes bulged as she nodded enthusiastically and tears began streaming down her face. Richard, just laid there in shock, trying to determine if he was awake or asleep.

"I presume you're Ms. Collins. And you. You must be Richard Chambers. Am I correct?" asked Johnson.

Liz and Richard nod vigorously against the firm grips of Davis' and Smith's strong callused hands clasped across their mouths.

"Mr. Chambers. We are concerned that you may not be willing to be rescued. Am I correct?" asked Johnson.

Shaking his head side-to-side, Chambers tried vehemently to assure Johnson that he wanted to be rescued.

"Mr. Chambers, I'm going to instruct Chief Davis and Smith to release the both of you. I assure you, if you put up any resistance or make a sound, they will not hesitate to terminate you here and now. Do you understand?"

Liz whimpered faintly as she nodded again and again her understanding. Richard, still wallowing in disbelief, nodded just once assuring Johnson he understood.

Convinced that Liz and Richard wanted to be rescued, Johnson signaled Davis and Wilson to relax their grip on the couple. Releasing their hold, Davis and Smith stepped back as Liz jumped from the bed and threw her arms around Johnson, hugging him tightly.

"Please Ms. Collins," whispered Johnson. "This isn't necessary. We have much to do and too little time. We must move swiftly," assured Johnson as he gently yet forcefully removed Liz's arms.

"Mr. Chambers, before we leave, we need to collect every bit of information possible. My team has already begun dismantling your computers, collecting the hard drives and scouring your paper-files. Is there anything we need that you are aware of?"

"Yes. Yes. There's a locked file cabinet in the work room," offered Chambers.

"Okay. Do you have access or do we need to open it?" asked Johnson.

"No. I don't have the key. Only Barakat's people have access," whispered Chambers as Liz pulled herself close to him.

"Richard. Richard," she whispered. "Is this really happening?"

"I guess so Liz. I guess so."

"Okay folks, get dressed. Please do so quickly and quietly. Do you understand?"

Under Johnson's watchful eye Chambers and his people feverishly began moving about dressing and gathering what little personal belongings they had.

"Hernandez, Freedom Leader, over," called Johnson over the radio. "What's the status of transportation?"

"Skipper, we've secured two vehicles. One truck and one armored carrier armed with a fifty cal and plenty of ammo. We're ready to go out front," replied Hernandez.

"Great. We're on our way. Be ready."

"Eagle's Nest. Freedom Team Over," called Johnson.

"Eagle's Nest, go ahead," replied Salem.

"What's the status outside?"

"Skipper, the area's clear. Over."

"Roger Eagle's Nest. We will be out in ten. Stand by," ordered Johnson.

Assembled in the common room, Chambers pointed out the locked file cabinet. Following Johnson's directions, once again Gonzales shaped a small ball of nano-thermite and pressed it into the lock that secured the fire-proof cabinet, then placed the magnesium detonator.

Gonzales advised the Autonomous Team to cover their eyes, and called out, "Fire in the hole." The room was momentarily illuminated by the swoosh of the ignited nano-thermite. As the chaos subsided, the molten slag dripped to the ground. Gonzales slipped his Ka-Bar in between the door and the frame and pried open the cabinet reveling the valuable contents.

"Take everything," ordered Johnson as Gonzales retrieved an empty pack and filled it with the contents of the cabinet.

"Let's go! Let's go!" ordered Johnson. "Move out!"

Swiftly Chief Davis and Johnson took the point as Chambers and his team congregated into a tight scrum behind the men with Gonzales taking up the rear. Davis scanned the corridor leading away from the common room, then slipped through the doorway and made his way to the connecting corridor. Once satisfied the path was clear, Davis raised his left arm and called the cadre forward. Except for the movies, Chambers and his people were unfamiliar with tactical procedures and progressed clumsily along with the seasoned professionals. Huddled behind Johnson and Davis, the pack scampered close behind.

"Command, Freedom Team, over," called Johnson.

"Freedom Team. Command. Go ahead."

"Freedom Team ready to mount transportation. ETA to extraction point twenty minutes. Over," declared Johnson.

"Roger Freedom Team. ETA twenty minutes. Your transportation is en route and will be on the ground upon your arrival," replied Command. "Advise when mounted and we'll call directions and traffic."

"Roger Command," replied Johnson.

"Gentlemen, let's go. Our rides are waiting."

Under the shadow of the dark North Korean moonless morning, thirteen souls emerged from the building greeted by Hernandez and Walker. Johnson and Davis quickly and efficiently assisted their charges into the vehicles. Claiming his rightful seat up front in the lead vehicle, Johnson gestured to Hernandez to move out. "Let's pick up Eagle's Nest."

With engines roaring, the two North Korean vehicles trundle along to collect Salem and Gray perched high above in the water tower. "Eagle's Nest. Freedom Team. We're clear, what's the status?"

"The area is clear," replied Gray. We're coming down and will meet you on the roadway."

Salem slung his rifle over his shoulder and began the short descent down the water tower's ladder. He dropped to the ground alongside Gray who was crouched low on one knee with his weapon positioned scanning the area.

"Well," chuckled Salem. "Now for the hard part."

"Really," laughed Gray. "Catching a flight out of North Korea. What a joke!"

"Johnson has never let us down before. Here they come. Let's go."

The two vehicles swung wide in a long arch with doors open, screeching to a halt in front of the two men. Without missing a beat Salem jumped into Johnson's vehicle and Gray took a seat in the other.

"Let's go! Let's go!" yelled Johnson as the men's feet barely left the ground.

"Command. Freedom Team. We are en route."

"Roger Freedom Team. We have you. Continue north for one klick then take the first left west on AH1. You have thirty klicks to go," instructed the controller.

Speeding away from the complex, the two vehicles barreled along the unpaved road at sixty kilometers per hour kicking up a cloud of dust in their wake.

"Freedom Team, ETA twenty minutes," called the controller.

"Roger, ETA twenty minutes," replied Johnson.

"Command. Freedom Air en route. ETA fifteen minutes," called the C-17's first officer.

Sitting on the edge of his chair, President Bennett watched the satellite image of Johnson and his men as they made their way to North Korea's main airport. "This is just crazy. Out of your mind crazy," exclaimed Bennett. "How are we going to pull this extraction off?"

"Well, Mr. President, the first phase of the mission is complete. Now all we need is a little luck," commented General James. "As you can see, the C-17 and its escort of eight F-35s are about to cross the border. We anticipate Freedom Team will encounter ground resistance at the airport and Freedom Air is likely to encounter the threat of surface to air missiles as well as aerial engagement. The F-35s are the most advanced aircraft in our arsenal. Along with the F-35s are Hellfire equipped MQ-9 Reapers on station to neutralize Surface to Air Missile threat and cut a clear path for the C-17."

"Freedom Team," called the controller. "ETA twelve minutes. The path ahead looks clear."

The general silence of the Command Center was suddenly broken by the alternating high low squeal of the alert klaxon. "Mr. President, North Korea has just scrambled a flight of six MIG-29Bs out of Pukch'ang en route to intercept Freedom Air.

"Freedom Team. ETA six minutes. Your ride is en route. ETA upon your arrival. Meet your ride at the south end of Runway One. Over," instructed the controller.

"Roger. ETA six minutes. So far, we haven't encountered any resistance but expect to at our destination," replied Johnson.

"Gentlemen we are almost there. Be ready!" declared Johnson.

Flying low and hugging the North Korean terrain, the C-17 and its F-35 escorts progressed toward their destination. "Command. Freedom Air. ETA three minutes," called the first officer.

"Prepare for arrival," commanded Major Samuels, piloting the massive transport.

Careening around the corner onto the airport access road, Johnson and his team made a mad dash toward the only resistance—a flimsy chain-link fence.

"Don't bother knocking. Just go through it. Just go through it," ordered Johnson.

"Roger Skipper," replied Hernandez. "Wilco!"

"Freedom Attack, Command," called the controller to Lt. Colonel Garrett Lynch commanding the flight of the F-35s.

"Roger Command. Freedom Attack. Go ahead," replied Lynch.

"You have six bogies, fifty miles and closing at your twelve o'clock," announced the controller.

"Roger Command. We have them. Are we clear to engage?" asked Lynch.

General James, looked at President Bennett awaiting his orders. "Mr. President, it's your call."

"We are fully committed. We have to get our people out. Engage," ordered Bennett.

James, acknowledged Bennett's order, and gave the go ahead to the controller.

"Freedom Attack, Command. You are go to engage."

"Roger Command. Freedom Attack is go to engage."

"Attack Two, Attack One," called Colonel Lynch. "You are go with Amraam launch against bogies. I'll engage lead bogie."

The two men slid their fingers across the massive full color touch-sensitive liquid crystal displays as they placed their cursors on their respective targets and established missile lock. Targeting confirmation was prominently displayed on their helmet's virtual heads-up displays, as their bomb bay doors swung open and their Ratheon AIM 120 missiles descend below the belly of their F-35s.

"Target confirmation," announced Lynch.

"Roger. Target confirmation," replied Lieutenant David Cranston flying Attack Two.

Lynch gave the fire command and both pilots flipped up the red safety cover protecting the missile fire control switch on the F-35s' throttles. In one fluid motion, their left thumbs pressed the fire buttons and two AIM 120 missiles dropped from their slings into the cold night air as their engines ignited. In the blink of an eye, the powerful Amraams began their journey toward their destination, dutifully plotted and displayed on each pilot's colorful display.

"Control. Missiles away," declared Lynch.

"Roger Freedom Attack. Confirm missiles away. ETA twenty seconds," replied the controller.

Five...four...three...two...one... the MIG-29s futilely tried to evade the most advanced air-to-air missile in the world. Their efforts, however, proved fruitless as they were vaporized in two balls of fire lighting up the night sky.

"Freedom Attack. Targets destroyed," called the controller. "Two are retreating and two are continuing on."

"Roger Command," responded Lynch. "Attack Two, target the northern bogie and I'll take the south," commanded Lynch.

"Attack Two. Roger," replied Cranston.

Once again, Attack One and Attack Two tapped their LCD screens selecting their respective targets.

"Fire," commanded Lynch as he and Attack Two pressed their fire buttons releasing two more Amraams toward their targets.

"These Aim 120s make our job too damn easy. Kinda takes all the fun out of it," chuckled Cranston.

"So true Attack Two. So true," agreed Lynch.

Freedom Attack continued pressing forward clearing the way for the C-17's imminent arrival at Sunan International Airport.

"Command, Freedom Team. On station," called Johnson.

"Roger Freedom Team. Your ride is inbound. Stand by, replied the controller.

"Skipper," announced Davis. "We have company."

"Okay gentlemen, let's stand our ground," ordered Johnson. "Keep the civilians in the vehicles."

"Freedom Team," called the controller. "We see unfriendlies converging on your position. Flight Attack is inbound to provide air support."

"Roger Command," replied Johnson. "We could sure use the help."

"Skipper. Look! Our ride is on final," announced Davis.

"So is our support. There they are. Go Navy!" smiled Johnson as he pointed toward the flight of F-35s.

Johnson and his team crouched around the vehicles in preparation to defend their position just when their attackers were consumed in a ball of fire from three Hellfire missiles deployed by the Reapers loitering high above.

"Outstanding!" exclaimed Salem. "Just outstanding!"

Freedom Attack's F-35s began orbiting the airport at five hundred feet, providing cover just as the C-17 passed low overhead, and moments later planted its wheels hard onto the tarmac. Immediately, the pilot dumped his flaps and the air filled with the roar of the thrust reversers as the massive craft's nose pitched downward with brakes smoking. Major Samuels brought the massive jet to a stop in less than two thousand feet and swung a hard right, followed by a high-speed taxi back down Runway One to where Johnson and his team were waiting. As the C-17 approached Runway One's threshold, once again the pilot pivoted the massive jet and lined it up for departure as the crew chief lowered the ramp in anticipation of receiving his passengers.

Holding their defensive position protecting their charges, Johnson instructed Davis and Hernandez to move Chambers and his people toward the waiting jet.

"Skip, we have more visitors," declared Gray.

"I see them. Hold your ground men," ordered Johnson.

Five troop transports sped to within one hundred yards of Johnson's people and came to a screeching halt as one hundred armed North Korean regulars swarmed the tarmac.

"Fire at will," ordered Johnson as three F-35s strafed the attacking troops. Two trucks immediately exploded, consumed in raging balls of fire as two of the F-35s hit their targets with 2,000-pound GBU-32 JDAM bombs.

"Awesome. Go Navy!" declared Gonzales.

While the men were consumed by the demands of the fire fight, the C-17's ramp touched the ground. Hernandez hustled his charges to the aircraft and up the waiting ramp.

"Let's get out of here!" commanded Johnson as they began falling back toward their waiting ride.

"Damn!" exclaimed Torres as he took a round in the leg. Swiftly, Miller and Smith grabbed their comrade under his arms and high-tailed it toward the waiting transport. The team scampered up the ramp of the jet then turned around and dropped to their knees, returning fire as the massive jet began its take off roll. Major Samuels guided the C-17 as the first officer quickly advanced the throttles.

"Captain, ramp still extended," called the crew chief.

"Retract as we go," ordered Samuels. "Were out of here!"

"Okay men. Hold on, this is going to be steep. Our job's done. Now it's up to the Navy and the Air Force," declared Johnson as the big jet accelerated down Runway One. Against the shaking and rumbling of the mighty jet's struggle to get air born, the fuselage was pelted with small arms fire, poking several holes in the fuselage, but fortunately not hitting anyone or anything vital. Committed to protecting Freedom Air, the F-35s continued strafing the attackers, giving the jet time to get airborne. At sixteen hundred feet down the runway, the massive jet's nose rotated skyward as Major Samuels executed an amazing short field takeoff, leaving Runway One far behind. Banking right, the big jet began a mad dash toward South Korea, only seventy miles to the south.

For Major Samuels, this leg of the mission was simple. Rather than piloting the massive transport and hugging terrain, as he did penetrating this sovereign nation, his job is far less complicated. As the sun began to peek over the horizon, Samuel's task was simply an all-out balls-to-the-wall dash to the DMZ, counting on the F-35s to run interference.

Bennett was ecstatic and exhausted. "I can't believe it! They did it."

"I am concerned for the security of our great Nation; not so much because of any threat from without, but because of the insidious forces working from within," General Douglas MacArthur

✖ ✖ ✖ ✖ ✖

# Chapter 24

◆

### Drone Assault Gaming

Like any other Starbucks, America's favorite coffee shop is jam-packed with people in a hurry, yet content to wait in the glacially slow lines. This line, trailing out the door did little to dissuade the coffee connoisseur, devotee, or aficionado in quest of the perfect caffeinated beverage. Unfortunately, the joy of anticipation is often tempered by the constant underlying and festering irritability. Irritability unique to coping with a line that for some inexplicable reason, day-after-day, moved so slow it gave rise to ever present sub-audible grousing and bellyaching or impersonal commentary among patrons. Commentary adding to the perpetual din of new-age music droning on in the background augmented by the one or two fellows who perpetually believed *everyone* was interested in hearing their thoughts and opinions.

Already ensconced in his favorite over-stuffed chair, Ricky Granger kicked back and enjoyed his Double Espresso Macchiato generously financed by Banger Mobile Games. Since discovering Drone On, Ricky hasn't paid a penny indulging his high-end coffee habit typically out of the economic reach of most high school freshmen. A daily caffeine fix satisfied for free. Free that is as long has he continued executing Drone On campaigns. "Hell," pondered Ricky. "Playing Drone On isn't all that difficult. And leveling up is easy." Smiling, Ricky mutters, "Crap, just show up and you get easy cash. Beats looking for a job after school."

"Hey Ricky," shouted Pete, as he navigated the obstacle course of humanity.

"Hi Pete. Here's your cappuccino. Courtesy of Banger," chuckled Ricky.

With his iPad in hand, Pete slid into the chair opposite his Drone On buddy. "Thanks Ricky," as he snatched up the hot cup of foamy ambrosia. "You know, I think I found a better deal," offered Pete.

"Yeah. What's that?"

"Last night I downloaded Drone Assault. In one campaign, I leveled up three times and earned twenty-five bucks. Can you believe it? Twenty-five bucks. You gotta download it."

"Are you kidding? Twenty-five bucks on one campaign? Cool. Give me a second to install it." Tapping his iPad with the agility of a concert pianist, Ricky installed the new app. "Ok...almost done. There! It's installed. Pete, we have a half hour before class. Want to execute a campaign?"

"Sure, why not? You pick the mission, I'll join you," replied Pete.

Ricky navigated Drone Assault's menus like a seasoned user and was automatically assigned the Atlanta campaign. "That was easy." With a chuckle, "Looks like they pirated Drone On. OK...I'm in. I just sent you an invitation to join me in the Atlanta campaign. Pete, there's one unassigned fleet. Quick, grab it before someone else does."

"Got the invite. Wait a minute. Almost there. Hold on. Hold on. OK! I'm in and in control."

"Super. Holy crap! Pete, you're not going to believe this. Our target is the Bank of America building. Just like in New York the other night."

"Who cares? I just want to make more bank. Let's do it commander," snapped Pete.

The boys maneuvered their drones. Pete southbound on US 85 with Ricky coming from the south, also following US 85 with two more fleets of drones inbound from the east and west.

"We're going to level this place, Pete," declared Ricky.

"You got it buddy. Absolutely...Mass destruction. Holy crap! Did you see that?" burst Pete.

"Yes. It looked like we were fired upon. I lost two drones," reported Ricky.

"They missed me. I'm descending to three hundred feet. Hopefully my drones will be under the radar."

"Me too," replied Ricky. "It looks like I'm just above the road. There we go. Targeting now. Do you have the target?" asked Ricky.

"Yep! Target lock! Right between the crosshairs," responded Pete.

"Great. All we have to do is follow the magenta line and form up from the south and follow Peachtree to the building. Let's stay left of the road to avoid the buildings on the right," suggested Ricky.

"Roger commander."

Ricky swept his right hand up to the Drone Assault control panel on his iPad and gently tapped the button titled Attacks. As his thumb made contact with the iPad's cold shiny surface, the Attacks button exploded into an animated bubble offering a generous list of options and scenarios. Like most fourteen-year-old boys, Ricky struggled with focusing. Whether attention deficit disorder, or Ricky just liked change, it doesn't much matter. He was always at the ready for something new. Fliting from one game to another, Ricky was drawn to anything novel and refreshing, like a moth to a flame. And there it was. Something he hadn't seen before. There, under the Attacks button he found what every fourteen-year-old boy sought and enjoyed: Chaos!! Difficulty Level 12.

"Hey Pete. Let's execute attack plan Chaos!!" called Ricky. "It's difficulty level 12. It should pay off big time."

"Bitchin'. Sounds perfect," said Pete. "Attack Plan Chaos!! it is."

Ricky commenced a mock countdown, "five...four...three...two...one...execute!" and both boys tapped the word Chaos!! on their iPads. Immediately, without a pause, their squadron of eighteen remaining drones climbed high, with Ricky's lead drone broadcasting what appeared to be real-time video of the squadron's attack on the Bank of America building this quiet morning in Atlanta. From the lead drone's perspective, Pete's and Ricky's machines were swirling in a tight, chaotic ball of technology and explosives while the other two flights of drones orbited directly over the target. Resembling a swarm of bees, the drones appeared to fly tight complex random patterns yet, in reality, they followed mathematically defined paths with the precision of electrons orbiting an atom's nucleus. Passing within inches of one another, the chaotic ball of drones grew tighter, each losing its personal identity as they melded together into a surging mass of chaos and destruction. The ascending ball of drones reached its apogee and suddenly, on order from a series of invisible 'ones and zeros' buried deep in Drone Assault's programming, the tight collection of destruction began a downward spiral with the Bank of America building and plaza centered squarely in the black and white Targeting Window. Positioned dead-center between the Targeting Window's cross hairs, Ricky's and Pete's target grew larger. The drones continued their spiral dance, then suddenly, without notice the compact ball of drones burst into a flurry of individuals each descending on a randomly assigned area of the Bank building. Each drone swooped and tumbled as if out of control giving meaning to this particular attack's name. As quickly as the tightly packed drones burst into a flurry of chaos, they each, without a moment's hesitation, dove into the building as the lead drone coldly broadcast the death and destruction. As if satisfied that the fleet of drones achieved its objective, the lead drone tilted forward and began its run at the Bank of America building in a final salute to a job well done. Mission Complete and Level Up flashed across both boy's iPad screens followed by a text message confirming their Starbucks cards had each been credited with twenty-five dollars.

Looking up from their devices, Ricky and Pete smiled and finally took a breath. As if on cue, the boys leapt toward one another converging in a raucous high-five that went unnoticed by the coffee loving throng absorbed in their quest for the ultimate caffeine experience.

### The Evening News

"Good evening. Welcome back to UNN's Evening Report. Gretchen, in the past twenty-four hours, once again America fell victim to more than a dozen drone attacks inflecting damage and injury across the country," said Stoddard.

"Yes Jeff. It's just so disheartening that these attacks continue. Today, a few of the attacks were devastating while, once again, for some unknown reason others resulted in minimal damage. Unique to today, the attack on the Bank of America building in Atlanta resulted in massive damage. In Atlanta, most of the drones detonated into the Bank of America building while a few crashed into Lake Clara Meer in Piedmont Park, two miles northeast of Bank of America Plaza. Truly confusing indeed," offered Gretchen Chen.

"Gretchen, equally interesting are the reports that something happened in North Korea today. According to a video posted by KCNA, North Korea's Central News Agency, American forces invaded North Korea attacking Sunan International Airport north of Pyongyang. Let's take a look at the video," offered Stoddard.

The image of Stoddard and Chen was seamlessly replaced by a chaotic scene, reportedly on the taxiway at Sunan International Airport, of a North Korean military contingent charging two vehicles clearly being protected by a team of a dozen unknown soldiers engaged in a firefight. As the two forces exchanged gun fire, the video showed low on the horizon what appeared to be a number of fighter jets circling the airport. Captured on video were two North Korean armored assault vehicles as they charged the forces protecting the vehicles at the end of the runway. Suddenly, the oncoming vehicles were consumed in a ball of fire, apparently from a missile attack.

The camera shifted position slightly to show a large transport jet, a United States Air Force C-17, arriving from the south with landing gear extended as it approached low over the two vehicles protected by what appeared to be U.S. Special Forces. The C-17 passed low over the two vehicles, then landed firmly with a cloud of smoke billowing from the tires as the massive transport strained to stop on the runway. Coming to a swift stop, the C-17 swung sharply to the right as six Navy F-35s strafed the oncoming North Korean military.

One after another the F-35s screamed in low over the airport, protecting the C-17 and the ground personnel as the jet transport taxied swiftly to the end of the runway, toward the waiting vehicles. As the C-17 approached the end of the runway, the gigantic aircraft began pivoting to the right and at the same time started lowering its rear cargo ramp. Just as the jet finished its turnaround, five people emerged from the waiting vehicles, accompanied by four armed troops, and then made a mad dash toward the waiting jet. Suddenly, one of the soldiers stumbled to the ground, apparently wounded, was swiftly picked up by two of his comrades and hauled up the ramp of the waiting jet. The remaining eight troops continued engaging the oncoming North Koreans as they backed up the ramp while returning gunfire. Just as the last member of the ground forces stepped on the ramp, the massive jet began accelerating down the runway retracting the cargo ramp as it rolled.

"Gretchen, this is simply amazing. Unfortunately, we have not been able to confirm the purpose of this mission or who the five people were that emerged from the vehicles. Regardless, North Korea's Supreme Leader, Kim Jung-Un, is not happy and is threatening to attack America and South Korea."

"Tonight, we're joined once again by UNN's military correspondent, General Arnold," said Gretchen as the General's image appeared on the right side of the screen. "General, what light can you shed on this exciting and dynamic situation in North Korea?"

"Gretchen, this is a very interesting situation to say the least. According to reports from North Korean news agencies, and the video coverage, it's obvious that U.S. Special Forces were on a mission to recover five people from North Korea. As to who these people are, one can only speculate. I can, however, presume that they are important. So important that President Bennett was willing to invade and attack North Korea."

"General, can you provide some insight into the events captured on video by KCNA?" asked Stoddard.

"Certainly Jeff. This was a classic extraction strategy. I can only presume that the twelve troops, likely U.S. Special Forces, recovered the five people being held somewhere in North Korea in close proximity to Sunan International Airport. The flight of F-35s provided air cover and very likely escorted the C-17 as it penetrated North Korean airspace. Likely from Osan air base in South Korea. My guess is the F-35s launched from the aircraft carrier George H. W. Bush, which is currently on station in the Sea of Japan. As for the massive explosion earlier in the video that destroyed the two North Korean armored vehicles, it looked like a Hellfire missile which may have been deployed by a UAV orbiting above, providing intelligence and coverage."

"Well General Arnold, as always, we appreciate your insights and explanations. Since this mission was so well covered, I anticipate we'll be hearing from the President soon," said Stoddard.

Nodding, "Jeff and Gretchen. The pleasure is all mine. God bless our troops. Good night," replied Arnold.

### After the Evening News

After watching the evening news with his parents, Pete sat in awe of what he had just heard. Suddenly, looking more than a little disturbed, Pete leapt from the couch.

"What's up Peter? You ok?" asked his dad.

"Uh...nothing Dad. Yes. I'm fine. Just going to my room. I, uh, remembered I have some homework to finish," explained Pete, clearly a little shaken.

Pete dashed up the stairs toward his room and swiftly closed the door behind him. For just a moment Pete was stalled in the middle of the room, dropped onto his bed, shaking and covered in sweat, stricken by the sudden realization that he and Ricky may have been involved in the drone attack in Atlanta. Crunched in the fetal position, Pete feared the worst when suddenly the chirping of his iPhone announced he had a WhatsApp message from Ricky.

*Pete, did you see the news?*

*Pete. Are you there?*

Hesitating out of fear and confusion, Pete finally picked up his iPhone and stared at Ricky's messages. Trying to contain himself, Pete began tapping out a message.

*Yeah. I saw the news. Holy shit. Was that us? Shit man! This has to be a coincidence. Right!?! Call me.*

Pete's iPhone rang with Ricky's crazy expression filling the screen. "Ricky, what's going on?"

Overwhelmed by fear, Ricky responded, "It has to be a coincidence. There's no way we had anything to do with this. No way!"

Tap…tap…tap…"Pete…please open the door," said Pete's Mom.

"Hold on Ricky. My mom is knocking at my door."

"Okay. Crap. My mother is knocking at my door too. What in hell is going on?" wondered Ricky.

As Pete slowly opened his door, he was confronted by his obviously upset mother. "Peter, there are two FBI agents downstairs wanting to talk with you."

Shaken, "Mom, I didn't do anything. Nothing! Why do they want to see me?" asked Pete.

"I don't know Peter. They didn't explain. They just want to talk with you. They're waiting in the living room."

Pete timidly descended the stairs behind his mother and made his way into the Zell's modest living room where his father was standing with two ominous and serious looking gentlemen.

As Pete entered the living room, the closest gentleman presented his FBI identification, "Peter Zell? I'm FBI Special Agent Summers and this is Special Agent Gates. "Please sit down, we need to speak with you."

Pete, overwhelmed with fear made his way over to the couch and sat down tentatively.

Unknown to Pete, the same scenario was playing out at Ricky's house.

Sitting on the couch across from Pete and his parents, Agent Summers began. "Peter. May I call you Pete?" he asked.

"Uh…Yeah. Sure," replied Pete. "Why not?"

"Well Pete, first, I want you to understand that you haven't done anything wrong. This is an informal interview to discuss your use of the mobile game Drone On. According to our information, you and your friend, umm…let me see, yes, Ricky Granger are active players of this game. Is that correct?" asked Summers.

"Yeah. I guess so. I didn't do anything wrong. Did I?" stuttered Pete.

"I understand Pete. Please relax. I assure you, you are not in any trouble," said Summers. "Apparently you and Ricky are pretty good gamers."

"Yeah. I guess so," said Pete.

"Well Pete, from the information we have, you and Ricky are in the top one percent of Drone On game players in America. Because of your skill level at Drone On we at the FBI want to speak with you."

"Wait a minute!" exclaimed Pete's father. "You're here about a game? What's going on here? Is Pete under arrest?"

"Not at all Mr. Zell. Peter is in no trouble whatsoever. The situation is very complicated and to say the least, unconventional indeed. What I'm about to tell you is a matter of national security and has to remain in the strictest confidence. Any disclosure of this conversation is a federal offense and will result in severe penalties. Do you understand Mr. and Mrs. Zell?" asked Summers. "Peter, do you understand?"

Pete and his parents nodded in agreement.

"Yes. We won't say anything to anyone. So, please Agent Summers, what's going on?" asked Pete's father.

"Well, Mr. and Mrs. Zell, Pete, I'm certain you're aware that America is suffering constant attacks from thousands of automated drones we believe conducted by Islamic State Jihadists embedded in America. The sad fact is, since these attacks began, the U.S. Government has been unable to implement any effective defense against these drones mostly due to their small size and speed. Basically, these vehicles fly under the radar, so to speak, making conventional defense options ineffective. That is, until now."

"Are you telling me that somehow Pete's playing of this game…what's it called? Drone On has something to do with these attacks?" asked Pete's dad.

"Yes sir. In fact, Drone On has proven to be the most effective response to neutralizing the drone attacks. Very simply, we've developed technology that allows Drone On players to take control of real drones within the virtual world of the Drone On game. As a result of game playing by people like Pete and his friend Ricky, many of the attacking drones have been neutralized."

"How is this possible?" asked Pete's father.

"Mr. Zell, I'm certain you can appreciate that the technology is Top Secret. Suffice it to say, when people, like Peter here play the game, the Drone On software guides many of the enemy drones, unbeknownst to the player, to safe areas where they crash away from people and property," explained Summers.

Pete, finally appreciating the implications of what he has been doing and that he's not in trouble, asked, "So me and Ricky playing Drone On caused real drones that are attacking a building to crash someplace else? You mean we stopped the attacks?"

"Yes Pete. That's it in a nutshell," replied Summers.

"So," asked Pete's father, "what brings you here tonight scaring the crap out of all of us?"

"I'm sorry about scaring you and your family Mr. Zell. That was never our intent. Unfortunately, it seems there is no unthreatening way for the FBI to knock on anyone's door. Whenever the FBI shows up, it's usually a little scary. But, tonight, we're here to ask permission for Pete to come with us to Washington to help us better understand how we can improve Drone On's effectiveness in responding to the Islamic State's continued reign of terror in America and worldwide. I promise you, Peter is not in trouble and will be treated with the utmost respect and courtesy. In fact, visiting Washington and FBI headquarters should be exciting for him. Mr. Zell, the simple fact is your son is a hero, and very likely the most effective deterrent against these heinous and ongoing attacks," explained Summers.

"We have a jet waiting to take Pete, Ricky and you and Mrs. Zell to FBI headquarters to meet with Director Teich to discuss their ongoing participation in advancing the Drone On initiative. Mr. Zell, I presume this is okay with you and your wife," asserted Summers.

"Well, Agent Summers, I can't leave work and my wife has to care for Pete's younger brother and sister."

"I understand. Mr. Zell, certainly we would like your consent, but, we have a Federal Order to take Pete with us this evening," as Summers removed a folded package of papers from his coat pocket.

"So, we really don't have any choice here?" asked Pete's dad.

"Basically, Mr. Zell, no you don't. I promise Peter will be well taken care of. Unfortunately, I'm sorry to pressure you, but we have to leave immediately in order to get Pete and Ricky Granger to Washington for meetings tomorrow morning. I assure you we'll take good care of him. Do you understand?" asked Summers.

Turning to his son, "Pete, are you okay traveling without us?"

"Sure dad. It isn't a problem. Is Ricky going to be with me Agent Summers?" asked Peter.

"Yes," replied Agent Gates. "I just received a text message confirming Ricky Granger is en route to the plane as we speak. Can Pete pack quickly, the jet is waiting at Springfield Air Services at Abraham Lincoln airport."

"Sure," replied Pete enthusiastically as he leapt from the couch bounding toward the stairs. "This sounds cool. I can be packed in five minutes."

While Pete rummaged around upstairs throwing clothes in his backpack, the Zells stood nervously with Agents Summers and Gates. Mr. Zell, quietly asked, "Agent Summers, are you certain that this is necessary and Peter's involvement will make a difference?"

"Yes, Mr. Zell. We wouldn't be here if we didn't think so."

Pete bounded back down the stairs two steps at a time, and announced he was ready to go. Quickly hugging his mother and father, he followed Agents Summers and Gates out to the waiting black Chevy Suburban parked at the curb with its engine running. Following Agent Gates, Pete jumped into the back seat of the Suburban then flashed a wink and a smile at his mom and dad.

"Call when you arrive Peter," yelled his mother as the door began to close on the ominous vehicle. Before the door latch had time to catch, flashing lights illuminated at the top of the windshield as Peter and the FBI sped away.

The high speed and flashing lights of the Suburban made for good time through the city streets, allowing Peter and his escorts to slide through the gate at Abraham Lincoln airport fifteen minutes later. Pete's FBI-transport bypassed security and sidled up alongside a gleaming white Gulfstream which stood stately on the ramp with its air-stair deployed awaiting Pete's arrival.

Pressing against Special Agent Gates, Pete leaned over to look out the side window. "Wow!" exclaimed Pete. "Is that for me?"

A little annoyed being sent on a babysitting assignment, Gates replied, "Kind of. Your buddy Ricky is already on board. Let's go, we have a schedule to keep," as Agent Gates pressed against Pete encouraging him to exit the vehicle. As Pete dropped to the tarmac, Agent Summers retrieved the backpack from the Suburban and tossed it to Pete as he ascended the jet's stairs three steps at a time. "Thanks," yelled Pete.

"Pete, over here," called Ricky as his buddy emerged through the doorway.

Dropping his backpack on the seat next to Ricky, Pete grabbed the window seat across from his Drone On buddy. "Holy crap Ricky. This is awesome!"

"For sure. When the FBI showed up at my door, my dad almost had a heart attack," declared Ricky.

"Mine too. I was certain these guys were going to haul me off to some jail or Gitmo or someplace equally scary," said Pete. "They told my parents that we are meeting the Director of the FBI. Do you believe it? What the hell is going on? What's going to happen to us?"

Agent Summers walked up to the two boys. "Guys, buckle up. We are going to take off very shortly.

"I don't know Pete. But I guess we're going to find out soon," said Ricky as the big Gulfstream accelerated down the runway destined for Washington, D.C.

# Chapter 25

———————◆———————

### *An Unhappy Barakat*

Abdul stormed into Barakat's chambers and began shaking him vigorously. "Emir! Emir! You must wake up."

Accustomed to living in the chaos of war, Barakat awakened, fully prepared to confront whatever it was that justified disturbing his sleep. "What is it Abdul?"

"Emir. They're gone. All of them are gone," announced Abdul.

"Who's gone my friend? What are you talking about?"

"The team. Chambers and his people. They are gone and our guards are dead," explained the frustrated Abdul.

"What!" exclaimed Barakat. "They can't be gone. We're in the middle of North Korea."

"Emir. I understand. But, the Supreme Leader's people just called and told me that the Americans invaded their country and left with five people. I went over to the compound and found it empty. Completely empty! They're all gone. The files are empty. The computers have been ransacked and hard drives taken," explained Abdul as he tuned the Korean Central Television Network on Barakat's television and were greeted by Hyun-Ae Yo, the network's most prominent anchor newswoman, ranting about America's invasion of their country.

The chirping iPhone distracted Abdul for a moment. Snatching it from his pocket, he tapped the screen and acknowledged the caller. "Yes. I understand. We will be ready in fifteen minutes. Thank you." Abdul returned his iPhone to the sanctity of his pocket, than turned his attention to Barakat who by now was completely engrossed in Hyun-Ae Yo's news report. "Emir. Excuse me. But, the Supreme Leader wants you to come to the palace immediately. A car is on its way."

"Very good. I want to talk with him as well. I can't believe the Americans successfully invaded this country and recovered Chambers and his people. Call Ko, we need to speak with him as well. Have him meet us at the palace."

Clearly frustrated and concerned, Abdul once again retrieved his iPhone. Before putting a call into Kang Ko, President of Korea Navigation Company, he paused for just a moment to remind Barakat the Supreme Leader's car would be arrive shortly. "Yes Emir. I will call Mr. Ko. Before I do, I am sorry to hurry you, but the Supreme Leader's car will be here in ten minutes. You must get dressed."

Rising from his cushion in front of the television, Barakat shook his head in disgust and acknowledged Abdul's prodding. "Yes. Yes. I understand. Make certain Ko is on his way. I will be dressed in a few minutes and meet you out front."

"Very good Emir," said Abdul as he slipped from Barakat's chambers while he awaited Ko's people to answer the phone.

### The President Greets Johnson

It had been a long day for President Bennett as he huddled in the Oval Office with Secretary of State Umberg, FBI Director Teich and various and sundry key advisors. Diplomats from across the globe have been pelting the White House on behalf of North Korea, and sabre rattling could be heard loud and clear from the justifiably angry tyrant. Fortunately, the fifty thousand U.S. troops recently deployed in South Korea are were the ready and supported by the U.S.S. George H. W. Bush Task Force with the U.S.S. Harry S. Truman en route.

Chief of Staff Kerns popped his head into the Oval Office, "Excuse me Mr. President. Sheriff Johnson is here."

"Outstanding. Bring him in," replied Bennett.

"Mitch, how is the debriefing of the Autonomous team progressing?" asked Bennett.

"Mr. President, they are happy beyond imagination and are providing unbelievable detail about the technology they created. Each of them are concerned whether they will be charged with any crimes," added Teich.

"We'll figure that out later. Right now, we need to learn everything possible to aid in defending against the continued drone attacks."

"Certainly Mr. President. Unfortunately, the drone attacks continue. At a higher rate," commented Teich.

The President paused for a sip of his coffee recently refreshed by his butler, Tyron Garner. "Is there anything else you need Mr. President?" asked his butler.

"No thank you Tyron. I'm fine."

Placing his coffee cup on his desk, Bennett turned to General James. "General, your people did a phenomenal job."

"Thank you Mr. President. Everyone did a fantastic job. But, it wouldn't have been possible if not for the incredible intelligence provided by the CIA. Thank you Director Haydon," said James.

"It's our pleasure General," replied Director Haydon. "I had no intention of repeating the Islamabad fiasco."

"Additionally Mr. President, with the exception of some enemy fire taken by the transport and a wound to Chief Torres' leg, the mission went off without a hitch. Chief Torres is currently recovering at Bethesda. Also, the Navy F-35 squadron and the Air Force's C-17 and MQ-9 Reapers did magnificent jobs both entering and exiting North Korea, not to mention the wonderful close-air support during the battle at the airport. Also, the F-35s performed well protecting the C-17 going into North Korea where they shot down two MIG-29's," said James.

"Yes General. Outstanding job. We need to award these men some medals," offered Bennett just as Kerns and Sheriff Johnson appeared at the door of the Oval Office.

President Bennett rose from his desk and swiftly strode across toward Johnson as Johnson snapped to attention and briskly saluted his Commander-in-Chief. Quickly returning the hero's salute, Bennett grabbed Johnson's hand and pumped it vigorously. "Graham, well done. Well done indeed. We are all so very proud of you and your team."

Johnson humbly accepted Bennett's praise, "Thank you Mr. President. My team performed superbly. It wasn't possible without them."

Directed by Bennett, the men shuttled over to the comfortable seating of the Oval Office as Tyron Garner served coffee. "Gentlemen, now that this phase is behind us, we cannot let down our guard. Mitch, what is the status of the Drone On people you've brought to D.C.?" asked Bennett.

"Mr. President, we have sixty-five individuals, ranging in age from fourteen to seventy, representing the top one percent of Drone On game players in America, at FBI headquarters being debriefed as we speak," replied Teich.

"Are any of them aware that they were controlling real drones?" asked Bennett.

"Mr. President, for the most part they were not. There are, however, two teenage boys we picked up last evening in Springfield, Illinois that grew suspicious after the Bank of America attack in Atlanta."

Flipping through his papers, Teich mumbled to himself after successfully recovering the boys' dossiers. "Here it is."

"The boys, Mr. President, are Ricky Granger and Peter Zell of Springfield, Illinois. Both are freshmen at Springfield High School. Over the past couple of months, we've been closely monitoring their activities. These boys are extremely bright adolescents and your typical technology nerds isolated from the mainstream high school community. More importantly, they are deeply entrenched in online gaming. According to their psychological profiles, they fit our requirements perfectly and both appear interested in our program."

"That's great. What's the next step?" asked Bennett.

"Mr. President, we're assembling the Drone On gamers for a group orientation in two hours. At that time, they'll be informed of our strategy and recruited. The good news is, with the exception of a small number, our preliminary observations indicate a majority of these gamers meet our requirements and are highly receptive to participating," explained Teich.

"Well Mitch, this is going to be interesting," replied Bennett.

Roger Kerns glanced at his iPhone, took advantage of the pause in the conversation. "Mr. President, we have to prepare for your press conference scheduled for six this evening."

"Yes, of course. Gentlemen, unfortunately we need to bring this meeting to a close. Job well done by all of you. Graham, America is forever in your debt for a magnificent job done by you and your team," offered Bennett.

### Drone On Defenders

Ricky Granger scored two seats in the front row of the FBI's auditorium as the collection of motley gamers poured in from four different doors; each escorted by stoic FBI agents.

"Pete! Pete, over here," called Ricky to his buddy he hadn't seen since arriving in D.C. on the Gulfstream.

Breaking from the group, Pete dashed over to where Ricky was sitting and vaulted over two rows of seats and plopped down in the seat next to his friend. "Hey buddy. What's been going on?"

"Nothing much. Just a lot of questions. It's been really weird. All they did was ask the same questions over and over," replied Ricky.

"Yeah. Same here."

The lights blinked twice as Agent Lane approached the podium and performed the obligatory and forever annoying microphone tapping. Once assured the audio system was working, Lane spoke loudly to overcome the cacophony of nervous conversations that filled the room. "Ladies and gentlemen. Ladies and gentlemen. Please settle down and quickly take your seats. We need to begin today's meeting."

"I want to thank you all for your patience and understanding. The purpose of today's meeting is to brief you as to America's strategy to defend against the ongoing drone threat and your possible role. Joining us today is FBI Director Mitchell Teich." Special Agent Lane moved away from the podium making room for Director Teich.

Director Teich, stepped up to the podium, laid down his notes and retrieved his glasses from his coat pocket.

*Ladies and gentlemen. I'm Mitchell Teich, Director of the FBI. Thank you for joining us here in Washington. I understand that the events of the past couple of days may be a little confusing. However, I assure you, this has all been in the best interest of the United States.*

*I am certain everyone is intimately aware of the Islamic State's commitment to bringing terror and devastation to America though the use of autonomous micro-drones. Like you, President Bennett believes this reign of terror has persisted much too long and it is time to do everything in our power to bring it to an end. Today, we're here to share with you President Bennett's strategy to combat this terror threat in a truly novel and innovative way. Before we proceed, I must inform you that what we are about to share is of the highest national security and is top secret. Divulging anything you learn here today is a Federal offense for which you will be prosecuted to the fullest extent of the law. Any of you unwilling to accept this responsibility please exit through the door at the back of the auditorium immediately, where you will be met by our agents to discuss your decision.*

The crowd stirred uncomfortably as a few people rose from their seats and headed toward the exit. Once the few choosing to leave exited the auditorium, the agent monitoring the passageway closed and secured the door, and took up his position guarding the exit.

*I want to thank all of you who have chosen to stay. Today, we're inviting each of you to join the President in becoming a critical part of the most innovative and potentially effective wartime strategy we have conceived of since the Manhattan project. Basically, we are taking the battle against the Islamic State's drone terror to cyberspace.*

*Over the past six months, many of you have been active players of the mobile game Drone On. From your point-of-view, Drone On is simply a game that allows you to command and navigate virtual drones against a variety of fictitious targets. However, in reality, the Drone On technology was developed for us and designed to do more than it appears. Drone On is integrated into a nationwide surveillance network that enables us to detect attacking drones, establish communications links, then inject these 'real drones' into the Drone On game environment alongside the virtual drones under your command.*

*By making the real drones indistinguishable from virtual drones, you are unaware whether you're controlling them or the virtual drones created by the software. It was our mission to create a technology that empowered you, Drone On Defenders, to take control of real-world attack drone squadrons away from the Islamic State.*

*As you know, in Drone On you direct your drones against targets which have real-world counterparts such as the Bank of America building in Atlanta Georgia. The genius behind Drone On is that the real drones that are injected into the game appear to you no different from the game's fabricated virtual drones. From your perspective, both the real and virtual drones are directed against their intended target. In the game, you, the Drone On Defender, has the impression that you have successfully crashed all your drones into your target. However, in reality, thanks to some very sophisticated computer programming, the real drones never make it to their intended targets and are actually redirected to safe areas we call False Targets. Apart from what you see in cyberspace, in reality the real drones, unbeknownst to you, are guided to our pre-defined False Targets far away from people and property where they are destroyed.*

*I am going to turn this meeting back over to Special Agent Lane who will explain the details, our training and operating procedures.*

Special Agent Lane once again moved to the podium to continue briefing the Drone On Defenders.

"Ladies and gentlemen, since you elected to stay for this orientation, I want to remind you that all you have learned today and will learn in the days to come is a matter of National Security. Any information you divulge will subject you to immediate and severe criminal prosecution. Now that you have been brought up to speed on America's Drone On initiative, over the next week you will receive in-depth training. Please note that your name badge is color-coded defining your training group. As you exit the conference room you will be directed to your training group's meeting room. Thank you."

### Presidential Press Conference

Like so many times before, the White House press room was standing-room only as Press Secretary Farnsworth approached the podium. "Good evening everybody. Thank you for joining us for this White House briefing. Please stand for the President of the United States."

President Bennett made his way up the two steps to the podium.

*Good evening. As you all know, the continuing terrorist drone attacks against America and our allies have been nothing less than devastating. Unfortunately, our efforts to mount an effective defense has been disappointing. Worldwide, hundreds of thousands of lives have been lost and billions of dollars in property damaged or destroyed. Furthermore, the effect on the world economy has been calamitous to say the least. This has truly been a very difficult time for us all.*

*In a stroke of luck, our collective intelligence agencies determined that the Islamic State was executing these attacks from a facility in North Korea supported by that government. As you've undoubtedly heard on the news, two days ago we executed a mission into North Korea in an effort to subdue the perpetrators and impair their ability to continue.*

*Sheriff Johnson, here with us today, and his team executed a very dangerous and courageous high altitude parachute insertion into North Korea and executed a textbook assault against the Islamic State's engineering facility. As a result of this mission, Sheriff Johnson and his team successfully recovered substantial information about the Islamic State's drone technology and just as importantly, they recovered the American engineering team from Autonomous Systems.*

*Thanks to Sheriff Johnson's brave team of patriots, this mission was flawlessly executed with no loss of American lives. Unfortunately, Chief Fred Torres was wounded in the leg during the extraction from Sunan International Airport and is resting comfortably at Bethesda Naval Hospital.*

*I assure you, this decision was not made lightly. To take an action against a sovereign nation is truly serious. However, North Korea made the decision to deal themselves into this game and as such, must take full responsibility.*

*According to Link, I have a little time to take a couple of questions. David.*

"David White, Associated Press. Mr. President, as it has been stated, only five members of the Autonomous Systems' team were recovered. Weren't there more? What happened to them?"

"Yes David, only five members of the Autonomous team were recovered. They were Richard Chambers, the Chief Executive Officer, Liz Collins, Gary Sasaki, Akio Chan and Will Schmidt. Two engineers, Mr. Kent Anders and Mr. Jeff Chaplain were murdered by their captors apparently to coerce the remaining team members to cooperate. The three members of the Autonomous Systems jet flight crew also were killed. They were Captain Jeff Taylor, First Officer Carey James and Flight Attendant Becky Reynolds," replied Bennett. "Stephanie," said Bennett as he pointed to a young woman in the front row.

"Thank you Mr. President. Stephanie Walker, TMZ. According to information we've received, Captain Taylor was in league with Moktar Barakat in abducting the Autonomous Systems engineers. Can you confirm this?"

"Stephanie. You know we don't comment on rumors. All I can say at this time is that Captain Taylor and his flight crew were killed as part of the abduction of the Autonomous Systems team."

Farnsworth leaned toward Bennett and whispered into his ear. Bennett nodded and returned to the microphone, "Thank you all. Good night and God bless America," as Bennett swiftly turned and exited the press room.

### The Supreme Leader and Barakat

Barakat, Ko and Abdul waited in the meeting room for the Supreme Leader's arrival.

"How could this have happened?" asked Moktar. "How is it the Americans were able to swoop in and simply make away with everything?"

"Emir," said Ko. "I understand that this is a disturbing turn of events. I assure you, we don't need Mr. Chambers or his engineers to continue our efforts. My team is more than capable of managing the design, engineering and manufacturing on their own."

"Mr. Ko. I have the utmost confidence in Korea Navigation's capabilities. You have done a commendable job. If you say we don't need Chambers and his people, then I believe you. I am concerned, however, that they will provide information to the Americans that could enable them to mount a defense against our drones. What are your thoughts?" asked Barakat.

"Yes Emir, you certainly have a legitimate concern. I have spoken with my engineers and they have assured me that they are capable of advancing the technology beyond that which Chambers' people created. More importantly, they are confident that they can develop more formidable drones," assured Ko.

"Well Mr. Ko, this is good news," responded Moktar as the door to the meeting room swung open and the Supreme Leader and his entourage flooded in.

Rising to their feet, the two men greeted North Korea's Supreme Leader.

"Emir, I am most disturbed by the American invasion. I assure you they will regret the day they set foot in my country," blustered the Supreme Leader.

"Yes, Supreme Leader. I appreciate your anger over these events. Fortunately, Mr. Ko has assured me that we can continue without Chambers and his team. I am confident in Ko's ability and thankful for your support," replied Barakat.

Turning to Ko, "Mr. Ko, you are certain that we can continue our mission without the American team?" asked Kim Jung-Un.

Bowing deeply, "Your Excellency, you have my promise and commitment," replied Ko.

# Chapter 26

◆

### *The Climate*

America, living under the oppressive pall of the Islamic State's twenty-first century capability, reeled unsteadily back on its collective heals. Until now, Americans enjoyed a peaceful existence, only to have it snatched away by lone-wolf Jihadists embedded deeply and invisible to passersby. For the first time in a very long time, the average American has developed a sensitivity, a new-found kinship toward its allies. Allies like Israel, which lives under the constant day-to-day threat of rocket barrages and suicide bombers. The sense of peace and security once enjoyed, thanks to the expansive Pacific and Atlantic oceans, has been swept away as terror continued to rain down from high above. That is, if drones flying three hundred feet overhead can be considered high. Regardless of altitude, this diabolical and frightening weapon of terror had thus far proven unstoppable. Unlike conventional military weapons, the Islamic State's drones are wielded by operatives casually walking among peaceful citizens. Operatives that are virtually invisible residing, deep within America's closet-communities. The image of one's neighbor as a benign fellow citizen has been painfully repainted in the American psyche, creating a canvas of distrust toward anyone that 'isn't like me.' A new age of doubt has permeated one's core and changed who we are.

As Islam continued to command attacks from afar, pillaging the American landscape with impunity, Congress has tried futility to respond to its citizens' call for solutions. But unfortunately, the obvious solutions that echo through history threaten to open the long-sealed Pandora's Box of an America back in the days of McCarthyism, when accusations of subversion or treason overwhelmed reasonable thinking — thinking in total disregard of the evidence. Behind closed doors, American Leadership entertains solutions that harken back to World War II when over one hundred thousand innocent people of Japanese ancestry, most of which were U.S. citizens, found themselves gathered up and confined behind barbed wire in places with innocuous names such as Manzanar, Heart Mountain and Topaz. Thinking driven by fear, confusion and prejudice. Thinking that has and will forever damage the American spirit. Thinking that makes citizens of Arab ancestry more than a little nervous.

One doesn't have to look far before recoiling at the paradox that is the American economy. Since President Bennett's decision to shut down the nation's constellation of global positioning satellites, businesses ranging from airlines to overnight delivery services suffered increased costs and eroded efficiency. In some cases, product lines became obsolete overnight. Yet, in stark contrast, two Silicone Valley rising stars—Banger Mobile Games and Millennial Games—were riding high. These new-age mobile gaming upstarts, each commanding more than twenty billion dollar valuations, were making their shareholders wealthy beyond imagination while at the same time repelling criticism from social observers questioning the morality of their exploitation of a suffering nation.

Each day, since the first attack against Lincoln, Nebraska, the Islamic State's drones have filled America's skies, raining down death and destruction with impunity. Even worse, month-after-month hundreds of thousands of victims arrive in emergency rooms exhibiting symptoms of RICIN poisoning. The harsh reality for many is they waited just a little too long and finally succumbed to this dreadful, yet treatable, unethical biologic contaminant.

Complicating America's way of life even further were the outright threats and saber rattling from North Korea resulting from the dramatic rescue mission executed by Sheriff Johnson and his team. Being six thousand miles away, America enjoyed a substantial buffer insulating it from any immediate threat. Yet, North Korea's five million active and ready reserve military is disturbing both to America and its allies in the Pacific Rim.

### The Evening News

"Good evening, welcome to United Network News' Evening Edition. I'm Jeff Stoddard."

"And, I'm Gretchen Chen. Jeff, the crisis in America continues. Like so many days before, today America and many of our allies once again have fallen victim to the Islamic State's continued drone attacks."

"Yes, indeed Gretchen these are truly dark days for America and our allies. Now, with the threat posed by North Korea, our future grows more and more uncertain. Perhaps, General Gary Arnold, UNN's military advisor, can shed some light on the current situation," suggested Stoddard. "General Arnold, thank you for joining us this evening."

As UNN applies the magic of technology, the image of General Arnold seated at a large desk framed between the American and Marine Corps flags slid into view. "Jeff, Gretchen, it is always an honor to join you. Yes, these are dark days for America. Dark days indeed."

Stoddard took the lead and posed the first question to General Arnold. "General, in the past few days, we've all learned that U.S. citizens were being held in North Korea. However, until the highly publicized rescue mission we knew nothing of this and had not heard a word about any diplomatic efforts. What are your thoughts? Do you think President Bennett acted precipitously, potentially putting America on the brink of war with North Korea?"

"Jeff, these are good questions. First, I believe it's important to understand that this was not simply a matter of U.S. citizens being held hostage. These innocent people were being held against their will and forced into serving the State of Islam as well as North Korea. Compound this with the fact we are in a state of war with Islam, at the very least North Korea and Kim Jung-Un are collaborators. From President Bennett's perspective, this clearly defines where North Korea and its Supreme Leader stand in our struggle with Islam. Jeff, the bottom line is simple; I fully support President Bennett's decision to mount a covert assault to recover the Autonomous Systems' team. Not only were these people rescued, I believe our enemy's technological capability has been severely impacted."

"Yes General Arnold," injected Gretchen. "Americans coast-to-coast are applauding the heroic rescue mission mounted by Sheriff Johnson and his team. My concern is what's next? Does North Korea pose a real threat? A nuclear threat?"

"Gretchen, Sheriff Johnson and his team are true American Heroes. Their rescue of the Autonomous Systems' personnel will be remembered as one of the most important and precise military campaigns in history. Regardless of what triggered North Korea's sabre rattling, the fact is they are casting overt threats which I believe are real and credible. Remember, North Korea has a large standing army, nuclear weapons, and some level of long-range delivery capability. All this adds up to North Korea posing a genuine threat. Not only to us, but also to our allies in the region: Japan and South Korea. I'm confident that President Bennett will not allow Kim Jung-Un to take action against our allies. Currently we have more than fifty thousand troops in South Korea and support from our allies ranging from Britain to China, all of whom want stability in the region and to put an end to the Islamic State's terror."

"Thank you General Arnold. As always, your insights provide great clarity and understanding," said Stoddard.

"You're welcome Jeff. It's my pleasure," replied Arnold.

As General Arnold's image faded away, Stoddard turned to the camera. "Gretchen, since President Bennett issued the executive order, along with Russia's President Nikolai Volkov, to shut down the civilian Global Positioning System, our economy has been in a constant state of turmoil. However, there is light at the end of this very dark tunnel. With us tonight is Commerce Secretary Jerome Price. Secretary Price, welcome to UNN's Evening Edition. Mr. Secretary, we understand there is good news on the horizon. What can you share with us tonight?"

The image of Commerce Secretary, looking distinguished and academic, faded into view. His taut-skin and bright smile engenders the sense that this man is much too young for a role so important in our government.

As he gazed into the camera, Price gave everyone watching the sense he was speaking directly to them. Clearly, this man is in line for greater things in American leadership. That is, if America survives.

"Jeff, thank you for inviting me on. Since the first drone attack in Lincoln, Nebraska on April 19th, every aspect of the American economy has been effected, but none as dramatically than air, land and sea navigation. Thankfully, thousands of engineers across the globe have been working selflessly to develop and implement the new Secure GPS system, SGPS. Over the coming months, as SGPS goes live, much needed and necessary commercial applications for GPS will begin to come back online," explained Price.

"This is great news Mr. Secretary," offered Chen. "If I heard you correctly, you said necessary commercial applications. What about personal GPS needs, such as street navigation? Aren't these necessary?"

"Gretchen, unfortunately, personal GPS use is the root of the problem. If GPS services are made available for everyone to use from their cars and smartphones, then what would prevent the Islamic State from using this technology for drone navigation? In order to protect our citizens, it was necessary to limit SGPS access to a definable and controllable body of users whose need can be controlled and monitored," replied Price.

"Well Mr. Secretary, in this dark and difficult time, like many of our viewers, I'm happy to take any good news whenever possible," offers Stoddard.

### Autonomous Team Back Home

The big transport landed at Andrews Air Force base just as the morning sun peeked over the horizon, completing a long and exhausting flight from South Korea. Just as quickly as they were recovered from the clutches of their captors, the Autonomous Team was awakened and shuttled into the black FBI SUVs waiting on the tarmac. Under the grey morning sky, the caravan swiftly covered the thirteen-mile trek between Andrews Air Force Base and FBI headquarters on Pennsylvania Avenue. One-by-one the SUVs slipped through the massive and well-guarded garage door of 935 Pennsylvania Avenue and were greeted by a cadre of well-prepared Special Agents, two for each of the Autonomous Team members.

"Now what?" asked Gary Sasaki, of the sun-glassed quiet FBI agent seated beside him.

"Please exit the vehicle Mr. Sasaki," encouraged the agent.

Chambers and his remaining team were escorted en masse through the empty hallways to a well-guarded secure conference room, two days after Sheriff Johnson and his team returned from their mission.

As the conference room door closed, the all-too-familiar forceful click of the electronic locking mechanism broke the silence.

"What the hell is going on?" groused Sasaki. "It's been two days and all that's happened is we've gone from one prison to another. Sure, the food is better, but it's still a damn prison. I want out of here."

"Dammit Gary! All you do is complain. Forty-eight hours ago we were prisoners in North Korea. Today we're in America. Why in hell can't you count your blessings?" chided Chambers.

Sasaki, glaring at Chambers with two years of pent-up resentment, "Yes, but…"

Stopping him in mid-sentence, Chambers raised his voice. "Yes, but my ass! Shut the hell up! I've been listening to your constant complaining for over two years. I wish they'd have put a bullet in your head instead of poor Kent's and Jeff's."

Gary, dropped his eyes toward the floor as if searching for some snappy repartee but was startled as the conference room door swung open allowing in a flood of strident looking souls followed by someone clearly important. The important gentleman made his way to the chair at the head of the table.

"Good morning! I'm FBI Director Mitchell Teich. On behalf of the President of the United States, I want to tell you all how happy we are to have you back in America. We appreciate all that you have been through. However, there is much we need to understand and accomplish. Over the next few days, you'll be thoroughly debriefed, put though a battery of psychological tests as well as receive a complete medical examination at Walter Reed Medical Center. To help you through this process, each of you has been assigned two Special Agents that will accompany you throughout the debriefing and the transition back to your normal life. Overseeing the entire process will be Special Agent in Charge Ralph Lane and Special Agent Janet Richards," as Teich pointed right toward Lane and Richards. "If you have any questions, ask the agents assigned to you or Special Agents Lane or Richards." Teich quickly scanned each of the five Autonomous Systems personnel, as if taking inventory. He rose from his chair then headed toward the door. "Again," pausing for just a moment, "welcome back."

As the door closed, Lane rose to his feet. "Gentlemen. Ms. Collins. Please accompany the agents assigned to you," the five remaining members of the Autonomous team were quickly escorted in different directions to parts unknown in the massive and intimidating Pennsylvania Avenue facility.

### Autonomous Team Debriefing

Gary sat uncomfortably alone in the sterile interrogation room buried deep in the bowels of FBI Headquarters. The question, "Now what?" rattled around constantly in his brain when the creaking of the metal door disrupted his thoughts as Agents Casey and Taggart slipped into the room.

"Good morning Mr. Sasaki. I'm Special Agent Casey and this is my partner, Special Agent Taggart. We appreciate that you're anxious to return home to your family. As such, we'll do our best to keep this interview process to a minimum. Are you okay with this?"

"What choice do I have? I haven't done anything wrong, yet I feel like a criminal. Why haven't I been allowed to call my wife?" asked Gary.

"Mr. Sasaki, your family has been notified that you are safe and back in America. The sooner we get on with this interview, the sooner you will be reunited with your family," replied Casey.

Casey slipped into the chair opposite Gary, and flipped open a file folder emblazoned with the words 'Top Secret' and began scanning through the pages. Pausing for a moment, the FBI agent turned to Gary, "Mr.

Sasaki, we're aware that you, Akio Chan and Will Schmidt were in communication with a Mr. Arman Deeb of Autonomous Systems while you were in the custody of Moktar Barakat. Is this correct?"

"Uh..mmm. Yes. I suppose so. I know that Will and Akio were sending messages back and forth. Is that a problem?" asked Gary.

"Not at all Mr. Sasaki. In fact, thanks to the messages we intercepted a great deal was learned about your captor's agenda and technology. What we're curious about Mr. Sasaki is the degree of cooperation Chambers and the rest of you provided Barakat?" asked Casey.

"I didn't do anything. I was afraid for my life. They had already killed Jeff and Kent in cold blood," said Gary with a quiver in his voice.

"That's Jeff Chaplain and Kent Anders?" asked Taggart.

"Yes. They murdered them in cold-blood right in front of us. Blew their brains out for no damn reason. Other than to scare us. Which they did. As for speaking with Barakat, none of us met with him privately other than Dick," said Gary.

"Dick? You mean Richard Chambers. Correct?" asked Casey.

"Yes. Richard Chambers. But, as far as I'm concerned, he's a dick!" asserted Sasaki.

"You don't sound pleased with Mr. Chambers," offered Taggart.

"Of course I wasn't pleased with him. He's just the typical useless CEO who makes all the money, takes all the credit while guys like me do all the work. That's how he treated us at Autonomous and that's what he did while we were in captivity. My bet is Chambers told Barakat that he was the genius behind our work and we were his little slaves," said Gary.

"So, am I to assume that Mr. Chambers met with Moktar Barakat regularly?" asked Casey.

"Absolutely. He regularly disappeared for private meetings with him. Whenever we asked him what was going on, he just said he was keeping us alive and we should just do our jobs," said Sasaki.

"Well Mr. Sasaki, based on local intelligence, it appeared to us that Mr. Chambers was doing a little more than just keeping you alive. In fact, we believe he was a willing collaborator." Taggart turned over some photographs and slid them smoothly across the shiny surface of the table toward Gary. Gary struggled for a moment to grasp the magnitude of Casey's accusation, as he stared at the three photos showing a man dressed in Arab garb kneeling in prayer. Pondering why some towel-head praying to Allah was important to the FBI, Gary suddenly realized that this wasn't just some towel-head, it was Richard Chambers.

"Do you recognize this man Mr. Sasaki?" asked Casey.

"Yeah. Of course I do. It's Chambers. Hell, we all were given crappy Arab cloths to wear. But none of us prayed to Allah. At least none that I knew of. But based on these pictures, it looks like Chambers is a damn Muslim. Bastard!" shouted Gary.

"Okay Mr. Sasaki. Let's move on," said Casey. "Are you aware how Barakat employed the drone technology you developed for him?" asked Casey.

"Not really. I presume he was using it locally to terrorize somebody. Who, I don't know," claimed Gary.

"Well Mr. Sasaki, would you please bear with us a moment and view this video?" asked Casey as he picked up the black remote control, which had lain unnoticed on the table, then pressed the play button. A vivid montage of death and destruction interspersed with a collage of news reporters played out before Gary, driving home the point that his drone technology was used for something more than 'just terrorizing some locals.'

Gary sat stunned by what had played out before him in vivid living color. "I had no idea. I don't know what Chambers' and Liz knew. All I know is Akio, Will and I had no idea what was going on. All we did was write code and implement the engineering of the drones. I don't even know where they were being manufactured. Believe me, we had no idea that they were being used this way. This is just horrible. What do you want from me?"

Agent Casey glared at Gary and paused for a long moment. "Mr. Sasaki, that's what we presumed. It was clear from our assaults on the facilities in Islamabad and North Korea that no manufacturing was going on at these facilities. We believe, however, that the drones were and are being manufactured in North Korea and Malaysia. What we don't know, is where. Is it your position that you don't have any information regarding drone manufacturing?"

"Yes. I don't have any idea."

"Do you believe Mr. Chambers has any information regarding their manufacturing?" asked Casey.

"I really don't know. You'll have to ask him. All I know is, we were kept in the dark about that. Obviously large-scale manufacturing was going on. As to where, I've already told you I don't know."

"Okay Mr. Sasaki. One last question. According to the information recovered from P'yŏngsŏn, the team was involved in the development of the mobile game known as Drone Assault. What can you tell us about this game?" asked Taggart.

"I don't really know that much. Drone Assault was Will's and Akio's project. It was my understanding they were creating a game to train people to fly drones. Since gaming isn't my area of expertise, I wasn't included in any of the discussions."

"Unfortunately Mr. Sasaki, Drone Assault was actually more than a training device. In actuality, the game Drone Assault enabled players to influence control over attacking drones to counter any effort America and our allies employed to defeat an attack. Currently, more than fifty million people worldwide are playing Drone Assault and actively directing the Islamic State's attack drones toward targets. Right now, Drone Assault represents a serious threat to national and world security," explained Casey.

"You're kidding. This is terrible. I swear, I had no idea. Also, I'm certain Will and Akio didn't know what they were working on. What can we do to help?" asked Gary.

"At the moment, Mr. Sasaki, we're just filling in the gaps. Rest assured, you, Mr. Schmidt and Mr. Chan will be called upon to help address this situation. For now, we'll bring this session to a close and continue in the morning. Agent Taggart will escort you back to your apartment," explained Casey.

"You mean prison cell," grumbled Gary.

"Not at all Mr. Sasaki. Rest assured, I know what a prison cell is and the accommodations provided by the FBI are far from prison cells. On behalf of the Director, thank you for your cooperation. We'll continue after breakfast in the morning. Have a restful evening."

After Agent Taggart pushed back from the table, Gary decided to follow his lead and rose to his feet. Gary paused for a moment, a little shaky, waiting for the circulation to return to his left leg that had gone to sleep from sitting in one place for too long.

"Follow me Mr. Sasaki," directed Agent Taggart.

"Yeah. Give me a moment."

# Chapter 27

———————◆———————

### *Breaking News – 8:00 PM Eastern Time*
Bleeeep! Bleeeep! Bleeeep! Went the annoying breaking news alert.

"Good evening. I'm Jeff Stoddard, and I'm here with my co-anchor Gretchen Chan. We interrupt this evening's programing to cover breaking news in North Korea. According to intelligence sources, it appears a nuclear armed intercontinental missile, believed to be a Taepodong-6, exploded on its launch pad approximately one hour ago, 7:00 PM Washington time which is 8:00 AM Friday in North Korea. According to scattered reports, the Taepodong-6 missile was being readied for launch when for some unknown reason, it simply exploded, devastating the facility located at Dandong on North Korea's west coast on the Yellow Sea about one hundred and thirty miles northwest of Pyongyang, the capital city."

"Yes Jeff," added Gretchen. "The launch facility, believed to be named after a nearby village, is known as Tongch'ang-dong. Based on seismic reports coming in from around the world, it's estimated the explosion was equivalent to one hundred kilotons — five times the size of the bomb dropped over Nagasaki, Japan in World War II — and likely devastated the complex and villages within twenty miles. As of yet, we have no reports on fatalities. In fact, the only report coming from the Central News Agency of the Democratic People's Republic of Korea is no such nuclear missile existed and no explosion occurred. More importantly, there is no information as to the alleged missile's intended target."

"Thanks Gretchen. Also, according to the information we have on the Taepodong-6 missile, it is believed to be North Korea's longest-range launch vehicle. It is capable of sub-orbital flight, providing North Korea with first strike capability anywhere in the world. Once again, one hour ago it is believed a North Korean nuclear tipped long-range missile exploded on the ground while being readied for launch."

"Gretchen and I will stay on top of this story and return with any breaking news. We return you to your regularly scheduled broadcast," said Stoddard.

### *White House 1745 Hours Eastern Time*
President Bennett sat quietly on the comfortable couch in the Oval Office, reviewing his speech scheduled to be delivered at the South

American Trade Alliance meeting in Borgata in two days, when Ruth Holcomb came into the office. "Mr. President, General James is here to see you. He says it's urgent."

"Certainly Mrs. Holcomb, bring the General in," replied Bennett.

With barely a pause, General James charged into the Oval Office, clearly out of breath as Mrs. Holcomb retreated and closed the door behind her.

"General, what it is?" asked Bennett.

"Mr. President, I rushed over as soon as possible. We have a terrible situation. Our MIDAS-3 has detected North Korea fueling a Taepodong-6 missile at their Yellow Sea launch facility north of Pyongyang," exclaimed James exhausted from his sprint from the Pentagon.

"Hold on. Let me get caught up. I don't recall, what is MIDAS-3 and what is a tabdong-6 missile?" asked Bennett.

"Sorry Mr. President. MIDAS-3 is the third generation of our low-earth orbit Missile Defense Alarm System. The missile is a Taep-o-dong-6, North Korea's latest long-range nuclear delivery system. They are fueling as we speak," explained James. "We have to react immediately."

"Okay! I get it. What are you suggesting?" asked Bennett.

"Mr. President, you need to authorize use of our satellite based anti-missile energy defense system; Talon-II. I assure you Mr. President, we must act immediately. Unfortunately, it takes thirty minutes to charge the Talon-II," replied James.

"How long do I have to make this decision?' asked Bennett—retreating to the comfort of his desk.

"At best we have upwards of an hour for them to achieve launch status. If we wait until they launch, we may have a fifty-fifty chance of destroying the craft in flight. Mr. President, our best option is to destroy the missile while it's still on the pad. The Talon's energy beam is imperceptible and the cause of the explosion would be unknown. This provides us maximum deniability," explained General James.

"This is horrible. If they launch, how long will it take to reach a critical target?" asked Bennett.

"Well, Mr. President, if their target is the West Coast of the U.S., it could take anywhere from forty-five to ninety minutes. However, if their target is one of our allies, such as Japan, they are only fifteen minutes away. Regardless, we project they will be ready to launch in forty-five minutes," replied James.

"So, I have thirty minutes to make this decision?" asks Bennett.

"No sir, more like fifteen minutes at best, and counting. I'm sorry, but a decision has to be made immediately," replied James.

Bennett picked up his phone and buzzed Mrs. Holcomb. "Mrs. Holcomb, get the Speaker and Senate leader on the phone immediately. Also, summon Roger as well," commanded Bennett.

"Yes sir. Will do," replied Holcomb as she hung up to make her calls.

The President began wringing his hands impatiently as he waited for the calls to go through.

"Mr. President," reminded James, "we have twenty-six minutes."

"I know," replied Bennett as Holcomb's voice came through the intercom. "Mr. President, I have the Speaker and Senate leader on the phone. Mr. Kerns is on his way."

"Thank you. Put them through," replied Bennett.

"Speaker Teasdale and Senator Palmer, we have an emergency. General James just informed me that North Korea is fueling a nuclear tipped long-range missile. Based on their recent sabre rattling, we can presume they are planning an attack on the U.S. or one of our allies. The situation is critical. We have a maximum of twenty minutes to make the decision to neutralize this threat before they achieve missile launch. In doing so, we can virtually guarantee successful destruction of this weapon. Unfortunately, if we wait until they launch, our likelihood of successfully destroying the missile while it's in the air is fifty-fifty at best," explained Bennett.

Speaker Teasdale spoke first, "Are you saying that we don't have any alternatives, Mr. President?"

"That's correct Mr. Speaker, none whatsoever. Senator Palmer, do you understand the severity of this situation?" asked Bennett.

"Yes Mr. President. If this is our only option, I assure you that you have the full support of the Senate," replied Palmer.

"And you Mr. Speaker? Do I have support of the House?" asked Bennett.

"Yes Mr. President. I wish we had more time, but unfortunately it appears we don't," replied Teasdale.

"Unfortunately, these are the cold hard facts. I need to issue the go order to deploy our Talon-II energy weapon immediately. In fact, the clock is ticking and we have less than fifteen minutes to issue the go order. We are heading down to the Situation Room. Meet us there," ordered Bennett.

"I'm on my way Mr. President," responded Palmer.

"So am I Mr. President."

Bennett tapped the hang-up button and turned to James standing at attention as Roger Kerns swooped in out of breath. "Mr. President, Mrs. Holcomb summoned me. What's going on?"

"Roger, we have a situation in North Korea. They are readying to launch a long-range nuclear missile," explained Bennett. "I need you to document my order."

"Yes sir."

"Mr. President," asked James, "are you issuing the go order?" as he pulled his cell phone from his pocket and tapped the speed dial button.

"Yes General. You have my authorization to use the Talon-II weapon," ordered Bennett.

"Hello. General James here. Security Code Six Seven Bravo Bravo Yankee Victor. You are go to deploy Talon-II on the assigned target," ordered James. "Yes! Security Code confirmed as Six Seven Bravo Bravo Yankee Victor. You are ordered to deploy Talon-II. Mr. President, we need to move to the situation room immediately," urged James.

Bennett, James and Kerns exited the Oval Office as three Secret Service Agents fell in close behind as the men dashed down the hallway.

After a short ride down to the Situation Room level, the elevator door opened and the six men emerged, struck by the glare of lights and buzz of activity.

*Talon-II deployment, T-minus seventeen minutes,* announced the controller.

Bennett and James took their reserved seats at the massive curved conference table to monitor the mission.

"Mr. President, the image on the center screen is from our KH15-B Hexagon satellite which has been monitoring North Korea. As you can see from the vapor trail, they are fueling the rocket," explained James.

"Yes General. I see that." How much time do we have?"

"The timer above the screen shows fourteen minutes till fueling is complete."

*Talon-II deployment, T-minus eight minutes.*

"Based on the Talon-II's charging requirement, we have six minutes of buffer," explained James.

"Oh my God. That's cutting it close General," exclaimed Bennett.

"Yes sir. It will be close, but we have enough time. Once the Talon is charged, we can initiate up to six long-duration pulses."

"How long will it take for the energy pulse to destroy the missile?" asked Bennett.

"According to our tests, the Talon only needs to be on target for thirty seconds before the rocket's fuel ignites," answered James.

Again, the elevator door slid open and Palmer and Teasdale stepped out and made their way toward Bennett.

Palmer, almost out of breath, "Mr. President, how much time do we have?"

*Talon-II deployment, T-minus three minutes. Initial charging phase complete.*

"I guess we have three minutes. Have a seat," replied Bennett.

"Mr. President. Prior to deploying Talon-II, you'll need to enter your go-code into the control pad in front of you," explained James as he gestured for Marine Major Jeffrey Fabian to come forward. Today, Major Fabian, Bennett's military aid, was charged with the responsibility to keep the football containing nuclear and strategic weapons' launch codes close at hand. In orderly Marine fashion, Fabian stepped forward and placed the briefcase on the table.

Pausing for a moment, Bennett placed his hand on the football's scanner as the device swept up and down to confirm his identity. The device's red light flashed and changed to green followed by a computerized voice requesting voice recognition.

Bennett leaned forward and spoke toward the football, initiating the voice recognition process. "Carlton Bennett. Go code Charlie Two Two Xray Seven Four."

The football's six LEDs began flashing sequentially as Bennett's identity was being confirmed.

"*Identity confirmed,*" announced the football as the computer-controlled latches disengaged, allowing access to the authorization codes kept safe and secure inside.

General James opened the football and retrieved the plastic sleeve emblazoned Talon-II. Breaking it in half, he extracted a benign looking card inscribed with the Talon's launch code. "Mr. President, please key in the following code."

Bennett's hand hovered over the keypad, ready to complete the process. "Okay. Let's do it."

"Mr. President, the Talon-II's go code is, Eight Eight Six Bravo Seven Bravo."

Bennett tapped the six characters into the keypad, each followed by a definitive beep, completing the authorization sequence.

*Talon authorization confirmed. T-minus one minute.*

"Here we go," uttered Bennett.

*Talon-II deployment, T-minus thirty seconds.*

"I hope to God this works," prayed Bennett.

*Talon-II deployment, T-minus ten seconds.*

"I hope we're in time," said Bennett to James as the ominous vapors continued to trail downwind from the missile.

"We are Mr. President. We are in time," replied General James.

*Talon-II deployment, T-minus five...four...three...two...one...Talon Deployed*

Target Lock flashed across the center screen, indicating the energy weapon had been activated.

"It's happening Mr. President. Please watch the central display," directed James.

Above the central display, the timer went from minus to plus.

*T-plus ten...eleven...twelve...thirteen...fourteen...fifteen...*

Before the controller could reach sixteen, smoke began to emanate from the Taepodong-6 launch vehicle. Suddenly a bright flash lit up the launch pad as a fire ball consumed the missile. In a heartbeat, the extreme light of the burning missile filled the Situation Room, as the visible rolling concussion of the explosion swept across the ground laying waste to everything in its path. As the chaos of the initial explosion subsided, the frightening mushroom shaped cloud, the symbol of the power we all feared, rose upward from where the missile once stood. North Korea's nuclear ballistic missile program was stopped dead in its tracks.

"That's the end of that Mr. President. We just set North Korea back ten plus years," announced James.

"I know it sounds horrible, but, I hope the Supreme Leader was at the launch site. He's a pain in the ass," exclaimed Bennett.

### Chambers in the Hot Seat

It's been a long twelve hours since Chambers and his team returned to U.S. soil. Although the team was happy to be back in America, it was disturbing how the ongoing debriefings and continued isolation were so reminiscent of the past two years. Certainly without the threat of a bullet to the back of one's head and better food and accommodations compared with those provided by Barakat. But, regardless of who their captor was, the fear of continued isolation from friends and family was disturbing. Aside from being separated from loved ones, the ever-present hopelessness of the past two years no longer lingers in the back of the Autonomous Team's minds.

"Mr. Chambers, we have a few more things to discuss," said Agent Lane. "I cannot begin to imagine how bad it was for you and your people. Being abducted and pressed into working for the enemy had to be terrible."

Nodding, "Yes it was. I'm surprised we survived," replied Chambers.

"Well, the good news is you did survive. The sooner as we can complete the tasks before us, the sooner you can return to your life. Are you up for it?" asked Lane.

"Agent Lane, I have been up for this since we were freed from Barakat's clutches," responded Chambers.

"Very well, Mr. Chambers. We understand Moktar Barakat kidnapped you and your people and forced you to work for them. Unfortunately, we are a little disturbed by some questions that need to be explained. Please take a look at this picture," as Lane slid a long-distance photograph across the table to Chambers depicting Barakat, his lieutenants and a man resembling Richard Chambers dressed in Islam garb. "Do you recognize these people?"

"Hmmm...Yes. That's Barakat," as Chambers tapped the photograph pointing at the man in the center of the picture. "And this man," on the right, "he's Abdul Fadel, Barakat's lieutenant,"

"Thank you Mr. Chambers. By the way, how about this man," as Lane pointed to the man standing on Barakat's right.

"Please Mr. Chambers, do you know this man?" repeated Lane.

"Yes I do."

Agent Lane stood still waiting for Chambers' response. After waiting long enough, Lane pressed Chambers once again for an answer, "Well Mr. Chambers. Who is the man?"

Chambers shifted nervously in his chair staring at the picture.

"Well Mr. Chambers?" pressed Lane.

"Yes. Yes, I understand. It's me."

"Based on the intelligence we have Mr. Chambers, we suspect that you voluntarily collaborated with the Islamic State. In fact, we believe you are an avowed Muslim and an enemy of the U.S."

Agent Lane took more pictures from his file folder showing Chambers in prayer, and slid them across the table to Chambers. "Well Mr. Chambers, what do you have to say about this?"

Staring straight ahead, Chambers, looking defiant began speaking in Arabic. "Alhamdulillah. La hawla wala quwata illah billah. Allahu Akbar."

Turning to Agent Richards, Lane asked, "What did he just say?"

"There is no strength nor power except Allah. Thanks be to Allah. God is the greatest."

"Mr. Chambers. Do you have anything you want to say?" asked Lane.

Chambers just sat stoic, staring straight ahead.

"Well Mr. Chambers, you leave us no choice," said Agent Lane.

Agent Richards, pulling handcuffs out from her belt, moved behind Richard Chambers and began cuffing him as Lane read him his rights. Rights as an American. "Mr. Chambers, you are under arrest. You have the right to remain silent. Anything you say can and will be used against you in a court of law. You have the right to an attorney. If you cannot afford an attorney, one will be provided for you. Do you understand the rights I have just read to you?"

Chambers just sat staring straight ahead.

"Take him downstairs," commanded Lane to Richards.

### Reunion

Special Agent Fernando Mendoza escorted Gary Sasaki through the FBI's sterile hallways to yet another of the now familiar interrogation rooms, euphemistically referred to as interview rooms. As Agent Mendoza opened the door, "Mr. Sasaki, please have a seat. Agents Lane and Richards will be with you shortly."

"Sure. Sure, more questions. I get it. All I want to know is, when do I get the hell out of here?"

"Please be patient Mr. Sasaki. Have a seat."

As Gary entered the room, for the first time since his return to the states he finds he is not alone. Today his fellow abductees, Will and Akio, sat quietly waiting for God-knows-what.

"Hey guys. What the hell is going on?"

"Your guess is as good as mine Gary," replied Will. "We just got here a few minutes ago."

"Yeah. It's anybody's guess," echoed Akio.

"I don't know about you two, but I am fed up with this bullshit. I want out of here and go the hell home. I'm afraid they're going to throw us in some gulag to rot. By the way, either of you seen that asshole Chambers or his squeeze, Liz?" asked Gary in his typical pissed-off tone.

Shaking his head, Akio replied, "Nope. Until now, I haven't seen anybody but the feds. Honestly, Gary, I don't think we're in trouble. How can we be? We didn't do anything wrong. We were kidnapped and forced to work for Barakat. How can anyone blame us? My guess is they just want more information. I think the better question is, why did they bring us together now? That's the mystery."

"Yeah, I haven't seen Dick or Liz either," replied Will. "My guess is they need us to clear up something. Something they believe only the three of us can handle."

"To hell with these assholes. I want out of here," bitched Gary. "We have rights!"

"Gary, trying to piss off Chambers over the past two years was a waste of your time," said Will. "Please control yourself. I don't need the feds pissed at us because you can't keep your mouth shut."

"Are you kidding?" replied Gary. "I have every ri..."

Cutting Sasaki off mid-sentence, "Gary, please knock this shit it off. I agree with Will, your attitude isn't going to help this situation. It didn't help us in Islamabad or North Korea and it isn't going to help us here."

Gary, bit his tongue and plopped down in an empty chair and crossed his arms defiantly just as the door opened and Agents Lane and Richards entered the room.

"Gentlemen," said Lane. "Thank you for your patience. I understand this has been a terrible ordeal since the day you were abducted. Rest assured we are close to bringing this phase to an end and we look forward to reuniting you with your families."

"It's about time," replied Gary as both Akio and Will glared at him disapprovingly.

"Ok guys. I get it. I'll shut up."

Taking a seat and placing his iPad on the table Agent Lane began. "Gentlemen, we want to thank you for all your help. You have been of tremendous value in tying up many of the loose ends in our investigation. However, we have a couple of matters to discuss. The first of which is the Drone Assault game. What can you tell us about it?"

Looking back and forth at each other, Gary was the first to speak. "I don't really know very much. That was Will's and Akio's project."

"Okay Mr. Schmidt and Mr. Chan. Let's get started. Tell us about Drone Assault." Recognizing the men's trepidation, Lane decided to be more proactive in this discussion, "Mr. Schmidt, may I call you Will?"

"Yes. Certainly."

"Okay, Will, give me an overview on the game's functionality," as Lane tapped the screen of his iPad activating the audio recorder.

For the next twenty minutes Will Schmidt rambled on ad nauseam explaining Drone Assault in minute detail. How it began when Chambers introduced them to the Drone On game and that Barakat wanted them to create a game that could counter the influence from Banger's game. Chambers had promised Barakat that the team could reverse engineer the technology and devise a way to hack into the game servers at Banger. Then, he dumped it in Akio's and my lap. Will continued, explaining that he and Akio didn't actually create the Drone Assault game but rather the underlying logic and the heuristics engine, creating an autonomous and self-adaptive artificial intelligence neural network that could out-smart Drone On. The actual game development was performed by Millennial Games.

"Thank you Will. I just want to confirm, the actual game programming was performed by Millennial Games then downloaded via the Internet. Once installed on a smartphone or tablet, the game communicated with Banger Mobile's game servers and was specifically designed to counter any control exerted by the Drone On game. Is there anything you wish to add Mr. Chan?" asked Richards.

Shaking his head, "No. Will explained it all," as Richards jotted notes on her iPad.

"Okay gentlemen. Let me explain the situation. We in the FBI truly believe you were forced to work for the Islamic State against your will. However, since Congress declared a state of war, unfortunately your cooperation is clearly an act of treason and subjects you to prosecution as war criminals," said Lane.

"Wait a minute," blurted Sasaki. "If we hadn't cooperated, they'd have killed us, just like they killed Kent and Jeff. Our brains would have been blown out."

"We understand Mr. Sasaki. Unfortunately, the American public probably doesn't share your sentiment. You have to understand, hundreds of thousands of U.S. citizens have lost their lives thanks to your technological expertise. I assure you, you will not be enthusiastically embraced by the American people. In fact, based on your collusion with America's sworn enemy over the past two years, it is doubtful that you will be able to find a job if not impossible, let alone live a quiet and peaceful life."

"What's going to happen," asked Will timidly.

"Well Mr. Schmidt, we have an answer which we hope you will embrace. The Director has been in discussions with the White House and the Justice Department. After great consideration of the exigent nature of your circumstances as hostages of the Islamic State, we are prepared to offer you immunity on two conditions."

Barely able to contain himself, Sasaki asked, "We didn't do anything wrong. Why do we need immunity? What conditions?"

"Unfortunately Mr. Sasaki, neither the Attorney General nor the people of America share your opinion. As such, your only options are to accept our terms for immunity or be prosecuted as war criminals."

"Great," lamented Gary, "Just great! This sounds just like the offer that asshole Barakat made. He also offered us two choices. Work for him or die."

"That is truly unfortunate Mr. Sasaki. The good news, Gary, Will, Akio, is that the government's offer is far less melodramatic. If you wish to be granted immunity, you and your immediate family will be required to enter the witness protection program under new identities. Rest assured, we understand that this isn't a simple decision. In doing so, you'll have to cut ties with everyone. And, I do mean everyone. Any violation of the witness protection conditions will void our agreement and you will be immediately prosecuted."

"And," asked Gary. "What's the second condition?"

"Fortunately Mr. Sasaki, the second condition is relatively easy. Since you're functionally unemployable, the second condition is that you'll work for the United States Government and will be subject to very stringent security requirements."

"Doing what?" asked Will.

"Mr. Schmidt, you will work in your field of expertise except for the United States instead of a private company. Beginning immediately, you'll join the engineering team working with the Homeland Security to develop viable defenses and responses to the Islamic State's drone strategy," replied Lane.

"So gentlemen," announced Agent Richards, "You need to understand something. This offer of immunity is all or none. All three of you have to agree to our offer of immunity or all three of you will be prosecuted."

"That's not fair," complained Gary.

"Shut the hell up Gary," exclaimed Will. "You sound like an eight-year old bitching that his father isn't fair. I for one want my life back and don't want to end up in some federal prison."

"What about Chambers and Liz?" asked Akio.

"Mr. Chan, Richard Chambers is not interested in accepting immunity. As for Ms. Collins, since she doesn't have the valuable skill set that the three of you possess, she is being dealt with separately," replied Richards.

### The White House Weighs In

"So Mr. President, over the past week we have conducted in-depth interviews with the entire Autonomous team recovered from North Korea. With the exception of Chambers, the remaining four have accepted our proposal and are being processed into the Witness Protection program," explained Director Teich.

"Thank you Mitch. Great job. What's the next step?" asked Bennett.

"Well sir, as you know we are completing the final training of the Drone On Defenders. In order to maximize our game-based defense strategy, it is imperative that Barakat's Drone Assault countermeasure is neutralized. In order to neutralize them we need to do so at the source—Millennial Games," explained Teich.

"We need to shut down Millennial Games?" asked Bennett.

"Yes sir, and do so immediately. Attorney General Santich has already secured arrest warrants for Millennial's management and we are prepared to raid their facility in Palo Alto by noon tomorrow and should have their servers disabled shortly thereafter. Finally, the SEC is prepared to delist them from NASDAQ by the end of business tomorrow, upon issuance of Justice Department's warrants. Do we have your authorization to execute the warrants?" asked Teich.

"Absolutely Mitch. Finally, I feel as if we are making progress against these bastards. Keep me posted. Okay?"

"Yes Mr. President. Special Agents Lane and Richards are on their way to San Francisco and they will lead the raid. I will call you as soon as I have word that Millennial Games is shut down," replied Director Teich.

### Millennial Games Raid

At 11:00am Pacific Time, Agents Lane and Richards assembled their team at Peers Park, two and a half miles away from Millennial's two hundred fifty thousand square foot high-tech facility on Page Mill road; considered by many as ground zero of the Silicon Valley. Fifty FBI agents and two hundred support personnel comprised of local law enforcement, Palo Alto SWAT, emergency services and fifty National Guardsman patiently waited the go order as Lane briefed the team leaders as two helicopters sat a hundred yards away, their rotors spinning, ready for departure.

"Ladies and gentlemen," began Lane. "According to the architectural plans, there are six access points. Upon arrival, the National Guard will encircle the campus and secure the area. Bravo through Foxtrot teams will position themselves at their assigned entrance points identified on the handouts. Special Agent Richards and I, along with Alpha Team, will enter via the main entrance and issue the warrants. Once the warrants are issued, the go order will be issued and the remaining teams will breach the building and secure all the occupants. Police One will land on the roof and secure the area as Police Two maintains its station above. Are there any questions?"

"Very good. People, let's mount up and move out," ordered Lane.

The convoy of busses, police cars, SUVs and ten Army Strykers trundle down Park Boulevard to put an end to Barakat's cyber capability. Within ten minutes, Millennial's glamourous office campus was encircled and the National Guard secured the area. Lane and Richards, accompanied by Palo Alto SWAT and five of the FBI's finest computer technicians, pulled up to the main entrance and proceeded into the lobby. Agents Richards and Lane, with badges and warrants in hand, the frightened security guard directed them to the executive suites on the third floor. Richards pressed her microphone button and gave the go order. In the blink of an eye, the assault team swarmed the facility. Ten minutes later, the FBI computer technicians took Millennial's servers offline, putting an end to Drone Assault.

"We must guard against the acquisition of unwarranted influence, whether sought or unsought, by the military-industrial complex,"
President Dwight D. Eisenhower

✖ ✖ ✖ ✖ ✖

# Chapter 28

———————◆———————

### *Drone On Defenders*

Over the past ten days hundreds of America's Drone On Defenders gathered daily in Washington D.C. doing little more than play Banger's mobile game. For hours, rooms filled with America's new front-line of defense strived to commandeer the enemy's drones and thwart attack after attack.

In general, America's Drone On Defenders were as varied as smartphone users themselves. However, the highest-rated and most successful of the new guard were mostly teenage boys who regularly saved the most lives and property. Other than racking up Starbuck's credits and a few 'attaboys' from FBI trainers, motivation for being a Drone On Defender was a combination of patriotism, pride and employment by Homeland Security.

To an outsider, these new American heroes were indistinguishable from any other teenager engrossed in their smartphones. But in reality, they had quickly evolved into something more. One FBI agent couldn't help but observe that these people were the first and almost comical step toward man and machine integration. Albeit not some cybernetic organism made famous by California's former governor, but a blending nonetheless of man and machine. In this new age of the Islamic State's autonomous and indefensible attack system, man and machine could not live without the other.

Night after night, news channels worldwide reported drone attacks on unsuspecting and often less than strategic targets. Targets where loss of life seemed to be the only mission objective. Since the first attack on Lincoln, Nebraska, the Islamic State's new-age strategic and indefensible weapon of mass destruction has proven to be nothing short of amazing. Regardless of the defenses America put up, a great number of these deadly mechanisms had successfully pummeled their targets. The only good news was America's cadre of Drone On Defenders were now forcing upwards of forty percent of the enemy's drones into ditches or vacant fields. Unfortunately, the remaining sixty percent were still reaching intended targets, wielding their deadly hammers with impunity.

The troubling fact was the battles taking place in Drone On's virtual world, between gamer and the real enemy, was less than perfect. Regardless of the Drone On Defender's increased success rate, attacks kept coming, night after night, day after day. In spite of the large number of drones falling to the wayside, pundits pointed out a disturbing fact: The Islamic State's drone strategy was simply a matter of economics—the cost to manufacture and deploy these deadly little machines was incidental; was under a thousand dollars each. When compared to the fifty million dollars America spent to purchase, maintain and operate a single MQ-9 Reaper drone, the State of Islam could deploy over fifty thousand of its micro-drones. If only forty percent—or twenty thousand micro-drones—reached their targets, the impact would be devastating and the Islamic State's cost, minimal.

At three on the afternoon of the tenth day of training, America's new frontline virtual defenders assembled in the FBI conference theater. Since the first day, twenty-three candidates had withdrawn from the program for a variety of reasons. However, the remaining fifty-seven were now fully trained and ready to receive their final instructions and pep-talk. The message they heard was simple—Play Drone On, play it often and recruit more players.

Agent Lane approached the podium. "Ladies and gentlemen, all of us at the FBI and Homeland Security want to congratulate you for jobs well done and welcome you into the family of men and women who are committed to protecting this country. This afternoon, Homeland Security Director Harold Simpson has a few comments to make and afterwards he'll administer the Homeland Security oath. Please welcome Director Harold Simpson."

Moving to the podium, Simpson began. "Good afternoon. America has never faced a more deadly and persistent enemy than we do today. An enemy that has infiltrated our borders with embedded lone wolf operators and employed the most unconventional and deadly weapon since the tragedy on 9/11. Every day, thousands of Americans and our allies are killed, injured or infected with deadly toxins in an effort to lay waste to our way of life. Until Autonomous Systems and Banger Mobile Games came to us offering a truly innovative and equally unconventional strategy, our efforts to counter this indefensible threat had been for naught.

Today you will be sworn in as the newest and most strategic members of Homeland Security's team. By taking this oath, you commit yourself to fight this enemy in this unconventional virtual world. Also, you will strive to recruit more Drone On Defenders until we thoroughly disrupt the Islamic State's ability to execute their mission. Ladies and gentlemen. Please rise and raise your right hand as I administer the Homeland Security Oath. Repeat after me,"

*I, [state your name], do solemnly swear (or affirm) that I will support and defend the Constitution of the United States against all enemies, foreign and domestic; that I will bear true faith and allegiance to the same; that I take this obligation freely, without any mental reservation or purpose of evasion; and that I will well and faithfully discharge the duties of the office on which I am about to enter. So help me God.*

"Congratulations. Welcome to Homeland Security. Go forth and make America proud. You're dismissed."

### Ricky and Pete

As the sun was setting, Ricky and Pete were the last remaining Drone On Defenders in the white Homeland Security Gulfstream as it departed Atlanta heading north to Springfield.

"This is really weird Pete," offered Ricky.

"Really? It's crazy," replied Pete. "These old farts want us to play Drone On and pay us thirty thousand a year."

"Yeah. Who cares? The cool thing is, if we get more players we make five hundred dollars more for each. I don't know about you, but I'm going to get everybody to play. Hell, I have over five hundred followers on Facebook and Twitter," said Ricky.

"Me too. We're going to make real bank," declared Pete.

"Yeah, a ton of money. Just to play a game," replied Ricky.

The boys sat quietly, luxuriating in the comfortable leather seats of the Gulfstream winging their way back home as the youngest sworn members of Homeland Security. Once again, America has changed.

### North Korea Continues Manufacturing

Ultimately disappointing to President Bennett, North Korea's Supreme Leader wasn't in attendance at their failed missile launch and was alive, well and infuriated back at his palace in Pyongyang.

"Your Excellency," said Pak Yong Sik, North Korea's defense minister. "I assure you, the missile failure was not the fault of my people. Prior to launch, the systems were performing flawlessly. Then suddenly, the fuel ignited and demolished the warhead. Your Excellency, I am certain this is a matter of sabotage or the use of some American weapon. I assure you Your Excellency, these are the only explanations."

Pounding his fist against the table, "When can we have another missile ready for launch against the U.S.?"

"Your Excellency, the lost launch facility will take over five years to rebuild. Also, we lost most of our enriched uranium in the explosion. We simply do not have an adequate supply to prepare another warhead. It will take at least two years of concerted effort to enrich more. Your Excellency, it is most unfortunate, but this tragedy has set us back at least five years."

"I will not let the U.S. get away with this. I want revenge. What are our options?" demanded the Supreme Leader.

Having waited patiently, Barakat saw his opening and chose to enter the discussion. "Excuse me, Your Excellency. If I may, I believe I have an answer."

"Emir, what is it?"

"If we increase drone production I believe we can swarm the west and rain down devastation beyond their imagination. Currently we are taking a dramatic toll against the west every day. By increasing production, we can bring the West to its knees. More importantly, we need to broaden our attacks across the globe, striking every American ally. Your Excellency, I believe we should immediately double or even triple our manufacturing efforts," explained Barakat.

"Emir, what do you need?"

"Very little Your Excellency. Just to secure more manufacturing capability beyond that which Mr. Ko and Korea Navigation Company can provide."

"But Emir, we lost the Americans. How are we going to make more drones?"

"Your Excellency, we don't need the American engineers any longer. Mine and Ko's people have complete understanding of the technology and can continue advancing it to higher levels without the Americans. In fact, I was close to eliminating the Americans anyway. I am certain we can move forward and step up our attacks."

Thinking for a short moment, the Supreme Leader turned to Seonu, his Commerce Minister, "assign drone production to every company that has the capability. I don't care what it takes. I want their resources dedicated to drone manufacturing and nothing else. They will be under the Emir's direct supervision. Understand?"

A little timid, Seonu bowed deeply, "Yes, Your Excellency. I will do so immediately."

"I want America brought to its knees," demanded the Supreme Leader. "I want those pigs destroyed."

### Months Later

"Good evening and welcome back. As has been mine and Gretchen's sad duty for so very long, once again we turn our attention to the continued drone attacks devastating America and our allies across the globe," began Jeff Stoddard. "Since we reported on the events in North Korea a few months ago, it is clear the number of attacks have increased dramatically."

"Yes Jeff," added Gretchen. "The number of drone attacks have almost tripled in the past ninety days. According to our count, more than fifty attacks are occurring daily in America alone, along with England, Israel, Australia and now we are hearing of more drone attacks in Russia and Japan.

"Thanks to whatever defenses that are being employed, a great many of the attacking drones continue to crash in deserted fields, farms, and out-of-the-way places. Let's bring in United News Network's military advisor, retired Marine three-star General, Gary Arnold. "General Arnold, thank you for joining us."

"You're welcome Gretchen."

Jeff began the discussion, "General, what are your thoughts regarding the drones that seem to be diverted from their targets?"

"Jeff, it's obvious to me that a systematic response is being employed. I assure you, these drones are not crashing away from populated areas by accident. It is simply too consistent, and automated systems do not act this way," assured Arnold.

"Do you have an explanation General?"

"Actually Jeff, I do. After extensive research and investigation by my Defend America Foundation, I believe we've identified the defense mechanism that is being used," replied General Arnold as he held up his iPhone.

"General, we see you are holding up what appears to be an Apple iPhone. Excuse me, but I am a little confused," replied Gretchen.

"Don't be Gretchen. It is a little confusing and truly unexpected. And yes, this is my Apple iPhone. However, it isn't your run-of-the-mill iPhone. My iPhone is unique in that I have installed the Drone On game app."

"Well General, so have millions of iPhones users," replied Chen. "Please, explain."

"You are correct Gretchen. Over one hundred million smartphone users have downloaded Drone On, making Banger Mobile Games one of the most successful technology companies in the world. And that's the point. I believe Drone On has been causing thousands of drones to be diverted from their intended targets."

"What!?! How?" asked Stoddard.

"Jeff, please bear with me a moment. According to our research at DAF, every time there's an attack, such as yesterday's attack against the First Merit Tower in Akron, Ohio, the target city suddenly becomes part of Drone On's virtual game. Yesterday, at the time of the Akron attack, the city of Akron Ohio appeared as one of Drone On's attack scenarios. Coincidence? I think not. More importantly, during yesterday's attack on Akron, upwards of forty percent of the observed drones never made it to the First Merit Tower, but crashed harmlessly in Grace Park a mile away. I'm sure this is not a coincidence."

"Are you suggesting that somehow people playing the Drone On game are causing the attacking drones to crash?" asked Stoddard.

"Jeff, that is exactly what I am saying. I believe this game, and Banger Mobile Games are integral to America's drone defense strategy. And if I'm correct, I applaud President Bennett for thinking outside the box and advance such an innovative solution for defeating this deadly technology. There is, however, a certain irony in fighting technology with technology. Since conventional defenses have proven ineffective, I believe Drone On is a truly brilliant response to the Islamic State's drones. The bottom line is simple. Drone On epitomizes American ingenuity at its finest," answered Arnold.

"So, what's next General Arnold?" asked Gretchen.

"The next step is obvious Gretchen. Assuming Drone On is America's defense strategy, I believe that more people playing the game improves the likelihood that drones will be diverted from their intended targets. Jeff and Gretchen, this is simply a numbers game. It is imperative that all of us step up and become Drone On gamers. In essence, take up arms against these deadly and indefensible machines. In doing so, we dramatically improve our chances of disrupting the Islamic State's capability. At some point, the state of Islam will not be able to afford to build more drones. The cost will simply be too high. I want to assure your viewers that I cannot overstate the importance of everyone playing this game. And, playing it often. This is truly a milestone in American history. For the very first time, Americans can defend this country against its enemy without putting one single life at risk," replied Arnold.

### What Now?

Cabinet members, General James, and select leaders from Congress waited in the oval office for President Bennett's arrival. Engaged in nothing more than nervous small talk, the group suddenly fell silent as the door swung open and Roger Kerns entered the office. "Good morning ladies and gentlemen," in Kerns customary efficient tone of voice. "Thank you all for coming. The President will be here momentarily. When he arrives, he expects a status report on the key issues outlined in this morning's agenda. Please keep in mind his schedule is very tight and the President will be departing for Camp David to meet with the Israeli Prime Minister at noon. So please be efficient."

Just as Kerns completed his statement to the attendees President Bennett walked in, coffee in hand, followed by FBI Director Teich. "Good morning everyone," as Bennett slid into his favorite chair. Pondering for only a moment, Bennett broke into a stern monologue. "After last night's UNN interview with General Gary Arnold, I was infuriated. My first reaction was that Arnold was a treasonous bastard and needed to change his name to Benedict. But, thanks to sage counsel from Director Teich, thankfully cooler heads prevailed. Director Teich reminded me that our best course of action is for more people to become Drone On Defenders. Mitch, please share your observations."

"My pleasure Mr. President. Since General Arnold's unplanned national announcement last night, over five million new copies of Drone On have been downloaded. More importantly, at any one time we have over two hundred thousand players of Drone On. As such, in the past twenty-four hours the effective drone engagement and destruction rate has risen from forty percent to fifty-two percent. The bottom line is, Drone On works and General Arnold did us a favor."

"Thank you Mitch. This is great news. Certainly I would have preferred to have been consulted prior to General Arnold's announcement, but alas, we are enjoying a positive outcome. Unfortunately, drone attacks continue and there seems to be no immediate end in sight. Jerome, how are things holding up over at Commerce?"

"Mr. President, thankfully deployment of the new Secure GPS technology has had dramatic improvement in some sectors, especially the airlines and shipping. Unfortunately, most consumer GPS-based businesses are struggling, since they are not eligible to log into the secure system. Hopefully a solution will be on the horizon soon, and GPS services can be restored for the masses."

Turning to the Attorney General, "Grant, now that SGPS is up, what's the status with home monitoring?"

"Mr. President, the new SGPS ankle bracelets are up and running. The biggest challenge has been finding the home detainees. Of the three hundred thousand people subject to home confinement, we have only been able to locate fifty thousand. Local, state and federal law enforcement has made this a high priority. Unfortunately, rounding up a quarter of a million criminals is a monumental task and will take some time. Until then, crime rates are up twelve percent," explained Grant.

"Mr. Attorney General, are you attributing the rise in crime rate to the missing home detainees?" asked Bennett.

"Not at all Mr. President. Certainly a significant percentage is likely a result of this population, however, over at Justice, we believe a majority of the increase is attributable to the rise in unemployment, exacerbated by the frustration and chaos due to the constant drone attacks."

"Finally, David, what progress has the CIA made in getting our arms around drone manufacturing and deployment?"

"Certainly Mr. President. What we know is that drones are being manufactured in facilities across North Korea and Malaysia, as well as the mid-east and South America. In the past thirty days, our operators have successfully destroyed two manufacturing facilities, one is Venezuela and the other in Syria. Unfortunately, these represented relatively small production. Since the technology is so easily duplicated and doesn't require exotic tooling or processes, these nasty little machines can be manufactured anywhere. Even in someone's basement. Our fear is that large-scale manufacturing will discontinue and embedded jihadists will simply be provided the few parts necessary to build their own."

"Folks, I know you are all tired. But, our resolve cannot waiver. We are fighting for our lives. Each day, America and our allies around the world are falling prey to swarms of drones casting dark shadows as they attack our society. North Korea and Barakat need to be stopped. General James and the Joint Chiefs are suggesting an all-out assault on North Korea. Until we have solid intelligence regarding manufacturing facilities, I am hesitant to issue this order. David, the burden rests square on the shoulders of the CIA. Get us the information so we can put an end to this plague."

"Will do Mr. President."

"Thank you all for your service. Keep up the good work."

Bennett's advisors filed out of the Oval Office, proving once again that the American Presidency is the loneliest job in the world. Carlton Bennett, snatching a private moment, decided to be just another citizen as he slid into his chair behind the *Resolute* desk. Leaning back, gazing at the portrait of George Washington over the fireplace, Bennett pondered the unique situation the world was in. Across the globe, tens of thousands of enemies in the real world are committed to destroying the West's way of life. In stark contrast, these enemies of western civilization are being challenged in the virtual world of Drone On by millions of people equally committed to defending it.

Bennett gently lifted his iPhone and rotated his chair as he noticed the surging dark cloud of drones against the southern clear blue morning Washington sky. Indulging his desire to not think about matters of state, Bennett tapped the Drone On icon prominently centered on his display. Almost immediately, he was injected into the virtual world of Drone On and assigned a fleet heading toward the Lincoln Memorial, less than a mile from Bennett's office. Bennett prayed that he and other Drone On Defenders would successfully impede the advancing fleet armed with explosives and very likely, something much worse. One by one Bennett's armada missed the Lincoln Memorial, only to end their journey in the cold waters of the Potomac. "Mission Accomplished – 71%" flashed across Bennett's phone.

"Today was a good day," thought Bennett. "Dedicated Drone On Defenders of Washington, D.C. took its toll against the Islamic State threat."

After enjoying a moment of personal glory, Bennett returned his iPhone to its charging cradle and began reading yet another CIA report. Only ten pages into the document, Ruth Holcomb's voice over the intercom broke the silence.

"Mr. President, Director Teich is on the phone for you."

"Put him through Mrs. Holcomb."

"Yes Mr. President."

"Long time no see," laughed Bennett. "Mitch, what can I do for you?"

"Mr. President, I have good news and bad news."

"Give me the good news first. I need a lift."

"Well Mr. President, thirty minutes ago we had three drone fleets attack D.C."

"I know, I was commanding one of them."

"Very good Mr. President. I'm certain thanks to your efforts, only a half dozen drones made it to their targets, causing minimal physical damage."

"Minimal physical damage? Mitch, what's the bad news?"

"Mr. President, as we've feared, these drones seemed to be carrying something more frightening than explosives and RICIN. According to the boys from the CDC on the ground, they've detected Class-A bio-agents."

"Class-A Bio-agents! That means it can spread people-to-people. What bio-agents?"

"Mr. President, just as we feared. Anthrax."

"Anthrax," muttered Bennett to himself. "Dear God!" Just when he had a sense that the gaming response to the drone terrorism was making progress, now this. "Mitch, keep me posted as to casualties."

"Will do, Mr. President."

Bennett was overwhelmed by the magnitude of the challenge that lay before him as he placed the phone's handset back into its cradle. Thinking to himself, "This is truly a dark age. A dark age indeed."

Tired from the growing burden on his shoulders and a nagging sense of impotence, Bennett did the only thing he could think of to provide him a sense of control. He tapped the Drone On icon on his iPhone and once again, took the battle to the streets….the virtual streets.

## The End

"The conviction of the justification of using even the most brutal weapons is always dependent on the presence of a fanatical belief in the necessity of the victory of a revolutionary new order on this globe," Adolph Hitler

✖ ✖ ✖ ✖ ✖

# Cast of Characters

———————◆———————

### Garner Ames
SEAL Team Six Weapons Specialist.

### Kent Anders
Autonomous Systems' Software engineer. Kent is twenty-eight years old.

### General Gary Arnold
General Arnold is a retired Marine three-star and is a Military Advisor for United News Network. Also, General Arnold is the founder and Executive Director of the Defend America Foundation a strategic and military think tank.

### David Banger
President and Founder of Banger Mobile Games, the creator of Drone On. Also, a college friend of David Kramer, Chambers replacement at Autonomous Systems.

### Moktar Barakat
Forty-four year old born and raised in Kabul Afghanistan. He is the creator and leader of the Islamic State's Drone Terror Initiative committed to destroying western civilization. Barakat earned his undergraduate degree in electrical engineering in 1995, from the University of Edinburgh and four years later he was granted his Masters and Doctorate in autonomous systems.

### Carlton Bennett
President of the United States. He is fifty-eight years old.

### Phillip Carlson
Anchor of United News Network's Early Edition.

### Richard Chambers
CEO and Founder of Autonomous Systems.

### Akio Chan
Autonomous Systems' Electrical Engineer. Akio is twenty-nine years old.

### Jeff Chaplain
Specialist in Autonomous Systems at Autonomous Systems. Jeff is forty-four years old.

**David Charmer**
Director of the Center for Disease Control.

**Gretchen Chen**
Co-Anchor with Jeff Stoddard on UNN's Evening Edition.

**Terrance Colby**
Vice President of the United States. Colby is seventy-one years old.

**Liz Collins**
Autonomous Systems' Drone Project Manager. Liz is twenty-seven years old.

**Carrie Connors**
UNN's Wall Street Business Correspondent

**Arman Deeb**
Software Engineer and head of network security for Autonomous Systems.

**Abdul-Ghaffar Fadel**
Abdul is thirty-five years old, born and raised in Kandahar Afghanistan and is Moktar Barakat's Shura (Advisor). Abdul earned his undergraduate degree in international studies from the University of Southern California.

**Link Farnsworth**
President Bennett's Press Secretary.

**Thomas Gomez**
Director of the Federal Aviation Administration.

**David Haydon**
Director of the CIA and is sixty-one years old.

**Ruth Holcomb**
President Bennett's Secretary and is fifty-two years old.

**Carey James**
Autonomous Systems' pilot and First Officer of Autonomous Systems' Falcon jet.

**Garland James**
Chairman of the Joint Chiefs.

**Graham Johnson**
Sheriff of Lincoln Nebraska. Former SEAL Team Six member. He served with Carlton Bennett in the SEALs.

**Mark Johnson**
Commander of SEAL Team Six.

**Roger Kerns**
President Bennett's Chief of Staff.

**Kang Ko**
Executive Director of the Korea Navigation Company and charged with the responsibility to manufacture and ship Barakat's drones.

**David Kramer**
CEO of Autonomous Systems. Replaced Chambers after the company's jet was lost.

**Ralph Lane**
FBI, Special Agent

**Jennifer Palmer**
Senate Majority Leader.

**Ron Parsons**
Autonomous Systems Project Manager.

**Jerome Price**
Secretary of Commerce

**Becky Reynolds**
Flight attendant on Autonomous Systems' Falcon jet.

**Janet Richards**
FBI, Special Agent

**Thomas Rolands**
Mayor or Los Angeles California

**David Sams**
Software Engineer for Autonomous Systems.

**Christopher Samuels**
Software Engineer for Autonomous Systems.

**Grant Santich**
Attorney General of the United States and is sixty-four years old.

**Gary Sasaki**
Autonomous Systems' Software Engineer. Gary is thirty-one years old.

**Rebecca Saunders**
UNN's New York based Financial Reporter.

**Will Schmidt**
Aeronautical Engineer for Autonomous Systems. Will is thirty-six years old.

**Harold Simpson**
Director of Homeland Security.

**Trudy Sloan**
Co-Anchor with Phillip Carlson on UNN's Early Edition.

**Connor Sterns**
Mr. Sterns is the Executive Director of the Free Skies Alliance and is an advocate for free use of personal and commercial drones.

**Jeff Stoddard**
Anchor of United News Network's Evening Edition.

**Jason Stuart**
SEAL Team Six Corpsman.

**Carl Summers**
Chief Technology Officer for Autonomous Systems.

**Robert Teasdale**
Speaker of the House of Representatives.

**Captain Jeff "Skip" Taylor**
Autonomous Systems' pilot and Captain of Autonomous Systems' Falcon jet.

**Mitchell Teich**
Director of the FBI. Teich is sixty-six years old and lifelong friend of Carlton Bennett.

**Anthony Umberg**
Secretary of State.

**Grant Underwood**
Anchor for UNN's Business Report

**Nikolai Volkov**
President of Russia.

**Bruce Walker**
SEAL Team Six Sniper.

*Rene Zane*
Communications officer for SEAL Team Six.

*Johnson's Team*
    **Brad Davis:** Jumpmaster
    **Albert Gonzalez:** Breacher
    **Peter Gray:** Surveillance
    **Richard Hernandez:** Ordinance
    **Willie Miller:** Heavy Weapons Operator
    **Bob Salem:** Sniper
    **J.P. Smith:** Small Arms Specialist
    **Randy Summers:** Corpsman
    **Fred Torres:** Communications
    **Garland Truman:** Point-man/Navigator
    **Grant Walker:** Interrogator

"A drone strike is a terror weapon, we don't talk about it that way. It is; just imagine you are walking down the street and you don't know whether in 5 minutes there is going to be an explosion across the street from some place up in the sky that you can't see. Somebody will be killed, and whoever is around will be killed, maybe you'll be injured if you're there. That is a terror weapon. It terrorizes villages, regions, huge areas. It's the most massive terror campaign going on by a long shot," Noam Chomsky

# Acknowledgments

◆

This book was made possible thanks to the encouragement, feedback and thoughts of a number of people near and dear to me.

First, I want to thank Melinda Richards Banks, my wife of twenty-five years and the mother of my two marvelous children. She has been a constant source of encouragement in everything I do, including the writing of Indefensible. Without her patience, incisive commentary and deft editing, the process of crafting this manuscript would have been impossible.

Second, I want to thank my best friend, Mitchell Teich, after whom I named a character in my book. Mitch has been a remarkable friend and was there that fateful Saturday morning, while drinking coffee and smoking cigars, when the idea for Indefensible popped into my consciousness. In the moments that ensued, I shared my ideas with Mitch and he did what he does best—encouraged and supported his friend.

Third, I want to thank my friend John Pickett, a fellow technologist and real-world nerd, who selflessly provided encouragement to complete the manuscript. I'm honored that John took the time to read every single word and offer me brutally honest feedback which I believe resulted in a better product.

Fourth, I wish thank my friend Joel Morris, cigar buddy and a good man with whom to discuss big topics. Joel was the first person on the planet to read the manuscript. I know Joel to be honest and direct. What better person would an author want to be the first reader of his manuscript?

Finally, to my new friend, Ace Hoffman, Owner & Chief Programmer of The Animated Software Co. in Carlsbad, California. Ace generously and selflessly scoured the manuscript for every typo, inconsistency and provided insight to enhance the quality of INDEFENSIBLE.

And to those too numerous to mention (you know who you are are) thank you.

Made in the USA
San Bernardino, CA
19 November 2018